Prolonged Exposure

His Bibliography

Westerns:
The Killer
The Worst Enemy
Leadfire
Timber Blood

The Bill Gastner Series:
Heartshot
Bitter Recoil
Twice Buried
Before She Dies
Privileged to Kill
Prolonged Exposure
Out of Season
Dead Weight
Bag Limit

Prolonged Exposure

Steven F. Havill

Poisoned Pen Press

Poisoned Pen Press

First Trade Paperback Edition 2001

10 9 8 7 6 5 4 3 2 1

Library of Congress Catalog Card Number: 200190168

ISBN: 1-890208-73-6

Poisoned Pen Press
6962 E. First Ave. Ste. 103
Scottsdale, AZ 85251
www.poisonedpenpress.com
info@poisonedpenpress.com

Printed in the United States of America

For Kathleen

Chapter 1

The late-afternoon sun angled across the sweep of the bunchgrass prairie, casting harsh shadows around mesas and on the lowlands where arroyos cut the sand into fantastic patterns. The wind gusted fitfully, as if nervous about the clouds forming over the San Cristobal Mountains to the south, along the Mexican border.

With my eyes closed, I could watch the changing patterns of shape, color, and texture. I could even see where an aging piñon clung in the loose, powdery soil on a distant rock outcropping, and I could see, in the shade under that piñon, a Saye's ground squirrel industriously sifting through the piñon-nut hulls for one that held a morsel.

The image was strong enough that I could smell the prairie, and hear it, and even, sitting there quietly in my chair, imagine that I could feel the ghostings of fine sand particles across my bare feet.

The landscape would hold as long as I kept my eyes closed. If I opened them, I'd see the hedgerow that marked the back property line of my daughter's home. And beyond that, if I cared to get up and stroll across a quarter acre of manicured bluegrass, I would catch a glimpse of power lines and rooftops, an expanse of suburbia that stretched, as far as I knew, all the way east to Lake Huron.

I had been sitting with a paperback novel open on my lap, head leaned back, eyes closed, soaking in the Michigan haze. The novel wasn't worth reading, but it was good for appearances. Otherwise, I sure as hell would have looked like an invalid. I'd lost a few pounds—I had plenty to spare still, but decent green-chili burritos were difficult to find in central Michigan, and I woke up each morning with the feeling that I was fading fast.

Were I recuperating in New Mexico, where I belonged, the lack of proper food could have been offset by doses of sunshine strong enough to bake lizards. But that wasn't the case, either. If the sun had been lit at all in Michigan that day, it was hidden somewhere behind a sky of flat, featureless stainless steel. So, with my eyes closed, I pretended.

My daughter Camille would have only chuckled if I complained, so I didn't bother. Her one concession during the past three weeks had been letting me keep the wheelchair longer than necessary, but even its usefulness was fading. The gadget would have been even more comfy with a nice knitted afghan to spread across my lap, but my daughter would never have allowed that. She was into power recuperation.

I didn't need the wheelchair, mind you. I took long morning and evening walks, sometimes in the company of one or more of my teenaged grandchildren, strolling around blocks of secluded, expensive homes with smooth black macadam driveways. There were no rattlesnakes, no goatheads to pick out of my socks later, no sand. I hated every step.

And for the past week, Camille had been making noises about sending the wheelchair back to the health-aids rental place from which it had come, but I had pointed out that of all the furniture on my daughter's patio, the straight-backed aluminum speedster was the most comfortable. If I had slipped into one of the low Adirondack chairs, I never would have been able to heave my bulk up and out. The other choice was even more unattractive. The white wicker love seat had enough sharp cane ends sticking out that no matter which way I sat, some article of clothing was speared.

Behind me, I heard the back door open.

"Do you want to take a call from the sheriff's office?" Camille possessed one of those voices that carried command in every sentence. If she had said, "It's a beautiful day," well then, by God, it had better just *be* a beautiful day, if it knew what was good for it. She was the oldest of my four children, and she had been boss since she was two years old.

"Why do they want to talk to me?" I asked, turning my head so I could see her. She shrugged, and waggled the receiver at me. She was wearing an apron, which meant that she was cooking something that would end up resembling health food. I frowned. "I don't even know what county we're in," I added.

I had a fleeting vision of the local police hopelessly stymied by a tough case. They knew that their only hope lay with the aging, ailing undersheriff, who happened to be in town visiting relatives and recuperating from having his carotid arteries reamed out. I could see the harried captain of detectives reaching for the phone, saying with arched eyebrow to his sweating lieutenant, "Let's call Gastner in." It was indeed a fleeting vision, the sort of thing the mind dreams up when there's too much free time.

"This is Genesee County," Camille said, "but you're off by about two thousand miles." She grinned, her dark face softening until she looked like her mother. "The acting undersheriff wants to speak with you." She put the receiver to her ear and said, "He hasn't decided whether or not to get out of his chair, Estelle. Hang on a minute while I beat on him."

My pulse jumped, not from the threat of pummeling, but from the mention of Estelle Reyes-Guzman's name. Camille saw the expression on my face. "The cord won't reach," she said, but I was already grunting myself upright.

"They make cordless phones now," I muttered, but I knew that on her husband's lowly earnings as an oral surgeon, they no doubt had to be careful about such luxuries.

Out of habit, I glanced at my watch and saw that it was 4:36. Flint, Michigan, was on eastern time, so it was siesta time in Posadas County, New Mexico. If I'd been home, I would have been just wrapping up lunch at the Don Juan de Oñate restaurant. But I wasn't home.

Camille handed me the phone as I reached the screen door.

"Gastner," I said, sounding for all the world as if I'd been busy with something important.

Estelle Reyes-Guzman knew better, even from two thousand miles away. "I hope I didn't wake you, sir," she said.

Her voice was soft and musical. I grinned and ambled back toward the kitchen, doing my best not to trip over the cord. "I was right in the middle of a high-level meeting," I said. "It's good to hear from you."

Estelle, chief of detectives for the Posadas County Sheriff's Department, had called several times during my convalescence, and I'd called her only two days before, enjoying a nice long chat at my son-in-law's expense. He didn't mind, and he even pointed out that what few calls I made were nothing compared to the communications havoc that his three teenagers could wreak.

In the background, I heard the squelch of the dispatcher's radio. Knowing that Estelle was at the office peaked my interest, and it was logical that she hadn't called just to chat.

"What's up?" I asked.

"There were a couple of things Francis wanted me to ask you, and now I can't remember what they were," Estelle said.

Her physician husband could ask his own questions, and no doubt would when next we met eye-to-eye. "Tell him that I've lost a hundred pounds and that I'm running eight miles every morning. And that I've given up Mexican food entirely."

"The latter I can believe, sir," she said, "As long as you're stuck up there."

"Ain't that the truth."

"I called because of a couple of things myself," she said. "First of all, do you remember Florencio Apodaca?"

I should have responded, "Well, sure, of course I do," but the name drew a blank. "Uh-huh," I said instead, a grunt that could be construed either way.

"Mr. Apodaca is the old man who lives at the end of Escondido Lane, in that old adobe with the steep metal roof and—"

I interrupted her as my memory kicked into gear. "Sure," I said. "Of course." Escondido Lane curved around behind my own property in Posadas. If my five acres hadn't been so choked with trees and brush, I could have looked out my den window and seen the Apodacas' house three hundred yards away.

"I used to see him and his wife taking evening walks, but that was a while ago. Did he die, or what?"

"No, he didn't. But we can't find his wife, Gloria."

"What do you mean, you can't find her?"

"Just that, sir. One of the neighbors told us that she hadn't seen Gloria in quite awhile…that she'd been ill, you know."

"It seems to me that she was frail a hundred years ago," I said. "Maybe she has Alzheimer's and wandered off. Did anyone ask?"

"Gloria would be in her late eighties, so that's entirely possible, sir." Estelle said. "One of the village officers stopped by to check, and Florencio told him that she'd gone. That's all he would say. Not that she had died, just that she'd gone. That's all he would say."

"Who was the officer who talked to him?"

"Chief Martinez," Estelle said, and I looked heavenward. Eduardo Martinez was kindhearted, understanding, gentle, and stupid.

"So let me guess. The chief assumed that when Florencio said 'She's gone,' he meant that his wife had gone to visit relatives or some such."

"Exactly."

"But you don't think that she did?"

"No, sir. A couple of youngsters were in the lot across the street, building a tree house in one of those old cottonwoods. They found a grave. We're pretty sure it's hers."

"Really? You think she died and her husband just planted her himself?"

"Yes, sir. There was a small cross, and her name was carved in the wood."

I shrugged. "Well, there you are, then. If you've got a grave, the odds are good you've found your corpse. So what's the deal? It's not illegal for her to die, and it's not illegal for him to bury her. Poor old guy. Where's the grave site? I don't remember their lot as being very big."

"It's not on their property, sir," Estelle said, and then repeated what I hadn't caught the first time. "It's across the lane, on yours."

I laughed. "You've got to be kidding."

"No, sir."

"You're saying that the old lady died, and Florencio dragged the body across the street, into my woods, and dug a grave…under one of my trees?"

"That's what it looks like, sir."

"I'll be damned. Brassy old cuss, isn't he? I wonder what put that notion into his head. And he even made a cross, too, you say?"

"Yes, sir. A simple wooden cross."

"Well, that's sort of sweet," I said. "It's not quite the way things are done these days, but what the hell." I chuckled. "Gene Salazar is going to be ticked that he's out a prep and burial fee. I wonder what Florencio used for a casket."

"I don't know, sir."

"Well, I don't care, I guess," I said. "I don't walk around back there much. In fact, I probably haven't been on that particular spot in twenty years."

"I didn't think you'd mind, but the village does. That's the area where they wanted to run the new water line, so there'd be service to DelSol Estates. They said that you'd given them an easement."

"Oh," I said. "Yeah, I guess I did. Well, we certainly don't want to stand in the way of progress." I chuckled. "Or lie in the way. I didn't know there had been any interest in that DelSol development, anyway."

"They're hoping, I think," Estelle said.

"I'm sure we can work something out that will make everyone happy. If that's the biggest problem you're having, things must be going pretty smoothly."

"That's one," Estelle said. "We're also having a rash of B and E's, sir. I think we've had something like eight residential burglaries in the past two weeks."

"Kids again?" I remembered that the last rash of breaking-and-entering cases that Posadas County had endured featured a thirteen year-old punk as the mastermind.

"Probably. We're not sure. Your house was one of them."

"Shit," I said. "You're kidding." That was a waste of breath, of course, since Estelle Reyes-Guzman was not the kidding sort.

"Apparently they gained access by busting out the bathroom window. They left the front door unlocked afterward. They did a thorough job of trashing the place."

I felt my blood pressure start its slow, inexorable rise. "So you need an inventory?"

"If you have one."

"I don't. I'm not sure there was much that was worth taking. Just a bunch of books. I'd have to walk through the place to jog my memory."

"Most of the books are scattered on the floor. The thieves dumped them off the shelves. They took the VCR but not the television."

"Small loss."

"And when you left, was the Civil War rifle and sword still mounted on the wall in your den?"

"Yes."

"They took them, too."

"Those little bastards."

"Yes, sir."

"Estelle, you might check that lockable filing cabinet just to the right of my desk. The little two-drawer unit. A couple of my handguns were in there, locked up."

"That was gone, too."

"The entire unit?"

"Yes, sir."

I closed my eyes and listened to the blood gurgling in my newly reamed pipes. "There were some papers in there that I can't afford to lose," I said finally.

"I'm sorry, sir. We've got a couple of pretty solid leads that we're following. If we come up with anything, I'll let you know. And by the way, I had Bob Torrez nail a stout piece of plywood over the broken window in the bathroom."

"Thanks. What about the garage? Any sign of entry there?"

"Apparently they didn't get in there. The truck is all right."

"That's the least of my worries," I said. "It's too bad they didn't steal it. It'd be a hell of a lot easier to trace that than the smaller stuff."

I reached across the kitchen counter and pulled the calendar toward me, flipping the page over to the next month, December. "I was planning on flying back to Las Cruces in a couple of weeks. On the third of December," I said. "That's a Wednesday. I could move it up and leave here the day after tomorrow. That's November sixteenth. I've got a couple of things to wrap up here, but that shouldn't be a problem."

"If you can manage, sir, it would be a help. Otherwise, I can go through room by room and we can settle over the phone."

"That won't be necessary."

"Are you doing all right?"

"*Nicely* is the doctor's favorite word now. Apparently cutting out a cheese burrito from each carotid artery made all the difference. Let me plan on catching a flight out of here on Sunday, then. That shouldn't be any problem to arrange. I've got a meeting with a man tomorrow that I really don't want to break, but after that, it should be fine."

Estelle Reyes-Guzman didn't ask me what the meeting was all about, but when I hung up the telephone a few minutes later, Camille appeared in the doorway, both hands on her hips in that "Oh no you don't" posture I knew so well.

Chapter 2

The plane touched down in El Paso to two surprises. The first was the weather. During the flight from Flint, Michigan, I had eagerly anticipated seeing the vast, sun-swept panorama of the Southwest. Despite her best efforts, the month that I had spent recuperating at my daughter's home seemed a lifetime, to a point where I was sure that I had grown mold cultures under my armpits. At least once during that sojourn in Michigan, the thought had crossed my mind that I might not be returning anywhere, ever.

As the jet entered Texas airspace, I could see a low, thick cloud layer that spread northward from the Gulf of Mexico, blanketing El Paso and muting the wonderful dichotomy between earth and sky to a solid, dismal gray. There was no break in the cloud layer to the west over New Mexico, either, and I sighed.

The jet sank into the stuff and I turned to glance at Camille to see if she had noticed the meteorological insult outside the plane. She was reading a book about the former prime minister of England. If she had any interest at all about her upcoming visit to Posadas, the little bleached New Mexican village where she'd grown up, that interest hadn't bubbled to the surface yet. Without missing a syllable in her reading, she lifted a hand and patted my arm in consolation.

"Wonderful," I muttered just as the airliner touched down. The tires threw up great clouds of spray, and I watched through the scratched plexiglas as rain pounded the jet's aluminum skin and ran back to fountain off the trailing edges of the flaps.

Of course the Southwest needed rain. It always did. That didn't mean I appreciated a homecoming greeted by a frog strangler, with no edges of the cloud on the horizon.

Camille closed the book, twisted slightly in her seat, and squinted out the window. "Isn't that a wonderful sight," she said, sounding as if she meant it. "Maybe you'll get some real snow this winter if this moisture continues."

I started to say that I couldn't think of a single reason why I would want to see snow, real or otherwise, but instead, I just grunted something that could have been mistaken for agreement. The airliner lumbered in toward the terminal, and I found myself looking for familiar faces behind the concourse's tinted glass.

The walk into the building was welcome exercise after three hours sitting in a seat far too small for my frame. The rain was loud on the thin skin of the concourse's accordion walkway, and I noticed that Camille and I were hardly setting the pace as passengers deplaned and hustled into the terminal. People flowed around us like water rolling by a rock caught in the middle of a stream. I would never have suspected that so many souls had an interest in reaching El Paso on a bleak Sunday in mid-November.

"Now if our luggage didn't go to Terre Haute, we'll be all set," I said. "And someone's supposed to be here to meet us." I had expected to see Estelle Reyes-Guzman's face in the crowd. That was my excuse for not immediately recognizing Posadas County sheriff's deputy Tom Pasquale's husky six-foot-two-inch frame.

"Welcome back, sir," he said. I stopped in my tracks. He thrust out a hand, and, knowing what was coming, I tried not to flinch as the crushing handshake threatened to dust my arthritic knuckles. "I'm your ride," he added.

I nodded and glanced over his shoulder, thinking that perhaps he hadn't traveled from Posadas to El Paso alone. He had. "Thanks," I said. "This is my daughter Camille." She favored the darkly handsome Pasquale with a radiant smile.

"I've heard a lot about you," she said, making the comment sound like an innocent compliment. She then had the good sense to drop the discussion of personal résumés right there. During my stay in Michigan, our conversations had occasionally touched on some of the Sheriff's Department personnel. I'd told her some of the high points of Pasquale's career, beginning first when he was a part-timer with the village's three-man department.

He'd caused more than his share of messes, but young Pasquale had determination, I gave him that. He had tried for three years to get on with the Sheriff's Department, and the road had been a rough one—made so as much by me as by anyone.

He'd finally made it—he'd graduated from the state law-enforcement academy and had been with our department for four months as a full-time officer. He still operated at a high state of eagerness. He hadn't yet been lulled into the bored stupor that made rural law enforcement so dangerous.

Despite his drive and ambition, he had no interest in working for a larger metropolitan department. Posadas had been his home since birth, and I had no doubt that he would work there until he was old and doddering.

"Estelle didn't come?" I asked, ansd started to trudge down the corridor toward the baggage-claim area.

Pasquale shook his head. "They've got a manhunt going on right now, and she couldn't break away." He said it almost as an after-thought. He was trying not to walk sideways, looking at Camille and me—mostly at Camille. I don't know what he had expected. Perhaps he had thought my eldest daughter would be a small, feminine version of me. That would have been a scary vision.

I stopped in the middle of the corridor and looked up at him. "A manhunt? For whom?"

"Ah," Pasquale said, shaking his head in dismissal. "A kid got himself lost up on Cat Mesa. Apparently he walked away from a hunting camp. They'll find him."

"How old is he?"

"I think they said he was three."

"Three? You're kidding. A local youngster?" I glanced outside at the glowering clouds. November in New Mexico could be lethal, even for experienced hikers who thought they were prepared.

I could feel pressure on my arm from Camille, doing her gentle best to shag me toward our bags. She was one of those rare people who could walk, talk, and even chew gum at the same time.

Pasquale nodded. "His mother's a woman named Tiffany Cole."

"That doesn't ring a bell."

"She moved here not too long ago, they were saying. Maybe a couple of years. Other than that, I don't know anything about her, except I don't see how she could just let a toddler go off like that."

"We don't know the circumstances," I said. "Where were they camped?"

"Up on top, just north of the Pipes." The Pipes were a series of jagged near-vertical rock outcroppings that stood in line like pieces of a giant limestone pipe organ. The local rock climbers liked to bruise themselves against the formations, struggling to the top, where there was room for two people to stand if they stayed really cozy.

I frowned. "A three year-old out there by himself is going to be tough."

"Well, there's no place for a kid to go up there in that country," Pasquale said with easy confidence, and then added again, "We'll find him."

"And they were members of a hunting party?"

Pasquale nodded. "That's probably what she was doing," he said. "Although with her, it might be hard to tell. She was camped with her boyfriend. We're not sure if anyone else was there or not."

"You know this woman?"

Pasquale glanced at me, a little uneasy. "No. I just meant that she didn't seem like the hunting type when I talked to her yesterday."

"I see," I said. "Maybe just more like a party, then." I pointed ahead at the sign for the baggage claim. I had checked one battered old leather suitcase, as much a museum piece as practical. Camille didn't believe in traveling light, and we waited until her mammoth blue garment bag and two hard-shell suitcases thumped onto the belt.

Pasquale picked up everything but the smallest suitcase as if they all were filled with helium. Camille took the remaining bag, and I followed along toward the rain, feeling useless.

He'd parked the county car in an "Official Use Only" slot, just a few steps outside the electric doors. I frowned again, and Camille caught the expression and assumed I was irritated at the weather. I didn't bother to explain to her. No doubt Tom Pasquale was only doing what he'd been told. The unmarked sedan wouldn't be much help in a mountain-terrain search, but Pasquale would be. With his long legs and stamina, he could cover acres of rugged ground without missing a beat.

Sheriff Martin Holman should have known better than to waste his manpower running a taxi service for me.

Interstate 10 was only minutes from the airport, and as soon as we were on the highway heading north toward New Mexico,

Pasquale drove so fast in the left-hand lane that even the trucks looked as if they were crawling. I didn't complain about the speed, and Camille had returned to life with the prime minister. If she heard my gentle sigh when we flashed into New Mexico, she didn't comment. The ride west from Las Cruces was even quicker.

The village of Posadas was a mile off the interstate, and tourists didn't stop often. There wasn't much more to see standing still in the middle of town than there was thundering by on the highway at seventy-five miles an hour.

A mile before the single exit, a large billboard announced the Posadas Inn, American-owned, family rates, and travel association-approved. Beyond that, a single sign with small lettering and a tiny arrow pointed to the off-ramp. That wasn't much of a greeting, but it was enough for me.

Deputy Pasquale braked hard for the tight curve of the ramp, and if I had twisted my neck, I could have seen the grove of trees that marked my property south of the highway. No doubt my house was a mess, thanks to the bastards who'd ransacked it.

At first, I had assumed that a gang of neighborhood kids had been responsible, tempted after they'd learned I was away from home. But Estelle Reyes-Guzman had said that my filing cabinet had been taken, and that didn't sound like the work of children.

We pulled to a stop at the intersection below the interstate overpass, and Tom Pasquale started to turn left, toward Escondido Lane and Guadalupe Terrace. I held up a hand.

"Why don't you swing by the office first for a few minutes," I said, nodding off to the right.

For someone who didn't appear to be paying attention, Camille had finely honed hearing. "He needs to go home before anything else, Officer," my daughter said quietly, taking her self-appointed role as my nurse seriously.

I'd enjoyed a twenty-year career in the Marines Corps, retiring as a gunnery sergeant. After that, I'd been in civilian law enforcement for a quarter of a century, with fifteen years spent as undersheriff of Posadas County. I was as used to giving orders as most people were to breathing.

Tom Pasquale glanced over at me, hesitated for two heartbeats, and turned left.

Chapter 3

I turned the key in the lock and pushed open the heavy carved door, glad that some little teenaged rodent hadn't taken a crowbar to the ancient worn wood in his efforts to gain entry.

The massive oak slab had originally guarded the entry to a wine cellar deep in the bowels of a seventeenth-century monastery near Tlaxcala, Mexico. After the monastery burned in 1846, the door had been salvaged, and then over the years, it had worked its way north from one admiring owner to the next.

The hinges swung silently and I stepped to the foyer. The brass hardware on the inside of the door still showed a generous dusting of fingerprint powder, and I avoided touching the metal. The cool air wafted from deep inside the old adobe. The place should have been stone-quiet, too.

"Is that your phone?" Camille asked, but she made no move to elbow past me. I didn't bother to say that it couldn't have been anyone else's. This wasn't a suburb of Flint, Michigan. There were no next-door neighbors here, no smell of someone else's barbecue, no screeching kids, no traffic except for the interstate in the distance. The only telephone whose ring I could hear would be my own.

If I had voiced the comparison, I suppose Camille would have been quick to reply that in Flint, people didn't bury their spouses in the nearest handy wooded lot across the street, either.

I turned and reached out to put a hand on my daughter's arm. "Stay here in the foyer a minute," I said. She looked up at me, puzzled, and I added, "I want to see the house before we touch anything else."

Despite the persistent telephone, I made no move toward the kitchen. "Do you want me to answer that?" Camille asked, and I grinned at her. She was from the generation that considered the jangle of a telephone some sort of imperative.

"If they want to talk to me badly enough, they'll call back," I said. After three more rings, the damn thing gave up, and I stood motionless, taking in the silence. That bliss lasted another four or five seconds before radio traffic from the patrol car in the driveway squelched it.

"I'll just be a minute, sir," Deputy Pasquale said. He had been standing in the doorway threshold, and he turned to walk to the car.

"You might as well head back to the office," I called after him. "Thanks for the lift."

"Our luggage is still in the police car," Camille muttered. She bustled after Pasquale. That left me alone in my house, and I sucked in a deep breath of relief. It was good to be home, even if a bunch of strangers had violated the place.

I ambled across the foyer's expanse of Saltillo tile toward the living room, an irregularly shaped seven-sided room with sunken brick floors and heavy, dark ceiling beams of ponderosa pine. Nearly thirty feet across at the widest point, the living room had been designed to suggest an Indian pueblo ceremonial kiva.

The room was a modern touch to an otherwise-traditional old adobe. An artist had lived in the house during the war, and in 1945, maybe in celebration, he'd knocked out a few walls, excavated, and plastered. The new living room and foyer that he had created split the house—a large den, two baths, and three bedrooms to the east; a kitchen, bathroom, and two more bedrooms to the west.

The artist had finished that project and then decided that Posadas, New Mexico, wasn't the heart of the modern-art world. He sold the house to me, and we were both delighted.

I had lined those living room walls with floor-to-ceiling bookcases built of dark oak by Simon Ortega, an alcoholic cabinetmaker in Posadas who did wonderful work when he had drunk just enough to forget his troubles and steady his hands, but not enough to blur his vision. It had taken him three years to finish the job.

Figuring that everyone hides valuables behind books, the little sons of bitches had swept the shelves clean, scattering two thousand volumes across the bricks. The VCR that had been on top of the television set was gone, but that was no great loss. I rarely used the damn thing anyway. The VCR and one movie tape had been a birthday present from my youngest son. I used the tape to put myself to sleep on occasion—and that one tape was still the extent of my video library. The tape lay on the floor, half out of its jacket.

I stood with hands on hips, surveying the familiar scene that I had investigated dozens of times in other homes during my career. And always before, I'd been able to survey the damage with a cool, professional detachment.

Anything that had been resting on a flat surface had been swept off. It was a thorough, workmanlike job.

I bent down and picked up a photograph mounted in an inexpensive silver frame. My son William, in full flight suit, with helmet tucked under one arm, knelt in front of a T2-C Buckeye naval jet trainer. His other arm hugged Kendal, his oldest son, just turned seven when the photo was taken. I put the picture back on one of the shelves and made my way through the mess to the den.

Being an open-and-dump burglar must have been hard on the back. It would have been easier just to open the drawer and look through its contents than to dump things on the floor and have to bend down and rummage around. But these kids had strong backs, and dumping was obviously their style. The den looked like the county landfill. And conspicuous by its absence was my filing cabinet, which normally nestled between the east wall and the end of my desk.

A deep scar was gouged into the desk's wooden top near one corner. I bent down to peer at the damage. The scar ended in a well-defined triangular cut in the oak finish, and I could imagine exactly what had happened. The intruders had picked up the filing cabinet, discovered how heavy it was, and slammed it down on the desk to regain their grip. Maybe one of them had blown a hernia or slipped a disk in the process. I could only hope.

I bent down, hands on my knees, and squinted at the polished wood of the desktop. With the light flooding across it at an angle, the well-defined dusting marks told me that one of the deputies had done a careful, patient job.

"All right," I murmured with satisfaction. On the desk corner nearest the wall was a clear shoe print, the fancy tread patterns clear on the dark wood, clear enough that we'd be able to match for brand, size, and wear marks. "We've got you, you little bastard," I said aloud.

One of the officers had drawn a set of four-corner bracket marks around the print with a dry-erase marker. They wouldn't have been able to lift the shoe print, but someone talented with a camera could sure as hell photograph it.

With an audible crack of joints, I stood up and looked at the wall. The Springfield .45–70 trap-door carbine was gone, as was the sword that had hung below it. To reach the carbine, I had to stand on my tiptoes, and I was five feet ten. The burglar had stepped up onto the corner of the desk to reach the weapon, leaving his shoe print behind.

I sighed. The sword was no great loss, but to a military history buff like myself, the carbine was. And it wasn't the weapon itself so much as where it had been and what it had done. Manufactured in 1874, the .45–70 had been issued, still packed in Springfield Armory's grease, to a young trooper named Gilbert T. LeSalle.

LeSalle hadn't been a famous military hero or a cutthroat villain. Just one of the thousands of young men who'd spent their lives in the Southwest, moving from one fort to the next, he rode one dusty, rocky trail after another, year after year after year. His military career spanned three decades, long enough to see the aging Springfields replaced by more modern weapons.

Whether he was technically allowed to or not, Trooper LeSalle had kept his .45–70 and taken it with him when he left the service. It hung over the fireplace of his home in Deming until he'd died in 1950 at the age of ninety-six.

I had purchased the carbine in 1973 at a garage sale for twenty-five dollars. Over the course of the next two years, I tracked down both the carbine's provenance and the military records of the trooper who had carried it.

All that paperwork, interesting only to someone fond of the little guy's place in history, had been in the locked filing cabinet.

Government paperwork was all replaceable, of course. A few items in the cabinet that I didn't want to think about were not, and their loss made my stomach churn.

Of more interest to a thief were a couple of handguns—including the .357 Magnum Smith & Wesson issued to me by the Posadas County Sheriff's Department. I grimaced, knowing damn well what kind of trouble a kid could get into with those. That wasn't all, of course. A lifetime's worth of financial papers, my own service records—the list went on and on. The more I thought about it, the sadder and madder I got.

I folded my arms across my chest and leaned against the desk, frowning. The faint marks of tape and print dust on every smooth surface told me that deputies had finished with their chores. Estelle hadn't cautioned me when we'd last talked, and I knew that procrastination wasn't part of her character. She probably had a thick file folder of glossy eight-by-ten photos of every corner of my home and its shambled contents. Camille and I could start the cleanup.

Out in the kitchen, the telephone sprang to life again, and I could hear Camille's steps on the foyer tile. "I'll get it," she called, her voice sounding small and distant through the maze of adobe walls.

I straightened up and left the den, reaching the living room just as Camille leaned over the kitchen counter to holler at me, her hand covering the receiver.

"It's Sheriff Holman, Dad."

I grimaced. "Tell him that I'll call him later."

She returned to the telephone, and after a brief exchange, I heard her laugh. I stepped up into the kitchen and she extended the receiver toward me.

"He says you must be feeling better."

"No doubt," I muttered, and took the phone. Finding one's home turned upside down wasn't my idea of a practical convalescence. "Hello, Marty."

"Hey, Bill. Welcome back, and I sure am sorry about the—"

"Thanks," I said, cutting him off before he got too far into the eulogy over the break-in. "Hell of a homecoming. Any news on the lost kid?"

"Not a thing yet. Pasquale filled you in?"

"In part."

"Let me tell you, the folks are getting worried sick."

"I can imagine. Listen, don't tie up any of the officers on my account. I'm not going to be much use to you for a while, and I sure as hell am not going to be of any use up in those rocks." I glanced back into the living room. "I can handle a residential burglary if I move slowly."

The least the sheriff could have done was manage agreement to that, but he didn't. After a moment's hesitation, Martin Holman asked, "What sorts of things are missing, besides the firearms?"

"Just personal papers. Nothing from the department."

"Oh," Holman said, and the relief in his voice was obvious. I could imagine Martin Holman worrying at night, as he lay in bed, that I had secret files at home, culled over the years—names, dates, indiscretions. Maybe even *his* name. Sheriff Martin Holman's specialty was worrying, even when he had nothing to worry about.

"Have you been up on the mesa yet?"

"All morning," Sheriff Holman said. "And by the way, there's a message here that a Stanley Willit wants to talk with you as soon as you're available."

"Stanley who?"

"Willit. W-I-L-L-I-T. That's the name on the note. I've never heard of him."

"Nor have I. What does he want? Did he say?"

"The note just says, 'Ref F. Apodaca.' That mean anything to you?"

"Sure. Reference Florencio Apodaca. The old gent who's using my back lot as his own private cemetery. I can't imagine who Stanley Willet is, or what he has to do with that, but I'll give him a call when I get down to the office."

I didn't look in Camille's direction when I said that, since she had made it abundantly clear that she would accompany me to Posadas and help me settle in *if* I promised that the Posadas County Sheriff's Department was off-limits.

"Well, shoot," Holman said. He was one of the few people I knew who actually said things like that. "You know, we've been so caught up in the logistics of the search up on the mesa that I didn't even remember the old gravedigger. Estelle told you about that, eh?"

"Yes. And all that's the least of our problems right now."

Holman laughed good-naturedly, assuming that I was referring to my health. "We jumped right back into all these things so fast, I haven't had a chance to ask you how you're doing. Did you miss us?"

"Like typhoid," I said. "And I'm doing fine. As the doctor in Flint said, I'm a new person now."

"That in itself will be something to see," Holman said. He could have meant any number of things, but I didn't pursue it.

Instead, I asked, "You said you'd been up on the mesa. Any sign of the boy at all? Any footprints, scraps of clothes, anything like that?"

Holman made a small groan of disappointment. "No, not a trace. We've got a good crew out there, though. We've got nearly two hundred people now. They brought in the dogs this morning, and the National Guard has three choppers out of Las Cruces."

"He's spent one night out?"

"Yes, a cold and wet one."

"Then you don't have much time, Marty. If he isn't found by morning, he's a goner."

"I know it. But it's tough. One of the rescue folks was telling me that a little kid like that will actually hide from the search party. He'll get frightened and do just the opposite of what would make sense."

"Just like a little frightened animal, Marty. Who knows what tiny rock ledge he's crawled under."

"I'll have Estelle give you a call as soon as she breaks free."

"You don't have to do that," I said. "She's up to her ears. But if I get a chance, I'll drive up on the mesa later this afternoon, if you haven't found the youngster yet. Getting out would do me some good."

After I hung up, I stood for a long time, staring at the designs in the countertop.

"It never lets up, does it?" Camille said. I looked over at her and she was smiling, her expression sympathetic.

"No, it doesn't," I said.

Chapter 4

My daughter's sympathy did not extend to agreeing to a trip out to the wilds of Cat Mesa. "They don't need you for that," she said flatly, and instead, she suggested that it might be nice if we worked to put to rights the wreckage of my home. She was right, of course, but I didn't have to like it. Every time I glanced at the mess, my anger returned. A trip to the mesa would have put it out of sight, out of mind.

I plugged in the coffeemaker and watched it brew while she started on the books in the living room. She paused when she came to the picture of her younger brother kneeling in front of his jet airplane with his son. "Billy looks about eighteen years old in this," she said, and grinned.

"He almost was," I said.

She carefully placed the framed photo back on the shelf, a colorful break between the tomes of Grant's memoirs on one side and Lee's on the other. "You don't have very many pictures, Dad."

"I've got lots of pictures."

"I mean out. Where you can see 'em."

I couldn't have told her why that one photograph of my youngest son rested there by itself. "I rotate," I said. "That way, I don't get confused by too many faces."

She cast one of her famous withering glances my way. "Do you want a cup of coffee?" I asked.

"No. And you shouldn't be drinking that stuff, either."

I poured myself a mug and walked down into the living room. I had arranged my considerable collection of books in general categories by wars: a section on the French and Indian, then the Revolution, 1812, Civil, and so on. Military history wasn't a passion, but it seemed a logical way to come to grips with a nation's progress.

I bent down to pick up one of my favorites, a book on Joshua Chamberlain that I had purchased not more than a year before.

"Let me do this, Dad," Camille said. Perhaps she had heard the grunt, or noticed that I concentrated on one title at a time. At that rate, the pickup would take a year. I handed her the book and she waved toward one of the leather chairs. "Sit and talk to me."

"I'd like to go out to the grave before it gets any wetter," I said, doing as she instructed. She stopped with her hand still on the shelved book and turned to look at me.

"The grave? You mean out back?"

I nodded.

"What on earth for?" She turned and held up a book. "This doesn't belong with the Spanish-American War stuff on this shelf. Where do you want it?" She examined the spine critically. "It's *Baumgarner's Guide to Injectable Drugs*. Charming title." She looked at me and raised an eyebrow.

I waved a hand. "Two shelves down, with the other cop stuff."

"Cop stuff," she said, stooping. "You don't have very much of that."

"Too much," I said. "And if someone buried his wife on your property, wouldn't you be interested?"

"I suppose so," Camille said. "In our backyard, it would be an all-star attraction." She glanced at another book spine. "Did Estelle say there was evidence that kids did this?"

"There might be."

She looked over at me and grinned. "He said, evasively."

"I'm not being evasive. It's just that you can never be sure. It looks like Estelle was able to lift one good shoe print in the den— where one of the little bastards stepped up on the desk to reach the rifle."

"How much did that filing cabinet that they took weigh?"

"Probably a hundred pounds. Maybe more. It was one of those fireproof things. A couple of stout kids could have moved it easily enough."

I watched her for a few more minutes, then got up. "I need to move around," I said. "I get stiff just sitting. And I miss my wheel-chair."

Camille put up a last armful of books and brushed off her blouse. "I bet. Come on, I'll walk out back with you."

It might have been easier to walk around my lot, taking Guadalupe Terrace north to Escondido Lane and then east, but instead we wound our way right through the grove of wild and snarled trees, a collection of stunted piñon, juniper, elm, sumac, and several massive cottonwoods.

It was anyone's guess where the undergrowth was sucking water from. Posadas County was dry as bleached bone most of the time, and I sure as hell didn't do any watering. If something wanted to thrive in my yard, it had to have the proper attitude. Maybe the roots had all bored northward, invading the village water lines.

After several minutes crisscrossing the northeastern quadrant of my property, we located the grave site. If someone from the Posadas County Sheriff's Department had actually been here, they'd left no trace. They certainly hadn't stretched any yellow tape, and that was just as well. There wasn't much to protect, and the yellow would be an attractive nuisance for neighborhood busybodies and kids.

Before we saw the grave, we saw the work of the industrious youngsters who'd reported Florencio Apodaca's clandestine work. They had nailed a series of short, mostly rotten boards up the wide flank of a cottonwood tree as a crude ladder. Using that, they'd carried more lumber up into the spreading limbs, managing to create a mess even a pair of ravens would have been ashamed of.

I could understand the attraction. From the tree platform, Escondido Lane was just a stone's throw away, literally.

Sometime in their work, the little contractors had looked down into the brush. A sharp pair of eyes had caught sight of the fresh earth and the carved cross.

The grave itself was a neat mound of the loose reddish sand, gravel, and clay mix that told geologists that most of Posadas had once been the bottom of a prehistoric lake or wandering streambed.

Standing at the foot of the grave, I could look through a screen of elm saplings, past a utility pole, and see Florencio Apodaca's front door.

"Nice spot," Camille said. She stood by a runty juniper that had lost half of its trunk fork to an ax, and not long ago. She shoved her hands in the pockets of her baggy chinos.

"Elegant," I said. "He could find the place by lining up with that utility pole."

The marker was a crude but sturdy cross made from two pieces of juniper, and the shavings and chips still littered the ground. The crosspiece, notched tightly into the upright, was further secured with a leather thong.

The wooden cross wasn't plunged into the ground quite straight, but tipped artistically, looking as if it'd been there for generations. He'd made the vertical piece about three feet tall, and I bent down to read what he'd carved into the crosspiece.

The wood was a rich reddish brown, and Florencio had taken some time to rub off the bark and polish the natural sheen of the juniper.

"'Gloria Espinosa Baker Apodaca,'" I read.

"No dates?"

"No date. Just the name. I wonder who Baker was."

"Florencio would know," Camille said helpfully.

"And no Willit," I muttered. I shook my head.

"And who's Willit?"

"Some character who's pestering our good sheriff. Marty passed him along to me."

"You don't need to talk to them, do you?"

"I suppose not," I said. Camille stepped closer and inspected the cross. "That's really very nice," she said. She reached out and rubbed the smooth wood. "Kinda sad, in a way. Two old folks so close that when the end comes, he can't bear to have her somewhere else."

I chuckled. "But she is somewhere else, my dear. This is my property, not the Apodacas'." I sighed and straightened up. "I could deed them a few dozen square feet, and we could put an old iron fence around this, and it'd be just fine."

Camille hooked her arm through mine and bumped my shoulder with her head. "That's sweet," she said. She pointed off to the west where an orange tag fluttered from one of the tree limbs. A metal stake was driven into the ground below it, with another tag, this one blue and white. "Except for the utilities," she added.

I grimaced. "I suppose." I turned and looked off to the east, searching for another tag. "It wouldn't kill 'em to put a little bend in the line, though."

"You think they'd do that?"

"Probably not." I shrugged. "The village attorney will make a fuss. And the housing-development lawyer will fuss."

"Let 'em fuss," Camille said, frowning. She bent so that she could see through the bushes to the house across the street. "How could he think this was his property, though?" Camille asked.

"Easy enough. He's lived across the way for a long time. That neighborhood was there before the interstate went through on the property behind them. Even the street here—Escondido Lane—was just a dirt two-track as recently as 1972, when we moved here.

"And Apodaca lived in that old house long before that. He stepped off his front porch, and what's he see? This property over here, just across the dirt lane. It was never developed, and then he got old and confused like the rest of us, and he just decided that the property was probably his." I shrugged.

"Who the hell knows. Maybe at one time, he actually did own the lot. Maybe he's forgotten that he sold it off. I don't much care, and when I bought this place in 1971, I didn't bother to do a title search beyond what the real estate deal required."

Camille looked sad. "And now I suppose the village is going to want her moved?"

"I don't know that," I said. "I really don't know what the law is for burials. It's not something that the department deals with every day." The cool, damp air was beginning to seep through my jacket and I shivered. "Let's walk back on the road." As we strolled along the broken macadam of Escondido, I kept looking toward the south. In only one spot was the vegetation thin enough that I could see, a hundred yards or more away, the dark hulk of my house.

Camille stifled a yawn, and it was contagious. I realized I was more tired than I cared to admit.

"Well, we've toured a trashed house and waded through the jungles to tour a grave site. Those are the highlights of current Posadas County attractions," I said. Camille laughed, but I got the impression that she probably agreed. "Mind if I take a few minutes and stop by the office?"

I felt her arm tighten in mine. "As a matter of fact, I do mind," she said. "You promised. And what I want to do most is go home and have a nice long, hot bath. I've been stuffed in a supersonic tin can, chauffeured on the interstate by a kid who thinks he's the next Unser, sorted dusty old books, and hiked through the mud." She managed a grin. "I'm tired and hungry, and that means you're ten times that. Let the office wait, Dad."

I shrugged. "I was just eager to find out from Estelle what's going on." That sounded about as flimsy as excuses come, and Camille waved it aside.

"She's probably still up on the mountain, and when she comes down, she'll be more wet and cold than we are. She'll call when she gets a chance."

I knew that, but patience wasn't one of my virtues. Still, Camille was tougher than I was, and I had promised. I reached over and patted her hand just as we walked into my driveway. "Commercial jets aren't supersonic, by the way," I said. "And you mentioned hunger. How's the Don Juan de Oñate sound after we get cleaned up?"

"Sounds fine," Camille said without hesitation, and that surprised the hell out of me.

We went into the house. The damn telephone was ringing.

Chapter 5

I would have ignored the damn thing had Camille not been first in the house. She slipped out of soggy running shoes, disappeared down the hall, and picked up the receiver in the kitchen after no more than five or six rings.

"We just got in," I heard her say. "Give him a minute."

"It's going to take more than that," I said, thumping down on the bench just inside the door. I was no acrobat, and if I tried my daughter's trick, I'd break an ankle before the first ten pounds of Wellington boots and mud came off.

"It's Gayle Sedillos."

"Ah," I said, taking a deep breath before bending down to pull on a boot again. A slimy dollop of forest floor came off on my hand. "Tell her I'll call back in five or ten minutes." I cursed to myself and wiped my hand on a recent copy of the *Posadas Register* that lay on the bench.

In stocking feet, I padded across Saltillo tile toward the kitchen. "Did she say what she wanted?" I asked, but I knew the answer before the words were out of my mouth. Gayle had worked as chief dispatcher for the department for five years, and in varying capacities for another five before that. Perhaps, in those ten years, she had wasted that many words.

"No, she didn't," Camille called, already disappearing into the dark quiet of the house to find herself a hot bath.

I punched in the number and Gayle Sedillos answered in the space between the first ring and the second. Her voice was husky and clipped.

"Sheriff's Department, Sedillos."

"Gayle, what's up?" I had asked her that same question a thousand times over the years, and it seemed a good way to start off after having been held hostage in Flint, Michigan, for a month.

"Sir, welcome back."

"Thank you." I knew she hadn't called for conversation, so I added quickly, "It's good to be back. What's going on?"

"Sir, I need to relay a message to Estelle, but apparently she's on her way down from the search area and either she's in a dead spot or she's got her radio turned off."

"That's happened before," I said. An automobile was a good place to mull things over if the interruptions could be eliminated. I'd made it a point to teach Estelle that over the years.

"I thought she might be stopping by your place before she checked in here."

"That's entirely possible. What can I tell her?"

"Dr. Guzman went to Tres Santos to check on Estelle's mother. Apparently Mrs. Reyes fell."

"Ouch. Is she all right?"

"We're not sure, sir."

"Is Erma with the children?"

"Yes, sir." Gayle's younger sister, Erma, had been working as *nana* for the two children in the Guzman homestead for several years. And work it was, too, with Dr. Guzman matching his own brand of strange hours as a vascular surgeon against Estelle's.

"Well, then, everything should be fine. If I see Estelle, I'll tell her. Did the good doctor happen to mention how seriously Estelle's mother had been hurt? What she broke?"

"I think her hip, he said."

"Oh my." Mrs. Reyes was one of my favorite people, even though I could barely understand a word she said when, on rare occasions, she chose to speak her own brand of fractured English. Ancient, tiny, independent, she lived in the same adobe cottage in Tres Santos, Mexico, where she had been born in 1910—and where Estelle had spent the first sixteen years of her life after the old woman had adopted her. The village was just twenty miles south of the border and an hour's drive from Posadas.

"When did Francis leave? Do you know?"

"He called here at sixteen twenty-one, so I imagine shortly after that. Erma told me that one of Mrs. Reyes's neighbors called her, and she called Dr. Guzman."

There had been occasions, as Mrs. Reyes became more and more frail, when I'd heard the Guzmans discuss medical care in Tres Santos, and the discussion never lasted long. Francis had mentioned the one resident physician by name, along with the words *snake oil* in the same breath. The forty miles wasn't a problem drive—most of it could be dusted off at a hundred miles an hour if need be. But the border crossing at Regal was closed at night. If there was an international emergency, it needed to happen between 6:00 A.M. and 6:00 P.M.

I assured Gayle that I would pass on the message, told her to keep trying the radio to contact Estelle, and then hung up. What I wanted more than anything else was a potful of strong coffee, but I knew I could have my fill at the restaurant in just a few minutes.

I dialed the Guzmans' and when Erma picked up the telephone, I could hear in the background the kind of organized bedlam that she loved best.

"Just a minute now. Don't hit me with that," she said, and I heard a giggle. "*Hijo,*" she said, and the warning was stern. "Guzman residence," she said to me.

"What's he going to hit you with, Erma?" I asked.

"Just a pillow. Is this Mr. Gastner?"

"Yep. Did Estelle get the message about her mother?"

"Oh yes," Erma said, the "yes" lilting with her heavy Mexican accent. "She came in the door about five minutes ago, and she left right away. I think they sent an ambulance to Tres Santos to bring her mother up here."

"That would make sense. Look, if they need anything, will you let me know?"

"I sure will. But I think everything will be all right."

As all right as being eighty-eight with a busted hip in a foreign country can be, I thought.

"Don't let the kids wear you down," I said, and Erma giggled.

After I hung up, I looked outside at the glowering sky. Slate gray and jagged-edged, the clouds scudded in from the northwest.

It wasn't going to be a pretty night for a three-year-old to be stuck out on a New Mexican mountainside.

I cleaned myself up, and by the time I walked back out into the kitchen, I felt almost human again. Camille was busy at the kitchen counter, fussing with a long plastic box. She glanced up at me and smiled.

"Would you like me to fix a nice salad here instead of us going outside again?" she asked.

"I need green chili," I said. "And there's nothing in the house anyway." I pointed at the box. "What's that thing for?"

She straightened up and tilted the gadget toward me and I squinted through my bifocals. I grunted with indifference when I saw that it was one of those compartmented pillboxes where the drugs can be arranged by the day, plenty of little cubicles to serve the needs of even the most spaced-out, helpless patient.

"Put the meds in here and it's easier to remember what's what," she said. "Just do it by the week."

"Oh, gee," I said. "Are you ready to go?"

She filled the last two compartments with a rainbow, then handed me a bottle of long blue-and-white concoctions. "You're supposed to take these with dinner," she said.

"Absolutely," I said, and tucked the bottle into my jacket pocket. We made it out of the kitchen, down the hallway, and across the foyer. I ushered Camille outside, and I was just closing the front door behind us when the telephone rang again.

"Do you want me to get that?" Camille asked.

"No," I said. "Estelle and Francis went down to Mexico, and Erma has everything under control. Five gets you ten it's just the sheriff. He has this mistaken impression that I want to be useful again." I turned the lock. "Let's eat."

The Don Juan de Oñate restaurant was across town, on Twelfth Street. It had been a favored haunt of mine for the better part of twenty-five years, still owned by Rosie and Fernando Aragon, their son Miguel, and his pudgy wife, Arleen.

Exactly what connection Don Juan had had in the early seventeenth century to the dust and sagebrush that would eventually become modern Posadas County was a puzzle to even the most ardent historians. Perhaps the explorer had walked through the place on his way north. Perhaps it was just because Rosie and Fernando liked the sound of his name. I didn't care.

We settled into a fake leather-upholstered booth, and with a perverse comfort I noticed that they hadn't fixed the broken springs in the seat. I rested my elbows on the table and my chin in my hands.

"Tired?" Camille asked.

"Just really glad to be home."

"I bet."

A waitress arrived whom I didn't know, and I tilted my head back so I could focus on her name tag. "JanaLynn," I said. "When did you join the Aragon forces?"

"Sir?"

She looked puzzled and I smiled, taking the menu she offered but leaving it closed. "How long have you worked here?"

"Oh," she said, and ducked her head. "I started last week."

"Well, welcome aboard." I folded my hands on top of the red menu with Don Juan and his skinny horse on the padded cover. "I'd like the burrito grande plate, smothered in green. And coffee."

"Salad with that, sir?"

"No thanks."

"A salad would be good for you, Dad," Camille said, then grinned at the withering glance I shot at her. She continued the grin up to the waitress. "He forgot to tell you to hold the cheese," she said.

A burrito without cheese is sort of like a chocolate ice cream soda without ice cream, but I didn't have the energy to argue. Camille mused through the menu, finally ordering a respectable dinner herself.

When the chips and salsa and water arrived, we both sat back, me contented, Camille no doubt plotting. Outside, the parking lot was a black polished sheen of chilly moisture. Not a single star poked through the overcast. I shook my head and sighed. "A bad night," I said.

"There's not much anyone can do, is there? For the child, I mean."

"Not at night, no. He's too young to build a fire to attract attention. I don't know. Maybe the National Guard helicopters could look for him after dark with spotlights if the weather was decent, but not in this soup. They'd be tangled in the trees in nothing flat. Search and Rescue might work the dogs all night. There's that possibility."

"I don't see how such a little toddler can just wander off like that without being noticed," Camille said.

I grunted and sipped the water. "The 'without being noticed' part happens all the time, sweetheart." Movement caught my eye and I looked out the window again. A county car had pulled into the parking lot, and an instant later, it was joined by a dark brown Buick.

"Our peace and quiet is over," I said. JanaLynn arrived with dinner, and I concentrated on inhaling at least a healthy sampler before the sheriff found us.

Chapter 6

"Do they know you're here, do you suppose?" Camille asked. I watched Sheriff Martin Holman walk across the parking lot toward the restaurant's entrance, head down, hands in his pockets. At five ten, the same height as I am when standing up straight, he was a head shorter than Sgt. Robert Torrez, who walked beside him.

Torrez was explaining something to the sheriff, and with Holman, it could have been something as simple as the time of day. The sheriff nodded, then nodded again, then shook his head.

"He knows all right," I said. "He would never eat here, given any kind of choice. The country club is more his style."

And sure enough, within the minute, JanaLynn appeared around the salad bar's divider, followed by Holman and the towering sergeant.

Martin Holman pasted on his widest smile, stuck out both hands, and shook mine like a long-lost brother. I didn't bother trying to get up by scrubbing my belly through my burrito. "Back in the real world," he said. He waved a hand at my dinner. "And this figures. A safe bet that it's the exact opposite of what the doctor ordered."

I shrugged and had the courtesy not to say something nasty about his preference for embalmed chicken and green beans. Instead, I said, "Sheriff, this is my eldest daughter, Camille. From Flint, Michigan. I think you two knew each other, back in the dark ages."

Martin pumped her hand, too, maybe for just a little too long. Camille's smile was radiant. "I'll be darned," she said, as if I'd never talked to her about the current sheriff of Posadas County. "You aren't that scruffy little kid that sat in front of me in Mrs. Dutcher's American history class."

"Not anymore," Holman said. He feigned mock hurt. "And I don't think I was ever scruffy."

I glanced down at his polished boots, still mint after a day up on the mountains, and the sharp crease of his gabardine trousers. Even the raindrop circles on his leather jacket were placed just so. "I don't think so, either," I said. "Join us." I pushed myself over closer to the wall, taking my burrito with me. "Robert, it's good to see you. Camille, this is Bob Torrez, the department's senior patrol sergeant."

Torrez nodded at me, then at Camille. He was handsome enough that he probably could have landed a Hollywood job, but instead he had settled into place, keeping tabs on his eight younger brothers and sisters. I'd suspected for years that the long-term arm's-length love of his life was our senior dispatcher, Gayle Sedillos. Maybe the two of them figured there was no hurry, since they saw each other as regularly as shift work.

Holman sat down beside me, and Torrez balanced his huge frame on the edge of Camille's bench seat, careful not to slide too close.

"You're still eating that stuff," Holman said.

"I'm still breathing."

"Uh-huh."

JanaLynn had sidled back around the divider and now looked at the sheriff expectantly. "Just coffee," he said. "Decaf."

"Bobby?" she said to Torrez.

"Nothing, thanks."

She left, and Holman leaned forward, his voice low. "*Bobby*? What's with *Bobby*?"

"She's my cousin," Torrez said without a trace of fluster. "They all call me that."

"I think he's related to half the county," Holman said, and he then turned to me, his arm on the back of the booth. "So. What do you think?"

"About what?"

"About being back."

I chuckled. "Long overdue."

"I should say so. What's first on the agenda for you?"

I looked sideways at Martin, wondering what he really wanted. "First, we're going to clean up the mess in the house. Camille made good progress today. And by the way, thanks for covering that window, Robert."

Holman leaned forward and folded his hands on the table. "Yeah. That was a hell of a welcome home for you."

I nodded. "What's the news on the youngster?"

Holman shot a glance at Torrez, then shrugged. "I just don't know. I really don't. That's one reason we stopped by. You weren't home, and at dinnertime there weren't too many other places you were apt to be." He grinned and craned his neck, looking around at the other booths in that section of the restaurant. They were empty.

"Are they going to go with a night search?"

Holman nodded. "The National Guard's going to keep after it, along with Search and Rescue. It looks like the weather is holding stable enough that they might be able to use the choppers with spotlights. And I've sprung all the personnel the county can afford. Bernie Tafoya even has his dogs up there. This will be the second night. I don't know. It looks grim."

"That's rugged country," I said.

"Yes, it is. About the worst in the county." He paused, then traced one of the patterns in the plastic tablecloth with his right ring finger. "And I get the impression that there's something about the whole thing that Estelle doesn't like."

"Meaning?"

Holman shrugged. "I don't know what I mean. She asked Bob here to coordinate things for our end. So he's been working with the Guard and SAR."

"Who's up there now, by the way," I asked, "coordinating things?"

"Eddie Mitchell, and he's got Tom Pasquale keeping him awake."

"He'll love that," I said. Eddie Mitchell had been with the Posadas County Sheriff's Department for nine years, after an unhappy stint with one of the big metro departments. I knew that the taciturn and efficient sergeant delighted in assigning young Pasquale to every dull civil-law job that came along, but I agreed with him—that was one way to keep the youngster out of trouble until he aged a bit.

"Estelle had a family emergency," I added. "That's going to be her first priority for a while. There's no problem with that."

Holman waved a hand. "No, no. I know her mother took a header. I know about that. No, what I mean is before that. Everyone is working out of a base camp, like right here, just east of the tip of the Pipes." He drew a little circle on the table, close to the edge. "That's about where the hunting camp was that the kid strayed from."

He turned and rested his head in his left hand as he looked at me. "I was hoping that being a young mother herself, Estelle's intuition might tell her where the kid went, right away. But she's got something else on her mind. She's not communicating with us."

I frowned and put my fork down. "She's not communicating with you? What do you mean?"

Holman shrugged. "Just that. You know how you used to joke that Estelle was half Oriental or something? She gets so damn inscrutable that no one knows what the hell she's thinking? Well, at a time like this, it just seems like she sure as hell should be talking to us. That's a little kid out there. I'd like to hear her ideas."

"Did you talk to her?"

"You bet. Her stock phrase for anybody in the search is 'Just cover every square foot.'"

"Well? Good advice, seems to me. What else is there to do?"

"Sure. But for most of the afternoon, she's off on the back side of the mesa, well out of the search area, doing who the hell knows what. Just before she got the call about her mother, I happened to catch sight of her standing off about fifty yards from the family's campfire site, leaning against a tree, staring off into space."

I chuckled. "That sounds familiar."

"I thought maybe you'd have a talk with her when she gets back."

"Of course. But I tell you, Marty, it's been my experience, and yours, too, that Estelle does things in her own good time." I took another forkful and chewed thoughtfully. "I've spent many a time waiting for her to decide what she wants to do. And she usually isn't wrong, either."

"It's not just my imagination, then."

I laughed. "No, Sheriff, it's not your imagination. So tell me about this family. Pasquale told me their name, but I've forgotten already."

"The Coles," he said, and looked at Torrez. "Tiffany, right?" Bob nodded. "Tiffany Cole is the mother's name. She moved here about a year ago."

"They were hunting?"

"No. Just camping. The campsite looked more like it was just a place to blow off a little steam."

"And just the three of them? Mom, her boyfriend, and the boy?"

"I assume so. She's a wreck, so it's hard to get any kind of answer out of her. Bob, you talked with her some."

"Just those three," Torrez said, his voice almost a whisper.

Camille looked puzzled. "It's hard to imagine a three-year-old covering enough distance to get himself lost."

"Yes, it is," I said. "But he doesn't have to travel far, as the sad experience we had about ten years ago with the Culpepper boy proved to us. That youngster was eleven years old when he walked away from a hunting camp over by Regal, and they found his bones six months later. He'd curled up under a rock snag less than two hundred yards from the camp." I shrugged. "Now he was eleven, and two hundred yards is close enough, on a still night, to hear normal voices."

"It wasn't a still night, though," Martin said.

"No, it wasn't. It was a goddamn blizzard, and the youngster apparently fell and fractured his skull. And it was so cold that he probably froze to death the first night, if the injury didn't kill him first." I put down my fork and pushed back. "And that's that. If this little tyke is only three, and this is his second night out, with the possibility of freezing rain, then he's had it. And a little body is just terribly easy to miss, even if you've got a thousand troops combing the place."

Holman sighed.

"And that's probably exactly what's bothering Estelle, Sheriff," I said. "Remember that her oldest boy just turned three himself. So this is up close and personal."

"You'll talk with her, though?"

"Sure."

Holman put his palms on the table and pushed himself to his feet. "Did you happen to talk with old man Apodaca about the grave in your backyard, by the way?"

I grinned. "No. Camille and I walked out there this afternoon. Damnedest thing I ever saw. I keep thinking that I'm just going to tell the village to put an oxbow in their goddamn water line and leave her bones in peace. I'll deed him the land, if that makes it easier."

"Whatever you want to do," Holman said, but he didn't sound convinced. "Let me know what Estelle says," he added.

"I'm sure Estelle will let you know herself," I said, and Holman looked heavenward.

"Nice seeing you again, Camille," he said. "How long are you staying?"

My daughter mumbled something noncommittal that I didn't catch, and Holman said something about having dinner with him and his wife if we got the chance.

As they started to move away from the table, Sergeant Torrez said, in his usual half whisper, "I'll be heading back up to the mesa after awhile, if you need anything."

I lifted a hand in acknowledgment, realizing that Bob expected me to reply that I'd be joining him.

Chapter 7

That evening after we returned from dinner, I made a mental note to call the Posadas village office the next day to see what their updated water-line aspirations were. With that information in hand, it would be time to stroll over and talk to old man Apodaca. I didn't really relish that idea, but it had to be done.

I suspected that Florencio Apodaca was an intensely private man, and now he had to be intensely lonely, as well. I didn't see a whole parking lot of relatives' cars over at his place.

What I really wanted was to hear from Estelle Reyes-Guzman, but the evening wore on and that didn't happen. I started to dial Erma Sedillos shortly before nine to see if Estelle and Francis had made it back from Mexico. I punched the first four digits and then thought better of it. Erma didn't need an extra phone call jangling the two sleeping terrors awake.

I walked a circle around the kitchen, stopping in front of the pillbox with all its stupid little compartments. They reminded me of just how useless I was. I turned, walked to the kitchen door, and looked outside. Gusts of wind rocked the cottonwood limbs, and the sky was starless. The thermometer tacked to the window casing read thirty-four degrees. Raw, nasty, and cold.

If anyone needed help, it was the kid lost on the mountain, and I knew damn well that I was useless up there, where the added altitude would make me wheeze, and my bifocaled night vision wouldn't be able to distinguish between a grove of trees and a battalion of National Guard troops.

That left the puzzling burglary of my home, and my mood brightened some when I discovered that when books were jammed back on the shelves, the living room looked about like it always had, minus the VCR—and that was a dust-catcher anyway. There was no telling what evidence Estelle had gathered when she and the other deputies combed the house after the break-in was discovered. I was anxious to talk with her about that, too, but I knew that a two-bit residential burglary was a long way down the list of priorities just then.

I held out until ten o'clock, then pushed myself out of my leather recliner with a grunt.

"Bed," I said to Camille, who was curled up on the couch, engrossed in the prime minister's life. She glanced up at me, her right index finger drifting down to mark her place in the book. "And I may take a run on down to the office later if I wake up." My daughter didn't look surprised.

Over the years, I'd come to first adapt to, and then to cherish my own special brand of insomnia. Posadas County was a wonderful, dark, quiet place at three in the morning, and there was no point in lying horizontal, staring at the ceiling, when I could be in a snug car, idling the back roads with the headlights and the radio off, windows down, listening to the quiet musings of the New Mexican prairie.

Camille knew my habits, and she didn't argue, but I saw her eyes flick toward the kitchen. I knew exactly what was on her mind, and before she could say anything, I added, "And I took my pills, all sixty-five of them."

I damn near set my alarm for 2:30 A.M., then decided against it, knowing my system wouldn't fail me.

Because it was my habit to grab a short snooze whenever the spirit moved, whether it be ten in the morning or five in the afternoon, my bedroom was the absolute dark of a room with two-foot-thick adobe walls and one thoroughly shuttered, curtained window.

I had about three sighs' worth of time to appreciate the comforting smell of the fresh pillowcase before I fell hard asleep. But in what seemed like just minutes, I awoke with a start, Don Juan de Oñate's coffee and green chili already beginning to work their magic. I got up to go to the bathroom and stopped short when I heard faint voices.

Puzzled, I opened the bedroom door and was hit smack in the face by a shaft of bright light that bounced down the hall from the living room. The sun was pounding the east side of the house, but I knew it couldn't be morning, since there was no smell of coffee. I retreated into the bedroom to find some clothes.

I put on my glasses and saw that it was a quarter after eight.

"Christ," I muttered, and quickly got dressed.

A couple of minutes later, I strode into the kitchen as if I'd been somewhere important. Camille was dressed and appeared to be fussing with things that looked like vegetables. The coffeemaker was silent, its one red eye blank, its pot empty.

"Good morning, sir," Estelle Reyes-Guzman said. She was leaning against the counter by the sink. I stopped short and glared at her.

"When did you get here?"

She smiled, but fatigue lined her dark features. "Just a few minutes ago. Camille said the smell of a green-chili omelette would wake you up." She pushed herself away from the counter, crossed the room, and hugged me so hard, I almost lost my balance.

"She's right," I said, and then stepped back, keeping my left hand on Estelle's shoulder. "You look beat, sweetheart."

She nodded. "It's been a long night."

"How's your mother?"

"She's a worse patient than you ever thought of being, sir," Estelle said. Estelle and I had known each other for more than a decade, and I could count on one hand the times that she had called me anything but "sir." Her physician husband had been able to break the habit now and then, and what it was that their two boys screeched as a name for me, I had no idea most of the time.

"She's here now, though? In Posadas?"

"Against her will."

"I can imagine that. What happened, exactly?"

Estelle took a deep breath and shook her head. "She went outside to toss a pan of water into the garden. She thinks she just planted a foot crooked when she went down that little step behind the kitchen. She busted her hip into a million pieces. Francis has her lined up for hip-replacement surgery on Monday morning."

I grimaced. "They're going to do it here?"

Estelle nodded. "Francis thinks it will go just fine. She's really in pretty good health, all things considered."

"And then afterward?"

Estelle ducked her head and gazed off in the general direction of the green chili that Camille was slicing on the counter. "I don't know, sir. We'll have to take it one step at a time."

I grunted and plugged in the coffeemaker. To my surprise, Camille didn't squawk. Instead, she pointed at the cupboard with her knife. "Coffee's in there," she said. "Toward the back."

"Maybe tomorrow," I muttered, and she glanced at me quizzically. "Tomorrow, no coffee. Maybe," I said. "One step at a time."

And in a few minutes, I felt better than I had in weeks. The green chili in the omelette was real, even if the eggs weren't. And the coffee even made the battalion of pills easier to swallow. I popped the last capsule and frowned at Estelle. "I need to ask your husband how many of these things are really necessary," I said. I poured a final cup of coffee, set the pot back on the machine, and added, "So tell me what's going on up on the mountain."

"You saw Sheriff Holman last night." It wasn't a question, and I just nodded. "He's pretty sure we're doing everything that can be done."

"But you're not so sure," I said. "Martin says you're being your Oriental self again."

Estelle smiled at the departmental joke. "Is there any chance you can come up sometime this morning?"

"Sure. What are you thinking?"

Estelle frowned, gazing down into the coffee. She cradled the cup in both hands. "I don't think he's up there, sir."

"Who, the youngster?" She nodded and fixed me with those bottomless black eyes of hers. "What makes you think that?" I asked.

She took a deep breath and held up her hands, tapping one index finger against the other. "For one thing, the search hasn't turned up anything except rumors. That happens when there aren't any traces, anything to provide a lead. Not even a scent for the dogs."

"What rumors?" Camille asked.

"For instance, yesterday someone said that they'd found a child's shoe print about two miles farther down the road."

"Two miles? We're talking about a three-year-old, aren't we?" I said.

Estelle nodded. "When that report came in, a whole sea of people flocked down that way. It wasn't a child's print at all. In fact, Bob Torrez said that the print was made by a woman's shoe, about size five or five and a half."

"It could have been someone on the search team, stopping for a break," I said, "or a hundred other possibilities."

"Sure. What is true is that the print was not that of a child—at least not this particular child. And then things begin to get even more bizarre. About two o'clock yesterday afternoon, just before I came down, we got a call that someone had seen the child riding in a white Ford van, heading down the mountain toward town."

"And let me guess," Camille said. "A white van with out-of-state plates on it."

I looked at her in surprise, and she shrugged. "It's always got to have out-of-state plates," she said. "If you watch all the crappy television docudramas, that's a staple. What good does it do if the van belongs to weird Uncle Louis down the street? That's too easily traced."

Estelle smiled, and that expression lifted half a ton of worry from her pretty olive-skinned face. Except for the aristocratic aquiline nose and narrow jaw, she might have been a younger sister to Camille. "No one actually saw a van. We checked on the rumor, and it was just that. And sir, that's what I mean. All these shapeless rumors," and she rocked her hands back and forth, "the sort of things that surface when the search is getting desperate and there just isn't a break of any kind."

"And you still haven't said why you think he isn't up there."

"He's too little, sir. I listen to all the theories—"

"Everyone's got one of those, or two."

"Yes, sir. But they talk about a three-year-old as if he's going to trek off across rugged country, maybe covering miles and miles, sleeping under logs, and all that sort of nonsense."

"Stranger things have happened, Estelle."

"Not to three-year-olds, sir. Now, an older child would walk, maybe even run. But a three-year-old? His legs are what, about this long?" She held her hands, one above the other, about two feet apart. "At most? That means a tiny little stride, if you can say that a three-year-old strides at all. And he's got no balance, not like an older child. He just can't manage rough terrain at any speed."

"How did he get separated from the camp in the first place?" Camille asked. "Three-year-olds don't go off on solo strolls at night."

"His mother says that he was playing beside the camp trailer. He was digging in the dirt with a stick, perfectly content, just on the edge of the light from the campfire. She said she and her boyfriend had been fussing with the fire, trying to arrange some baking potatoes in the coals. Then her boyfriend went into the camper to get his guitar. The mother says that it was getting late, and she wanted little Cody by the fire, sitting in her lap while her boyfriend sang."

"And she looked around and the child was gone," I said.

Estelle nodded.

"Just like that."

She nodded again.

"He never cried out?" Camille said. "A child's voice would carry at night like a ringing telephone."

"It was blustery, and the campfire was roaring," I said. "And somebody was tuning a guitar."

"No," Camille said, and shook her head.

"No what?"

"Just no," she repeated. "From the time she last noticed the kid playing in the dirt to the time she realized he wasn't there, how many minutes could it have been? Two, three? Maybe ten at the most if mommy was really numb? I mean, isn't that a rule of three-year-old ownership, that you have to pay attention every second?"

"Sure enough," I said, "So the choices are limited. Either the tyke wandered a few yards and fell among the rocks or he wandered where the walking was easiest for his tiny legs, on the road. How far could he go?"

"Not *could*. It's how far he *would* go, Dad. Remember, it was dark. How many brave three-year-olds do you know?"

I grinned, then reached over and patted Estelle on the forearm, thinking of her oldest, my godson. "One," I said. "The kid would walk from here to Cleveland if there was a reason."

"Maybe not," Estelle said. "Francis is beginning to think that there are monsters in the dark now." I found it hard to imagine Francis Guzman, Jr., three years old, as darkly handsome and intelligent as both his parents, afraid of anything.

"So what are the other choices?"

Estelle rested her head in her hands. "I don't know."

"Do you think someone picked him up?"

"I'd hate to think that, but it's a possibility. And I guess that's why I wanted you to go with me this morning. I've got some things I want to show you."

"Sure," I said again. "I don't know what I can tell you that your instincts haven't already covered."

"You never know," Estelle said. She frowned. "Do you mind if Francis goes with us?"

"If he can get away from the hospital, of course not."

Estelle smiled again. "No. I mean *the kid*." She used the nickname I'd adopted when the child was born. As Francis junior's *padrino*, I figured I was entitled. It was a name that was easy to remember.

"That country's no place for a child," I said, "especially in this weather."

"That's exactly what I was thinking," Estelle murmured. She looked at Camille. "Can I talk you into going up with us?"

"I wouldn't miss it," my daughter said.

Chapter 8

The sunshine that morning had been a false promise, a tantalizing little blast of morning light squeezed through a thin rent in the clouds just above the horizon. The rest of the sky was dull lead, with the bottoms of the clouds torn and fragmented by winds aloft. It was going to be a cold, miserable day, the kind that duck hunters love, where the targets show up nice and black against the uniform background of the sky, with no sunshine in the shooters' eyes.

We took my Blazer so that Estelle could use a child's seat for Francis. Camille cheerfully sat in back with the kid, no doubt thankful that she didn't have to stare out through a cop car's backseat security grill.

Radio traffic was intense by Posadas County standards, and dispatcher Gayle Sedillos was handling the various agencies effortlessly. Search and Rescue operations were generally a mess anyway, since no one except the National Guard got enough practice, and everyone wanted to be lead dog. In this particular SAR episode, Sheriff Martin Holman was the commander—his first stab at that kind of interagency organization.

Just before the landfill north of town, Estelle turned west on State Highway 78. A mile farther and the chain-link fence along the airport property grew out of the red sandstone. Enough junk plastered itself to the fencing that it could be mistaken for the landfill.

A Huey chopper in sober New Mexico National Guard colors waited at the end of the runway. The Huey was probably older than the kid who was flying it, but the young pilot was having a good time despite the seriousness of his mission. He held the aging helicopter in a hover a foot off the ground, rock-steady, its wide blades thumping the air so hard, it shook the Blazer.

A second Huey whumped out from the apron in front of one of the hangars, nose slightly down as it followed the taxiway toward its waiting buddy.

"The heavy guns," I said, pointing. Just in front of the hangar, a third chopper crouched, its blades just beginning to spool into motion. A couple of generations separated it from the two fat old Hueys. I didn't recognize the model, but it had enough gear hanging off and poking out to make it as menacing as anything out of Hollywood.

"Lookit," a small voice said, and I turned, to see young Francis straining against his belts, eyes huge as he stared at the show of airpower. I glanced over at Estelle and wondered if she was thinking the same thing. If I were three years old, lost and scared, and that thing arrived over the trees, blowing down a rain of dead leaves, sticks, nuts, even squirrels, I sure as hell would dig a hole and stick my head in, hoping that such a nasty monster would go away.

With the airport safely tucked behind us, we had a thousand yards of peace and quiet. And then Estelle said, "Here comes Robert." She was looking in the rearview mirror, and even as I twisted in my seat, one of the Posadas County patrol cars shot past us so fast, I could feel its wake.

I recognized the hulk of Sgt. Robert Torrez's shoulders, and our radio barked twice as he keyed the mike.

"Three oh eight," the small voice behind me said soberly.

"How do you know that?" Camille asked. She was sitting skewed sideways, her hand resting lightly on the kid's left shoulder. I wondered the same thing. The three-inch squad car numbers were displayed high on the back fenders. If Torrez had been parked and I'd had a pair of binoculars, I could have read them, too.

"'Cause," Francis said. "*Ese es quien es.*"

"In English, *hijo*," Estelle said, but in English or Spanish, that was all the kid wanted to say on the subject. "He knows the car numbers of all the deputies," Estelle added. "Valuable information every three-year-old needs to know."

In another two miles, we turned north on Forest Road 26, a road that was wide, smooth crushed stone for the first hundred yards and then narrowed to ruts, rocks, and dust for its climb up into Oria National Forest.

There wasn't much forest in the Oria. Why the U.S. Forest Service wanted the acreage, I had never figured out. A sparse fringe of trees softened the jagged prow of Cat Mesa north of Posadas, mostly junipers and slow-growing piñons. There wasn't a tree worth either managing or cutting for anything other than firewood within a hundred miles.

I didn't know any rancher foolish enough to want that country for his livestock, although once in a while cattle did wander up into the jagged escarpments that locals called "the Pipes."

With a commanding view of prairie, mesas, and dry riverbeds all the way south to Mexico, the rim of Cat Mesa was a favorite camping spot, despite the twenty miles of kidney abuse it took to get there. We took our share of that abuse as the road snaked up the face of the mesa, then turned sharply west, cutting through a meadow with several abandoned water-catchment structures. As we started to turn toward the edge of the mesa, we heard helicopters in the distance, and our radio came to life.

"Three ten, three oh eight."

I reached forward with a grunt and pulled the mike off the dashboard clip. "Three ten."

"ETA, three ten?"

I glanced at my watch. "About four minutes."

"Three oh one requests that you meet him at the cattle guard."

I acknowledged, and almost as soon as I slid the mike back in the clip, I caught a glimpse of white through the trees. Sheriff Holman was parked just off the road, next to the fence. Estelle idled the Blazer to a halt without pulling off the road, just over the steel rails of the cattle guard.

Holman stepped out of the county unit and leaned on my door. "Brought the whole family, eh?" he said, and nodded at Camille. "He's got you running around already?"

My daughter shrugged good-naturedly and remained silent. He looked at Francis and then at Estelle. "I kinda wondered what was up when Torrez said you were bringing your son out here."

Estelle nodded, but she didn't offer an explanation. Holman raised an eyebrow. "Nasty weather and a nasty place," he said, and I half-expected him to add, with an official rap of his class ring on the door, "Keep the kid in the car."

If the good sheriff had spent the early hours of the morning in the nasty weather combing every cranny of the nasty place, he hadn't collected any scuff marks. Holman was dressed in his mail-order outdoorsman's clothes, with neat waffle-soled boots, expensive chino trousers, and a down vest over a conservative wool shirt.

"Any news?" I asked.

"Nah." Holman wrinkled his face in disgust and pushed the brim of his Stetson up off the bridge of his nose. "The Guard has a high-tech unit in this morning that's shooting with infrared. They claim that if there's anything living on the hill, they'll find it. Or anything that hasn't been dead more than a day or so."

"Really. It would have been nice if they'd brought that up the first day."

Holman glanced at me, skeptical. "I guess we have to get desperate first. And maybe the thing works like they say it does. One of the troopers was telling me that they can trace anything that's been dead as much as a week, but I don't believe that."

"I don't know," I said. "Technology is amazing. But I'd rather find him alive on the first day than be impressed that we could find him dead a week later."

"It's not for lack of trying, Bill." Holman waved a hand in the general direction of the mesa edge. "Bernie Tafoya has his dogs up there, but they haven't found anything. In fact, we've had dogs since day one, and not a trace."

"How many troops are searching the area?"

"About two hundred, give or take. All the vehicles are parked just down the road a little bit, off in one of the pastures." He leaned down and looked across at Estelle. "We've been pretty successful at keeping people out of the original campsite. It's cordoned off, and I've got somebody from the auxiliary there all the time."

"What about the youngster's family?" Estelle asked.

"That's what I wanted to talk with you about, off the air," Holman said, and I nodded with satisfaction. During his first years as sheriff, he was so enamored with the damn radio that he forgot that half of the county was listening at any given time. Now he'd swung the other way, so tongue-tied that he preferred to relay messages in person whenever he got the chance.

"Both the mother and her boyfriend are up at the site. The mother—"

"That's Tiffany Cole?" I asked.

Holman nodded. "And her boyfriend is a guy named Andy Browers. I don't know him, but Torrez says he works for the electric company. And I gotta tell you, Ms. Cole is a basketcase. I don't think she's gotten any sleep in the last forty-eight hours. One of the nurses who works with Search and Rescue is trying to keep her quiet, so maybe she'll drift off for a while."

"And the boyfriend?"

"He's about to drop himself, but he wants to be out there, looking under every rock. I put Deputy Pasquale with him. That should keep him busy."

"What about the boy's real father? Have we heard from him?"

Holman shook his head. "We know the father's name is Paul Cole. He and the mother have been divorced for almost three years—since shortly after the child was born."

"And where is he?"

"He's a coach up in the northern part of the state somewhere. Bernalillo, I think. Or maybe southern Colorado. I'm not sure." He ducked his head and looked across the truck at Estelle. "You checked him out, didn't you?"

Estelle nodded. "He coaches in Bernalillo."

"Have you talked with him?" I asked.

"No, I haven't," Holman said. "You think we should?"

I shrugged. "Depends on what happens in the next day or so, I guess. Someone should have called him in any case."

"I guess I assumed Tiffany Cole would take care of that," Holman said.

"She might," I said. "When she can think straight."

"Well, anyway, Sergeant Torrez said you were headed up this way, and that he thought you had Francisco with you." He nodded toward the sober-faced Francis. Holman's accent made the little boy's name sound like someone from Cleveland running the

California city's name through his nose. "I wanted to intercept you before you wheeled in. If mama catches sight of him, she's going to go ballistic."

"Then do us a favor," Estelle said. "Take Mrs. Cole down to the SAR headquarters and get her involved looking at maps or something. Or sleeping. We'll be at the campsite for about fifteen minutes."

"Doing what?" Holman frowned.

"I'm not quite sure yet," Estelle replied.

"Not a return of *Tom Sawyer*, I hope," the sheriff said, and when he saw the puzzled look on my face, he added, "Remember the missing marble? Wasn't that what it was? A marble? A cat's-eye?"

I looked askance at Holman, who pushed himself away from the Blazer's door and straightened up. "See, now you should read some of the classics, Bill. Tom Sawyer and his buddies lose a marble, and Tom's heard this old wives' tale about how they should throw another one after it, saying, 'Brother, go find your brother.' The idea is that the second one will land next to the first, and you'll find 'em both."

"Did it work in the book?" I asked.

"I don't remember," Holman said.

"It took three tries," Camille said quietly from the back.

"We're not sending Francis out to look for another three-year-old, Sheriff," I said, and he nodded. He still glanced at Estelle again, ever hopeful that she'd tell him what was on her mind.

Chapter 9

Yellow marker tape was grotesquely attractive mingled with the deep browns and greens of evergreen trees, with the plastic snarled in the mistletoe-stunted limb wood and looping from trunk to trunk.

The camper had long since been moved, but one of the deputies had strung the plastic tape so that the area where their truck had been parked was included within the boundaries. If the auxiliary officer Holman had mentioned was on duty, he was invisible.

Estelle stopped the Blazer on the two-track road and leaned forward on the steering wheel, hands clasped together, frowning out through the windshield. If we didn't turn and look out the rear window, where we could catch glimpses of half an acre of parked vehicles two hundred yards down the road, we could have imagined that we were alone on the mesa.

"What are you thinking?"

She grimaced. "Beautiful spot, isn't it?"

"No," I said. The ground was strewn with trash, from yellow plastic oil jugs to the ubiquitous beer cans to part of an old sofa that was nestled between two piñons. Several scrap pieces of lumber had been nailed between two other trees close by, forming a crude shelf. I could picture myself trying to shave while standing in front of that shelf on an icy morning, dipping my frosted razor into a blue enamel pan water was beginning to sport a frozen skim on the soapy surface. "I haven't seen too many hunting camps that were things of beauty."

Estelle climbed out and walked around to my side to unleash the kid from the backseat. I grunted my way out and leaned against the Blazer.

"Smells good, though," I said. And it did. The juniper was rich, especially where the truck had brushed against the limbs. Through the trees, I could hear dogs and voices where the searchers combed the Pipes just to the north. Farther away, a dull thudding marked where one of the Huey helicopters worked the edge of the mesa.

"Do you need your jacket, Dad?" Camille asked.

I don't know why that irritated me, but it did. She sounded like she was taking care of some old man who was convalescing and fragile, sure to come down with a fatal something if an errant breeze tickled him the wrong way. That was unfair, of course, since she'd been pretty good so far—a quiet traveling companion and not too pushy about my habits.

She held out the jacket, and I shook my head.

"This is where they were camped," Estelle said. She had unbuckled the kid, and they stood hand in hand, Francis looking tiny and helpless framed by those ancient gnarled trees. Estelle walked forward a few steps and knelt by the ring of campfire stones. "Just far enough in from the rim that they had some protection from the wind."

I walked up and stood beside Francis. He was exactly the right height for me to rest my hand on the top of his head without bending down. When I did that, he shifted his weight so that he leaned against my leg, and I grinned.

Francis was as brave a three-year-old as I'd ever known, including four of my own at various times in the distant past. And his first reaction to this spot was to snuggle close. Whether or not Estelle had other reasons for bringing the youngster along, his behavior was certainly enough to feed her intuitions.

I took a deep breath and went down on one knee, the kid between me and Estelle. I heard a small click behind me and turned my head, to see Camille winding her camera.

"Oh, that's nice," I said, and she made a face.

"Tiffany Cole said that this is just about where they were sitting," Estelle said. She stretched out an arm. "The truck was over on that side, between the fire and the two-track. That means that little Cody was playing over by those trees." She stood up, keeping Francis's hand in hers. "The truck tracks are clearly visible." She walked slowly away from the fire circle, her son in tow.

After ten yards, she stopped and looked back at me. "This is a nice soft spot, under this grove of junipers," she said.

"You said that the youngster was digging? Digging with a stick was how you put it."

"Right. That's what his mother said. Just on the other side of the truck. And there are plenty of marks around here, even after all the adult feet stamped things flat." She swiveled at the waist, gazing off into the trees. Francis leaned against her, still tightly clutching her hand. "Come here, sir," Estelle said, and beckoned me.

I trudged over and she indicated the ground under the nearest piñon, soft and inviting with the thick scatter of needles. It *looked* soft and inviting anyway. Before I had a chance to remind her that those cussed things could be as sharp as carpet tacks and as sticky as old gum on a hot sidewalk, she sat down, cross-legged, and patted the ground. "If I get down there, I'm going to need a crane to pick me back up," I said.

"It's a good place to rest," Estelle said. I glanced back at the Blazer. Camille was rummaging in her voluminous handbag, no doubt for more film. I took the plunge before she could record the episode on film.

Estelle encircled her son at the waist, hugging him close. As she talked to me, her breath whispered right beside the child's ear. "Suppose he's playing right here. This is the only spot that makes sense, and this is where his mother remembers him being." She lifted one of Francis's arms as if he were a rag doll and pointed with it off to the left, past the Blazer. The youngster giggled and squirmed closer. "That's the direction of the fire." She swung Francis's arm and pointed off into the woods. "In the dark, it would be just about impossible to walk in that direction."

I ducked my head and looked past them at the dense limb wood. Both piñon and juniper were the kind of evergreens that went for the tender parts of the body, with sharp prongs, wild shapes, and lots of dead limb wood to cut, grab, and scrape.

"He wouldn't have gone far, that's for sure."

Estelle nodded, hugging Francis. "That's for sure." She lifted the kid's arm once more, pointing in the direction we'd come in the Blazer.

"Now, that way, it's easy walking," she said, bending her head close to her son's. "Look way down the road, *hijo*. Do you see where we turned the corner by those trees? See where the fence comes in and then crosses the road?" Francis nodded. The fence was no more than thirty yards away.

Estelle pushed her jacket cuff back and held up her watch. "Show *padrino* how fast you can run down to the fence and back."

Francis straightened up and turned to look at me, his dark eyes big and round, as if I'd made the strange request, or at least as if it was my fault. "Better him than me," I muttered, and Francis heard me.

He held out a tiny hand, as if his thirty-five pounds could hoist my two hundred-plus to my feet. I grinned, seeing the same gesture mirrored that his mother had used with him earlier.

"You go," I said. "You'll be there and back before I even get up." He didn't buy that one. I turned my head to see what Camille was doing. She was reloading the camera, forehead furrowed in concentration. "Camille, take a picture of Francis."

That was a miscalculation. Showing off his track-and-field skills wasn't on the youngster's agenda, especially in front of a camera. He said something in Spanish and collapsed against his mother's knees, head down behind, out of sight. Estelle rubbed his back. I found it hard to believe that this was the same perpetual-motion machine whose standard speed setting at home was set at "Cyclone."

"I don't think so, sir." She craned her neck, looking up at the canopy of contorted branches. "Especially in the dark. I can't imagine him straying *away* from the campfire, especially if there was something going on, like music. Fire attracts. Children can't ignore it. I'm sure you've seen the looks on kids' faces when they're staring into a bonfire. Every spark is a fascination."

Francis pushed himself up and leaned against her knees. He regarded me soberly; then I saw his eyes shift. He giggled and ducked his head a fraction of a second before I heard the click of Camille's camera.

"Estelle's right, Dad," she said.

"I'm not arguing," I said. "It's just that we don't know every-thing that went on that night. For instance, if the fire had been burning for a couple of hours, the youngster might have just got-ten bored and wandered off."

"At that time of day? Wandered into the dark? I don't think so. He'd have just gone to sleep," Camille said.

"Maybe." I turned and looked at Estelle. "What are you thinking?"

She frowned. "The easiest thing that could have happened is that someone picked him up."

"How is that easy? It would be impossible not to hear another vehicle."

"Unless they parked down out of the trees, maybe even down by the cattle guard where Sheriff Holman was."

"All right, suppose they did that," I said. "They sneak through the trees, or up the two-track, trip over the Cole youngster in the dark—he's playing fifteen feet from his mom. He's not going to utter a word?"

"Sneak?" Camille said. She stood in front of us, camera in one hand, other hand on her hip. She surveyed the stunted, gnarled caricatures of trees—little trolls compared with the towering hickories, oaks, maples, fir, and spruce of Michigan. "Cloudy as it's been, it would have been black as pitch up here at night. And the moon's just past quarter now anyway, even if the clouds did break. How is anyone going to sneak?"

"It's not hard." I looked at Estelle. Both she and I had spent more than our share of time picking our way one cautious step after another over country far rougher than this. "They could even use a light here. With the family sitting by a fire, with their backs to the camper, and the intruder's approach behind the vehicle, they wouldn't notice a flashlight anyway, especially if the beam was kept low."

"I don't think so, Dad. Someone coming to take the child just doesn't make sense. In the first place, there's a larger question, even if you allow that someone wanted the child badly enough to risk kidnapping. How did they know the family was camping here?"

I shrugged. "Don't know, don't know, don't know."

Camille crouched down beside me, balancing herself with one hand on my shoulder. "I think it's something simple."

"Like what?"

She stood up and pointed. "I think he's somewhere close. Where's the edge? The mesa edge?"

"About fifty yards straight ahead," I said. "Or even less."

"I'd be willing to bet that he's somewhere within a hundred-yard radius of this campsite."

I rolled to my hands and knees, then pushed myself to my feet. Francis grabbed me around my left knee and I damn near lost my balance.

"*Hijo...*" his mother said, holding out a hand.

"He's all right," I said, and clamped my left hand on his head, using him like a small squirming cane.

"They've combed every square foot of the mesa face, Camille," Estelle said. "Dozens of times."

"What was the child wearing?"

"His mother says he was dressed in jeans, T-shirt, and a bright blue down jacket. And sneakers."

Camille frowned, gazing off through the trees. "I admit, it's hard to see how they could miss a bright blue coat."

"Let's walk out to the edge," Estelle said, and I glanced down with more than a little apprehension at Francis.

"You stay close," I said, and he grabbed my hand.

Matching our pace to the boy's, we wound our way through the trees. That pace was just dandy with me. The air changed as we approached the rim, and I could hear the sweep of wind and, in the distance, the rhythmic thumping of a helicopter.

The view was extraordinary. The overcast was ragged and multilayered, with small rainsqualls breaking loose from the higher clouds and pummeling the prairie to the south. I could see the steep saddle of the San Cristobal Mountains, and the pass where State Highway 56 snaked through the mountains and then shot down to the tiny border village of Regal.

"Whoa," I said, and pulled Francis to a halt. Directly in front of us was a jumble of sandstone rimrocks, each smooth as an elephant's back, rounded and forming the cap of the mesa. Over the centuries, great chunks had broken loose and tumbled down, forming a jagged slope where only a few lucky junipers managed to find something to dig their roots into.

I scooped up the youngster, grunting at the unexpected weight. He hooked an arm around my neck, and we stood quietly, looking out at the valley below.

"Would you like to climb down those rocks?" I asked as I turned and looked off to the west.

"You go, too," Francis said, and I chuckled.

"Not a chance, kid," I said.

Estelle and Camille stood altogether too close to the edge, with that sure balance enjoyed by the young. Estelle knelt down and pointed. "The first thing they did was grid this whole area." She held her hands to form a box. "That way, they were certain that they hand-searched every square meter. There were more than two hundred searchers on this rimrock, all day yesterday, and most of the night."

Camille climbed down into a small crevice and stood with her hands on the broad flank of two enormous boulders.

"Slow work, I can imagine," she said. She turned and looked at me and Francis. "I have to agree with Estelle, Dad. I don't see how a three-year-old could even climb down here. And if he fell, he'd either holler out or they'd find him when they combed the place." She scrambled back up. "We used to party up here when I was in high school."

"Here and the lake," Estelle said. "The two favored spots."

In the distance, I could hear one of the choppers, and it sounded like he was working well in from the treacherous rim.

"Not favored by three-year-olds," I said, and I was about to add something else when we heard a loud dull thud from the northwest. It was several seconds before I realized that I was no longer hearing the rhythmic thudding of the helicopter's blades.

"Oh no," Estelle said, and she turned away from the edge and dashed back through the woods toward the Blazer.

Camille stricken face told me she'd been listening, too. "Let's go," I said.

"Let me take Francis," she said, and neither the boy nor I argued.

By the time we reached the truck, Estelle had the engine going and was talking on the radio.

"Get back to me when you know for sure," she said. She racked the mike.

"What is it?" I asked.

"They think one of the Hueys had a catastrophic mechanical failure of some kind," she said. "Nobody hurt, but it was a hard landing. They took out a couple of trees, so the chopper is junk."

She tapped on the steering wheel, forehead deeply furrowed. Camille struggled with the seat straps for Francis, but Estelle didn't seem to notice.

"So what else?" I said. She was still staring off through the windshield as if she was mentally computing something that didn't add up. "This is me, remember?" I said, and grinned.

She turned to look at me, smiling lamely as she did so. "Sorry, sir. That was Bob Torrez I was talking to on the radio. They found a blue jacket. That's where the chopper was circling when it went down."

"Child's jacket?"

"Yes, sir." She glanced toward the backseat, saw that her son was secure, and pulled the truck into gear.

Chapter 10

As the crow flies, the helicopter crash site was less than a half mile from where we had been standing on the rim of Cat Mesa. To reach it by truck, we had to snake our way northwest on the rough two-track as it followed the rim, then jog along a section fence line.

We were suddenly in the middle of a convention. If there had been two hundred searchers on the mesa, at least that many and a few dozen more had materialized, and they were still flooding out of the trees. Where they all came from was anyone's guess, and how they got there so fast would have been a good case study for a military tactician.

The flight crew of the chopper didn't have long to relish their privacy. As far as the helicopter was concerned, there wasn't much to see. The Huey was olive drab junk. It looked as if the pilot had done a wonderful job of backing it down into the trees, where first the tail rotor and then the wide black main rotor had each taken a turn trying to chew piñon and juniper.

There had been no fire, but a Forest Service truck was standing by, its crew and the four Guardsmen from the chopper nervously circling the cooling, ticking machine, watching for smoke.

After the first few minutes, though, the wrecked helicopter was no longer the main attraction. No one was dead or even bleeding; nothing was going to blow up. The Huey was just another piece of debris that would be a problem to haul down off the mesa. Maybe the National Guard would strip out the usable parts and donate the rest of the bent hulk to local hunters as a base camp. It was at least as attractive as the old sofa and wash rack.

Estelle pulled the Blazer to a stop and I turned to Camille. "Will you stay here with Francis?"

"Certainly," she said, and it sounded like she really wanted to say something else, but I didn't give her the chance. I couldn't keep up with Estelle, and I didn't even try. I plodded after her as she threaded her way through the scrub, making her way toward a convocation that had surrounded a grove of small oak saplings.

I could see Sgt. Robert Torrez, almost a full head taller than anyone else. He'd already made sure that a yellow tape had been strung, and I was sure that irritated the sea of eager faces. A hand plucked at my elbow, and I damn near lost my balance as I turned to see who it was.

"Undersheriff Gastner? You're back?" I grinned in spite of myself. Marjorie Davis looked as if she had dressed for an expedition to the north woods, rather than just a jaunt into the wilds of her own county. Under normal circumstances, I was a fan of the *Posadas Register*, the biweekly official newspaper of Posadas County. Marjorie had worked for the school district for a dozen years before deciding to join the wild world of newspaper reporting.

I glanced at the fancy camera that hung around her neck.

"Marjorie, how the hell are you?"

"Fine. What have we got up here? Do you know?"

"No," I said, stepping carefully. "I don't know." I nodded toward the helicopter. "Bent metal over there. Page-one sort of stuff."

"I got that. I was glad nobody was hurt." I glanced sideways at her, but she sounded serious. "When did you get back from Wisconsin?"

"Michigan. Yesterday." I stopped, thinking better of wading through the crowd of people whose attention was focused on the oak grove. I didn't have any answers or theories, and I wasn't in the mood to tell the same old story to a dozen of the familiar faces I saw ahead of me—yes, I was back; yes, I was probably still undersheriff, nominally at least; and no, I didn't have a goddamned clue about what was going on.

Sergeant Torrez and Estelle Reyes-Guzman were in the thick of things, and I hung back, resting under a fat old piñon that knew more than I did.

Marjorie Davis wasn't so content to loaf in neutral, and when I showed no inclination to move into the center of action, she said, "I'll talk to you later."

"Sure enough," I said, and watched her blend into the crowd.

What had been discovered deep in the little grove of contorted Gambel's oak dashed everyone's theories. I watched the ripple effect as word spread out through the assembled people as necks craned and eyes squinted for a look.

It wasn't much to look at—just a tiny blue coat, western-style yoke, quilted insulation, zipper up the front. The oak grove, a collection of a hundred or two saplings, none of which was more than three inches in diameter, was about the size of half a tennis court. The jacket was a third of the way in on the northwest side.

How it came to be there was certainly not evident, but I was sure the jacket would start a flood of speculation.

I heard Bob Torrez's voice, and he did a passable imitation of a drill sergeant. "Now listen," he bawled, and the woods got pretty quiet. "I want everyone who isn't working law enforcement to step back, then turn and walk back on the trail to the main two-track. We've got too many people here, and we're going to lose evidence. Law enforcement, I want you to just stand still until we get things sorted out."

I could see by some of the faces that Torrez's message wasn't what they wanted to hear. No, by God, they all wanted to stand around and exchange stories about what *they* thought. I grinned.

In short order, Torrez, Estelle, and a couple of the other deputies and troopers had an orderly line of people walking back the way they'd come, back toward the field of vehicles in the clearing. They looked like a bunch of well-dressed refugees.

I stood where I was, trying to look as inconspicuous as a fat man in a black windbreaker can.

After a few moments, we were left with a grove of oaks, a small jacket, and eight police officers of various ranks and departments— and reporter Marjorie Davis, who made herself small and quiet off to one side, camera at the ready.

I shoved my hands in my pockets and walked slowly toward the yellow ribbon, head down, watching where I put my feet. Dale Kenyon, one of the Forest Service cops, stepped forward and held out a hand. "It's about time you decided to get back to work," he said, grinning. "We're glad you showed up."

"Thanks," I said. "I just got in."

Estelle Reyes-Guzman had picked her way through the oak grove one step at a time, eyes like radar. She knelt beside the jacket and lifted one corner of it with a pencil. "No blood that I can see," I heard her say. She looked up at Bob Torrez. "Would you have one of the deputies go back to the undersheriff's truck and get my camera bag?"

"In the clearing by the helicopter," I said to Eddie Mitchell, and the deputy set off at a fast jog.

I tried to picture a three-year-old dressed in that jacket, trotting down the trail. After a bit, he got warm, and he took off the jacket, dropping it in the center of an oak grove.

A three-year-old, trotting *away* from camp, at night? Not likely, I thought, and about as likely as him stumbling through all those rough tree trunks to shed the jacket.

"Sir?" I realized that Estelle was looking at me, and when she had my attention, she beckoned.

"Sir," she said quietly, "doesn't this look like a knife slice?"

I put one hand on her shoulder and lowered myself to a kneel. She lifted the jacket with the pencil. From the top of the right shoulder, down across the back yoke for perhaps five inches was a deep slice, deep enough that the quilted insulation was seeping out. The deep slice was the second in a series of four cuts, all the others shallower and shorter.

"A little more," I said, and she lifted the jacket. I peered down, then moved the fabric to one side with a careful finger. "It goes all the way through, but only for an inch or so."

"And no blood," Estelle said.

"Right. No blood. And the other cuts don't even go through."

She dropped the jacket and tapped her lips with the pencil, then turned and gazed at me. Her voice was so soft that I had trouble hearing, and I bent close.

"Are we supposed to think that this looks like a series of tears from a bear claw, sir?"

I looked at her in surprise, then down at the jacket. The cuts were roughly parallel. And they were clearly blade cuts, not the sort of thing inflicted by a bear claw, no matter how sharp. "Maybe the jacket was torn before. We need to talk with mama."

Estelle nodded. "Maybe. But these aren't tears. They're cuts."

I held out my hand, and she handed me the pencil. I moved the jacket just enough that I could see the front half, which was on the ground. A single long rent tore the fabric from just inside the left armpit diagonally across toward the zipper, stopping just to the left of center. A portion of that tear penetrated the coat for a distance of an inch and a half, but again, there was no blood.

"I don't know," I said. "Under a microscope, you can tell for sure if the fibers are cut or torn."

"They're cut," Estelle said, more to herself than to me.

I pushed myself to my feet with a grunt and twisted at the waist to look at the others. I shrugged and said to Sergeant Torrez, "She'll want photos of the jacket in place. And after that, we need a shoulder-to-shoulder line to sweep this area. First time through, put the oak grove right in the center of the sweep. See what you can pick up."

Behind me, I heard Estelle Reyes-Guzman mutter, "They won't find a thing." I agreed with her, but at least the maneuver gave the troops something to do. She took photos of the jacket, and Marjorie Davis took photos of her. When it became clear that the searchers weren't going to turn up anything else, Marjorie walked back toward the vehicles, no doubt with deadlines to meet.

Estelle completed her series of close-up photos, then backed away from the grove and took several more, finally moving so far away that the jacket would be just a tiny touch of blue in the middle of the negative. She stopped at the sound of voices, and we turned, to see Deputy Pasquale walking through the trees toward us, in company with two civilians.

"Great timing," Estelle said.

Chapter 11

The woman walked with the exaggerated stability of the practiced drunk, her boots hitting the ground flat-footed and graceless. Small wonder, I thought as she drew closer. Her eyes were puffy and red, and despite what her clothing said, she was no more at home in the boonies than I was.

One of the state troopers materialized out of the trees to her left, and the woman startled, almost losing what little balance she had.

I had never seen her before, but I knew her escort. Andy Browers walked at her right elbow, his lean face haggard and pale. He still wore his Posadas Rural Electric Co-op work clothes, now soiled and wrinkled from his long hours on the mesa. Deputy Pasquale, looking fit and eager, rested a hand lightly on the woman's left shoulder. He steered her over to where I was standing.

"Undersheriff," Deputy Pasquale said, "this is Mrs. Cole." I nodded and extended my hand.

"Ma'am," I said. She wasn't looking at me. Her eyes were locked on the yellow tape a few yards ahead of us.

"Andy Browers," the lean man said, and shook my hand. Up close, the bags under his eyes could have been used to transport his belongings. I nodded.

"The deputy said that you've found something," he said, his voice was deep, smooth, and pleasing, with just a hint of the Deep South. He gestured toward the yellow tape. "Is that it over there?"

"We'll need an identification," I said, and reached out a hand to take Tiffany Cole by the elbow. Her blond hair was dirty and her clothes smelled of wood smoke. "We think that we've found the boy's jacket."

Mrs. Cole whimpered something unintelligible, and Browers and I walked her toward the oak grove. "And ma'am, you need to understand that we don't know what this all means," I said, but she didn't care. Her eyes were locked on the jacket, and when she reached it, she sank to her knees, picked it up, and hugged it as if the child were still inside.

"Jesus," Andy Browers said. He pivoted at the waist and looked off toward the southeast. "This is a good half mile from the campsite, at least. I don't understand what the hell…"

"We don't either, sir," I said. I glanced across at Estelle. She and the others seemed perfectly content to let me do all the talking. I didn't blame them. They'd been on that damn mesa for forty hours or more and had probably fielded hundreds of useless questions. "Is that your son's jacket?"

I suppose that was a stupid question, considering Tiffany Cole's agony right there in front of me. In her condition, it wouldn't have taken much to open the floodgates—any piece of child's cloth-ing, her son's or not, might have done the trick.

"I don't understand," Browers repeated. "Why would Cody take off his jacket on a cold night?"

"I don't know."

"And why would he wander way in there? Jesus."

"We don't know," I said. "At least it gives us something of a lead. A general direction anyway." I motioned with my hand to-ward the northwest.

"I don't see why we didn't see this before," Browers said. "There must have been searchers going by here before this." I didn't have an answer to that, and Browers added, "What's down that way?" He stood at his girlfriend's side, one hand resting on her shoulder. He didn't try to help her up, didn't try to pry the jacket loose.

"Well," I said, and turned to find Dale Kenyon. He was walking toward us through the trees, a black plastic folder under his arm. "Let's check a map."

"I can't believe we're still looking at maps," Browers said.

He had every reason to be snappy, and I could imagine just how frustrated he felt. "Maps keep us organized," I said pleasantly. "If we knew exactly where a lost three-year-old would go, then the boy wouldn't still be lost, would he?" Cole's forehead furrowed, and I saw a flash of color that was more than exertion. "All of these folks have damn near lived up here for the past two days, same as you. I'm the newcomer on the block, and I need a map. Leave me alone up here for two minutes, and you'll be looking for me, too."

"Here's a topo map of the area," Kenyon said, and he spread the plastic-coated map out on a level spot. "Here's where we are, right in from the rim." His finger followed the contours where they bunched together, indicating the steep country. "You can see that in another quarter mile or so, the country opens up some."

"What's this?" Browers asked, and when he knelt, his knees cracked like an old man's.

"Turkey Springs," Kenyon said. "It's an old water-catchment system that's been abandoned for years. The permittee on that section drilled a well farther east."

"That's Boyd?" I asked, and Kenyon nodded.

"Johnny Boyd. Right."

I cracked off an oak twig and used it as a pointer so I wouldn't have to kneel. "His place is about three miles north and west. Right there."

"And this is the closest road," Browers said, tapping a faint dotted line.

"That two-track runs along the edge, then cuts down the mesa," Kenyon explained. "It joins up with Forest Road Thirty-three at the base of the mesa, and Thirty-three winds farther on down, eventually joining up with County Road Fourteen. And by the way, we've had search teams sweep right along this mesa in that general direction, all the way to that two-track, and all the way to Thirty-three. So I don't know."

"Shit," Andy Browers said, and stood with his hands on his hips, as if he could discipline an answer out of the piñons.

I stepped around the map and knelt by Tiffany Cole. Her eyes were closed and her face was still muffled in the jacket. I was afraid for a moment that she'd gone to sleep. "Mrs. Cole, can you answer a couple questions?"

She nodded and lifted her face out of the polyester. "That's your son's jacket?"

"Yes." Her voice was small and distant. Her lip quivered, but she wouldn't look directly at the jacket she held in her hands. Instead, her eyes—and they would have been pretty had they not been shot through with so much red—were focused somewhere off on the horizon.

I put a hand on the tiny garment, and Mrs. Cole jerked as if she feared I was going to take it away. Instead, I just gave it a pat, leaving my hand on top of hers. "Was the jacket torn? The last time you saw your son, did his jacket have these tears in it?"

Then she focused, her eyes following the four parallel rents down the back of her son's coat. It was as if I'd pulled the plug on whatever small energy source she had left. She crumpled backward before I could catch her, her head hitting the base of one of the little oaks with a thump.

Andy Browers was at her side in an instant, as were Deputy Pasquale and Dale Kenyon. I backed off to give them room. Movement to my right attracted my attention, and I glanced up, to see Estelle Reyes-Guzman walking back through the trees, toward the spot where we'd left the truck, Camille, and little Francis.

Mrs. Cole needed a hot bath, a massive sedative, and about two days in a soft, warm bed. And none of that would make it any easier. We still didn't have a clue about the boy's whereabouts. And now, every time she drifted back to the real world, Tiffany Cole would think of that jacket and wonder what the hell had taken a swipe at her son—and if whatever it was had ever come back to finish the job.

I didn't blame Estelle a bit for wanting to go hug Francisco.

Chapter 12

The search teams spent the rest of the day on the mesa, systematically enlarging the search area, and now concentrating to the northwest of the campsite. The mood was grim when we left, and I could imagine every pair of eyes nervously flicking to any small shadow or trace of color, fearful that they'd find another clothing remnant, this time with a chunk of little Cody Cole still inside.

I caught up with Estelle as we approached the Blazer. I was carrying the blue jacket, holding it gingerly by the inside collar. "I've got a large evidence bag in the back," I said. "You're going to want to take this with you, I assume."

She nodded, and I could see that Estelle wasn't buying the rumor of a wild animal, which was the current mesa favorite. I hadn't mentioned her misgivings to anyone, and neither had she. But I could tell that was on her mind. Her black eyebrows damn near touched over the bridge of her nose, so fierce was her concentration. She brightened a bit when she saw her son.

"I'm sorry we took so long," she said to Camille, but this time it was Estelle and I who were interrupting the action. My daughter and little Francis were busy. Camille had folded down the backseat, and they were in the midst of a board game—using rules that had never occurred to the manufacturer.

Camille looked up and grinned, her eyes shifting to me as I bagged the jacket and scrawled my initials on the tag. The grin faded.

"Just that?" she asked.

I nodded. "So far. No blood, no signs of injury. No nothing."

"God," Camille whispered.

"What are you doing?" I said, and she looked down at the fistful of red plastic hotels in her right hand.

"These are all ore trucks," she said, as if I'd know just what she was talking about.

"Where did that come from?" I asked. I knew more or less the contents of my vehicle, and a board game wasn't on the list. Camille motioned toward Estelle's voluminous backpack.

"His aunt in Veracruz sent him that," Estelle said. "He just got it yesterday." I cocked my head, leaned closer, and got the thing within range of my bifocals. Sure enough, it was the Spanish version. And just as deeply as he'd been occupied by the game, Francis just as quickly came unglued. He stood quickly, upending the board and scattering pieces.

"Oops," he said, and then helped as much as any three-year-old could as Camille and Estelle gathered houses, hotels, and metal players' pieces from the cracks in the Blazer's anatomy.

"The reporter was nosing around," Camille said quietly as Estelle finally slid the lid onto the box.

Estelle nodded. "I saw her walk over this way."

"She apparently knows Francis?" She tucked an arm around the kid and held him in a hammerlock.

Estelle shot a quick glance at me, and her eyebrows furrowed again. "She did a feature story on me before the election last year, and of course"—she shrugged—"she covered the election itself. She talked us into a family picture for that first story."

"She took my picture," Francis said.

"That's right," Estelle said, "she did, didn't she? You and Papa and me. You didn't have a baby brother yet." It was a decent photo, too. I had a copy in my scrapbook. Estelle may have had a fetchingly photogenic family, but that hadn't been enough for an election win. *Progressive* had never been an adjective I would have applied to Posadas County, and the electorate had declined the opportunity to elect New Mexico's first female Mexican sheriff.

"No," Camille said. "What I think he means is that she took a picture or two of him just a few minutes ago."

"Why would she do that?" I asked. "How could she take a picture through the glass, anyway?"

Camille grimaced. "Bad timing, Dad. We were outside." She gestured at two small junipers and a piñon that snuggled together.

"Potty time. I promised I'd wait right here by the truck while he went over there."

"All of fifteen feet," I said.

"Yep," Camille said. "We were just about to climb back in so I could beat him in round two when Miss Photog showed up. She snapped a picture of Francis climbing into the truck, with me standing by the door, looking stupid."

"Ah, well," I said.

"And maybe another one after that." Camille released Francis so his mother could help him clamber his way into the seat belt shoulder harness that secured him in the small seat, looking like a miniature jet pilot ready for ejection.

"And she asked if you'd call her later," Camille added.

Estelle nodded and turned to look at me. "How are you holding up, sir?"

"I'm fine," I said, and leaned an arm on the Blazer's door. "I've been watching you think, so you're the one doing all the work. What's next?"

I could have predicted the result of that question. Estelle Reyes-Guzman played her cards close, even with me.

"Sir," she said, pulling the last of her son's belt tight, "We're going to have to talk with the Coles. In private, away from the rest of the audience."

"All right," I said.

"I'd like you to be there. And Sheriff Holman."

That surprised me, and Estelle grinned when she saw my expression. "He actually has an astute streak, sir."

"However narrow," I said. "Just say when."

She glanced at her watch. "About eight this evening would be just about right. It'll be dark by then; they'll be exhausted and willing to come off the mesa for a while."

"At the office?" Camille's face didn't show a flicker of annoyance when I said that. Perhaps she hadn't heard.

Estelle nodded. "I need to talk with my husband for a few minutes. And I've got some other odds and ends to wrap up this afternoon." She walked around the truck and climbed in the driver's seat. She put the key in the ignition and hesitated. "This morning I put out a bulletin for the child," she said. "I probably should have done that last night."

"There's always a chance," I said. "Who knows. Maybe they'll find him today. Maybe they're heading in the right direction now."

"He's not up here," Camille said quietly. I cranked around to look at her, and Camille shook her head. Her right arm had drifted over so that her hand rested lightly on the nape of little Francis's neck. "He's not up here," she repeated.

"No," Estelle said. "He's not."

Chapter 13

MY office door was locked when I arrived that evening, and it took a moment to fumble for the right key before I pushed the door open. The interior of the Posadas County Public Safety Building—a grand name for an aging adobe—had been remodeled the previous year, making room for the updated computers, wiring conduit, massive files, and more computers.

Posadas County residents hadn't paid a cent in raised taxes for the expensive renovation. The gleaming hardware, updated information-retrieval systems, and even the new furniture were all testimony to Sheriff Martin Holman's grant-writing talents. No one had ever convinced me that a tiny New Mexican county with fewer than eleven thousand residents needed any of it, but I had learned to keep quiet.

Parts of the renovation I liked. Parts of it made me grimace.

In most places throughout the building, the floor was beautiful polished tile that didn't generate either static or warmth. It was easy for a lackadaisical trusty to mop clean, and drunks could vomit all over it, or even bleed on it, and it could be wiped clean in a jiffy. On a cold winter's day, it was as comforting as an ice cube.

The tile ended outside my door, and I could walk across aging boot-polished wood to my leather swivel chair and oak desk. But sure enough, time marched on. A single computer terminal perched on my desk, its bland face dark.

And it stayed dark, most of the time. In spare moments the previous spring, Gayle Sedillos had surreptitiously helped me explore some of the machine's surface mysteries. When things were

really slow—say in deep February on a weekday night—it was
sort of fun to watch the toasters float across the monitor's face.
Sheriff Holman had been quick to point out that the screen-saver
program, flying toasters and all, was somehow more economical
that just leaving the damn thing turned off.

That was as far as I'd gotten. Estelle Reyes-Guzman could make
the computer do magic, of course, and that was just fine with me.

That evening, Gayle followed me to the door of my office. She
waited patiently while I found the correct key. "Sir," Gayle Sedillos
said as I headed for my desk, "there are a couple of messages that
came for you this afternoon."

"Aren't you due to go home?" I asked, taking the yellow slips
of "While You Were Out" paper from her.

"I thought I'd stay for a few minutes and give Ernie a hand,"
she said. Ernie Wheeler, our other senior dispatcher, didn't need
any hand. He was as steady as they come.

I glanced at the clock and saw that it was after seven. "Don't
wear yourself out," I said. "Something may break tomorrow. We'll
need you sharp."

Gayle nodded and turned to go. "And Estelle just called," she
added over her shoulder. "She wondered if you were here yet."

"I'm here," I said. My daughter had indeed overheard the
conversation up on Cat Mesa that promised a visit to the office,
and as part of a compromise package with Camille, I had agreed
to spend most of the day resting. At first, it had seemed like a
waste of time, but then I got a lot of thinking done.

I looked at the papers Gayle had handed me. One of the slips
was from Marjorie Davis, asking if I'd call her at home when I got
in. After twenty-five years of watching reporters work, I knew
damn well what the problem was. It wasn't just that the youngster
was lost on the mesa.

The *Register* had a midweek edition coming out, and that meant
Ms. Davis was staring at a deadline, with editor/publisher Frank
Dayan staring at her. If something broke and they missed it, all
the metro dailies around the state would beat the little *Posadas
Register* to an important local story, and the *Register* would end up
looking lame and late playing catch-up the following Friday.

I dropped the note on my desk blotter, near the phone, and
grinned. The double whammy was that Wednesday was the day

the grocery stores ran their full-page ad spreads. That meant lots of readership for the right story, if it broke in a timely fashion.

"Marjorie, Marjorie," I said, and looked at the other notes. One was from Sam Preston at Preston and Sons Real Estate, and I knew what he wanted. The third was from Stanley Willit, with an out-of-state area code. Gayle's neat handwriting recorded that he'd called at 4:45 P.M. I had been in the middle of a nap at that time, and if Willit had managed to find out my home phone and had rung the house, my daughter Camille hadn't admitted to fielding the call.

I got up and walked out to the newly designed skylight area that included the dispatcher's console, electrically controlled access doors to the rear lockup area, the sheriff's office, and the personnel lounge.

"I thought you were going home," I said. "But as long as you're here, this Willit person…" Gayle nodded. "Is he related in some way to the Apodacas? Holman mentioned that he's been calling."

"I think so," Gayle said. "I think he's actually Mrs. Apodaca's stepson from a previous marriage. I think that's what Sergeant Torrez said."

"That makes as much sense as anything, I suppose," I said. "And Bob would know." Gayle smiled. Bob Torrez kept track of things like family trees. He had plenty of practice with his own. "Did he say why he wanted to talk to me?"

"He didn't say, sir. He just called a little while ago. I guess maybe it's because it's your land that's somehow involved."

"Well, let's call him and find out," I said. "Maybe he wants some kind of memorial marker erected, or some such."

Gayle nodded.

"Or a neon-lighted mausoleum," I added, and Gayle nodded again. "This is an interesting world we live in," I said, and walked back to my office.

I settled back in my leather chair, pulled the telephone within reach, and dialed. A male voice answered on the fifth ring.

"Yello?"

"Stanley Willit, please. This is Undersheriff William Gastner from Posadas County, New Mexico."

"This is Willit."

I waited for a couple of seconds, giving him a chance to collect his thoughts, since he'd been the one who had called first. The line stayed dead, though, so I said, "Mr. Willit?"

"Yep. This is Willit."

"What can I do for you, sir?"

"Who'd you say you were?"

I took a deep breath and repeated myself, adding, "I'm returning your earlier call."

"Oh, good."

"What can I do for you, sir?"

"Say, can I call you back in just a couple minutes?"

"Sure," I said, and started to give him the number. Before I'd gotten through the area code, I'd collected a dial tone. With a shrug, I punched another line and dialed Marjorie Davis's home number. She answered on the second ring.

"Marjorie? This is Gastner."

"Oh, good, I was hoping you'd return my call."

"What can I do for you?"

"Can I be direct with you?"

I chuckled. "Do you mean there are times when you're not?"

"Well," she said, then let it drop. "Was there some special reason why Estelle had her little boy with her up on the mesa this morning?"

"You'd have to ask her that, sweetheart," I said. "But if I were to hazard a guess, I'd think it's because they're related, somehow. They hang out together a lot, she and the kid."

"Come on, sir. Please."

"Marjorie, let me suggest the obvious. Give Estelle a call, and ask her."

"I did. Erma Sedillos wouldn't let me talk with her."

I chuckled again. "I guess I could have predicted that. And by the way—not that it's any of my business—what are you planning to do with the pictures you took of my daughter and the youngster? Is that front-page stuff?"

"Frank wants to use it."

"Well, then, far be it from me to suggest to you and Frank how to do your jobs." I kept my tone gentle and even jocular, but an uneasy feeling settled somewhere in the pit of my stomach.

Gayle Sedillos appeared in my doorway and held up two fingers, and I nodded. I covered the receiver with my hand and mouthed, "Go home!" She waved a hand in agreement.

"Marjorie," I said into the phone, "Estelle will be here in about half an hour. I need to take another call, so why don't you either ring back or, better yet, come on down in person. We'll figure something out."

"Do you think she'll talk with me?"

"I don't know, Marjorie. I gave up trying to read Detective Reyes-Guzman's mind a long time ago." That wasn't strictly true, of course.

I punched the button for line two and prepared myself for Stanley Willit. But in the past two minutes, he'd become a new man.

"Undersheriff Gastner, Stanley Willit. Listen, sorry to cut you off like that, but in this crazy country, you just never know." He waited a heartbeat or two for me to agree, but I let the line hang silent, and he continued. "I don't know if you remember me or not, but Gloria Apodaca—that's Florencio Apodaca's wife—is my stepmother."

"Yes, sir," I said. "So I understand." Sgt. Robert Torrez's lineage chart for Posadas relationships maintained its reputation for accuracy.

"Gloria Apodaca's second husband was Howard Willit. He owned a big furniture store in Las Cruces for years and years. Howard Willit was my father. His wife, my real mother, died when I was born, and just a short time after that—oh, I suppose I was two or three years old—he married Gloria."

"I see."

"Then about 1945, my dad was killed in a car crash up in Alamogordo. About a year after that, Gloria sold the store and all of my father's holdings and moved to Organ. You know that tiny little village just east of Cruces? Up in the hills?"

"Yes."

"That's where she met Florencio Apodaca, and they got married sometime in 1948. I don't remember exactly just what the date was. I was about twelve years old, I suppose."

"And then your family moved to Posadas?"

"No, no. We lived in Organ for, gosh, close to fifteen more years. Florencio had a business where he made old-fashioned-style Mexican furniture. You know, that adobe hacienda *casa* stuff. He had himself quite a business going, when he wasn't drinking himself unconscious. Then we moved to Deming, and then when I went off to the military, they moved a couple more times. They finally settled in Posadas around 1970 or so."

"Mr. Willit, all this is fascinating, but just what is it I can help you with?"

"Well, see, that's just it. My mother—that is, my stepmother, although she was always like a real mother to me—Gloria had a good deal of money in her own name. From the sale of the store and all. She always kept that aside—for her old age, she used to say."

"They were elderly," I said, remembering the two of them hobbling down Escondido Lane on warm evenings, usually arguing with each other.

"Well, she finally gave in here a year or so ago, and she transferred her account to their joint bank account. I don't know who convinced her to do it, but she shouldn't have." I heard a rustle of papers. "I've got a whole slew of documents here, letters from mother. After she made that initial transfer, the first thing Florencio did was go out and buy a new pickup truck."

"That was a long time ago," I said. "He's been driving the same old truck for years."

"That was just the beginning," Willit said, and for the next ten minutes I sat patiently and listened to a litany of purchases, most petty, all paid for with old Howard Willit's furniture-store money.

"And so," I said to cut Stanley Willit short, "what can I do for you? There's nothing wrong with a man spending his wife's money, especially if it's in a joint account."

"That's my point," Willit said. "Last year, she told me that Florencio had started buying land around Posadas."

"That's a thought," I said, Posadas had never made any of the "fastest-growing communities" lists.

"He's got at least three sons from a previous marriage of his who are all starting to come out of the woodwork. So I guess he figures to set them up. Anyway, my mother said she was going to pull her money—what there was left of it—out of the bank and put it somewhere safe. She said that's all she and Florencio argued about anymore. Money, money, money."

I almost said, "But she isn't your mother," but I caught myself in time. "She was well into her eighties, wasn't she?"

"Eighty-four. Florencio is two years younger, I think."

"But then she died," I prompted. "And by New Mexico's law, right of survivorship gives her estate to her husband, unless she directs otherwise in her will, and as long as they were legally married. Did she leave a will?"

"That's one reason I'm calling. I don't know. She said she was going to write one. I don't know if she ever got around to it."

"The elderly often don't, Mr. Willit. Have you asked Florencio?"

"He won't talk to me."

"Ah. By law, I don't suppose he has to, either, sir. Under 'joint tenants,' he's free to do as he likes."

"Maybe so, but I want you to listen to this last letter. Wait a minute." More shuffling followed. "Here we go. It's dated September twentieth of this year. I won't bore you with all the chitchat, but right here, it says, 'It's very sad what he said he might do. I don't care, old as we are. There's still a little more,' and right here I can't read what she wrote, but I guess she's talking about her money."

"Did you hear from her after that?"

"No. That's the last letter I got."

"Did she normally write to you regularly?"

"Oh, once or twice a year, I suppose. Maybe four times, counting Christmas cards and so on."

"Did Florencio write to you, or contact you in any way, when your mother died? When Gloria died?"

"I didn't know she had died until last week. I telephoned, hoping to talk with her, and Florencio said that she'd passed away. He told me that she hadn't wanted a funeral service of any kind."

"I see. Have you talked to him since then?"

"No. He won't talk to me. But listen. It doesn't make any sense that he'd bury my mother just across the street in some vacant lot like that. Good God. And she was a devout Catholic. She'd have wanted services of some kind, I'm sure."

"Well, sir, it's hard to tell what he was thinking. The very elderly sometimes get a few screws loose, and what seems simple and logical to them is pretty bizarre to the rest of us. Actually, it's not a vacant lot, if you remember correctly. It's a quiet, shaded spot, almost like a park." I thought of the jumble of low shrubs and realized my description was a bit optimistic. "There's no law that says he had to use the cemetery, and with all you've mentioned about his ways with money, maybe the whole idea appealed to him."

"Well, it doesn't appeal to me. I mean, there's no protection for her grave from possible future development, no care, no maintenance. And from what the sheriff told me earlier, it's not even Florencio's property. It's yours."

"True enough."

"And we haven't settled a more important issue, anyway."

"What's that?"

"I think he killed her."

"That's hard to imagine," I said, trying to keep the grin out of my voice.

"Well, it's perfect," Willit said. "She's very elderly, so no one suspects because of that. He prepares her grave all by himself, like some innocent, half-senile old fart, and even carves a crude cross for special effects. People look at it and say, 'Isn't that sweet,' and he's home free."

"I don't think so, Mr. Willit." But I shifted uncomfortably in my chair. Words similar to Willit's prediction had been spoken as Camille and I visited the grave the day before.

"Why not? Two, three years, who's going to know the difference? Especially if she's just wrapped up in an old bedsheet or something like that. The body will be decomposed before long. That's why I'm going to Posadas this week. Tomorrow, if I can make arrangements. I want a court order signed. It'll make things a lot easier if you'd sign a statement saying that you don't want her buried on your property."

"I really don't care one way or another, Mr. Willit, but a court order for what?"

"Exhumation. I want to find out what killed my mother."

Chapter 14

"We're ready, sir," Estelle Reyes-Guzman said, and I damn near jumped out of my chair. I had swiveled it sideways and was gazing out the window, lost in thought somewhere. She frowned. "What's wrong, sir?"

I got out of my chair with a grunt and waved a hand at the telephone. "Nothing." I didn't have a clue how long I'd been wool-gathering. On the chance that it hadn't been too long, I added, "I just got off the phone with Gloria Apodaca's stepson."

"That's the Willit person that's been calling?"

I nodded. "He wants a court order to exhume the body. He thinks that Florencio Apodaca did her in."

I thought Estelle might laugh, or maybe chuckle, or even smile—just a little maybe. But the corners of her mouth didn't twitch and the little lines around her eyes didn't deepen. She stepped into my office and closed the door behind her. "What did you tell him?"

"Well, I didn't give him a definite answer. He's flying in from California sometime in the next day or two." I thrust my hands in my pockets and looked down at the old wooden flooring. "I guess it's something that's got to be settled one way or another. If I refuse, then Willit will take old man Apodaca to court, and we'll be tied up that way until he finds enough evidence to convince a judge. And I'm sure he'll find some excuse. I was thinking of going over to talk with the old guy. Maybe I can convince him that Gloria needs to be buried properly, out of the way of future water lines. That way, Stanley Willit can have his look-see, and the old lady can rest in peace." I shrugged. "It won't hurt to talk to him. See what he says. You want to go along?"

"Sure." She frowned and shook her head. "I've seen Gloria Apodaca in church a few times."

She didn't continue, so I prompted her. "And then?"

"Being practicing Catholics, being buried in unconsecrated ground would raise all sorts of clamor with relatives."

"Maybe she was and he isn't," I said.

"And that would make all the more reason to agree with Mr. Willit, sir. I think you should talk with Florencio. Maybe tomorrow, if nothing else breaks."

I nodded and she stepped aside to let me out into the modern world of tile, fluorescent lights, and electric doors. "Let's see what Mrs. Cole and her boyfriend have to say."

Had the young couple been interested in their surroundings just then, they would have been impressed with Sheriff Martin Holman's office. He had every computer gadget on the planet stuffed into a single piece of furniture that looked like an oversized entertainment center. The snarl of wires and cables lead down to a power source beside his steel desk that looked adequate to drain Posadas Rural Electric Co-op bone-dry.

Tiffany Cole had recovered from her head-thumping faint, but she was a wreck in every other respect. Andy Browers sat beside her, his large brown hand covering both of hers.

The sheriff indicated that I sit in his chair behind the desk, and I took him up on the offer. He perched on the edge of the desk, hands clasped in his lap, composed as hell and looking as if he was about to say, "Now, what will it take for you to drive home that new car today?"

"We're not getting anywhere," he said by way of preamble, and I was surprised at his honesty. "You've spent the same hours up on that mesa that we have, and other than the jacket, we haven't turned up a thing." That pronouncement didn't do a lot to make Tiffany Cole and Andy Browers any more cheerful.

"I think it's time to face the fact that the youngster is not on the mesa," the sheriff continued. He saw the quiver of Tiffany Cole's lower lip and added quickly, "That doesn't mean that we're not going to continue the ground and air search." He clapped his hands once, softly. "Even enlarge the sweep of the search to the west, north, and east."

Browers's voice was husky. "What do you really think, Sheriff?"

Holman hesitated and glanced at me, then at Estelle. "We think," he said slowly, "that the child was abducted."

Tiffany let out a little strangled cry and stuck her left fist in her mouth. Her eyes brimmed. I hoped that she wasn't going to go backward out of the chair.

Holman took a deep breath and plunged on. "You have to consider some main features of that country. It's rugged, and we just don't think that the child would walk very far. That means he'd hear voices, and he'd probably holler for help. He didn't do any of those things. But in addition to all that, there are several access roads to the general area where you folks were camping. It would be easy enough for someone to drive a truck up there, maybe even fairly close. It would also be fairly easy to slip through the trees to where you people were camping and, when it was clear that the youngster was by himself, pick him up."

"You don't really believe that," Browers said. If his hand clamped Tiffany's any harder, we would have heard bones starting to crack. "What about his jacket?"

Sheriff Holman spread his hands. "Detective Reyes-Guzman and I spent quite a bit of time this afternoon going over the possibilities, including the problems presented by the jacket," he said. He got up and walked toward the window, his hands on the small of his back. True to form, he wasn't wearing a gun—at least not one that was visible. "And let me tell you what doesn't make any sense. What doesn't make sense is that the child is still on the mesa. We've used dogs, helicopters, infrared heat-seeking equipment. Enough manpower to comb an area ten times that size. I'm sorry. I don't think he's up there."

The sheriff nodded at Estelle. "Do you agree?"

"Yes, sir." That's all she said, and Holman returned to the desk perch. "Let's take it apart. You provided articles of the boy's clothing so the dogs could pick up a strong scent. They followed the scent just a few feet from where your truck was parked and then lost it. They didn't follow it toward the area where the jacket was discovered." Holman spread his hands again, and Browers took the opportunity to speak.

"It's been raining, though. That screws up the scent for the dogs."

"It hasn't been raining that much," Holman said. "And the dogs are proven in dozens of searches, some in far worse weather than this."

"What if he's fallen over the edge somehow? Hurt real bad, maybe even…maybe even so bad, he can't cry out?"

"The search teams covered every square inch of that mesa face, folks. And I mean covered it. So did you. I spent four hours in the area immediately below where you were camped, in an area no bigger than a football field. The child isn't there. And the National Guard's infrared equipment agrees with us. He isn't there."

"But who?" Tiffany Cole said, and it was the first time I'd actually heard her voice.

"That's the primary reason we wanted to talk with you folks today," the sheriff said.

I cleared my throat. "Mrs. Cole," I said, "who knew that you and your family were going camping this weekend?"

She looked puzzled. "I don't know who we told," she said. "All kinds of people, I suppose. I mean," she added, and her voice took on a petulant edge, "it wasn't some kind of secret."

"Of course it wouldn't be," I said. "Let's try to narrow it down. When did you decide to go? Was it a spur-of-the-moment thing, or something you'd been planning?"

She looked at Browers and he shrugged. "We'd been wanting to go camping for a while, but we never seemed to get around to it. Cody was having so much fun this summer camping out in the backyard with some neighborhood friends." She looked up quickly. "Not overnight. He's too little for that. But they played with the tent and stuff like that. He's even got a little sleeping bag, and he's so proud of it." She sniffed. "Earlier in the week, we just decided that we ought to go out at least once, before the weather turned really bad."

"And with your camper, this kind of weather is no big deal," I said. "Kind of fun, I suppose."

They nodded.

"Were you hunting?"

Browers shook his head. "I don't even know what's in season right now, if anything. We just wanted a big fire, cook hot dogs and marshmallows, and have a good time."

"So it was a spur-of-the-moment sort of decision," I said.

"Exactly. None of this seems possible," Browers said. He leaned forward. "And what about the jacket?" When he said that, Tiffany Cole winced.

"The tears in the jacket are consistent with knife cuts," Estelle Reyes-Guzman said. Tiffany Cole's hand drifted back toward her mouth. "There was no blood on the fabric around the cuts, even though at least two of the cuts penetrated all the way through the garment. If the child had been wearing the jacket at the time the cuts were made, he would have been injured." Perhaps Tiffany Cole wouldn't have blanched quite so much if Estelle hadn't sounded like a bored coroner talking into a tape recorder.

"I don't understand," Browers said. "Are you saying that someone cut up the boy's jacket just for kicks?"

"No," Estelle said. "I don't know why the coat was left behind, or why it was cut."

"We were told that animals probably tore it."

"No," Estelle said flatly. "The cuts weren't tears from an animal's claws, or from a raven's beak, or from anything of that nature. I examined them under a microscope this afternoon, and it's quite clear. The fabric was cut. Four slashes in the back," and she made stabbing motions with her hand, which turned Tiffany Cole another shade paler, "and one cross the front."

"But why?" Browers asked. His voice was a half choke.

"The only thing that makes sense is that someone wanted us to think that wild animals were involved. It's not too hard to imagine. But wild animals were not involved, Mrs. Cole." Her tone was soft and matter-of-fact. "There are only four animals in this country that would be physically capable of taking a child."

It was clear that the parents didn't want to hear what Estelle had to say, but she continued anyway. "Black bears could but wouldn't. This isn't the time of year for cubs, and that's when people get crossways with sows. Mountain lions could, but you had a fire and were making lots of noise. The cats are shy and wouldn't have been in the same area. That leaves coyotes, and if they'd been in the area, you'd have heard them. They can't keep a secret."

Browers wasn't amused. "You said four. That's only three."

"There have been one or two reports of Mexican jaguars on this side of the border. I don't know anything about their hunting habits. But it doesn't matter. None of the animals I mentioned have knife blades instead of claws. It was a human animal that was responsible."

"You're sure?" Browers asked.

"Yes." She nodded at Holman. "I think the sheriff is right. Someone saw your fire, approached, saw an opportunity, and took Cody."

"But that couldn't happen," Tiffany said, and some strength had crept back into her voice. "We would have heard. He would have cried out."

"Maybe," I said. "If someone approached and clapped a hand over his mouth, he wouldn't have had a chance. One hand over his mouth, one hand around his waist, and he's gone. Just like that."

"Or, it could have been someone he knew," Sheriff Holman said. "If that was the case, he might not cry out."

Browers looked at him in astonishment. "You're really saying that someone abducted Cody? You're serious?"

"I'm saying that's the most logical explanation," Holman said. "What about the boy's father, for example?"

"Don't be ridiculous," Browers snapped. "He can have custody whenever he likes." He shook his head. "It's not logical at all. Who the hell would take a child from a campsite on a pitch-dark night? We didn't hear any vehicle, or see any headlights. I don't think it's possible that someone could sneak up on us, unless they knew we were there all along and had planned it all out."

The room fell silent. Finally, Andy Browers said, "But that's what you think happened?"

Holman nodded. Browers looked across at Estelle, and she nodded.

I said, "That's why we need to know every single person you've come in contact with during the past few days—from the time you first decided to go on this camping expedition. Everyone you can think of. We already have a bulletin issued, so every law enforcement agency in the Southwest has been alerted, and they all have Cody's photograph."

Tiffany Cole rose slowly to her feet, her eyes closed and her head shaking from side to side. "No," she said as Andy Browers took her by the elbow. "I'm going back up. That's where Cody is. I know that's where he is."

"Ma'am," I said, but Mrs. Cole was headed out. Sheriff Holman beat her to the door, but it was Estelle's voice that stopped her.

"Mrs. Cole," Estelle said, "there are one or two more things I'd like to ask you before you leave." Tiffany Cole turned and looked at her, one hand still reaching toward the doorknob. Estelle pointed at the chair. "Sit for a minute," she said, and the woman did.

Estelle leaned forward, her face not more than a foot from the other woman's, and when she spoke, it wasn't much more than a whisper.

"When was the last time you saw your husband, Mrs. Cole?"

"My husband?"

"Paul Cole."

The woman shook her head. "August. He had Cody for a weekend in August, just before school started."

"He works in Bernalillo?"

Tiffany nodded. "That's where he was."

"But you have custody of the child?" I said.

"Yes. Of course."

"How long ago was your divorce from Paul Cole?" Estelle asked.

"Almost three years," Tiffany Cole said.

"And what kind of arrangements were worked out as part of that?"

"I have custody of Cody," the woman said. "Paul can come see him whenever he wants, but he hardly ever does. Just that one weekend in August, and even then he called to cancel one day of Cody's visit."

"Is there any unusual bitterness between you and your former husband that you're aware of?" I asked.

She shook her head. "But he just doesn't care." She looked up at me. "I called him the day all this happened. I called him because I thought he had the right to know. But I couldn't get through to him. I left a message on the machine in the coaches' office at the school, in case he stopped in there, and on his answering machine at his house. He never returned the call."

"We'll talk with him," I said. "Is there anyone else in your life who might have a grudge against you for any reason?"

"No," Tiffany Cole said, and stood up abruptly. "And I don't think anyone took Cody."

"Mrs. Cole," Sheriff Holman said, "we need that list. We really do."

She lifted black-circled, bloodshot eyes and gazed at Martin Holman, her lips pressed into hard, thin lines. "My child is somewhere up on that mesa, and this will be his third night alone," she said, and pushed past him.

Andy Browers followed her, and as he passed the nonplussed Holman, he said hoarsely, "We'll get the list for you, Sheriff."

The door closed on soundless hinges, and Holman shook his head. "I don't think she heard a word we said."

"That's not surprising," I said. "The woman is distraught. More than distraught. She's panicked sick. I would be, too."

"If that were true, then she'd be willing to grasp at any straws we held out to her," Estelle Reyes-Guzman said quietly, and I turned, surprised.

"No one is going to welcome the news that their child's been abducted by some creep," I said.

"No," Estelle said, "but even Tiffany Cole should be able to understand that the odds of an injured child still being alive after three November nights, with off-and-on rain, are slim to none."

"We don't know if he was injured," I said.

"If he wasn't, then he'd have been found," Estelle said. "It's that simple. If he's up on that mesa, he's dead. It's that simple. If he was abducted, then there's a chance he's still alive. That's what Mrs. Cole needs to understand." She stood up and snapped her notebook shut. I glanced at the wall clock and saw that I was fifteen minutes overdue on my promise to Camille to be home in time to gulp down another handful of medications.

"Do you have time to stop by the house for a few minutes?" I asked.

"Let me swing by the hospital first and check on Mama," she replied, and then turned to Martin Holman. "Sir, if nothing turns up by this time tomorrow, I think that you can pull the primary search teams."

"Mrs. Cole is going to go ballistic," Holman said. "But you're right. What are you going to do now? If the child was taken just because some wacko child molester saw an opportunity, it's going to be tough following the trail."

Estelle grimaced. "That doesn't fit," she said. "Child molesters don't drive around the wilderness at night. Shopping malls, schools, neighborhoods—yes. Not mesas. What we need is a list of names. A list of the people who would stand to gain something by taking a three-year-old child."

I grunted to my feet as she continued. "Common sense would say that after a divorce, the noncustodial parent is the most likely to abduct. It happens all the time."

"Paul Cole?"

Estelle nodded. "That's a good place to start."

Chapter 15

Estelle was relieved when Sheriff Martin Holman agreed to follow up on Paul Cole that evening.

"This is what I think we ought to do," he said, standing behind his desk, pen in hand, looking down at the yellow legal pad filled with circles, doodles, and random jottings. "I'll call the Bernalillo Sheriff's office and have them make contact with Paul Cole. See if they can round him up for a few questions. Maybe we'll get lucky."

"Maybe," I said.

Holman frowned and regarded me. "I can't help wondering why he isn't down here already. I mean, we're not exactly working in secret down here. This search has been all over television and the city newspapers. Maybe what his ex-wife said is true. Maybe he just doesn't give a shit. What do you think?"

"I just walked into the middle of this mess," I said. "I don't think anything." I didn't say that whenever Marty Holman started acting like a cop, I got nervous. "Just be careful that he doesn't get spooked."

"What do you mean?"

"Make sure that the Bernalillo deputies don't give him any information that he doesn't need to know. None of the circumstances of what's going on up on the mesa. Nothing about what we might suspect, or don't suspect. Just have them tell Cole that his son has gone missing while on an outing with his mother."

"I would think he's heard about the search already anyway, from the television reports."

"Maybe," I said, "but they might not have used the youngster's name yet. One lost kid isn't statewide news until something unusual happens. It's entirely possible that he simply doesn't know."

"We'll play it by ear, then," Holman said, and that should have made me really nervous. But I was as tired as everyone else, perhaps with less reason, and Martin Holman needed to dive into his job headfirst, without me holding his hand. I had other concerns.

Estelle hadn't left the hospital by the time I arrived home, and even though it was nearly nine o'clock, I was restless. I suppose I should have chugged a handful of medications and gone to bed, but that was a repulsive notion on both counts. Camille knew my habits, and she knew better than to nag.

Still, it surprised me when she agreed to accompany me on a visit to Florencio Apodaca's. The old man might not care one way or another what his stepson thought, or what Stanley Willit planned to do, but I had a feeling that whatever was about to happen between the two parties, I was going to be caught smack in the middle.

"Why don't we walk?" Camille said, and I stared at her.

"Walk?"

She grinned. "It's one block, Dad. The fresh air will do you good. Maybe it'll make you sleepy."

"Under ordinary circumstances, I would," I lied. "But the suggestion has been made that this is more than a friendly neighborhood burial. I'd feel better having a radio and transportation close at hand."

She held up a hand in surrender. "Are Estelle and Francis coming over? Have you had a chance to talk with them both?"

"I told her to stop by. We'll just have to see. I don't know what their schedule is. But we'll be gone just a few minutes. I'll leave a note for them."

We drove around the loop and I parked in front of Apodaca's house—a small settling adobe. At one time in the late sixties, a peaked roof had been added to the structure. The loft had created a home for pigeons, bats, squirrels, and the previous tenant's grandchildren.

When I knocked on the door, the only light I could see was the blue cast from a television. I knocked again, then heard a chair scrape against the wood floor.

Florencio Apodaca's face and figure showed every one of his eighty-plus years. He opened the door and stood behind the dilapidated screen, squinting out at me.

"Mr. Apodaca, I'm Bill Gastner, from across the way," I said.

He nodded. "Yes," he said, pulling the word out long and heavily accented.

"Do you mind if I come in?"

"Well, I guess that's all right." He turned and shuffled back inside without opening the door. The hinges squawked, and after I stepped inside, I was careful not to let it slam. I glanced back at the Blazer and could imagine Camille sitting in the dark, holding up her left wrist and tapping her watch at me.

Florencio Apodaca had made his way back to the blue light, and he was already seated in the remains of a recliner when I entered the room. He looked away from the television and nodded at a rocking chair. "Sit down. You want some wine?"

"No thanks," I said. The chair groaned under my weight, and I balanced gingerly, trying not to capsize backward. "What are you watching?"

He pointed at the set with his chin. "They got this show here," he said, as if that just about covered it.

I took a deep breath, made sure the rocker wouldn't collapse, and said, "Stanley Willit called me today."

Florencio regarded me with rheumy eyes. "What did he say?"

"He's worried about his mother."

The old man frowned and looked back at the television. "You know," he said finally, "I don't understand most of these programs that they have now. It's getting so I don't understand most of them."

"They're pretty bizarre," I said. I looked at the screen and saw that he was watching a sitcom featuring a brassy fat woman who had a perfectly timed slice-to-the-bone retort for every comment that came her way. She was enough to make even the most hardened traffic cop cringe.

"He lives out in California now," Florencio said.

"Willit, you mean?"

"Yes." He pronounced it *gess*.

"I told him I had no objection to the burial on my property."

He turned and regarded me again. "You own that land across the street?"

I nodded.

"I thought I owned that." His eyes went back to the screen.

"That's not really the problem, Mr. Apodaca. Mr. Willit is concerned with the circumstances of your wife's death—with how she died."

"That's what he said."

"He called you?"

Florencio Apodaca raised a hand in limp dismissal, then pushed himself out of the chair with surprising speed. "Let's have some wine." He left the television blaring, then returned in a few minutes with two small juice glasses filled to the brim with red wine. He handed one to me, his hands steadier than mine.

"He'd like to know how his mother died," I said.

"She's not his mother," Florencio muttered, and he sat down with a loud cracking of knee joints. "But that's a long story. You know my oldest son?"

"No, I don't."

"He's a cabinetmaker down in Cruces." Florencio sipped his wine. I wet my lips, just enough to discover that the stuff tasted just as rank as it smelled. I held the glass carefully in both hands, resting my forearms on my knees. "He makes all kinds of things."

"I see." I didn't, and added, "How long has it been since you've seen Willit?"

"The last time I saw him was…" He paused and looked up at the ceiling, examining the tin sheets with the pressed floral pattern. "I don't know. It was some time ago."

"When exactly did your wife pass away, Mr. Apodaca?" Chief Eduardo Martinez's incident report might include one version of that information, but I hadn't read the paperwork yet. The chief had interviewed the old man shortly after the grave was discovered, but I doubted that his report would tell me much more than I was learning from the old man's wandering memory.

He concentrated on the television, now featuring a commercial for a fancy pickup truck that leapt dunes, sand cascading from the undercarriage.

When the advertisement ended, he said, "You know, my oldest son has himself a nice shop."

"Uh-huh," I said. "Was it just this past week or so that she died?"

"You could ask the police," he said. "They were here."

"I suppose." I set the glass of wine on a small table. "Mr. Willit said he was coming to try to straighten all this out. We'll have to wait and see what he wants to do."

Florencio frowned and gazed at me appraisingly. I didn't know what he could actually see through the crusted spectacles, but he took his time.

"There's nothing for him here."

"He just wants to know about his mother, that's all. You can understand how he might want to do that."

"She's gone."

"True enough," I said.

"Where do you work?"

"For the county," I said.

"They're the ones who want to put a water line along the road over there?"

"That's the village."

"What do you mean, 'the village'?"

"Village, county—they're two different things. It's the village that wants to put in the line."

"Do I have to let them?"

"It's my property, Mr. Apodaca. And no, I don't have to let them."

"How much you want for it?"

"It's not for sale. If you want me to deed you a small plot of land that includes your wife's grave, I'll be happy to consider doing that."

He nodded and took a sip of wine. "I thought I owned that."

"I'm afraid not. But the village can put a kink in the water line, for all I care. The only thing I ask is that you clear up the circumstances of your wife's passing."

"What do you mean?"

"I need to know how she died, and when. The circumstances."

"The circumstances." He said every syllable as if it were a separate word.

"Yes. And I think that Stanley Willit has the right to know, too. It's only a courtesy."

Florencio Apodaca set his half-empty glass down beside mine. "He only wants the money," he said with surprising venom. "If he causes any trouble, I know a good lawyer."

"I'm sure that won't be necessary," I said.

The old man waved a hand. "That's how these things go." He turned back to the television. "She passed on. That's all he needs to know. That's all anyone needs to know. It's none of their business."

I sighed. I could see, highlighted by the pulsing light from the television, the muscles in his cheeks flexing. He was digging in, ready to play the mule. I stood up carefully, making sure I didn't topple the old rocker.

"I'm going to run along," I said. "I'll see what I can do."

"You want some more wine, you come over. Anytime you like." He got up and hobbled to the television and stood there, one hand on the corner of the cabinet. He extended his hand and his grasp was surprisingly strong. "You tell Stanley Willit not to waste his time bothering me."

"I'll do that."

As I moved toward the door, he said, "Who did you say you worked for?"

"The county."

He nodded as if it were all crystal-clear. "The county."

I made my way back to the Blazer, careful not to trip over the uneven bricks of his walk.

"Success?" Camille asked as I slid behind the wheel.

I grinned. "His oldest son owns a shop in Las Cruces."

Camille looked blank. "And…"

I shrugged. "That part was free. The rest of it, he's going to ignore until it goes away."

"And is it?"

"I don't think so. By the time it's all over, my guess is that Stanley Willit is going to wish he'd stayed in peaceful, logical California."

Chapter 16

When we returned home, I inspected the temporary plywood replacement for my bathroom window and decided to call Andy Sanchez the next morning to have a new frame installed. That took ten minutes. I was tired but not the least bit sleepy, and I finally settled in my leather chair in the living room.

Camille settled on the sofa next to the television, the prime minister's life near at hand.

"I was thinking of going back on Saturday," she said.

I nodded. "That gives us four more days." I grinned. "I'm going to miss having you around."

"Well," she said, "I'm guessing that Mark will have reached his limit of endurance." I tried to picture Camille's husband, the quiet, sober Mark Stratton, arriving home from his dental office each day to a home managed by three teenagers. "Did you have a chance to call Sam Preston this afternoon?"

"No. Well, that's not true. I had the chance, but I didn't do it. You never want a real estate agent to think that you're too eager, you know."

"Your mind's still made up, though?"

I nodded. "This old hacienda is too big for me. And I don't see any of you guys moving back to Posadas anytime soon to take it off my hands." Camille kept her expression politely blank, but I added, "Or ever, for that matter. And I really like the Gonzales place. So..." I shrugged. "You want some coffee?"

"No thanks. Will you take me over there tomorrow? I don't remember it at all. I can't picture it."

"Sure," I said. I started to push myself out of the chair, then stopped. "In fact, there are a couple of photos of the house right on that table by your elbow."

"I saw those earlier," she said. "It's neat." I wasn't sure what she meant by that, but the two Polaroid photos were typical real estate efforts, making the house look tiny, flat, and unattractive. "You want me to get that?"

"Get what?"

"The door." She was up and halfway down the front hallway before I had gotten to my feet.

I saw the look on Sheriff Martin Holman's face from twenty paces away, despite the harsh shadows from the light over the door and the single high bulb in the foyer. He would have made a lousy poker player.

"Good news?" I asked, and waved him inside. He advanced a few paces into the foyer and took off his tan Stetson while he exchanged pleasantries with Camille—altogether too pleasant on his part, I thought. And for a fleeting moment, I found myself wondering what Martin Holman would look like in faded, torn blue jeans and a grease-stained T-shirt, with his hair cut in a burdock buzz. Or even just without a tie.

"Would you drink some coffee if I made it?" I asked, and apparently Holman was more astute than I gave him credit for.

"Sure," he said. "If it's not too much trouble."

Camille grinned and shook her head in resignation. "I'll make it, Dad," she said.

"So what's up?" I lead the sheriff into the kitchen.

"This is a nice place," he said, repeating the same line he had uttered every one of the dozen or so times he had been in my home.

"Thanks. Any news on the youngster?"

He shook his head. "But what's interesting is that the deputies couldn't find Paul Cole."

"What do you mean, couldn't find him?"

"Just that. First, a detective went to his home. He lives in one of those new developments down by the bosque." Holman pulled a small notebook out of the inside pocket of his suit coat and thumbed pages. "Neither he nor his wife were home."

"He's married again?"

"Less than a year ago. One of the neighbors said that she thought the wife went to Santa Fe with a girlfriend for a couple of days of shopping."

"A couple of days? Wow. And Cole?"

"Well, that's the interesting part," Holman said. "Paul Cole has two vehicles registered to him. One is a 1996 Pontiac Grand Am, custom tag that says BEAT 'EM. Is he a coach, or what?" Holman grinned. "The other vehicle is a 1972 GMC four-by-four pickup that's missing an engine."

"And both were parked in his driveway," I said. Holman looked up sharply, and I added, "Just a guess."

"They were. So the detectives figured he was out for an evening run or something. They checked again an hour later, and still no sign of him."

"There could be a thousand explanations for that," Camille said.

"Sure could be," Holman agreed. "But." He held up the notebook for emphasis. "The Bernalillo detectives contacted the principal of the school where Paul Cole works, figuring that, with the way coaches hang out at school all the time, she might have some information. You know what she said?"

"I have no idea," I murmured, watching the coffee beginning its rapid drip. Camille had cleaned the pot so that it actually looked like glass instead of crusted concrete.

"Paul Cole took five days' professional leave to attend a coaching clinic and conference in Anaheim, California."

"This past week, you mean?"

"From Monday through Friday. The principal said that she thought he was scheduled to fly out last Sunday, and that he was planning to return yesterday or the day before."

"Football must be even more important than I thought," I said. "But let me guess again. He hasn't returned yet." I shrugged. "What did the airline have to say?"

Holman grinned, and I got the impression that he was distinctly proud of himself. "He was never booked out of Albuquerque—on any airline that goes anywhere close to Anaheim."

"Or booked back to Albuquerque, either?"

Holman shook his head. "They have no record of him flying anywhere."

"Maybe he drove out with friends," Camille said. "It's only a twenty-hour drive nonstop."

"If he rode with someone else, that would explain both his vehicles being left at home," Holman said, "but no one else from the school was scheduled to attend the conference. The principal said that as far as she knew, no one else went."

"Other schools going?" I said. "Did he ride out with coaches from other schools?"

Holman leaned forward across the kitchen table, his voice lowered conspiratorially. "There was no conference in Anaheim."

"Why did I think that might be coming?" I muttered.

"But it gets even more interesting," Holman said. "The detective—his name's Richard Steinberg, by the way—he chatted with a couple of neighbors. One of them, and she's an elementary school teacher in the same district, said that Cole was excited because he'd been able to get an elk permit in Wyoming."

"A what?"

"He drew an elk permit for a hunt in Wyoming. She thought that he was planning to go but that he was worried about taking that kind of leave from school. She said there was a stink a couple of years ago when a teacher took a week off to go deer hunting. And she said that Cole's wife was petrified that he'd get in trouble."

I leaned back and watched Camille pour the brew into first Holman's cup and then mine. The coffee looked a few shades weaker than I would have liked, but what the hell. There it was.

"So he either flew up to Wyoming or drove up with a friend," I said.

"He didn't fly up."

I sipped the coffee and couldn't resist a grimace at the wan bouquet of decaf. "You've been busy," I said, and set the cup down.

Holman grinned his best used-car salesman's grin. "What I figure is that he either skipped out from school to go elk hunting or he skipped out to do something else."

I was tempted to say, "Well, duh," but instead I asked, "What was his football team's record this year?"

Holman looked puzzled. "I don't know the answer to that."

"In any event, the season should have been over. I don't know when the state championship was, but if his team wasn't a contender, then that's a complication out of the way. I don't care what he's up to, but no football coach is going to miss a play-off, elk or no elk."

"Do you think he might have taken his own son?" Camille said, and I realized it was the first time anyone had come right out and said it.

"I don't know. My first guess would be that he didn't," and as soon as the words were out of my mouth, Martin Holman looked disappointed. "For a couple of reasons. For one thing, if he just wanted his son, he could have driven down almost anytime, picked the kid up, and gone back home, all in a single day. Making a week-long conspiracy out of it would just attract attention. I know the kid's only three years old, but there must be a thousand opportunities during the course of an average day when the father could slip in, grab the youngster, and be gone. And there's always this: The boy's mother said that Cole isn't interested in the kid. He won't even take him for visits when there's the opportunity."

"So it doesn't really make sense that he would do the bit up on the mesa, at night," Holman said.

"No, it doesn't. What makes sense is that Paul Cole went hunting with buddies on school time, and made up the conference nonsense to cover his ass. Did you happen to check with the Wyoming Department of Fish and Game to find out if there was an elk season in progress?"

Holman nodded vigorously. "I checked the net. There is an elk hunt in several parts of the state. Stretches to the end of the month."

"Checked the net?" I said. "Meaning what?"

"Computer, Bill. They have a Web site. You need to join the twenty-first century."

"No, I don't. And the next step is to call Wyoming and find out if he actually has a license issued in that state. Cole's principal is a woman, you said?"

Holman consulted his notes. "Dorothy Nusburger."

"Then Dorothy Nusburger needs to get a little tighter grip on her staff," Camille muttered.

"If she's like any other principal in this state, there's some pressure to have a winning team," I said. "It's the American way of life, let's face it. So if her head coach says he wants to go to an important conference, then she'll send him. Athletics might be an area that isn't her field of expertise. If she trusted Cole, maybe she didn't look too closely or ask too many questions."

"Then that fits," Holman said quietly.

"What fits?"

"Nusburger told the detectives that the school couldn't afford to pay for Cole's travel, and that he then agreed to pay his own way. He told her that the school board would probably think the conference was a luxury but that it was important enough that he was willing to pay his own way."

"And that makes it simple," Camille said. She sat down at the table opposite Holman. "He doesn't have the problem of turning in receipts, or per diem, or any of those other things schools would require for bookkeeping." She looked at me. "I wouldn't be a bit surprised if Nusburger knew where he was going all along."

Holman smiled broadly. "You ought to come work for us."

Camille looked heavenward. "I don't think so, Marty. But it doesn't take a genius to figure out that Mr. Cole thinks he's pretty slick. And I can image his wife being furious with him, especially when he doesn't come home on time. So she takes a day or two for expensive shopping out of town with her girlfriends. Payback time."

Holman glanced at me, maybe a little hurt knowing that he hadn't been elected to genius rank yet. He took a deep breath. "Lieutenant Steinberg said that he was going to nose around a little more and find out where Cole went, for sure. One way or another, he needs to know about his son."

"And if he went hunting, then he was due back in school today," I said. "Maybe he'll show up in the next few hours. No message sent to his school today?"

"Apparently not."

"That's interesting. Thanksgiving break doesn't start for another week or more in most schools. So it's not like he's just taking another couple of days to nose into the vacation time."

"In the meantime," Holman said, "I think it's a good idea to keep the search teams up on the mesa. You know, we've got all these theories, but the whole thing is really"—he made swirling motions with both hands—"pretty nebulous. We don't have a damn thing to go on, other than the youngster's jacket. I'd hate to pull the search off and have the bones found next spring by some turkey hunter. What do you think?"

I shrugged. "It was interesting watching Estelle today. I don't think there's any doubt in her mind that Cody Cole was abducted. And after watching the way her own youngster behaved up there, I'm ready to agree with her."

"Yeah," Holman said, and sighed. "But she's got a lot on her mind right now, with her mother and all. I'm not so sure she's thinking straight."

"There's that possibility, but I wouldn't count on it," I said. "And think of it this way. By leaving the search teams on-site, all you risk is the budget. If he's up there and alive, all Cody has going for him is that no one gives up. So it's worth it until we know for sure."

Holman showed signs of rising, and I added, "By the way, we need to ask Judge Hobart for an exhumation order."

"You've got to be kidding," Holman said.

"No. I went over a bit ago and talked to the old man. There's some kind of grudge he's got against his stepson. And the stepson—"

"That's this Willit guy who called from California?"

I nodded. "He's coming in a day or two. It's a mess. And it's just going to be simpler to move the old lady off my property and plant her in a proper cemetery. That way, everyone will be happy."

"Except Mr. Apodaca," Holman said.

"He'll come around," I said. "He said he'd file a lawsuit to prevent having the grave disturbed, but he's got no legal recourse. And any lawyer will tell him so."

"And you don't think this Willit person will give in, either? Maybe just drop the issue?"

I shook my head. "No. He thinks his mother was murdered."

"Well, shit," Holman said, and stared at me. "Murdered?"

Holding up a hand to reign in Holman's active imagination, I added, "That's just what the stepson thinks. He's dreaming, but you know how it is once somebody like that gets an idea in his head."

"Dad, is what Mr. Apodaca did actually legal? I mean, can you just bury someone in this state without any formal procedures?"

"Well"—I ducked my head—"that's the way it used to be, anyway. The state's dotted with thousands of little family plots, some consecrated, most not. Technically, I suppose that Florencio should have contacted some authority when his wife died, but he didn't, and Chief Martinez didn't press the issue. And technically, the old man can't just dig graves on his neighbor's property, either. But in this case, *I* didn't press the issue, and there wasn't anything surreptitious about what he did. He dug the grave, even marked it in his own fashion. And he told me that he thought he owned the property. So"—I shrugged again—"it's no big deal."

"Unless he murdered her," Camille said.

"Exactly. He's not supposed to do that," I said.

"If he'd buried her in his own backyard, his stepson couldn't force an exhumation, could he?" Holman said. "Unless the stepson could show cause and get a judge to go along?"

"It doesn't matter where she's buried. He'd have to show cause," I said.

"I don't understand why he buried her across the street, then," Camille said.

"He told me that he thought it was his property. Other than that, I don't have a clue, except it's more isolated. It's been a woodlot for generations, and the old man probably figured it would always be." I pushed my empty coffee cup away. "At first, I was just going to deed a small chunk of land that included the grave site over to the Apodaca family. But I got to thinking about it, and I don't want the nuisance. I don't want my property encumbered with some crazy complication. So we'll move the old lady, and that will be that."

Chapter 17

On Cat Mesa, two hundred weary, depressed searchers took a deep sigh of relief when the morning dawned bright, sunny, and windless. By eight o'clock that Tuesday morning when I walked into the Posadas County Sheriff's Office, it was already pushing fifty, with a promise of much higher temperatures. Deputy Tom Pasquale was coming off graveyard shift, and with the typical endless energy of the young, he was changing clothes in preparation for a day on the mesa.

"At least if he's still alive, this change in weather might stretch his chances some," Pasquale said, and I was sure the same sentiment would fire up the search party's enthusiasm for the rest of the day.

And as the weather improved, so did the number of leads, some fanciful, some ridiculous, some just plain worrisome. Every one had to be followed through on, though, and that sapped manpower and time.

Shortly after nine, one of the Search and Rescue coordinators was standing on a ridge north and east of the rim, sweeping the terrain with binoculars. Movement caught his eye, and he zeroed in on a small moving object and no doubt sucked in enough breath to choke.

The child was walking on a narrow Forest Service road, then disappeared over the horizon before the man could fumble his radio off his belt.

Ten minutes later, hopes were dashed when half a dozen Guardsmen caught up with the kid and discovered that he was actually twelve years old, in perfect health, other than being startled by the sudden appearance of troops, and belonged to a family who was cutting wood on the far north side of the mesa.

Shortly before noon, two members of the Posadas Volunteer Fire Department, working the mesa face almost down at the base road, discovered several small bones that, with an active, desperate imagination, might have been mistaken for those of a child.

Despite what common sense should have told them, the discovery created enough furor that search coordinators raced to the scene with one of the medical examiners. The bones were scattered remnants of a mule deer fawn that had met its fate months before.

With the door of my office ajar, I listened to the radio traffic with half an ear. Each new surge of adrenaline that pumped through the search team's veins kept them eager and interested, but it wasn't going to be long before each surge pumped the men just a little less, and then a little less.

The top of my desk was nearly clear when the telephone lit up. "Well, well, well, well" came out as a rumbling chuckle from the other end, and I relaxed back.

"Sam, what's up?"

"I'm supposed to ask you that," he said. Sam Preston had been selling real estate in Posadas for thirty years. I'm not sure what the thrill was of selling the same weed-infested, dusty lot over and over again, but Preston was good at it. "You got time to jaw?"

"No," I said, and the Realtor laughed.

"You haven't changed," he said. "Have you figured out what kind of schedule you're lookin' at on the Gonzales place now that you're back?"

"Sam, you're supposed to say 'Welcome back' first."

"Welcome back. The surgery went well?"

"I don't want to talk about it."

Preston laughed again. "See? I was just saving us time."

"I told Camille I'd like to take her out to look at it today."

"That'd be fine. Time?"

"I don't know. I'll give you a buzz when we're ready."

"Do that. Any word on the youngster?"

"No."

"What a terrible, terrible thing. The parents must be going nuts."

"I would think so."

"Just let me know," Preston said. "And by the way, it really is good to have you back. What you need to do now is retire and start spending all that stash you've been accumulating over the years."

"Thank you, Sam. I'm touched."

"You call me, now."

"I will."

I hung up, jotted one last remark in the margin, and shoved the last of the paperwork for the proposed January budget into its folder. I did so without hesitation, even though my name appeared several times in the personnel section as a full-time employee. That could be changed with a simple pen stroke, and I confess that the thought gave me a certain amount of comfort.

"Sir?" Gayle Sedillos appeared in the doorway and I looked up. "Sir, you might want to know. Eddie Mitchell is checking out an RV that's parked in the back of the Posadas Inn's lot. The sheriff said he wanted at least one deputy available now, while the others are tied up with the search. Eddie was working central and spotted it."

"And?"

"Apparently it has a Bernalillo County tag. There is also a small child inside. There don't appear to be any adults in it at the moment."

My pulse hammered, even though I knew perfectly well what the odds were.

"What's the tag bring up?"

I followed Gayle into Dispatch and looked at the computer readout. "Registered to a Niel Bronfeld, Corrales, New Mexico." I took a deep breath. "And no wants or warrants." I straightened up and looked at Gayle. "Has Eddie talked to them yet?"

"No, sir."

"Where is he now?"

Gayle slid into her chair, leaned forward, and pressed the mike bar.

"Three oh seven, PCS. Ten-twenty."

"PCS, three oh seven is at Trujillo Shell."

"Ten-four."

"Tell him to stay there," I said, and reached across in front of Gayle to slip the keys to 310 off the board. Forcing myself to take my time, I trudged out to the unmarked patrol car, unlocked the door, and slid behind the wheel. The last person to use the car had been a smoker, and I grimaced and buzzed down the windows.

It had been five weeks since I'd last sat behind the wheel of 310. Although common sense would explain to even the most feeble-minded that the county couldn't afford to let expensive patrol units sit idle, I was still irked. I'd driven 310 almost exclusively for the past year and a half and 89,000 miles.

As I pulled out of the parking lot on to Bustos Avenue, the main east-west arterial of Posadas, I turned on the radio.

"Three oh seven, three ten. ETA about a minute."

"Ten-four."

I turned south on Grande Avenue and immediately could see, a mile ahead, the interstate ramps. Art Trujillo's Shell Station was nestled beside the westbound off-ramp, and I saw the county patrol car parked near the car-wash bay on the north side.

Eddie Mitchell lowered his window as I pulled alongside.

"It's the scruffy-looking WorldWide by the utility pole," he said. It was no surprise that the deputy had located the RV. Every deputy I'd ever known had a favorite pastime, a way to keep the long, dull hours from piling up to crushing, job-wrecking boredom. One of Eddie's quirks was cruising parking lots.

Whenever Mitchell was on duty, the dispatcher could count on continuous keypunching as he called in plates.

"And you saw the youngster?"

Mitchell nodded. "I swung around the RV, between it and that retaining wall. He looked out at me through the small back window."

"Did he wave?"

"No, sir. He just looked at me and then disappeared. He didn't look happy."

"No adults?"

Mitchell shook his head. He held up his clipboard and tapped the five-by-eight photograph of three-year-old Cody Cole. The little kid was grinning mischievously, as though he'd just slipped his brussels sprouts under the dinner table to the dog. "I didn't see him for long, but the resemblance was close enough that I wanted to double-check."

"How long have you been here?"

Mitchell looked at his watch. "Twelve minutes."

"They're probably eating lunch inside," I said. "Without the kid. That doesn't make sense, since it'd be a risk to leave the boy unattended. He could attract all kinds of attention."

"I'm not sure a three-year-old would understand that," Mitchell said quietly.

"Let's do it this way," I said. "I'll go inside and find this Mr. Bronfeld and have a chat. You might go park near that whale just in case there's someone inside who's got a driver's license."

Mitchell nodded and I idled 310 across the street to the motel, parking between a custom van from Colorado and a Texas Pontiac station wagon.

"PCS, three ten will be ten-seven at the Posadas Inn."

"Ten-four, three ten." If Gayle was feeling any apprehension or excitement, she kept it off the air.

Noontime did not bring a crush of diners at the motel's restaurant. I stepped inside and Buzzy Ortega grabbed up a menu and greeted me with an enormous smile. The inn had the best iced tea in town, but that was the extent of their accomplishments. The local Lions Club met there, but that was because they didn't want their meeting interrupted by too much attention being paid to the food.

"Buzzy, how ya doin'?" I said.

He managed to maintain the smile. "I guess walking is good for me, Sheriff." He patted his midriff. Judge Hobart had jerked his driver's license for a year after one too many DWIs, but Buzzy Ortega was one of the few people I'd met who'd been able to cope with the inconvenience without getting into even deeper trouble.

I waved away the menu. "I'm looking for a gentleman named Bronfeld," I said, and stepped past him to look into the dining area. "He's either checking into a room or eating lunch here."

"You want me to check the register for you?"

"Just a minute," I said. Only five of the tables were occupied. One was an elderly couple, a walker standing beside the woman's chair. Two tables west, a man wearing a trucking company's logo on his sleeve was eating his way through the soggy, awful burrito special that I'd learned to avoid years before.

Near the window were two young women in animated discussion about who knew what. The table nearest the salad bar was commandeered by five National Guardsmen, looking well rested and clean. A few hours up on the mesa would take out some of the creases.

That left a family two tables behind them, including mother, father, and two children. Both kids were blond.

I ambled over toward them, my hands in my pockets.

"Mr. Bronfeld?"

The man looked up sharply as if I'd jerked his head at the end of a leash. "Yes? I'm Niel Bronfeld."

I smiled and nodded at the woman sitting beside him. She was pretty and looked ten years younger than she probably was. I kept my voice down and my back to the Guardsmen behind me. "I'm William Gastner, with the Posadas County Sheriff's Department."

Bronfeld frowned and extended a hand. His grip was limp and nervous.

"Sir, is that your RV out back?"

He leaned over and looked past his wife, out through the elegant fake-wood slotted blinds. He started to nod. Then he saw the county patrol car parked just a few feet in front of the unit, and he turned back to me, concern knitting his brows.

"What's wrong, Officer?"

"May I talk with you for a few minutes?"

"Sure." He got up and patted his wife on the shoulder. "I'll be right back."

"How are you guys doing?" I asked as we passed the Guardsmen. They all nodded, mouths full.

Outside, Bronfeld and I walked toward the RV. As we approached, Mitchell got out of the patrol car.

"Deputy Mitchell, this is Niel Bronfeld." Shaking hands with a fat old man dressed in a casual flannel shirt and chinos was one thing. Facing a uniformed, unsmiling deputy was another matter. Bronfeld didn't offer to shake hands.

"What's going on?" he said softly, and walked to the RV's door. "Leigh?" He rapped a knuckle on the door, and after a moment it was opened by a rumpled, sleepy-eyed teenager who was a carbon copy of the woman in the restaurant. "Is David still asleep?"

"He's awake," the girl said, and looked at me and Deputy Mitchell. "What's going on?"

"I don't know," Bronfeld said, and turned to us. I liked the guy already. "What can I do for you gentlemen?" He walked away from the RV and glanced down its mammoth flanks. "Did something fall off?"

I laughed. "No, sir. The deputy was making a routine check of the parking lot, and apparently a young child looked out at him through the window. The RV did not appear to be tended, and he wanted to double-check that everything was all right."

"Oh my God," Bronfeld said, and his shoulders slumped. "This is near where that youngster went missing, isn't it?"

"Yes, sir," Mitchell said, and the tone of his voice made it clear that we were still interested in the contents of the camper.

"We read about that in the Sunday paper." He stepped up into the doorway and Leigh backed out of the way. "Come on in, Officer."

I followed him and instantly realized that RV living wasn't for me. A family of six would have to love one another every minute of the day to avoid a homicide before the vacation was over.

"David is our youngest. We're not sure if he's just a little carsick, or what. Leigh was keeping him company. David?"

The child appeared from one of the cramped bunk units. From a distance, he could have passed for Cody Cole. Up close, I could see his mother's pug nose and freckles. He was pale and sober, the way little kids get when they're not feeling well.

"Mr. Bronfeld, I'm sorry for the intrusion, and we appreciate your cooperation," I said, but he shook his head.

"No, no. No trouble at all. I'm sorry we gave you a start."

I grinned wryly. "You folks have a good vacation."

"Oh, I'm sure we will. Going on down to Tucson to see my parents. We pulled the kids out of school a few days early to give us a head start."

Leigh tried to smile as I slid past her. "You're the designated baby-sitter, eh?" I said pleasantly.

She made one of those teenaged "I'm cool, but the rest of my family's not" faces, and I stepped back down to the parking lot.

"You folks have a nice day," I called, and patted Deputy Mitchell on the arm as I walked by. "Good eyes," I said. "Keep it up."

I sounded confident, but other than giving the Bronfelds something to talk about during dull moments on their trip and pumping my blood pressure up, we hadn't accomplished anything. And I knew damn well the odds of seeing little Cody Cole alive, sober-faced or not, were slim to none.

Chapter 18

Sam Preston looked from me to Camille and then back at me. I waited for Camille to say something—anything at all that would let me know what her first impressions of the Gonzalez place might be. We stood in the November sun, Sam Preston leaning on the hood of the Suburban, waiting.

"Can we look inside?" Camille finally said, and her tone was flatly neutral. Not "This house is perfect," or even "Oh, how cute." Just "Can we look inside?"

Sam glanced at me, and when the Realtor is skeptical, you know you're in deep water.

He led the way down the dirt lane to the front door, the pathway dappled in shade by a grove of cottonwoods whose crackling brown leaves still clung stubbornly. The six rooms of the tiny adobe had been built one at a time, added as the need arose. Hector Gonzalez had built the first room, thirteen by thirteen feet, in 1890. He'd married Sara Montano the next year, and by the time the first child arrived, he had completed two more rooms. In 1920, when Sara's elderly and ailing mother moved in with them, he added two more wings, one off each end. Shortly after, someone in the family decided that indoor plumbing was here to stay, and the final room was added as the bathroom.

"This is a storybook house," Sam said as he opened the door for Camille.

"Some story," she muttered. The place was clean enough, in its own dark way, about as clean as any place can stay when it stands vacant for half a dozen years.

"Hector Gonzalez's son was the last one to live here," I said to Camille. "Remember Rudy?"

"Is he the guy who used to sit in Pershing Park playing the guitar all the time?"

"That's him," Sam said heartily. "He'd walk up there every day. It's what, two miles? Maybe a little less?"

Pershing Park was a grandiose name for a tiny triangle of land framed by the skewed intersection of Bustos, Grande, and Pershing. I could remember seeing Rudy Gonzalez sitting on the grass, leaning against the steel treads of a vintage army tank that was displayed there—the tank an olive drab testimonial to all the simpleminded ways the U.S. military had tried to catch the Mexican bandit, Pancho Villa. A bright yellow state historical marker implied that Villa had strayed into Posadas sometime in his checkered career.

Camille leaned against the bathroom doorjamb and surveyed the utilities, such as they were. The tub looked as if pack rats had been the last ones to use it. "What do you think?" I asked.

"I think it's awful," Camille said matter-of-factly. "You must be out of your mind. But then this part of the country is not featured regularly in *Better Homes and Gardens* anyway. What's out back?"

We went out the kitchen door. As the trees shed their leaves, the view to the south and west was impressive, a great sweep of prairie and in the distance the San Cristobal Mountains. The cottonwood grove continued back to the irrigation ditch, a park of great thick-trunked trees whose crowns mingled and filtered the November sun through leaves turning to crisp brown.

"This part of the deal is impressive," Camille said. "I love these trees." She turned and looked at the dull brown of the little house. "I'm sure a couple of good contractors and about fifty thousand bucks could work wonders with the house, too."

"Now there you go," Sam Preston said. "This is a smart daughter you've raised, Bill."

"I was thinking more along the lines of hiring a cleaning crew for a couple hundred," I said, and Camille grimaced.

Sam Preston's beeper shrieked at him, and he held up a hand. "Let me run and get that," he said. "Don't go away."

Camille linked her arm through mine and lead me to one of the old wooden benches by the back door.

"You're sure you want to do this?" she said.

"No."

"And at least once when you were up at our house, you said you weren't even sure you wanted to stay in Posadas when you retire."

"I'm not."

"And so…"

I took a deep breath. "The trouble is, I don't have anywhere else in mind to go, either. I like Posadas as much as I like anyplace."

"There isn't a lot to do here."

"And if there were, I probably wouldn't do it." I looked at Camille and grinned. "I've kind of gotten used to my own company over the years, sweetheart. If I get the urge to get up at three-thirty in the morning and roam the county, then that's what I do. I'm not sure that's something I want to change."

"Four horses are going to tie you down, though."

I nodded. "They'll give me something to think about, that's for sure." I looked off toward the cottonwoods, trying to picture the mammoth Percheron draft horses ambling among the gnarled, armored tree trunks. "And I think maybe I need that, too."

The horses had been my own private version of the white light that some folks claim to see just when their hearts give up.

In my case, it had been visit to an Octoberfest north of Flint a week or so before my surgery. I hadn't particularly wanted to go, but Camille and family had convinced me that if I liked beer, this was the place to drown in it. That part didn't sound half-bad, although I detested the loud polka music and the crowds that went with such an event.

I went, and I stood rooted and mesmerized as the great horses competed in deadweight pulling competition. Great concrete blocks were set on the enormous rude wooden sled by a smoke-belching diesel front-loader. Between each round, as they waited for the tonnage to be increased, the handlers walked their teams of horses around the churned arena, and the immense creatures were as docile and plodding as old fat men.

Their heavy leather harnesses were rigged to a single tow bar with one stout iron hook that hung down like a claw. As soon as the driver began to maneuver his team toward the load, the animals came alive, broad hooves smashing into the dirt in a frantic dance.

The man had to fight the reins, yelling at the animals at the same time, while a second handler grabbed the tow hook. He had the most dangerous job, since the horses lunged the instant they heard the clank of iron against iron, and he needed to dive to safety.

Four tons of horses lunged into the harness, snapping the front of the sled out of the dirt and surging the pile of concrete weights into motion.

The winning team had pulled twenty-eight tons the measured distance. And in the process, they had captured my imagination as nothing else had in half a century.

After the horse pull, I'd met the owner and driver of the winning heavyweight team, and we'd talked while we stood in the shade of those massive beasts. I'd never made a decision so promptly that didn't involve arresting someone.

He agreed to sell me a matched team of fourteen-year-olds, animals that were approaching retirement and would need a nice, quiet, shady spot. As the idea took root in my mind, I had let go of what little common sense had been nagging me. I also agreed to buy an eight-year-old mare and her foal.

And in the course of several conversations over the next couple of weeks, he'd agreed to several other things, too. He would deliver the animals himself when I was ready. Perhaps most important, he agreed to take them back, at no charge, if I happened to drop dead one day.

Camille, of course, had thought at first that I'd gone certifiable, but given enough time and argument, she at last shrugged. Horses weren't new to me, after all. The first eighteen years of my life had been spent around them, including a lot of time at the dumb end of the reins while my father's Belgians, Hugo and Fred, plowed nice straight furrows in the North Carolina soil.

I had always liked the Gonzalez place, and I had driven by at least half a million times in the past twenty-five years. And I knew that it was for sale—and had been for months. The entire deal had been predicated on my surviving what the doctors had planned for me. That accomplished, I had wasted little of my convalescent time. Telephones were wonderful gadgets.

I heard the clump of Sam Preston's boots coming back through the house. "That was Detective Reyes-Guzman," he said. "She wants to stop by if you're going to be here for a few minutes."

"We are," I said. "Why don't I talk with you later on this afternoon, back at the office?"

Sam nodded. "Place is open. Just make yourselves at home. If you would, be sure the front door locks when you leave, although I don't guess there's much to take here yet."

After he left, Camille hooked her arm through mine again. "What does Estelle think about all this?" She gestured out at the cottonwood paddock.

"I haven't had a chance to tell her yet," I said. "It all happened pretty fast, and since we've been back, there hasn't been time for chitchat."

"Ah," Camille said. She pointed toward the west. "Let's walk back to the irrigation ditch." We did, our shoes crunching the leaves under the cottonwoods. What I had started calling the paddock included seven acres, a vast park that was a delight to the eye. We reached the ditch, now, just a berm on either side of a weed-choked channel.

"Hasn't been water through here in awhile," Camille said.

"A long, long time."

"Where did the water come from? The Salinas is too far west, isn't it?"

I nodded. Rio Salinas was a seasonal and undependable little rivulet itself. "There used to be a series of springs. But they dried up in the early 1960s, when the mine was getting started."

"So where does the water come from now?"

"The house has a well—a very good one. I'll pipe water back to the paddock."

I collected another of those skeptical glances from Camille. She stood on the bank of the ditch, hands on hips, looking back toward the house. "Quite a challenge," she said.

"That's a kind way of putting it. But look at it this way. The grandkids can visit one at a time and ride the horses."

Camille laughed. "One at a time. I like that." She shook her head. "You're hopeless, Dad. I'd like a photo of that, though. A little kid would need a stepladder to climb up on the back of one of those beasts." She pointed at the house. "That must be Estelle," she said. "Let's see if she thinks you're as crazy as I do."

Chapter 19

Estelle Reyes-Guzman saw us as we walked toward the house, and she sat down on the bench by the back door. She was wearing a tan suit, and from a distance, she blended in with the adobe behind her.

As we approached within speaking distance, she stood up, a smile brightening some of the fatigue on her dark face. Camille gave her a small hug around the waist with the one arm, keeping the other linked through mine.

"Sam Preston told me you were out here," Estelle said, and her gaze swept the property. I could see the mental gears working.

"Anything new on the youngster?" I asked.

She shook her head. "Eddie told me about the folks in the RV."

I laughed. "We made their day, I'm sure."

"Holman doesn't want to pull the search teams for a while yet," Estelle said. She examined the corner of the old house where the stucco was badly cracked.

"That's probably just as well," I said.

She ran her hand down the rough finish. "Are you buying this place?" She turned to look at Camille, and I walked over to the bench and sat down, leaning back against the wall, feeling the warmth of the old adobe filter through my flannel shirt.

"She's not. I thought I might."

"I see," Estelle said. I grinned, amused at this accomplished detective's complete lack of nosiness.

"I'd like to own some horses," I said. "This place is on the market, and it's cheap." I reached around and patted the thick adobe wall. "The house is basically sound."

"You mean you're going to live here?" She didn't try to conceal the incredulity in her voice.

"Yes. That's what I was thinking."

"Oh." Estelle walked a step or two closer to the back door and stopped. "Well, it's farther from the interstate," she said.

"That's one plus."

She gazed at me, and I felt as if I were being CAT-scanned. I took a deep breath and said, "I've been thinking about offering the hacienda to you."

"Me?"

"To you and Francis." Up to then, I hadn't been able to imagine how I was going to broach this subject with Estelle. I'd thought about it for months, playing various conversations through my mind. But now that I'd started, the words tumbled out in a rush.

"You've said several times that your place on Twelfth Street isn't anywhere big enough. Hell, my place is big enough for three families. And I don't know what you've decided about your mother, but if you wanted her to stay with you, there's enough room for her to have her own apartment there, and you'd never know it."

Estelle looked down at the ground and made her way to the bench. She sat down with her hands clasped between her knees.

"How is she, by the way?" I added.

"Francis has her scheduled for hip-replacement surgery on December second."

"Ouch. That's a long time to wait."

Estelle nodded. "There are still some heart irregularities that they're trying to get under control first, so they postponed the hip. Nothing life-threatening, Francis says. But worrisome. She's reasonably comfortable."

The dark circles under Estelle's eyes were worrisome as well, and I said, "Maybe this isn't a good time to talk about the house. But I'd sure rather know you guys were living there than a bunch of strangers who didn't understand the place."

"Complete with cemetery in the backyard." Estelle chuckled.

"That's going to be resolved. The old lady's going to be moved, whether Florencio Apodaca likes it or not."

Estelle reached over and put her hand on top of mine. "It's a beautiful home, sir. And I'm touched that you'd even consider such a thing." She hesitated and glanced at Camille. "But I don't think we're in a position to take on something like that."

"If you're talking about price, that's not a problem," I said. I indicated my daughter. "None of the kids want the place, as Camille will tell you. They've all got their own complicated lives at the far corners of the country. And I don't need the money. Hell, you can have the hacienda for a dollar, if you want it. Just say the word. It would make me feel good, knowing that you and Francis and *los niños* were enjoying the place. It would keep it in the family."

Estelle looked down at her hands, and her forehead was wrinkled in a frown. She blinked once or twice and I thought I saw her swallow hard.

"But it's nothing that needs to be decided overnight," I added quickly.

She looked at me, and, as usual, I couldn't read what was deep in those inscrutable dark eyes. "You've got horses coming?"

"Well," I said, waving a hand, "I've made a tentative deal. Let me put it that way. It's not like they're arriving tomorrow. Probably in the spring, after I've had a chance to get this place shipshape."

"Saddle horses?"

"No." I shook my head. "It'd take a derrick to get me up on a horse now. Workhorses—Percherons."

"You never mentioned them," Estelle said, not as a rebuke, but just as a statement of fact.

"It was one of those love-at-first-sight things," Camille said. "We made the mistake of taking him to a county fair-type October-fest when he was visiting us."

"You used to drive horses when you were younger, didn't you?" I nodded. "Much, much, much younger."

Estelle shook her head slowly, gazing out into the paddock. "That will be a lot of work."

"It'll be good for me," I said. "And when he's a few years older, I can hire the kid to do all the hard stuff." By the time little Francis was old enough to do the hard stuff, I reflected, I'd be pushing eighty years old—or perhaps daisies. But it was a nice thought.

Estelle patted my hand again. "I'll talk with Francis," she said. "I know he loves your place as much as I do. But I don't think he'll change his mind."

"Change his mind? About what?"

Estelle hesitated for a long moment. "He's accepted a position at another hospital."

"You're kidding," I said. "What, Cruces?" Dr. Guzman had spent a good deal of time driving between Posadas and Las Cruces, doing whatever it was doctors did when sharing hospitals.

"No." Estelle took a deep breath. "He's accepted a position at the Mayo Clinic."

"Mayo? As in Tucson?"

"Rochester, Minnesota." A heavy silence settled on our little patch of sunshine and adobe.

I didn't know what to say, so finally I settled for "That's a hell of an opportunity."

"Yes, it is. There's some teaching involved, too. And research."

I smiled with a great deal more enthusiasm than I felt. In fact, a great black hole was growing in my gut. "It snows up there, you know. Except during the two days of summer."

"Yes, I know. Francis and Carlos are going to go crazy."

"They can learn things like ice skating," I said. "All kinds of cold, bleak, soggy pastimes. Your kitchen floor will always be covered with boots and wet socks."

Estelle grinned at that.

"When?" I asked, and I didn't mean it to come out so bleakly.

"His appointment begins June first."

"Ouch," I said. "And your mama?"

Estelle shook her head. "Assuming everything goes well, there are dozens of extended- or acute-care facilities in that area."

"Of course there are, but that's not what I meant. She's going to hate it, you know. You're going to have to be your persuasive best."

"I've got seven months to work on her," Estelle said. "Who knows. Maybe she's like you. Maybe she's ready for an adventure."

"Maybe," I said. I stood up and brushed off the seat of my pants. I felt Camille looking at me, but I couldn't meet her gaze. "We'd better get back," I said. "Camille, would you go through the house and make sure the front door is locked?" I walked around the side of the house, hands in my pockets, looking like I was examining the structure of the walls.

The truth was that I didn't want to see the inside of that dreary place.

Chapter 20

Camille was silent on the short drive home, and I was grateful for that. I hadn't been ready for Estelle's curveball, and my mind was a wallow of ridiculous thoughts that bordered more on self-pity than anything else.

Estelle had never mentioned the possibility of her physician husband accepting a position elsewhere, but I realized I was foolish to assume that a young, talented surgeon would set his sights on nothing more than a career in Posadas, reaming varicose veins. Somehow, I'd allowed the assumption to grow and flourish in my head that Estelle, Francis, and my two godsons would always be a part of my existence in Posadas.

But goddamn Minnesota? Even before I had pulled into my driveway on Escondido, I had transferred my worry to Estelle. What was *she* going to do in that bleak, cold, chililess land? I hadn't asked, either, and that irritated me even more.

I didn't know anything about the state, and I wasn't sure I wanted to, but common sense told me that Minnesota probably had just as many counties as New Mexico, if not dozens more—and each one had a sheriff's department. And there was the state police, and the city police, and village constables—and any department would jump at the chance to hire an experienced female minority officer who was bilingual, and talented to boot.

"We'll have to send them care packages full of sand, green chili, and piñon smoke," I muttered as Camille and I went inside. Standing in the foyer of my rambling home, I realized just how scruffy the Gonzalez place was. My daughter didn't respond to my lament, heading for the kitchen instead.

I tossed my jacket on the bench by the front door and ambled down the hall, eyes locked on the polished Saltillo tile floor, old and buffed to a gleam like polished saddle leather. In the living room, I found my road atlas and idly turned the pages, pausing here and there without really looking until I landed in Minnesota. The city of Rochester was in the southeast corner. By squinting and shifting my glasses, I could almost read the fine print.

It looked like Olmsted County included the city. I wondered who the Sheriff of Olmsted County was, and if he was a former used-car salesman like Marty Holman. "Posadas, where?" he'd ask, and he probably thought that he would need a visa to visit.

"You want a snack?" Camille called from the kitchen, and I closed the atlas and slid it back on the shelf.

"Sure," I mumbled.

"You know, I had a thought," Camille said. I stopped beside the table, looking at the array of hors d'oeuvres she'd assembled. "You've got plenty of room here."

"Here? For what?" I asked, and sampled a miniature nacho—a nuked chip with cheese and a slice of jalapeño on top. It was so hot, it made my eyes water.

Camille stepped to the kitchen door and looked out toward the five-acre jungle. "You've got enough room for horses right here, Dad. All it would take is hiring some kids to clean out the undergrowth."

"What a job that would be," I said.

"Less than what you've got in mind for the Gonzalez place," my daughter replied. "And the biggest job is finished. You've got a marvelous home here."

I shrugged. "Yep."

She hefted the coffeepot and poured two cups. I could tell from the aroma that it was the real thing. "I wonder if Sheriff Holman knows yet," she said. "That she's leaving, I mean."

"Well, if he doesn't, he will soon enough. And he's got until June first to do something about it. When Estelle leaves, so does our entire detective division."

"Is there anyone you'd care to move into her place?"

"I'm not sure. Probably Eddie Mitchell. When he and Skip Bishop work together, they make a pretty good team."

"What about Bob Torrez?"

I shook my head. "He runs the Patrol Division. We'll ask him, but he's never shown any inclination to move out of uniform." I ate another nacho. "Our problem is that we're a tiny department. I mean, I say Patrol Division, but that means only a handful of uniformed deputies. We're up to seven now, to cover three shifts, seven days a week. Plus Martin and myself. That's nine of us, and that's hardly a 'division' of any kind.

"You and Martin Holman, then." Camille said.

I grimaced. "The halt and the blind. You're too kind." I ate another nacho, particularly savoring the cheese. "Despite everything, Marty Holman is doing a fair-enough job. He doesn't know much, but he's a fast study. He's been sheriff now for nine years, and already he's learned that if he rubs a latent fingerprint off a piece of evidence, there's no way we can put it back."

"Awesome."

"Indeed." We sat in comfortable silence for a while. "The hardest part," I finally said, "is remembering that an institution functioned perfectly well before we arrived on the scene, and that it will probably function perfectly well long after we leave."

Camille nodded but didn't respond. I rested my elbows on the table, folded my hands, and rested my chin on them, gazing across the kitchen toward the window that looked out on the backyard.

"That doesn't make it any easier, sweetheart. Holman keeps telling me that I should take up golf."

"Ugh," Camille said.

"You can't see me doing that?"

"More important, I don't think *you* can see you doing that. I think you were on the right track before."

"What's that?"

"You saw those draft horses and it lit a passion, that's for sure," Camille said. "I saw your face. Everyone will think it's silly, of course, because it involves a lot of work and time and money. But what everyone else thinks doesn't matter. The work is good for you; you've got the time, and you've got the money. What's silly is feeling that you have to give up this place."

"I don't feel I have to. I just thought that it made sense, that's all. Estelle and Francis need the space a lot more than I do."

"And they're moving, so that's no longer an issue," Camille said. "You have a housekeeper who comes twice a week to keep the place spotless for you, so it doesn't matter if the building itself is a thousand square feet or five thousand. Just enjoy it."

"Maybe so."

"And out back, those five acres are big enough that you could have a neat two-acre paddock, a small barn and arena, and still have enough space left over so that the whole complex would be hidden on all sides by whatever strange things are growing out there."

"And a small cemetery to boot."

Camille laughed. "And with everything here, you'd have room when company came to visit."

I looked at Camille in mock horror. "Visit? Who's coming to visit?"

"You never know when a grandchild might want to come and spend a week or so with his crazy grandpa."

"They never have before," I groused.

"That's because you're always working," Camille said, and she looked at me as if to add, "So there."

I took a deep breath, eyeing the nachos. "I'll think on it," I said.

I was about to reach for the tempting morsel when Camille reached over to the counter and picked up the pill organizer. "Here," she said. "Have some. It's time."

Chapter 21

I was walking across the foyer in my stocking feet when I heard the crunch of tires on gravel. I glanced out through the single slender window beside the front door and saw Martin Holman and Eddie Mitchell climbing out of a county car.

"What the hell would they have done if I'd stayed in Flint?" I said, and opened the door.

"We were in the neighborhood," Holman said affably as he climbed out of the car. He was holding a clear plastic evidence bag and wearing another of his enormous smiles. His days were clearly marked by the joy of small individual victories. "I was hoping we'd catch you." He held up the bag. "How about this?"

He handed the bag to me, and I took it by the closure. "Well, well," I said. "Come on in." I shut the heavy door with one hand, holding up the bag with the other. The revolver inside was a Smith & Wesson, a perfectly run-of-the-mill .357 Magnum, four-inch-barreled Model 19. The letters PCSO were engraved on the rightside plate, just under the manufacturer's logo.

"Mine, I assume," I said, and Holman nodded. I turned the bag and saw the deep scratch across the bottom of the left grip where I'd snagged a barbed-wire fence a year before.

"Where was it found?"

"Well, that's the interesting thing," Holman said. "You know Deann Black?"

"Sure. She runs that day-care center, over behind the hospital."

"That's right. She found this in her son Jason's sock drawer."

"Under the socks," I said, and looked at the Magnum again. It was fully loaded. "Maybe that's where I should have kept it. How old is Jason?"

"He's ten," Eddie Mitchell said, and I glanced up at the deputy. He was no taller than I was, and probably weighed nearly the same, little of it fat.

"A ten-year-old? Well, that explains the brilliant hiding place. Was the little terrorist in on the burglary, or what?"

Mitchell shook his head slightly. "I don't know. His mother discovered the weapon this afternoon when she was sorting laundry. She called us right away. And she's pretty smart. She didn't move it, or touch it. Dispatch sent me over there. Then she went and checked her kid out of school so he'd be there, too."

"What did the kid say?"

"He claims he found the weapon over behind Guilfoil Auto Parts on Bustos."

"Sure, that's likely," I said. "And mom?"

"She'd like to believe him, but I don't think she does. She gave me permission to search the kid's room. I didn't turn up anything else."

"And the kid maintains that he just found the gun lying in the alley?"

"Behind one of the Dumpsters. Right."

"Prints?"

Mitchell shook his head again. "I haven't run anything yet. Might be interesting, though."

"Unless the kid's watched too many movies," Holman said. "Then he's wiped it clean."

"We'll see," I said. "Eddie, in the meantime, give mom a call back and tell her that we want to have the kid come down to the office for a chat. Ask her to come along, as well. Who is Mr. Black, by the way?"

"They're separated. He works over at Posadas General. I think he's a custodian."

"You might get ahold of him, too. Maybe the kid relates to him better than he does his mother. You never know," I said. I glanced at my watch. "Set something up for three-thirty. That gives us half an hour. We don't want this kid having too much time to think. It'll be interesting to see how creative he can get."

"By then, prints might tell us something," Mitchell said.

"Were you going to go to the office today?" Holman asked. "I mean, other than at three-thirty?"

"I wasn't planning on it. Why?"

"There were a couple of budget matters I wanted to talk over with you, but they can wait. And by the way, Estelle's checking out a report from Alamogordo about a youngster someone saw in a white van. Apparently the kid was in some kind of distress, and someone got suspicious and tipped off the police. I don't know more than that."

"Well," I said, "we're going to hear all kinds of things. She's right to check it out, though. We can't let anything slip by."

"It's interesting to see how it works," Holman said. "There aren't very many members of the search party who really believe that Cody Cole is up on that mesa."

"Except Mrs. Cole," I said. "A mother's intuition is a powerful thing."

Holman nodded, then held up an index finger. "I almost forgot. We got some really interesting information from the Wyoming Department of Fish and Game. Paul Cole is not on record as holding an elk license from that state, or any other kind of license, for that matter."

I frowned.

"And I guess we should have expected that," Holman added. "All the licenses are awarded in drawings, and those take place early in the year. It's something he would have had to have been planning for months and months."

"Maybe he has been," I said.

"What do you mean?"

I shrugged. "Remember what Camille said? It sounds like there's some kind of war going on between Cole and his new wife. I wouldn't be a bit surprised." I held up a hand in resignation and handed the bagged revolver to Holman. "Wherever he went, he didn't go alone," I said.

"How do you know that?"

"Because both his vehicles are parked in his driveway, Martin. When we find him, it's going to be interesting to hear his story."

"His wife's going to be interested, too," Holman said.

Chapter 22

Jason Black was a slender kid, tall for his age. He moped into the Posadas Public Safety Building, walking a step or two behind his mother, as if it she was the one who had business there and he'd just been forced to tag along.

His reddish blond hair was slicked back from his forehead, lying flat on his skull, thanks to liberal applications of something shiny that stuck it all in place. The sides were cut short, up to the tops of his ears, though, making his hair look like some kind of bizarre helmet slipped over his head.

I watched from my office as mother and son presented themselves at the window that separated our dispatchers from all the weird folks who showed up at all hours of the day or night. The woman's jaw was clenched tight, and she spoke to Gayle Sedillos in monosyllables.

Gayle was used to handling parents who had reached their limit of stress, and she greeted Mrs. Black graciously, then pointed across the hall at the closed door marked CONFERENCE. The woman marched her son across the hall.

Jason Black managed to look indifferent and bored, but I saw him hesitate just a bit before following his mother into the conference room. He was trying his best to get an early start into the bizarre world of teenagers. Interesting times lay ahead for his mother, I mused.

The door closed behind them, and I elected to let them sit and stew for ten or fifteen minutes. It took that long to shag Deputy Mitchell back in off patrol.

Sheriff Holman led the assault, despite my suggestion that we wait until Estelle Reyes-Guzman could be present. I'd never met a kid whom she hadn't been able to reduce to gelatin. But she was at the hospital with her mother, and I didn't want to press into her time there.

Holman was in his usual good-humored form, and Jason misread that cue from the very beginning. The kid regarded him with studiously lidded eyes while the sheriff introduced everyone. Holman sounded much too reasonable, too much like a kindly guidance counselor. If the kid thought that he could get away with murder, he would elect to try it under the watchful, kindly eye of the Posadas County sheriff.

The kid sat with his shoulders hunched, part of the newfangled blend-in-with-the-crowd posture that had become so inexplicably popular. He avoided looking at Eddie Mitchell, whose expression was cold and blank, and he only let his gaze stray across to me one time. That was when I came into the room, tossed a manila folder on the table, and sat down with a scowl, obviously pissed.

The good sheriff was the only ally that the kid had in the room, other than his own mother. Jason shifted in his seat as Holman gently explained to both mother and son how deep the shit was that the boy was in.

"Jason," the sheriff said finally, after rattling on for five minutes about responsibility and the rights of other people to own their own property unmolested, "The Posadas County Sheriff's Department is considering filing charges against you that include possession of stolen government property. That's a serious felony."

If Mrs. Black had been planning to tough it out, that plan ended when she heard that. The mothering instinct was just too strong. I could almost hear her thinking, How could such a reasonable man say such an unreasonable, harsh thing as that?

"But Sheriff," she said, "if he just *found* the gun..."

"We know that's not what happened," I said brusquely. "It's that simple. Someone who walks into a particular alley, *finds* a loaded handgun, and then hides that weapon in his room obviously has plans of some kind."

"Jason," Mrs. Black said in her best "Son, how could you" tone.

I saw a faint quiver of the boy's upper lip and added, "If he had been concerned with following the law, he could have simply reported what he *found* and that would have been that." I turned to Eddie Mitchell, whose rattlesnake eyes were still making both kid and mother nervous. "What are the fingerprint results, Deputy?"

"Three sets," Mitchell said, and his eyes never left Jason's. "The computer is running matches now. It'll be a few minutes. Mrs. Black said that she did not touch the weapon at any time. She opened the drawer, and in trying to reorganize the socks, she uncovered the weapon, realized what it was, and called us. Since she did not touch it, I don't expect to find a match to her prints. When we book Jason, we will fingerprint him, as usual, and at that time, I expect to find a match."

Mitchell droned all that out in one breath, flat and emotionless, as if we did this sort of thing on an hourly basis. No one had explained to young Jason Black that the police couldn't just stuff unknown latent prints into a computer and be handed a match within minutes, if ever. If the kid thought that's what we could do, so much the better.

"Obviously, one of the sets of prints is Jason's," Holman said, "since the only way the weapon could get in his dresser drawer is if he put it there. But maybe Jason wasn't alone when the gun was discovered." I almost grinned at that nice word, *discovered*, making a loaded Magnum seem like some kind of pirate treasure. "Maybe," Holman said, "several people were involved, and several people handled it. Maybe someone talked Jason into just *hiding* the gun for a while. Is that about what happened, Jason?"

"Pete Harkins and Melody Perez," Jason blurted, and tears came at the same time as the names. For just a fleeting moment, Marty Holman looked almost disappointed that he wouldn't have to use any of the other tools in his arsenal of persuasion. It was like someone walking onto a car lot, pulling out a checkbook, pointing at a car, and saying, "I want that car. How much is it?"

"Pete Harkins and Melody Perez," Holman repeated. "Just those two?"

"Yes." The word was a miserable little bleat, and ten-year-old Jason Black's first venture into the world of crime came to an abrupt end. Once he started talking, there was little need for prompting, and mom, bless her, just sat back and let Jason ride on alone. Holman remained the patient, kindly prompter; Mitchell and I sat silently, watching and listening.

Pete Harkins, Jason Black's best bud, lived just off Grande at the Ranchero Mobile Home Park. That put his residence less than five hundred yards from mine. Pete and Jason had recruited Melody Perez, a tough little number who lived on the other side of the interstate, on MacArthur. The two boys liked Melody, Jason said, because she wasn't afraid to do anything.

They had busted into my house, Jason recalled, because they had heard a rumor that I owned a huge coin collection—which I didn't—as well as a bunch of other "stuff," which I probably did.

The three kids, all coldly calculating, chose my house because it was vacant, secluded, and scary, whatever a ten-year-old meant by that. It was simple enough to bust the bathroom window and squirm inside.

I looked at Jason Black skeptically. He was resting his arm on the table, relieved that he'd managed to talk his way out of an immediate trip to Leavenworth. I could have encircled his biceps with my thumb and index finger. I tried to picture the three of them wrestling to move my filing cabinet. Maybe Melody had carried it by herself.

"How'd you move the cabinet?" I asked.

Jason looked at me out of the corner of his eye and shifted slightly away, as if I might hit him. "We took the cart thing. The one that was right there by the garage."

"You sneaky little bastard," I wanted to say, but instead I settled for saying, "You mean the wheelbarrow?" He nodded. "And where did you take the file?"

Jason explained how they had managed to grunt the cabinet out of the house, into my own wheelbarrow, and trundle the whole affair on down Guadalupe Terrace until the lane ended in the arroyo that ran south, paralleling State Road 61.

"We were thinking that like if we dumped it into the arroyo, it would burst open when it hit the bottom."

"And did it?"

Jason shook his head. "We used that old ax."

"Old ax?" I wasn't in the habit of leaving axes outside.

"The one that was with the wheelbarrow."

"Ah," I said. Ax, pickax, hoe, shovel—same thing. "So you took the pickax and busted it open."

Jason nodded. "It came open pretty easy," he said. "A lot easier than we thought."

"What did you do with the papers?"

"We seen they wasn't money or nothing, so we left 'em."

"And the other gun?"

"Melody gots it."

I looked at Eddie. "It's a little Colt three eighty. It's in the inventory I gave Estelle." I took a deep breath, regarding Jason Black. "And you took the rifle, too? The big one that was up on the wall?" I slipped the eight-by-ten glossy of the shoe print out of the case folder and slid it across the table so it parked right under the kid's nose. He didn't have a poker face, and if it wasn't his own shoe, at least he recognized whose it was.

"Melody gots it. That and the sword. She said she knew somebody who'd buy 'em from her."

"And the VCR?"

"Pete took that. He was going to sell it to Predo Gonzales after a little while."

"What else do you have?"

"Nothing." He saw my eyes squint and hastily added, "Honest. Nothing."

Martin Holman managed to sound almost helpful when he looked at a miserable Deann Black and said, "While we're waiting for Judge Hobart, ma'am, it might save us some time to go ahead and book Jason. Get the fingerprinting process out of the way."

She looked horrified. "But he admitted—you mean, if this is all cleared up, he's still to be charged?"

"Ma'am, this is a serious business. We have pretty solid information that the burglary of the Gastner residence isn't the only incident involving these youngsters." My estimation of Martin Holman clicked up another few notches. "What happens will depend on how cooperative your son remains," he added.

"While Deputy Mitchell takes care of that," I said to Holman, "maybe you'd take a run out to the trailer park and bring in Pete Harkins. It'd be a good idea to have Debbie Mears go along when you pick up Miss Melody." Debbie was the wife of one of our deputies and served frequently as an on-call matron. I got up from the conference table. "I'm going out to the arroyo and check this young man's story. If he's telling the truth, I'll let Deputy Mitchell know."

As I opened the door, I turned and said, "And by the way, don't take any officers away from the search. We can walk through this thing if it takes all night." I nodded at Jason Black. "And don't let the three of them associate with one another in any way. Keep 'em separated. Separate cells."

Jason's face had been pale enough, but I have to admit I enjoyed seeing it go another shade lighter when I said the word *cells*.

Chapter 23

Jason Black hadn't been lying. I parked at the end of Guadalupe Terrace, walked two dozen paces, and stood at the edge of the arroyo. It was a grand view. Ahead of me rumpled chaparral stretched all the way to Mexico, studded with acacia and creosote bush, old car hulks, doorless refrigerators—all the things that made the southwestern desert so charming.

A few hundred yards off to my right was the back fence of Florek's Auto Wrecking, one of the premier businesses of Posadas, located on the east side of the highway, just beyond the point where Grande Boulevard lost its village designation and became simply State 61.

And ahead of me, down in the gravel of the arroyo, amid a blizzard of other junk from other eras, lay the gray hulk of my filing cabinet and my wheelbarrow. It only made sense that once the burglars were finished with the wheelbarrow, it, too, should be tipped down into the arroyo.

"Watch your step, Dad," Camille said, but the warning was unnecessary. We made our way down the steep, crumbling sides of the arroyo, grabbing the dry stumps of *chamiza* for purchase.

In places, the bottom of the arroyo had been swept clean down to the bedrock, and small pools of water from the recent rains would remain until the sun fried them dry.

The cabinet lay on its side and I was thankful for that. A handful of papers had remained inside, sheltered from the weather. Most of it was replaceable and didn't matter anyway—several insurance policies, a brown envelope containing my military papers and a

ribbon or two, birth certificate, vehicle titles—the sort of things
that were incomprehensible and of no value to three kids hunting
for gold.

I squatted down and rummaged while Camille commenced a
systematic search of the bushes and niches surrounding the spot.

By the time it was twilight, we'd assembled a fair stack of papers
and documents, envelopes and packets. I felt more relaxed than I
had since arriving home. If I couldn't remember what else might
be missing, I reasoned it obviously didn't matter much.

I got to my feet, brushed the sand off my knees, and picked up
the framed photo that I had placed on top of the rescued items.
Camille reached out and I gave it to her. She wiped a bit of moisture
off the unbroken glass, letting her fingers trace gently around the
narrow wooden frame.

"I'm glad you were able to recover this," she said. "The rest
probably doesn't matter much."

I nodded. In the fading light, the photograph could easily have
been mistaken for Camille herself, rather than her mother.

She looked up at me. "And this is the only picture you've got?
Of her, I mean?"

"Yes."

She examined the photo again, taken during a vacation twenty
years earlier in Acajutla, in El Salvador. Her mother had consented
to posing on a mammoth sea-polished rock, the water almost
emerald green behind her. That particular rock hadn't been chosen
at random, nor was this her first time to perch on top, knees hugged
tightly, the entire reach of the Pacific in front of her.

I could remember the circumstances of taking the photograph.
I could remember perching on the side of the rock and hoping
that the barnacles wouldn't slice my trousers to ribbons while I
focused and cropped and tried this angle and that, until I had the
light on her face just so, until the wind had positioned her hair.

If I had swung the camera slightly to the right, the picture
would have captured her family's home, where it nestled a long
stone's throw away from the constant murmuring of the sea.

She had been friends with that rock since she had been old
enough to clamber up the twelve feet to its pinnacle above the
surf. She had no photos of herself as a child, certainly none of her
perched upon the rock. So, in middle age, returning to her home

for a visit, she had consented to struggling up there one more time.

"This is the one you were always going to make copies of for each one of us, weren't you?" Camille said.

"Yes." I shrugged. "One of those things I never got around to."

"Would you mind if I took it in tomorrow? I think that the film-processing place at the video store can make copies right there, without the risk of sending it through the mail."

"Sure," I said, feeling an instant pang of uneasiness. But I shrugged it off. If the photograph—frame, glass, and all—could survive a nighttime assault by three little hoodlums and a dumping in a rock-strewn arroyo, then it could most likely survive a twenty-four-hour photo shop.

As the light failed, we made our way north along the arroyo bottom to a spot where we could clamber out without difficulty. There were probably other items of mine that the wind had picked up and hidden here and there in the arroyo bottom, under rocks or bushes along the edges. Now that I had the photograph, I didn't much care about the rest of it.

That night, as if a switch had been flipped by the emotional upset of losing and then recovering the only photograph that I owned of my wife, my system settled back into its comfortable, erratic schedule.

I awoke at 2:30 in the morning on that Wednesday and lay for a few minutes on my back, listening to the quiet sounds of the old house as the wooden vigas creaked and the two-foot-thick adobe walls breathed.

After awhile, I got up, dressed, and left the house. The air was sharp, but there was no wind. I slid into 310, started it, and backed out of the driveway. With my window down, I let the car idle up Guadalupe Terrace, turning first onto Escondido and then Grande.

At that hour, the wide, deserted street looked like something out of a cheap science fiction movie, one of those films where no one is left alive in a devastated city.

In comparison, the dispatcher's station in the Public Safety Building was bursting with activity. The dispatcher, Ernie Wheeler, was absorbed in a paperback novel. He was sitting with his chair tipped back, long legs stretched out under the computer console.

He looked up and did a double take when he saw me, and I grinned.

"Evening, sir," he said. "I didn't expect to see you out and about tonight. Welcome back."

"Thanks. I couldn't sleep," I said. "But what else is new. What's going on?"

"Absolutely nothing. No night ops anymore up on the mesa, the sheriff says. I guess they're going to continue the search come morning, but most of the troops have pulled out." He shook his head. "Doesn't look good."

"No, it doesn't. Did you happen to hear if Tiffany Cole is still up on the mesa? Or Andy Browers?"

Wheeler frowned. "I don't know. Sergeant Torrez has been keeping track of that mess. He and Skip Bishop were talking earlier when I came in, but I didn't pay any attention."

"Any messages for me?"

Ernie shook his head. He leaned forward and looked at the desk log. "You missed the commotion earlier in the evening."

"Commotion?"

"Mitchell and Tony Abeyta brought in a couple of juveniles in connection with the burglary at your place." He leaned back and grinned. "Turns out their little prints are all over. They've admitted to breaking into six other homes, all down in that general area."

"So what was the commotion?"

"One of 'em didn't want to be booked, I guess. Melody Perez? You know her?"

"Never had the pleasure."

"Well, she didn't see what the problem was. Quite an attitude for a twelve-year-old. Her mother and father ended up apologizing for her."

"That certainly makes it all hunky-dory, then," I said. "As long as the parents are sorry. Did Deputy Mitchell happen to mention to you if my rifle was recovered? The Civil War relic?"

"He said it was. They need to hang on to it for awhile, though."

"Of course," I said. "As long as somebody knows where it is." My mailbox was clear of all those annoying little "While You Were Out" messages, and no one was waiting for me in my office.

"I'm going to wander," I said to Ernie. "Who's on tonight?"

"Mears. Abeyta was on until two, and then he went home."

I nodded. "If you need me for anything, I'll have the radio on." On the way out to the car, I stopped in my office and checked an address in the phone book.

Tiffany Cole's address was listed as 392 North Fifth Street. I jotted down the address and the telephone number. I thumbed back a few pages and found Browers, A. L., listed at 407 North Fifth. Perhaps they met at a block party, I mused, and slipped the notebook back in my pocket.

Pershing Park was illuminated harshly by too many streetlights as I drove up Grande. More stores were empty than not, reflecting the limping economy of a village that had put too much stock in a single large mining company.

Salazar Mortuary looked prosperous, and I turned on Hutton Street just beyond the mortuary's circular driveway. Most of the houses on Hutton had been built in the late 1950s, and at that time they had probably looked bright and cheerful. Now, they were slumping cinder block and peeling paint, with the kind of metal-framed crank-out windows that let in a trail of dust every time the wind blew.

I crossed Fourth Street and slowed the car to a crawl, with both front windows down. At the intersection of Hutton and Fifth, I let 310 roll to a stop along the curb, the headlights off.

Andy Browers's house, across the intersection and two houses down, looked like every other. One-story cinder block, flat roof, narrow macadam driveway sloping up to what had once been a garage but now was another bedroom, or den, or playroom.

Except for a small outboard motorboat on a trailer, the driveway was empty.

The boat and trailer almost hid the grille and front bumper of another vehicle that was backed in beside the house, scrunched between the building and the block wall separating the property from the neighbors.

I pulled 310 away from the curb, swung right through the intersection, and slowed to a crawl. The vehicle was a large motor home, about the same size as the one used by the Bronfeld family, although older and more angular. I swiveled the spotlight and clicked it on. The beam lanced out and illuminated the house and

RV. I could see jacks under the front axle, propping up the front end so that the monster sat level.

Browers had been using a camper that slid into the back of his three-quarter-ton pickup, a wise choice for Cat Mesa. The big RV would be fine on the open road, sticking close to the nearest cable-television hookup. It would be helpless on the narrow, winding, rock-studded paths up on the mesa.

I drove around the block, retracing my tracks to the same intersection, and this time turned the other way. The third house on the left was 392.

Two vehicles crowded the narrow driveway. One, a light blue Corsica, was dwarfed by Andy Browers's huge GMC truck and camper.

It appeared the exhausted parents had called it quits for the night. That surprised me, since Tiffany Cole hadn't shown any weakening of her stubborn streak earlier. But fatigue has a way of building until it finds the weakest link in a person's constitution.

I jotted down the license number of the Corsica, thumbed the mike, and jolted Ernie Wheeler out of his paperback.

"PCS, three ten. Information request on New Mexico Tom Lincoln Paul one niner seven."

"Three ten, PCS, stand by." I grinned. Ernie Wheeler sounded as if he'd been poised over the microphone, expecting my call.

While I waited for the computer to spit out what it knew, I drove on down the street to the intersection of Fifth and Blaine and turned around, punching off my headlights as I did so. No sooner had my wheels scrubbed the curb than the radio crackled again. I buzzed up the windows so our conversation wouldn't be public knowledge on the quiet street.

"Three ten, PCS. Be advised that New Mexico Tom Lincoln Paul one niner seven is issued to a 1996 Chevrolet Corsica, blue over silver, registered to Alicia T. Cole, Three ninety-two North Fifth Street, Posadas. No wants or warrants."

"Ten-four, PCS."

I drove past Tiffany Cole's house, my headlights still off. I had seen Browers's truck up on the mesa and didn't bother running its plate. But the big RV in Andy Browers's yard interested me. With the vehicle hidden in the dark shadows two houses down from the nearest streetlight, it was impossible to tell if it was just a corroded-out hulk waiting restoration or a newer unit waiting for its first outing.

I pulled up to the curb three or four houses farther on. If one of the deputies had stopped to check out a vehicle without calling in, I'd have given him a withering reprimand. But that was them.

With flashlight in hand, I got out of the car and strolled across the street. I stepped up on the rough sidewalk and ambled down toward the house at 407. The night was so quiet, I could hear the occasional tractor-trailer on the interstate, a full mile to the south.

No dogs barked, no nothing. I stopped by the rear of the motor-boat and turned on my flashlight. The RV hadn't been there too long, either that or Andy Browers was meticulous about snipping weeds. The rear tires had pressed obvious tracks in the gravel.

Moving carefully, one hand on the block wall, I made my way along the RV until I came to the rear, as high and square as any diesel bus. The New Mexico license was current.

Holding the flashlight under my armpit, I jotted down the number. The only other identification was a dealer logo mounted just above the bumper beside the left-rear taillight. I wrote down the logo and moved around the other side of the unit.

In the poor light, with shadows from my flashlight harsh, I damn near tripped over the power cord. It snaked out of the house from what had to be a bathroom window, and it was plugged into the side of the RV, just in front of the right-rear duals.

"Huh," I muttered. The unit would provide damn near all the comforts of home, that was for sure. And once again, I found myself admiring Andy Browers's good judgment. He had never tried to navigate Cat Mesa in it. If he had, the monster would probably still be up there, mired up to its fancy hubcaps in mud, or trapped between a couple of oak trees when he discovered there was no space to turn the flagship around.

Watching my step, I made my way back to 310. The patrol car burbled to life, and I keyed the radio. "PCS, three ten. Information New Mexico recreational vehicle tag Baker Echo zero zero one."

"Ten-four, three ten. That'll be a couple of minutes."

"Ten-four." I had nothing but time. I turned west on Hutton and followed it all the way to Twelfth Street, where I turned south, driving past the Don Juan de Oñate Restaurant after a couple of blocks.

I drove past the Guzmans' home on South Twelfth and noticed that neither Estelle's county car nor the good doctor's Isuzu was in the driveway. I knew what that meant, especially since Erma Sedillos's little worn-out Toyota was parked at the curb. With a sigh, I turned and headed toward Posadas General Hospital.

Just as I was pulling into the parking lot, Ernie Wheeler returned from the computer errand.

"Three ten, PCS. Be advised that New Mexico RV tag Baker Echo zero zero one should appear on a 1991 World Rambler L-Ten, white over silver. That's registered to a Bruce Elders, Two nine two nine Paseo del Sol Terrace, Corrales, New Mexico. No wants or warrants."

"Ten-four, PCS. I'll be ten-seven at Posadas General for a while. Hold that printout for me, if you would."

I didn't know who Bruce Elders was, but right then, I didn't care much. For both Estelle and her husband to be at the hospital at 3:00 A.M., the news couldn't be good.

Chapter 24

Three A.M. at Posadas General Hospital was a time of muffled noises—things like rubber-soled shoes on polished floors, muted whispers among white-cloaked staff members, and the soft swish of mop on linoleum.

I stepped around the little yellow CAUTION sandwich sign, and the custodian smiled at me and avoided slapping my shoes with the mop. Whatever potion was in his mop bucket had the same cloying sweet smell shared by all the other hospital disinfectants, and it was a smell that brought back all the wrong memories.

I'd been there a half dozen times as a patient, and hundreds of times for other reasons. At one time, head nurse Helen Murchison had half-jokingly called Posadas General my "home away from home." That was a grim notion.

No one was at the reception desk, and I steered around it and walked past the darkened coffee shop. When someone might need coffee the most, the place was closed. No one was in the Financial Services Office, and no one was in the X-ray Department. Where another hallway intersected, the walls gave way to the glass panels of the nurses' station.

A young man whom I didn't recognize looked up from his charts and raised an eyebrow. I suppose he didn't get a lot of walk-in traffic at 3:00 A.M.

"May I help you?" he asked. His voice sounded muffled and distorted behind the glass.

"Is Detective Reyes-Guzman here? Or her husband? Or both?"

"The last time I saw them, they were both down in ICU. If not there, you might try—"

We both saw Dr. Francis Guzman step out of a room at that moment. "Thanks," I said to the nurse. Francis had taken to sporting a full beard, trimmed short. It filled out his normally lean face and made him look professorial. He saw me and grinned.

"How are you doin'?" he said, and his grip was strong but gentle. He didn't let go of my hand right away, his black eyes looking out over the tops of his half-glasses, boring deep into mine, as if he could read some truth hidden there. "I haven't had a chance to welcome you home. Estelle tells me that everything went fine, and that you're already doing too much."

"As a matter of fact, I feel next to useless," I said ruefully.

He nodded sympathetically. He was almost a head taller than I was, his black hair and beard peppered with premature gray. He took off his glasses and slipped them in the breast pocket of his lab coat. "I've been meaning to call you," he said. "Estelle didn't know who was monitoring your medications." The crow's-feet at the corners of his eyes deepened. "Or how many you were taking."

"A shitload," I said. "Camille bought one of those little boxes to put 'em all in."

"A medications organizer?"

I nodded.

"Did you happen to request that your records be sent back? If not, I can request them by phone or fax, but it would really be helpful to have the whole background of what they did to you."

"No, I didn't do that," I said. Francis didn't look surprised. He knew damn well that I was far from the most helpful patient in the world. "And she just mentioned today the bit about Mayo."

The good doctor looked almost apologetic, and he leaned one shoulder against the polished wall tile. "It's just too good an opportunity to pass up, Bill."

"That would be foolish," I said. "If you turned it down, you'd keep asking yourself what you might have thrown away. Hell, some of the world's greatest medical advances must come out of that place." I didn't want to talk about Minnesota, despite my generous words. "Is Estelle still here? How's her mother?"

Francis sighed. "She's sleeping down in room one ten. Estelle, that is. She wouldn't let me give her a sedative, but she finally just pooped out." He grimaced and pulled his hands out of his pockets. "She was walking around here like a zombie. She worries so much about her mother that she can't eat or sleep, and she's worried about that missing youngster. Any word, by the way?"

I shook my head. "Nothing."

"She was talking about the case this afternoon, but we got sidetracked. There were some real problems stabilizing Carmina's condition earlier this evening. It was touch-and-go. We've got a real unstable heart activity that's causing considerable distress." He shook his head. "That, and her kidney function is less than it should be. That's worrisome." He looked at me. "Lump all those things on top of a busted hip and you've got a real mess."

"She was frail even ten years ago," I said. The last time I had seen Carmina Reyes was at Carlos Guzman's *bautizo* the previous spring. Eighty-seven years old and shrunken like a raisin, Carmina had held the hand of her other grandson, Francis junior, while his brother's infant head was doused with holy water. I had thought then the tiny woman wasn't a whole lot taller than little Francis.

Francis nodded. "If she doesn't give up, I think she might make it. It's going to be touch-and-go."

"Does she know about Minnesota?"

Francis looked down the hall toward the ICU ward. "No. Not yet. I think part of her problem is that she knows perfectly well that she's never going to be able to go home. Not unless there's some kind of miracle that we're not equipped to provide. She wants to be around her family, but not in the same house. To her, Tres Santos is a perfect compromise—in another country, but just thirty miles away." He chuckled. "She's never understood the pace of things in the United States."

"Maybe it'll all work out," I said lamely, knowing full well that old age wasn't something that "worked out," except in the final sense.

"Estelle mentioned that you were thinking of selling your house."

I saw no reason to hedge, since the good doctor's X-ray eyes would see through me anyway. But I didn't want to end up sounding like a spoiled child, either. "I wasn't going to sell it," I said. "I was planning to give it to you and Estelle. There is this other place I've had my eye on for a while, and the swap made sense. But Estelle told me about Minnesota, and Camille came up with an alternative, so, as I said before, it'll all work out, one way or another."

"Thank you for the thought," Francis said softly. "If we were staying here, I'd be ready to draw up the papers tomorrow." He glanced at his watch. "Hell no. Today."

The door opened behind him, and Estelle Reyes-Guzman appeared, her long black hair tousled and her eyes squinting against the harsh fluorescent lighting of the hallway.

"Wow," Francis said. "Twenty whole minutes."

"Just right," she said. "I zonked right out." She looked about twelve years old. She let the door close behind her and leaned against the metal door frame. "Any changes?" Francis shook his head.

"You look like twenty hours sleep would be about right," I said.

She smiled and stood up straight. "And you, of course, are home sleeping soundly yourself."

"I was, but I got bored. I drove by Tiffany Cole's place just a few minutes ago. It looks like both she and Andy Browers are down off the mesa for a little bit." Estelle nodded, and I couldn't tell if it was a nod indicating that she knew about the exhausted couple or if she just wanted me to continue before she fell back asleep herself.

"I also drove by Browers's address just a few houses up the street. There's an enormous RV parked beside the house. It's even plugged in with an extension cord through what looks like a bathroom window."

"Bruce Elders," Estelle said. She covered up an enormous yawn with both hands and then blinked back tears. "Excuse me. I saw that thing, and I ran a check on it earlier this afternoon."

"Ah," I said, feeling as if I was about a lap behind. "And who is Bruce Elders?"

Francis held up a hand, and we both stopped and looked at him. "I need to do a few things. But I'll be within buzzer shot if Carmina needs anything. And there's a nurse with her all the time. You ought to go home for a while, before you fall on your face." He looked at me. "You, too."

"And I don't even feel tired," I said after his white-coated figure had disappeared down the hall.

"He gets that way," Estelle said. "You want to go somewhere for coffee?"

"Sure. And you need to bring me up to speed. Who is Bruce Elders?"

"I have no idea. Let me get my bag." She ducked back into the room and emerged with her brown purse. "There's that little staff lounge just past the nurses' station. They've always got something brewing there."

I had been thinking more along the lines of an early-morning breakfast burrito, but I nodded in dumb agreement.

"I haven't had a chance to talk to Browers yet," Estelle continued. "Maybe he's just storing it for someone. Or planning to buy it. Any number of things. It's up on jacks, so it's been there for a while."

"I saw those," I said. "I just got curious, is all. I would guess a unit like that one is fairly expensive, although that's a used one."

"More interesting to me, though," Estelle said as she pushed open the white door marked STAFF ONLY, "is what Francis said about Mrs. Cole."

I followed her into the room. The place looked like an advertisement for white plastic garden furniture. The countertop was white. Even the cabinet doors were white. In a blast of independence, the flooring contractor had cut loose and installed a black-and-white checkerboard pattern.

"Now this is a cozy nook," I muttered. The coffee urn was full, its red light on. I poured a cup and offered it to Estelle, even though I knew damn well she wouldn't take it.

"No thanks," she said, and we sat at one of the three small white garden tables.

"What did Francis say about Mrs. Cole?" I asked.

Estelle raised one eyebrow and said, "You're going to think I'm crazy, but I think her faint up on the mesa was fake."

I had started to sip the coffee and stopped with the brim of the cup a half inch from my lips. "Fake? A fake faint?"

Estelle nodded. I placed my cup on the table carefully, lest I slosh a droplet of the brown stuff on the white surface. She remained silent, watching me. I tried to rerun in my mind the scene of Tiffany Cole's backward topple. I remembered the whites of her eyes and the thud of her skull on the warty-rooted little oak sapling.

"It didn't look fake to me," I said. "Her eyes rolled up, and she even smacked her head against a tree trunk." I frowned and added, "Don't do that." Estelle's beautiful eyes looked as awful as anyone else's when they were rolled back.

"You close your eyes a little and look up, and that's all there is to it. Anyway, I happened to be looking directly at her when she fainted, sir. When her head hit the root, she grimaced. Not much, but a little. She caught herself."

"I didn't notice."

"If she had truly fainted, she wouldn't have felt her head hit the tree. She wouldn't have grimaced."

"Thin, Estelle. Thin."

"That's why I talked to Francis. It's called syncope."

"I know what no blood to the brain is called, sweetheart. I'm an expert in that field."

"Yes," Estelle said, and she started to move my coffee cup across the table. "And Francis said that fainting, or syncope, is caused by insufficient blood supply to the brain."

I retrieved my cup before she had removed it out of my reach. She clasped her hands together and leaned forward. "If her pulse was racing, strong and racing, why would there be insufficient blood supply?"

I looked askance and sipped the coffee. It wasn't bad for hospital brew.

"How do you know her pulse was strong and racing?" I asked.

"For one thing, I saw it. The way her head was turned, I could see the artery in the side of her neck...."

"The carotid," I said expertly.

"Right. For another thing, Deputy Pasquale took her pulse right away, and if you recall, he said, "Her pulse is strong. Just get her head down.""

"I don't recall him saying that, but I'll take your word for it. So she had a strong pulse."

"She wasn't sweaty or pale."

"She looked pretty awful to me."

"Sure, because she'd been spending a lot of time doing the same thing as all the rest of us. Combing every square inch of that mesa for her son." Estelle leaned forward farther and lowered her voice to a harsh whisper. "But she wasn't *sick*-type pale. She wasn't shocky pale."

"I wasn't looking that closely," I admitted. "So what did Francis say, exactly?"

"He said that syncope in an otherwise-healthy person could be caused by fatigue, shock, severe mental distress—almost anything that lowers the blood pressure suddenly."

"The vessels dilate," I said. "Okay. And any of the reasons you've listed would qualify. She was so tired, she could hardly see straight, and all of a sudden there's her son's coat, all sliced to ribbons. That's shock and distress in spades."

"So she faints."

"She faints. She didn't faint when she first picked up the jacket."

"No."

"And she didn't faint while you, Dale, and Browers looked at the Forest Service map. She just knelt there, hugging the coat."

"True."

"She fainted when you knelt beside her and asked her about the tears in the fabric."

"I guess so. I don't have that good a memory, but I'll take your word for it. If that's the way it happened, it sounds like a 'last straw' thing to me. She's lost her son, finding his jacket takes away most of her hope, and then she sees ugly tears in the fabric, which can mean only awful things." I drained the rest of the coffee. "It's perfectly logical to me. It all built up to a head and, bingo, she faints."

"With you right there to catch her."

I laughed. "Estelle, come on. I can't remember the last time I grabbed a fainting maiden. Sure as hell I'd miss if I tried now."

"She didn't know that." Her dark, finely boned face was expressionless, the way she became when she'd turned inward and was perfectly sure of herself. She would have made a terrible cheerleader. Every time the home team scored, the stands in her section would be dead silent, nothing but dark, bottomless eyes watching the game.

"Let's consider something," I said finally. I leaned back in the white plastic thing and felt it flex with my weight. Afraid that it might dump me on the floor, I relaxed forward again. "Let's assume that you are one hundred percent correct with this notion. Let's assume that Tiffany Cole was faking." I held my hands up, framing an imaginary marquee. "The Academy Award for best screen faint goes to Tiffany Cole. Why would she do that?"

"I don't know, sir."

"But you can guess."

Estelle Reyes-Guzman nodded. "I think that she knows more about her son's disappearance than she's letting on."

I rested my head in my hands and gazed at the remarkable woman sitting across the table from me. She was either so far ahead of me that we were working different cases or she was completely, dreadfully wrong.

"Well," I said, "Is that the direction you're going to go with it?"

"Yes." There wasn't a instant's hesitation in her response.

I sighed and stood up. "And now, I'm tired," I said.

"I'm glad you got your wife's picture back," Estelle said.

I tossed my cup in the trash and turned to look at her, puzzled. "How did you know that?"

"Camille called here earlier. About an hour ago."

"I'll be damned."

"That's what daughters are for," Estelle said.

"She doesn't need to worry," I said.

"That's what I told her. I said that your working all night was a sign that you were all better. All back to normal." She grinned and patted my arm as she held the door open for me.

I stopped and looked at Estelle for a long moment. "I hope that you'll be very sure of your evidence before you initiate anything against Tiffany Cole."

"Yes, sir. I just wanted you to know what I was thinking."

I smiled widely. "That's always a treat, Estelle."

Chapter 25

The light of day on Wednesday brought two unpleasant surprises. The first was the *Posadas Register*.

Marjorie Davis had done more than her share to fill the front page. I paused with a fork halfway from plate to mouth. The elegant breakfast of fake eggs mixed with green chili was Camille's way of making up for being a surreptitious nag the night before. She wasn't about to give up, though. A small paper cup of pills rested beside my coffee cup—decaf coffee.

Across the top of the paper was a screamer headline, usually reserved by editor/publisher Frank Dayan for the end of the world. SEARCH ENTERS FIFTH DAY it bellowed in letters an inch high. Under the headline and covering the top quarter of the page, little Cody Cole's face beamed out at the world.

He was a fetching youngster, that was for sure. At the time the shutter was clicked for that picture, he'd been a genuinely happy little kid, with wide grin, sparkling eyes, dimples, the whole works. The tiny white cowpoke hat sat rakishly on his head, holding down a thatch of golden locks.

I sighed and flipped the paper over. Balancing the picture of Cody was another photo, this one positioned down in the lower-left quadrant. It was wonderfully composed, and I nodded in admiration at Marjorie's skill. The sunlight streamed through the trees and brush, and just off center rested the tangle of a shattered helicopter.

Ms. Davis had waited for just the right moment of drama. A Guardsman on the left was gesticulating to someone off-camera, his mouth caught in full shout. On the right, framed by a grove of trees and the wreck in the background, was a New Mexico State Police Officer and a National Guardsman, both kneeling in front of another soldier, who was holding a bandage to his forehead.

"No metro paper is going to compete with this," I murmured.

"Look at page four," Camille said, and I put down my fork and did so.

"Jesus," I said. In addition to various illustrated sidebars about the boy's parents, quotations from every agency involved, and pleas for information, another large picture at the top of page four riveted my attention.

I read the caption aloud. EVERYTHING POSSIBLE, the lead-in said. "In an effort to duplicate the possible behavior of the missing child, Detective Estelle Reyes-Guzman brought her own son to the mesa early Monday. Despite all efforts, the only trace of the missing youngster is the discovery of a blue jacket thought to belong to the boy."

"I'll be damned," I said.

The photo was one that Marjorie had taken when she saw little Francis and Camille waiting by the Blazer. The photo was cropped so that Francis appeared to be walking, head thoughtfully down, an adult's hand resting on his shoulder.

"Incredible," I said. At the bottom of the page was a large display advertisement promising a thousand-dollar reward for information on Cody Cole's whereabouts. The telephone number was that of the *Posadas Register*.

"Anything that helps," Camille said.

"I suppose," I replied. "But I hope Marjorie actually talked to Estelle before running that caption."

"The child was there," Camille said. "Francis, I mean."

"I wish she'd gotten a photo of Mrs. Cole hugging her son's jacket," I said, remembering my conversation with Estelle long before the sun came up that morning. "That would have been good for a tear or two."

"Dad," Camille said with considerable exasperation. "The newspaper's got a right to cover events in its own way."

"I know they do." That didn't mean I had to like it. I folded the paper and put it down, concentrating on my breakfast. I had slept fashionably late, and I was hungry enough to eat several dozen fake eggs.

I still smarted just a little from discovering that I was plodding along many steps behind Estelle. She had known about the big RV all along, even as I was stalking about in the dead of night, jotting ridiculous little notes under the beam of a flashlight.

"Do you want to help me do a little surveying today?" I asked.

Camille held her coffee cup delicately in both hands and looked at me over the rim. "Surveying what?"

"I'd like to do a little tramping out back here, with the horses in mind, and see if the whole thing will really work. I was thinking that if there wasn't room, I could just buy some pasturage somewhere, but then I decided that wasn't a good idea. The whole idea is to have the horses close at hand, not half a county away."

"I'd be happy to do that," Camille said.

We both would have been happy to do that, except the damn telephone rang. Maybe there was a higher purpose in that. As long as I was answering a telephone call, I was alive and kicking. An old friend of mine who owned a gun and tackle shop contended that the reason he'd lived so long with only half a functioning heart was that he always had something coming mail order. How could he kick off when there was something exciting arriving in the mail?

I glanced at my watch, saw it was 9:15, and said as I picked up the receiver, "It's got to be Marty Holman."

"It is Marty Holman," the voice said, and I grinned at Camille "Good morning," I said.

"Stanley Willit is sitting here in my office. He's got a bunch of paperwork that looks really interesting. I think you should come down."

"I can't wait," I said.

"I thought you'd say that," Holman said.

"Give me ten minutes," I said, and hung up. "We'll survey another time. The weird stepson just hit town."

Chapter 26

I don't know what I expected Stanley Willit to look like, but I certainly wouldn't have picked out of a crowd the man sitting in Sheriff Martin Holman's office. Perhaps his real parents had been from Lebanon, or Syria, or Iran.

Stanley Willit turned black eyes to regard me as I walked into the office. He got up and extended a hand.

"Ah, Undersheriff Gantner," he said. "I'm Stanley Willit. We spoke on the telephone." His handshake was limp and fleeting.

"Gastner. Yes, we did."

He smiled and his black mustache split, showing perfectly even white teeth. His face was square, with a broad, prominent jaw and high forehead. By noon, he'd need another shave and a fresh turban.

"I was just telling the sheriff that I've been able to assemble considerable documentation," Willit said. His voice didn't fit his appearance, sounding more like a prissy little accountant.

"Documentation of what?" I asked, and sat down in the chair at the end of Holman's desk.

"First of all, I have the letters written to me by Gloria Apodaca, in which she makes reference to threats from her husband, and allegations that he was beginning to make moves that might result in her inability to access her own finances."

He started to reach for a file folder that he had placed on Holman's desk, but I waved a hand, impressed as hell with that "inability to access her own finances." He made the two elderly folks sound like a couple of multinational corporations.

"Wait, Mr. Willit. Let's cut to the chase on this thing and not get mired in paperwork. I decided, after I gave the matter some thought, that it's best for all parties if Mrs. Apodaca's remains are moved from my property."

"So you've already instituted litigation to that effect?" Willit's eyes narrowed like a ferret's, and I decided I didn't like him very much.

"No, I didn't institute litigation. That would be ridiculous. She was buried on my property without my knowledge or consent. The best place for her, I would think, is in Our Lady of Sorrows Cemetery."

Willit shifted in his chair, the folder in his lap. He really wanted to open it and use all that ammunition. The cover flapped tentatively. "It's my understanding that he plans some sort of litigation should you make any efforts to exhume my stepmother's body and move it elsewhere."

I laughed, deciding that Stanley Willit loved the sound of the word *litigation*. Martin Holman leaned back in his chair and said, gazing up at the ceiling, "That's a case I'd love to hear. 'I buried my wife on your property, and if you move her, I'll sue.'" He looked at me and chuckled.

"Let him litigate," I said. "I agree with the sheriff."

"Perhaps the correct strategy is to take the first step in this and file a suit demanding that the body be moved," Willit said, rubbing his chin.

I laughed again. "No, Mr. Willit. That's not the correct strategy. There's no point in any lawyers making pocket change out of this ridiculous situation. Florencio Apodaca is a senile old man who's confused. That's the extent of it."

"What do you suggest, then?"

"I'm not suggesting anything," I said. "This is what I plan to do. This afternoon, I'm going to hire Chris Lucero and his backhoe. He will gently and skillfully open the grave on my property. I don't know how deeply your stepmother is buried. I plan to ask Gene Salazar to have a hearse swing by to transport Mrs. Apodaca over to Our Lady of Sorrows, where Chris will dig another grave with his backhoe. Your stepmother will rest in peace over there. Someone can even arrange a memorial service with Father Gilbert, I'm sure."

I paused to take a deep breath. "If Florencio has any objections, he can hoot and holler all he wants. If he's got a better idea that makes sense, he can say so."

"A better idea? Like what?"

I shrugged. "Maybe he'd prefer having her planted in his own backyard. I'd have to check the ordinance to see if his lot is big enough, but if it is..." I shrugged again.

Willit's olive cheeks showed signs of high blood pressure. "I don't know why everyone is so casual here, but I really think an autopsy should be done."

"Since we don't know how she died, one probably should be," Martin Holman said easily, enjoying one of his brief excursions into law. "Are you planning to swear out a criminal complaint against your father?"

"He's not my father."

"Stepfather, I mean."

"I haven't decided yet.

Unfortunately, a criminal complaint didn't require any litigation, so I could understand Stanley's hesitation.

"That would make an autopsy almost automatic," Holman continued. "Judge Lester Hobart signs an order to that effect, and that's it. Period. Takes five minutes, especially if we request it."

"Will you?"

"What, request an autopsy?" I shrugged again and looked at Holman.

He shrugged back. "Technically, it's not our case, Mr. Willit. Chief Martinez, the village chief, conducted the investigation. As I showed you in his report, the death was listed as natural causes and the case closed. But that's not to say the judge can't order it reopened."

Stanley Willit deflated a bit with satisfaction. "How long will all this take?"

"I'll make the telephone calls now, if that's soon enough," I said. "I can't guarantee the autopsy schedule. If they do it here, at the hospital's morgue, it won't take long. If the body has to be shipped to the medical examiner's in Las Cruces, it will take longer."

Stanley Willit clutched the folder to his chest and stood up. He was a big man, well over six feet tall, with solid broad shoulders and no taper at the waist. "Than that's what we should do," he said. "I would like to witness the exhumation personally."

"Of course you would," I said. Willit shot a glance at me, but I kept a straight face. Holman was smirking. "Where are you staying?"

"The Posadas Inn, room twenty-nine."

I ushered Willit to the door. I patted his shoulder and he cringed. "I'll call you as soon as the action starts."

"What do you suppose he does for a living?" Holman said when the door of his office was safely shut.

"Sells Persian rugs," I said.

"Or real estate. That's my guess."

An hour later, Judge Hobart flourished his silver ballpoint pen on the appropriate form and then glanced up at me. "How do you get yourself into these messes, Bill?"

"I made the mistake of leaving town for a little while," I said.

"That'll do it every time."

Things moved quickly, at least by Posadas standards. By two o'clock that afternoon, Chris Lucero's big yellow Case backhoe came belching into my driveway. Willit had telephoned three times from the motel, and it was with considerable relief that I called him back and told him the exhumation was about to begin.

Because Florencio Apodaca wasn't going to be happy, I had copies of the exhumation order and the court order for the autopsy delivered to him personally by a uniformed deputy—in this case, Tony Abeyta, who spoke fluent Spanish.

The autopsy had postponed the need for Gene Salazar's mortuary services. So, with the exception of the Posadas EMS ambulance standing by, as well as two units from the sheriff's office, we could have been mistaken for a city crew digging up a water line as we gathered out back. Sheriff Holman looked like the foreman who would never let the wood of a shovel handle touch his hands.

"You know how deep?" Chris Lucero shouted over the clattering idle of his machine.

I shook my head. "The old man wouldn't say. Just take your time."

"Is there a casket or anything?"

"I don't know." I shrugged and Chris looked heavenward as he climbed back on the backhoe. Deputy Abeyta had tried to talk Florencio into coming outside to supervise, but the old man just took the papers and waved him away.

Abeyta and I carefully uprooted the juniper cross.

"You think he's going to want to keep that?" Holman asked.

"I have no idea," I said. "We just keep it out of harm's way for now."

Chris idled the machine into position and the massive outriggers crunched into the soil. As delicately as a child digging with a fork, he swept the teeth of the bucket the length of the grave site, raking no more than an inch into the soil.

When he had what he thought were the grave's dimensions marked, he began excavating in earnest. With the first scoopful, I had a mental picture of the eighteen-inch-wide bucket coming up out of the earth with half of the old lady dangling from its teeth. I glanced over at Stanley Willit. He had on a really nice camel hair coat over his dark suit—he could have been the mortician. His face was impassive.

The soil was easy digging—especially since someone had been there first the hard way, with a pick and shovel.

Chris hadn't dug deeply enough to sink the bucket when he stopped the machine with a lurch. "Wood," he shouted. I stepped forward and at the same time felt a hand at my elbow. I turned, to see both Camille and Estelle Reyes-Guzman.

Estelle stepped close and spoke just loudly enough that I could hear her over the machine. "Where's the old man?"

"He wouldn't come out of the house," I said.

"Do you want me to talk to him?"

"It wouldn't hurt. Tony Abeyta was over there to serve the papers. He tried, but the old man just waved him off."

"I'll go see."

I nodded. "Take Tony with you."

Chris waited patiently while I walked to the edge of the hole and peered down. Eighteen inches wasn't much for a grave, but it had probably seemed a mile to Florencio Apodaca.

Martin Holman walked to within a yard of the grave and frowned.

"Why don't you see what that is," I said to him. "See if it's the top of the casket or just an old board, or root or something."

"Here, let me," Camille said. "I've got grubbies on."

Holman didn't pretend to protest. His gleaming shoes had been saved from soil for another day. Camille stepped into the shallow pit, then crouched down, gently swishing dirt away.

"It's a flat board. Maybe the top. I'm not sure."

Chris tapped the throttle of the Case for attention and indicated that he'd clean out a little more. Camille scrambled out of the way. As slick as can be, he shaved the dirt from the top of what looked like an old narrow door.

He took one more partial bucket, swung the boom out of the way, and settled it to the ground, shutting off the machine as he did so.

The little wooded area was suddenly still.

"I got a shovel in the truck," he said.

"This reminds me of when we had to dig up Todd Sloan out on the old Fuentes place," Holman muttered. "You remember that?"

"Indeed," I said. "I think the circumstances are a little different, though." Sloan had been a teenager who'd been murdered by his mother's boyfriend—and then had been buried out in the country where no one would ever find him. Except that we had, much to the killer's disappointment. "That was a December ceremony. This is only November." And we hadn't had a backhoe, and Holman hadn't done any of the digging.

Holman grunted something and backed up a step while Chris Lucero jumped down in the hole and swept the remains of the dirt from the wooden door.

He put the point of the shovel underneath and it lifted easily. "I don't think it's attached to anything," he said. "You want me to lift it up?" He sounded as if he really wanted me to say no.

"Sure." It was a door, an old weather-beaten Z-braced door barely eighteen inches wide and five feet long, the sort of door that would grace an old-fashioned woodshed. Chris lifted it and Camille took it by one edge, laying it down on the ground next to the hole.

"Hmmm," Chris said, and stepped up out. I didn't know if he was reacting to the fragrance or just the idea of an occupied grave. "He didn't dig too deep, did he?"

I heard twigs snapping and looked up, to see Estelle and Tony Abeyta working their way back through the underbrush.

"Ladrónes de tumbas," she said. "That's what he called us— grave robbers." She walked to the edge of the grave and knelt. The corpse was wrapped in a dark blue blanket, head facing the street. The blanket had been wrapped so neatly that I could see the outlines of the hands, folded together, no doubt clutching a rosary.

"That's one way to do it," Chris Lucero observed, "Just like in the old days. He didn't have enough wood to make the whole casket, so he just used the cover."

"Probably couldn't bring himself to shovel dirt on her face," I said. "Let's get her moved."

"Let me take photos first," Estelle said. "It'll only take a minute." While she did that, I waved at the two paramedics who had been lounging near the chrome back bumper of their immaculate red-and-white unit. Lugging the stout gurney, they followed the crude path the backhoe had made trampling down the underbrush.

Estelle took more photos than I thought necessary, but her motto was that film was cheap. Most of the time, she was right.

One paramedic grasped the body by the shoulders and the other took the feet. Working in perfect unison, they lifted the mortal remains of Gloria Apodaca up and out of the shallow grave.

"Whoa," Estelle said when it looked as if they were going to strap the body on the gurney.

She stepped close and knelt, hugging the camera with one hand. "Sir," she said, and I stepped around the grave. As soon as I bent over, I could see what concerned Estelle.

"If she died of natural causes, I don't think the blanket would be soaked with blood," she said quietly.

And sure enough, the blue blanket at the back of Gloria Apodaca's skull was the deep rich brown of dried blood.

"Oops," Martin Holman muttered.

Chapter 27

That was not the most inspired, thoughtful comment the sheriff could have made with members of the interested public watching and listening. Its very utterance admitted the possibility of some error, however small, on our part.

And I knew damn well how *error* translated in Stanley Willit's mind. His dark eyes narrowed and he took a step sideways so that he could see the bloodstain for himself without having to venture any closer.

"Will you make an identification for us?" Sheriff Holman asked him. Willit's composure paled a shade.

"Shouldn't her husband do that?" he said.

"He can," Holman said agreeably. "It would just expedite matters, is all."

Willit screwed up his courage and nodded. Estelle gently lifted the corner of the blanket and folded first one layer and then the next back, being careful that the dirt was shaken away from the corpse's surprisingly tranquil face.

Gloria Apodaca's hair had been wiry, steel gray, worn most of the time up in a bun. I stepped close, staying behind Willit in case he keeled over. He thrust his hands in his pockets, took a deep breath, and bent down. Estelle remained crouched at the gurney's side, and Willit peered over her shoulder.

"That's my stepmother," he said, and straightened back up.

"Thank you," Estelle murmured. She continued to ease the blanket away from the woman's head until the corpse was exposed down to midchest. She motioned to me, and I ushered Willit out of the way. Estelle waited until I had bent over, my hands on my knees, before saying quietly, "There appears to be significant bleeding from the back of her skull just above the spine." She glanced up at me. "I don't see any other obvious injuries to the face or head, but the ME will have to tell us for sure."

"Are you saying my stepmother was struck from behind?" Willit said. His hearing was sharp, no doubt honed by years of listening for verbal indiscretions that could be turned into profit.

"No," Estelle Reyes-Guzman replied. She stood up. "I'm saying that there's a considerable amount of blood that appears to have come from the back of her head."

"Same thing," Willit said.

"Is it?" Estelle's voice was pleasant, as if Willit actually had information she needed to know.

"What else would explain it?" Willit asked. The two EMTs began to shift position toward the gurney, and Estelle held up her hand. They stopped and waited.

"That's exactly what the medical examiner will tell us, Mr. Willit," she said. She turned and completed her photo series, and when she was satisfied, Mrs. Apodaca's mortal remains were carried off my property and placed in the ambulance.

"I assume that the next step is to arrest Florencio Apodaca," Willit said, and I turned to look at him with interest. If he planned to dog our heels every step of the way, his presence was going to be tedious at best.

"Mr. Willit," I said, and placed a fatherly hand on his shoulder. He cringed but held his ground, and I gave his shoulder a couple of squeezes. The camel hair coat felt smooth, soft, and expensive. "At the moment, we don't know any more about the circumstances of your stepmother's death than you do. The medical examiner has to examine the body to determine the cause of death. Then we have to piece together exactly how that death happened. It's not always a simple process, as I'm sure you can appreciate."

"What do we need to do to speed things along?"

I smiled. "The most constructive thing you can do is to stay out of our way, Mr. Willit."

"Are you planning to talk to Florencio?"

"Of course."

"May I come along when you do that?"

"No."

Willit didn't like the finality of that, and his eyes narrowed. "Why not?"

"Because you're not a police officer, for one thing."

"I won't be in the way."

"How true," I said. "Mr. Willit, just what is it that you do?"

"Do?"

"For a living."

Willit ducked his head, perhaps wishing he could say something that would impress the hell out of us. "I manage a restaurant franchise."

"Ah," I said. "And I'm sure you're very familiar with the operation of that restaurant, aren't you?"

"Of course."

"And as manager, I'm sure that you prefer that the operation of that restaurant is carried out in a smooth, organized fashion, with very little left to chance." This time, Willit settled for just a slight nod. "That's pretty much how we operate on our own turf, Mr. Willit. We have certain ways of doing things. For example, your stepfather is elderly and frail. Whatever has happened here, however it happened, we're not going to bust into Florencio Apodaca's home like a bunch of storm troopers."

He straightened his shoulders and looked down his patrician nose at me. "Even if he committed murder?"

I squeezed his shoulder again and then released him. "That sort of charge requires evidence, Mr. Willit."

Willit's snort was a curious combination of indignant cough and bleat. "I'd certainly say that a bashed-in skull was evidence of a crime, Sheriff."

Holman glanced at Willit, but the comment was clearly addressed to me. "Perhaps. But we aren't blessed with X-ray vision, Mr. Willit. I, for one, can't see that your stepmother's skull is bashed in, as you suggest. In fact, you seem to be the only one here who has the answers. That in itself makes me a little uneasy."

"Now wait a minute," Willit began.

I held up a hand. "Relax, sir. If there's an injury, it could also happen from a fall down stairs, or a hundred other ways that none of us can imagine." I shrugged. "We have our procedures, just as you do. That's all I'm trying to make clear."

I started to turn away, then stopped and held up a cautioning hand. "Also, Mr. Apodaca has made it clear in previous conversations that he doesn't much like you, Mr. Willit. It only stands to reason that your presence during questioning would be a hindrance."

"When will you be questioning him?"

I glanced at my watch. "Directly. If you don't wish to wait at your motel room and have nowhere else to go, perhaps you'd like to wait in the lounge at the sheriff's office. That way, you'll be on hand should we need you, and you'll be among the first to be informed of any progress we make." I smiled and tried to keep it sincere.

Willit watched the backhoe pull away, and then he stepped back as Deputy Tom Mears spun a yellow crime-scene tape around the area, fencing in the small grave.

"I'll do that," he said, and made his way through the brush toward his rental car parked on Escondido.

Holman nudged me. "Now I remember why the hell we miss you so much when you're gone," he said, grinning broadly.

I looked at him. "Oh?"

"And I bet it's fried chicken," Holman said without explaining himself. When he saw the blank look on my face, he added quickly, "Willit's restaurant."

"Fish," I said.

"Maybe you're right. What's the game plan? Wait for the ME?"

I nodded. "When we know what killed Gloria Apodaca, and when, then we can work on the who. In the meantime, we've got more important things to do, like finding a lost three-year-old. Accident, murder, whatever, none of this is going anywhere. It can wait."

"Amen," Estelle muttered.

Holman's eyebrows shot up. "By the way," he said, and stepped close, as if the trees shouldn't hear. I saw a smile on Camille's face as she stood outside the circle of yellow tape, waiting for us to finish up. "Do you know anything about that big RV that's parked next to Andy Browers's house? I drove by and saw that, and I ran the plate."

"Other than that it belongs to a Bruce Elders of Corrales, no, we don't," I said, and watched Holman's shoulders slump a fraction. He had wanted me to say, "What RV?"

"You want me to work on that? I've got some contacts up there."

"Fine," I said. "Let me suggest a simple approach first, though. Ask Andy Browers."

"Sure," Holman said, nodding as if that had been first on his list. "I just thought it was odd, is all. Here he's got a big camper that fits into the back of his pickup truck, and other than the electric company's truck that he uses all the time, that's all he's got."

"He owns a motorcycle," Estelle said.

"That, too." Holman nodded without skipping a beat. "And here's a late-model land yacht that must cost seventy-five grand parked next to his house, owned by some guy upstate. It doesn't make any sense to me. It's probably nothing, you know? But you're always lecturing about not ignoring any of the little pieces."

The sheriff left, and I watched Estelle pack her camera gear and make final comments in her notebook. "Do you want to meet somewhere for dinner?" I suggested.

"Oh please," Camille interrupted with immediate protest. "Dad, your only 'somewhere' is the Don Juan." She grinned at Estelle. "Why don't you guys come over when all the dust settles. Let me make something. Fancy pasta maybe. Bring the kids. Bring Erma."

Estelle sighed and slung the heavy camera bag's strap over her shoulder. "You know, that sounds like a really nice idea. I'll give Francis a call and make sure he isn't tied up, and I'll probably drop by the hospital for a few minutes. What's a good time?"

"Just whenever," Camille said.

It did sound like a wonderful idea at the time.

Chapter 28

At 5:00 P.M. that Wednesday, Sheriff Martin Holman officially announced the end of the mesa search for little Cody Cole. Four days and thousands of man-hours had produced nothing other than the torn jacket.

The event even attracted a live-news crew from one of the major television stations, and we watched the announcement on television while Camille put the finishing touches on enough food to feed an army.

"At this time, I regretfully announce that search efforts for three-year-old Cody Cole have been terminated," Holman said. I could see the front door of the Public Safety Building directly behind him. He was frowning, and he looked directly at the reporter, rather than into the camera. "In the absence of further leads, the risk to search teams both on the ground and in the air makes continued operations unacceptable."

The reporter tipped the microphone back and asked, "Sheriff, what does your department intend to do now that the search has been halted?" The cameraman was alert, and he panned to show the wind blowing the young woman's hair, giving her that tousled, on-the-scene look. Martin Holman was perfectly coifed and neatly pressed, as usual.

"The Posadas County Sheriff's Department, in cooperation with the United States Forest Service, the New Mexico Department of Fish and Game, the New Mexico State Police, and other agencies, will continue to monitor developments from a central command post in Posadas." He took a breath. "Limited search activities will continue on Cat Mesa until further notice, although without the involvement of National Guard aircraft."

"What do you think happened to the child?"

Sheriff Holman wasn't ready for that question, and he hesitated for just a fraction of a second. "I don't think that speculation is productive," he said.

"Do you think that Cody Cole is still on Cat Mesa?"

"As I said, speculation isn't going to find the missing youngster," Holman said, and nodded to end the interview.

The reporter persisted. "Sheriff, if you felt there was any chance at all that the child was still alive on the mesa, would you cancel the search?"

"History is being made," I said. "Martin Holman gets to field a question so stupid, even he should be puzzled."

Holman managed a pained expression for the camera, then said, "Thank you." He stepped out of camera range.

The television reporter signed off, and a final pan of the camera established that her channel had the scoop. "It's quite a day when live-news cameras come to Posadas," I said.

Camille laughed and clattered dishes. "They should have been out at the grave site earlier. That would have been photogenic. Marty could have refused to speculate on how the old lady's skull got bashed in, too."

"We don't know that's what happened yet," I said.

"Bet you twenty bucks."

"No." The telephone rang and Camille glanced around at me. "You want to get that? My hands are full."

"Even money says it's Martin Holman, wanting a review."

"No bet." Camille chuckled.

I picked up the phone. "You did really well, Sheriff," I said, and was greeted by silence at the other end.

After a few seconds, Holman said, "Did you catch the news?"

"Yes. Like I said, you did really well. You sounded like one of those people who work for the Pentagon."

"I'm not sure that's a compliment, but I'll pretend it is. Listen, two things. First of all, is Estelle there yet?"

"No. She and Francis are going to come over in a few minutes, though. We were going to see if we could actually squeeze in a dinner. Do you and Meg want to come, too?"

"No thanks. Let us take a rain check. But I wanted to pass along some preliminary comments from the medical examiner."

"That was fast."

"Express service. First of all, as far as the ME is concerned, it's a definite homicide. It appears that Gloria Apodaca was killed by a single blow to the base of the skull. A really hard blow, the ME said."

"What was the weapon?"

"You don't sound surprised," Holman said, ignoring my question.

"I'm not easily surprised anymore, Martin—except by the notion that Florencio Apodaca has enough gumption to swing any tool hard enough to crush in a skull."

"The ME thinks that the murder weapon was something like a shovel."

"Well, that makes sense, if Florencio did it. A shovel handle makes for a lot of speed at the blade."

"You're saying 'if Florencio did it.' Do you have doubts?"

Camille left the kitchen, and I switched ears so I could turn and look toward the front door. Estelle and Francis Guzman appeared in the foyer. "We need to talk with the old man now, Sheriff. But of course I have doubts, until we see some evidence. Who knows. Maybe Stanley Willit was here last week and killed her, then planned this performance."

"That's unlikely."

"Of course it is. But it's possible. Maybe one of Florencio's children. Maybe the son who owns the wood shop."

"What wood shop is that?"

"It's a long story. All I'm saying is that we need to be very sure of ourselves. There's no doubt in my mind that Florencio knows what happened, and who swung the shovel, or whatever it is. But whether he did it is another question." Estelle and her husband stepped down into the living room, and I could see Camille making hand signals about appetizers. "We need to move on this, though. Estelle and I can go over there this evening. Talk to the old man, see what he says. He may loosen up and spill the whole story."

"I'd like to make another suggestion, Bill," Holman said. The tone of his voice sank a notch into his administrative mode, the tone he used when he was feeling self-confident and forceful.

"What's that?"

"Let's let Sergeant Torrez and Deputy Pasquale go over there this evening. They both speak Spanish, if that's a help, and Bob is about as steady as they come. He's not going to do anything rash, and he sure isn't going to let Tommy Pasquale out of his sight."

I started to say something, then thought better of it. "All right," I said instead.

There must have been some hesitation in my tone, because Holman added, "I think sometimes we underuse Torrez. Certainly underestimate him, anyway. And Pasquale needs the experience."

"Fine."

As Holman began to speak again, I caught Estelle's eye and looked heavenward. She grinned. She and Francis were relaxed on the couch, stretched out, with their feet up on the ancient slabwood coffee table. "And you know, eventually you and I are going to have to sit down and discuss how we're going to reorganize things around here with Estelle leaving in May."

"She told you, eh?"

"Yes. I can't say I'm very happy about it. She's going to be difficult to replace."

"Yes, she is."

"Maybe they'll get sick of the north country and be back. I give them one winter up there."

"Yep," I said, and shifted my weight to the other foot. "What was the second thing you wanted to tell me?"

"Oh, I almost forgot. Another reason I wanted Torrez to visit the old man this evening. Stanley Willit was showing me some papers a few minutes ago. Interesting stuff. Bank records, mostly. It appears that his stepmother was in the process of transferring funds out of her and her husband's joint account. She had established a separate account, and what's more, Willit has a signed power of attorney for all of Gloria Apodaca's affairs should she become indisposed."

"Or dead," I said.

"Or dead. Convenient, isn't it? That would block Florencio from accessing those funds under joint tenancy. At least for a while, anyway."

"Did you explain all this to Torrez? So he doesn't walk into this mess without some prior knowledge?"

"No, but I plan to."

"And make sure that Willit does not accompany the officers to Apodaca's," I said.

"He seems content next door," Holman said.

"In the district attorney's office?"

Holman chuckled. "He asked if he could use the county's law library. I think he's trying to figure out who to sue next."

Normally, all one had to do was suggest the idea of litigation involving the Sheriff's Department to Martin Holman and his forehead began to sweat. He evidently thought Stanley Willit was as much of a fruitcake as I did.

"Well, it was my land that provided the burial site, so no doubt he'll sue me. And Florencio did the burying, or says he did, so he's on the list, too. And you're the one who said 'Oops' when we exhumed the body, so you're on there, too."

"Did I really say that?"

"Yes, you really did. Perhaps it would be prudent to tell Mr. Willit that the county offices are now closed, including the DA's law library. Let him go stew in his motel room."

"I'd rather have him where I can keep an eye on him," Holman said.

"Tell Bob to call me if he gets in a bind," I said. Camille was holding up a bowl of guacamole dip.

"One last thing," Holman said. "I put Tom Mears on the Cole situation. He said he wanted to keep somebody up on the mesa anyway, just in case. I told him that was a good idea. He'll be following up leads from here. We're spread pretty thin, but the Forest Service is going to help out, I think."

"Good idea. Keep me posted."

I hung up, my ear hot from the receiver.

"That was the sheriff?" Camille asked, and she handed me a small glass of red wine.

"His nibs," I said. "The changing of the guard."

"The changing of the guard?" Camille asked, and then she saw the expression on my face. "Oh," she said.

"He's sending someone over to talk with Mr. Apodaca?" Estelle asked.

"Torrez and Pasquale," I said, and took a long swallow of the wine.

"They'll do fine," she said. It would have been nice, I thought, if she had hesitated just a bit before saying that. Francis Guzman, who over the years had grown as perceptive of my various moods as anyone, pushed himself to his feet.

"Let's see what meds they've got you taking," he said. I know how he meant it—as a helpful diversion—but checking prescription labels wasn't my idea of recreation. It was too damn close to what old men in nursing homes did.

Chapter 29

We managed just over two hours of relaxation—enough to eat far too much of Camille's pasta primavera, several salads, all of which bordered dangerously close to health food, and a low-fat raspberry cheesecake that was really pretty good.

Two telephones sounded simultaneously—a startling cacophony that prompted me to look at my watch. Dr. Francis Guzman carried one of those small holstered cellular telephones on his belt—a New Age progression from beepers. His belt phone chimed just as the telephone in my kitchen jangled.

"So much for peace and quiet," I said, starting to push myself up and out of my old leather chair.

"Let me get it, Dad," Camille said, and she was in the kitchen before I was upright. Francis migrated toward the foyer, the ridiculously small instrument at his ear. His voice was soft and muted, but Camille had never been muted in her life.

"Good evening," she said, and then waited. I twisted around and saw the frown on her face. She was listening intently, but then she pulled the receiver away from her ear and glanced at it, as if she wasn't hearing correctly.

"Who is it?" I asked.

She held up a hand, then said, "Is someone on the line?"

"Cranks," I said, and turned away, grinning at Estelle. "Remember the days of the old party lines?"

"Dad," Camille said, "maybe you'd better listen to this."

By then, Francis had finished with his call, and he held up his hands in resignation. "Duty calls," he said, adding, "Camille, thanks for the dinner. I've got to run." He kissed Estelle on the forehead and waved at me. "And I'm sure you folks will be getting the call, too. Someone got themselves shot."

By then, I was on my feet. Camille handed me the receiver. "It sounds like falling furniture, with a youngster crying way in the background," she said.

As soon as I put the receiver to my ear, I could hear the lusty screams of a child, muted with distance, and then a series of heavy thuds close to the telephone, like someone thumping a book against a hassock.

"That's a really hurting child," Camille said.

I listened again, but obviously I didn't have Camille's fine-tuned mother's ear. It sounded like a child who was unhappy about something, but that was normal for most kids the majority of the time. Estelle pushed herself up from the couch, an eyebrow raised in curiosity.

"Gastner," I said into the receiver. A mighty crash was followed by more howling from the distant kid. It sounded as if the whole side of the room, telephone and all, had collapsed. "Jesus," I said. "Hello?"

I was about to hand the receiver to Estelle when I heard a muffled cry, an urgent "Mmmmph."

"This is Undersheriff William Gastner," I said again. "Is someone there?"

"Mmmmmph. Mmmmmph. Mmmmmph." And in the background, the child continued to cry, stirred on by whatever was making the wild thumping and banging.

"Can you understand me?" I said, and abruptly the ruckus stopped, followed by another string of grunts and moans.

"Grunt once for yes, twice for no. Are you hurt?"

"Mmmph, mmmph."

"Is the child with you hurt?"

"Mmmph, mmmph." Whoever it was put considerable urgency in those grunts, and then a slow, dim light began to glow somewhere in my dull brain.

"Are you using an automatic dialer?"

"Mmmph."

"Estelle," I barked, and I handed the receiver to her. She'd heard my side of the conversation and she didn't bother with background explanations. I could see by the look on her face that she recognized the voice of the howling child, if nothing else.

"Erma?" she said, and my pulse jumped. She got a single loud "Mmmph," loud enough that I could hear it standing three feet away. "I'll be right there." She thrust the phone at me and said, "Keep her on the line."

"Erma, do you need an ambulance?" I shouted. Estelle was already racing toward the front door.

The two "Mmmph" 's that came then were more like a whimper than a cry for help.

"Are you in any immediate danger?"

"Mmmph, Mmmph."

"Why can't you talk? Are you gagged somehow?"

"Mmmph."

"How about the kids? Are they all right?"

"Mmmmmph, Mmmph." I could hear the anger shouted right through the tape, or sock, or plastic bag that was covering her mouth.

My blood ran cold. "Hang in there," I said. "Is it safe for you to break the connection?"

The two screams were as immediate as a cry from a hot poker.

"All right, I'm here, and Estelle's on the way. It'll just be a couple of minutes." I put my hand over the receiver and looked at Camille. "Go into my bedroom and get my handheld radio." She took off like a shot. "Erma, now listen carefully. Is someone else there with you, other than the children?"

"Mmmph, Mmmph."

"Was someone there?"

"Mmmph."

She was crying, and I could hear her breath coming in jerky sobs. I could envision all kinds of nightmares, and one of them was Erma Sedillos choking to death. "Are they there now?" I knew damn well that the intruders weren't going to be sitting there, watching her grunt into a telephone, but they might have been in the yard.

I took a deep breath of relief when I heard the two choked grunts, and Camille handed me the handheld radio.

"Hang in there, Erma. Everything is going to be all right." I twisted the power button on, switched to channel three, and barked, "PCS, Gastner."

The response was instant, and I recognized the clipped, efficient voice of Ernie Wheeler.

"Gastner, PCS."

"PCS, I need a backup unit at Four-ten South Twelfth Street. Code Thirty-three."

"Ten-four, sir. What's your twenty?"

"I'm home, damn it."

"Sir, all units are responding to a call at the motel...."

With a curse, I grunted to my feet, not hearing the rest of our dispatcher's message. "Erma, are you still there?"

"Mmmph."

"All right. Listen, is there any danger to Estelle when she arrives?"

"Mmmph," and then, after a pause of five heartbeats, "Mmmph."

"She'll be there in just a minute. I'm leaving now, and I'm going to have my daughter Camille stay on the line with you. Do you understand me?"

"Mmmph."

"She's got a radio direct to the Sheriff's Department, so you're not alone. All right?"

"Mmmph."

I thrust the phone at Camille and planted the radio in front of her on the kitchen table. "If you need to call Dispatch, just push the talk button. I'll have the radio on in three ten, and I'll have the other handheld with me everywhere else, so you can talk to me, as well. All right?"

She nodded and sat down, as white as a sheet.

"You're sure you're all right with this?" I said.

"Go, go," she said. "And be careful."

If I could have sprinted, I would have. But motions repeated over the years until they were second nature sufficed. Three ten hit the asphalt of Escondido with a loud bellow, and then, with a wrench of the steering wheel, I launched north onto Grande.

Estelle's home was five blocks south of Bustos, the major east-west artery of Posadas. The fastest way to get there was to avoid all the side streets, heading straight north on Grande for a mile and then west on Bustos. I passed the intersection of Grande and MacArthur still accelerating, staying in the left-hand lane, hugging the center median.

The intersection with Bustos was four lanes wide, but I still didn't have enough room. The county car squalled sideways through the intersection, and for an instant I had visions of planting 310 upside down on Pershing's tank. Everyone and everything stayed out of my way, and I straightened out and headed west on Bustos.

My heart was hammering when I slowed for the left turn onto Twelfth, and as soon as I turned the corner, I could see Estelle's county car parked at the sidewalk three blocks ahead.

As I pulled up behind her car, I palmed the microphone. "PCS, three ten is ten-ninety-seven, Guzman residence."

"Ten-four, three ten."

I slammed the gear lever into park, eyes scanning the front of the house. I don't know what I expected to see, but nothing appeared amiss.

The engine died and I got out of the car. The Guzman home was one of those neat out-of-a-can tract homes that had been built during the mining boom. It was attractive and unpresumptuous. A decade before, the house next door had burned, and the previous owners of the Guzman home had had the foresight to purchase the lot, remove the charred ruins, and double the size of their own yard. That was the feature that had attracted the Guzmans when the place had come on the market a handful of years later.

As I walked to the door, I looked left, along the chain-link fence that enclosed the yard. Neither Francis nor Estelle had time to garden, and they'd settled for planting trees and bushes. On a summer's day, the place was a densely shaded arboretum.

The neighborhood was so quiet, I could hear the hot engine of 310 ticking behind me. Estelle couldn't have arrived more than a minute before me.

The front door was ajar. I pulled the screen open and sidled inside. The foyer opened into the living room, and Estelle was on her knees beside Erma Sedillos. A table was overturned, and the telephone unit and answering machine were on the floor.

From a back bedroom, I could hear the lusty voice of little Carlos.

"He's okay," Estelle said, and she was working frantically and gently to free the duct tape from around Erma's face, hands, and feet. She was trussed like a turkey. "They took Francisco," Estelle said over her shoulder to me.

"They what?"

Estelle shot a glance at me, and for the first time since I had known her, her voice shook. "Francisco. They took him."

Chapter 30

"He came in the back," Erma cried, and her tears were an equal mixture of agony and anger. She was no frail, shrinking violet. In an arm-wrestling contest, she'd probably break my elbow before tearing every muscle out of my shoulder. "We were in the kitchen, and he came right through the door." She followed Estelle into the back room, and in a moment they returned, Estelle holding the red-faced Carlos.

Less than a year old, Carlos was in no mood to understand or cope. He howled.

"When did this happen?" It was a simple-enough question, but Erma couldn't get the words out. She was sobbing and collapsed down on the sofa, her hands over her face. Estelle knelt beside her and hugged her shoulders with one free arm, then stroked her hair.

She had Carlos on one side and Erma on the other. "Come on, now, *hermana, think* for me." She gripped the girl's shoulders and shook her gently. "Come on. Pull yourself together and think for me. How long ago did this happen?"

"I…I looked at the clock in the kitchen as soon as I knew he'd gone. 'Cause I knew you might still be over at sir's. It was three minutes after six."

I glanced at my watch. An hour and forty minutes. The bastard had an hour-and-forty-minute head start. With that much time, he could be in Mexico. The Regal crossing closed at six, but we were a scant hour and a half from the twenty-four-hour crossing at El Paso. Or he could almost be in Arizona. Or he could be back in his hole somewhere in Posadas. The possibilities were endless, and all grim.

After looking at the clock, Erma had squirmed painfully from kitchen to living room. Something as simple as a telephone on a table had been a monumental feat for her. She had managed to worm against the table, pushing it against a chair until the whole thing capsized. And then she had pressed the automatic dialer with the only part of her anatomy that wasn't taped tightly in place—her nose. That trip and task had taken more than an hour.

"Now think hard," Estelle said. "It was just one man?"

"Yes." Erma wiped her eyes and looked imploringly at Estelle. "I thought that it was Francis. The back light wasn't on, and I thought he was Francis. The way he knocked on the door." Carlos heard the magic name and his cries subsided into hiccuppy whimpers. Estelle held him firmly; his arms were around her neck.

"The same size as my husband?"

Erma nodded. "He was maybe six two or three. And heavy. Not fat, but heavy and strong. Broad shoulders. When I saw him standing outside, I really thought it was Francis. I didn't even think. He rapped on the door frame, like he'd forgotten his keys. Oh, Estelle, there was nothing I could do."

"I know. Now try to think clearly." Estelle was talking to herself, and to me, as much as she was to Erma. She glanced at me and indicated the telephone. I jerked into action as if someone had slapped my face, and I punched the autodialer for the Sheriff's Department. Despite its crash to the floor, the phone still worked.

Ernie Wheeler answered on the third ring, an eternity. "Sheriff's Department. One minute please."

I wasn't about to wait while he diddled with someone else. "Jesus Christ, Ernie, answer the goddamn phone," I bellowed, and apparently he heard me over the radio traffic in the background.

"Sir?"

"Now listen, Ernie. Someone's abducted Estelle's son. We don't know who yet, or why. But you get on the horn and get some troops down here. And stay off the goddamn radio with it."

A brief pause followed. Ernie didn't bother to say anything inane like "You're kidding," or all those other things humans fill dead air with. "Sir, almost everyone is down at the motel. There's been a homicide there."

"I don't care if the goddamn thing is burning to the ground. Get a hold of Bob Torrez. And call the FBI office in Las Cruces."

I tried to force my brain to think in an organized fashion. "And call the Border Patrol with a description of the boy. We have no idea where this son of a bitch is headed, but south makes sense." "You think that's most likely?"

"How the hell should I know? I don't know what's most likely. The son of a bitch has had almost a two-hour head start. Just do it. And then call all the public transportation you can think of, especially Las Cruces International. Right now, we only have evidence that one person is involved, a big individual. Beyond that, we don't know. I'll get back to you. Keep the lines open. And call the state police. In fact, do that first. As soon as we have something, we'll let 'em know what to look for. Hang on."

I nodded at Estelle. "Sir," she said, "we have one man, large, heavyset. He was wearing blue jeans, a white knit shirt, like a golf shirt maybe, and an insulated denim jacket. He had on a ski mask, red and yellow stripes."

"He was wearing a ski mask and you thought he was Francis?" I snapped, then instantly regretted it.

Erma covered her eyes. "He was standing back from the door, off to the side, sir. It was dark. I heard the light rap, and I opened the inside door before I really checked. The backyard is fenced, and I just thought..." She pulled a deep, shuddering breath. "The jacket's insulation was blue and black checks, I remember," she said.

"Good girl. Did you see a vehicle?" I asked.

She shook her head. "The second I opened the back door, he yanked the lock right out of the screen. And when he left, I was all tied up on the floor."

"Did you hear anything? When he left, that is. What did you hear?"

"I could hear a car leave from farther down the street."

"Might not have been his," I said. "But nothing with a characteristic sound? Nothing you could identify? Car versus truck, that sort of thing?"

Erma shook her head.

"Did you hear any other people at any time?"

"No."

"What about his hands?" Estelle said. She reached up and coaxed Carlos's left hand away from her neck and held it out toward Erma. "His hands."

"His hands?"

Estelle nodded. "His skin. What could you tell about his complexion?"

"He was wearing brown gloves. Like the kind cowboys wear? Work gloves? He took them off when he was taping me. I think he was fair-skinned, because the hair on the back of his hands was blond, I think."

"His voice. What about his voice?"

Erma frowned and shook her head. "He never said a word."

"He never spoke to you?"

"No."

"Was there anything familiar about him that would lead you to believe that he was a local? Anything at all—even his smell. Anything that makes you think you might have seen him somewhere?"

Erma shook his head.

"No one like that in the neighborhood?"

"Doesn't sound familiar to me, either," Estelle said. "And we know everyone who lives on this street."

"All right." I put the telephone to my ear again. "Ernie, this is what we've got so far. It's a white male, six two to six three. Probably well over two hundred pounds. Maybe alone—we don't know. Unknown vehicle. He's wearing jeans, a denim jacket lined in blue and black, rawhide gloves, and maybe a ski mask." I turned to Erma. "What color was the mask?"

"Yellow and red, I think," she said.

"Yellow and red," I said. "He'll be in company with a three year-old Hispanic youngster—hell, you know what Francis junior looks like."

"Is the boy injured?" Ernie asked.

I started to answer and found I couldn't form the words. I managed a simple "We don't know."

"What was he wearing, sir?"

"Just a minute." A brief conference established that little Francisco had been in his pajamas, ready to go to bed. "Flannel pj's, Ernie. The kind with built-in booties. They're light blue with dark blue jackrabbits on them."

Estelle's face was pale, and if she hugged Carlos any tighter, the poor kid would suffocate. But he didn't seem to mind. "Erma,"

I said gently, "that's all the child had on when the man took him out the door? No coat? No shoes?"

She shook her head and then covered her face with her hands again.

"That's all we've got, Ernie. Get the state police working first, then the Border Patrol. Then go with the airports and the FBI. I've got the handheld here on channel three. Don't let anyone tie up lines."

I hung up the telephone, pulled the radio off my belt, and turned the volume up. "Show us what happened, now."

Erma led us out into the kitchen. The back door was closed, as if nothing had happened. The door had both a standard lock and a dead bolt. Despite the appearance of security, a properly aimed kick probably could have busted both out of the thirty-year-old wood frame.

"Francisco was sitting here," she whimpered. A box of cereal was open, waiting. A spoon was on the floor under the table. "I was at the sink, rinsing out his bowl." She picked up the only bowl that would work as far as the kid was concerned—blue stoneware with a line of jackrabbits bouncing around the rim.

"I heard a light rap and turned to look." She pointed at the door. "I could see a figure, but the back light wasn't on. The way he knocked, it just seemed—"

"Show me how he knocked," I said.

"It was just a light, friendly rapping, like this." She used the knuckle of her right index finger and imitated the familiar seven-note refrain—five and then two, shave and a haircut, two bits—of greeting. "Just a few minutes before I set the garbage out, and I hadn't turned the lock yet. I didn't think." The tears rolled down her brown cheeks. "I opened the door and then he just yanked the screen open."

I turned the knob and opened the back door. The screen's closure piston kept it firmly shut, but I could see the bent aluminum lock. That didn't mean much. A dedicated child could rip open a screen door. I flipped on the back light.

The Guzmans' back door opened onto a brick patio, the bricked area extending twenty feet or so back to the sandy rubble that was Francisco's playground. That was surrounded by trees and shrubs of various heights, keeping the place sheltered from wind and sun.

The chain-link fence was four feet high, adequate for children and dogs, but not much of a deterrent for an adult.

"And then what happened?"

"He burst inside, then grabbed me and threw me down on the floor. He threw me down so hard, I thought I'd broken my arm."

"That's when he taped you?"

"No," Erma said. "He moved so fast. When I fell, he just stepped right over me and went to Francis. He had this role of tape, and he just went around Francis three times." She made circular motions with her hands. "Just so fast. Around the boy and the back of the chair. I screamed at him, and by the time I got to my feet to try to stop him, he grabbed me. Because of the tape around him, Francis couldn't run away."

"And he never said a word?"

"No. I could hear him breathing and grunting, but he never said nothing. He threw me down, jerked my hands behind me, and taped my wrists. Then he threw me down again and taped my feet together. I tried to kick him, but he had me on my stomach, and I couldn't. Then he pulled my feet up and taped them to my hands. And then he taped my mouth." She stopped and wiped her eyes. "What are we going to do?"

"He left you here in the kitchen?" I asked.

"Right there on the floor," she said, pointing. "And then he pulled the tape off Francis so he could get him loose of the chair. He lost him then for a little bit, and Francis took off. The man, he grabbed Francis by one arm, but he fought as much as he could."

"Three years old and forty pounds," I said. "Did he just carry Francis out of the house?"

"He taped his hands, in front of him, like this." Erma held her hands together. "And then he taped his feet together at the ankles. Then he just picked him up like a...like a..."

"Under his arm?"

Erma nodded. I keyed the radio. "PCS, Gastner."

"Gastner, go ahead."

"I need some people, Ernie."

"Ten-four." I could hear other radio traffic in the background on the main patrol channel. "Undersheriff, three oh eight and three oh seven are responding. ETA about a minute."

"Tell 'em no lights or siren. Did you get hold of the state police?"

"Ten-four. They wanted to know what your suggestions were about roadblocks."

I cursed. Posadas wasn't at the end of anyone's road, but it sure as hell was on the road to a lot of places. The east-west interstate passed by less than a mile outside of town. Four state highways either intersected in or passed close by the village. Within that framework was a web of paved, gravel, or caliche county roads, as well as an additional network of U.S. Forest Service roads and trails that laced through Oria National Forest.

"Tell 'em to cover every one they can. Every one. Hell, there are still truckloads of Guardsmen left in town, or close to it. Shut everything down."

"Ten-four." Ernie's voice sounded strained. I knew what he was thinking. If whoever had taken little Francis had a two-hour jump on us, there wasn't much point in blocking roads ten minutes outside of Posadas.

A car slid to a violent stop at the curb, and I went to the front door. Robert Torrez came up the sidewalk at a dead run. Even as he did so, Deputy Mitchell's county car turned onto Twelfth from Bustos, its engine pushing hard.

"We don't know who or why, Bob," I said. "Someone broke in and abducted little Francis. He left the baby. Erma said the man's Anglo, big, built about like Dr. Guzman. He's dressed in denim— jeans and lined denim jacket. He might be blond. That's all we know."

Torrez turned as I was speaking, surveying the neighborhood. Lights were on in every house, small wonder with all the traffic. "What kind of head start does he have?"

"Since three minutes after six."

Torrez looked at his watch and grimaced. "Erma have any ideas?"

"None. Total stranger, as far as she's concerned. The description doesn't ring any bells with Estelle, either."

"All right. Between Chief Martinez and his men and one or two of our specials, we can bottle up the village pretty tight."

It had been a long time since Eduardo Martinez had worked nights in Posadas. His three-man police department turned the town over to us after four—and a lot of the rest of the time, too.

"Shag someone up the hill," I said. County Road 43 led out of town to the north, winding up past the landfill and the abandoned Consolidated Mining boneyard, passing by the old water-filled quarry. Now on Forest Service property, that place was the handsdown favorite of locals for parties, booze, necking—anything that didn't need an audience. The thought of this freak parked up there with my godson was enough to make me vomit.

Chapter 31

When I walked back inside the Guzmans' house, I found Estelle sitting on the couch, her arms still wrapped around tiny Carlos. He had stopped crying but continued to pop a hiccup now and then.

From what Erma had told us, the infant hadn't uttered a peep all the time that the intruder was in the house. Carlos had been asleep in his crib in one of the back bedrooms, and only he knew exactly when he had awakened and what he had heard.

Only when Erma Sedillos had begun creating her hour and a half of thumping, banging mayhem did Carlos let loose, standing in his crib and screaming.

I didn't blame him. I'd have done the same thing if it would have brought my godson to the front doorstep.

By the look on her face, though, Estelle was far, far away. Her dark brows were closely knit, and her rocking and cooing to Carlos were distracted.

"I told Robert to have someone pick up Francis at the hospital," I said. "He'll be here any second."

I didn't know if that was true or not. If Dr. Guzman was in the midst of delicate surgery, it was going to be hard for him to drop the scalpel and run. Unlike a large metro hospital, there wasn't a plethora of vascular surgeons who could just step in and take over.

And, as so often happens, a ridiculous thought, unbidden, came to mind. If Florencio Apodaca was guilty of actually murdering his wife, and if he was even half-cogent, he must have been wondering just how patient he was going to have to be with the Posadas County Sheriff's Department. I wondered what stage of

Bob Torrez's preliminary interview with the old man had been interrupted when the deputies got the call to break away.

"This has to be someone who knows our family," Estelle murmured. "He knew exactly what he wanted, and didn't waste a step." She turned tortured eyes to me. "He wanted Francis, sir."

"It appears that way," I said. "He knew the layout of your property. You can't really see your back door from the street unless you're looking for it. With the back light off, it would have been even harder."

"And there's no gate in the chain-link fence," she said.

"I don't know too many people who can vault over a four-foot fence with a child under one arm."

"And he didn't search through the house," Estelle said, nuzzling Carlos on the forehead. As if sensing that now wasn't a good time to interrupt, the child had released his hold on Estelle's neck and sat like a silent beanbag doll, his dark face sober and eyes watchful, as quiet now as he'd been noisy a bit earlier.

In the next few minutes, he had lots of things to watch. Camille arrived with Gayle Sedillos, Erma's older sister. This was my daughter's first visit to Posadas in nearly twenty years, and already she seemed a perfectly natural fit—part of her talent for remaining a stranger for only a few seconds.

"Gayle," I said, "Make sure that no one ties up any of the telephones. The phone in the bedroom is listed to Dr. Guzman in the directory. Until we get some recording equipment over here, I'd rather they weren't even answered. Camille, I'd like you to use the cell phone in my Blazer to keep in touch with the hospital. We want Dr. Guzman here the instant he can break free."

"Three ten, three oh one on channel three."

I jerked the handheld from my belt, recognizing Martin Holman's voice and at the same time dreading what he might blab out over the air for all of Posadas County to hear. "Go ahead."

"Ten-eighty-seven at Posadas Inn."

For an instant, I couldn't even remember what the hell 10-87 meant, and I frowned at the radio as if the translation would pop up in the little frequency window. My mind snapped into gear, but my frown deepened. The motel was the last place I was interested in visiting at the moment. A drunk getting himself killed in a parking-lot brawl was just not one of my concerns at the moment.

"Sheriff, that's negative. We've got a mess here."

"Three ten, stand by."

"I don't know what the hell he wants," I said to Estelle.

"He doesn't know about Francis yet," she replied.

"I'm sure he knows by now. Torrez is good at keeping things off the air, but—" The telephone rang, sounding so loud that we all jumped.

I picked up the receiver, not knowing what to expect.

"Bill," Martin Holman said, his tone clipped and businesslike. "You need to get down here ASAP. I know what you've got going there. Mitchell told me. There's something here that ties into the boy's abduction, and I want you to see it for yourself. Hustle. And bring Estelle with you."

"She's not going to want to leave Carlos," I said.

"Then bring him." The line went dead. I realized it was the first time Martin Holman had ever cut short a conversation with me.

"What is it?" Camille asked.

"I don't know," I said, then turned to speak to Estelle. "Sweetheart, we need to go down to the Posadas Inn. Holman's got something he wants us to see. He says it ties in somehow." And for the first time in our working relationship, I saw Estelle Reyes-Guzman hesitate. Two car doors slammed and I stepped to the entryway.

Deputy Tom Pasquale's long stride was matched by Dr. Francis Guzman. The young physician's face was grim. "Thank God you're here," I said.

"You need to go to the motel," Guzman said as he brushed by me. In two or three long strides, he was kneeling beside Estelle. "Go with him," he said to his wife. He disengaged Carlos from her embrace. "I'll be here, and Tommy's been assigned to stay here until we know what's going on. From what the sheriff told me, it's really important that you go to the motel. Then come right back."

Estelle nodded, stood up, and shook her head as if breaking loose from a tangle of cobwebs. She turned to Camille and Gayle. "Can you both stay?"

My daughter nodded. "Good," Estelle said. "We won't be long."

We left the house, Estelle at a dead run. She started toward her own unmarked county car, then thought better of it and climbed into the passenger side of 310. Across the street, I saw a heavyset woman—the wife of the county road superintendent—standing on her front step, watching the action. When she saw me, she started a step or two toward the sidewalk. I ignored her, and by the time I'd grunted myself into 310, she'd gone back up on the porch.

The telephone circuits around Posadas would be buzzing, if they weren't already. There would be a lot more ammunition for gossip before the night was over.

The Posadas Inn was just off the interstate on Grande, less than four blocks from my house. During the two minutes it took to cover a little less than three miles, I didn't have much time to reflect on what could be so important that Martin Holman would summon us both.

Chapter 32

Approached from the interstate, the Posadas Inn looked about as cheerful and clean as neon and plastic could make it. The front of the motel faced southeast, with a covered portal. The generous parking lot circled the building. As we approached from the village, I could see the flutter of yellow tape under the harsh illumination of the parking lot's sodium-vapor lights.

The barricade had been set up to include a service entrance, the sidewalk in front of it, and about a third of an acre of the parking lot itself. A November night hadn't attracted many guests to Posadas, and if anyone had parked around behind the motel, they had evidently been asked to move.

Under normal circumstances, a homicide would have attracted enough patrol cars to equip a sizable fleet. Every law officer in whistling distance would want a share, or, at the very least, a private tour—if for no other reason than to break the monotony.

But the place was damn near vacant. I recognized Martin Holman's brown Buick, and one of our department's older marked units. Parked on the opposite side of the roped-off area was one of the Posadas Village Police units, its red lights pulsing.

Sheriff Holman, a portable radio in one hand and a cellular phone in the other, stood near the door marked SERVICE ONLY. He was in animated conversation with DeWayne Sands, the night manager of the motel, gesticulating over his shoulder as he talked.

DeWayne did not look happy. He was well over fifty and going to flab. Standing outside in the chill November night while watching police take over his motel to find out who had whacked one of his guests was enough to make his blood pressure go over the top. I recognized all the signs, even from across the parking lot.

Holman saw us and said into the handheld radio, "Back door over here, Bill." By then, I was already out of the patrol car, concentrating on keeping up with Estelle's dogged pace. She ducked under the ribbon when she reached the sidewalk that skirted the bank of heat-pump units.

"DeWayne," Holman was saying as we approached, "you're going to have to make doubly sure that no one comes or goes until we say otherwise. And I mean no one, and I mean from the entire motel. I don't care if their room is a mile away on the other wing. No night staff, no maintenance crew, no patrons. If you've got a long-haul trucker who needs to leave, make sure you clear him through me or Chief Martinez. No one comes and no one goes. Understood?"

"Well, sure, but—"

"No buts," Holman said, and he steered Sands away from the door. Sands trudged off down the sidewalk, muttering to himself. "In here, Bill, Estelle."

The service door opened into a small foyer. Immediately on the left was a flight of stairs. Yellow plastic taped it off top and bottom. Directly ahead of us, a hallway stretched beyond the limits of my eyesight, ending eventually, I knew, in the front foyer, with restaurant to the left and check-in desk to the right.

Another hallway took off to the right, beyond the game room and the ice and soda machines, and that's where Marty Holman led us. He walked on the right side of the hallway, sticking close to the wall.

"The victim's name is Roberto Madrid," he said over his shoulder. "At least that's what some rental-car paperwork we found in the room says. Other than that, we don't know."

The rooms began with 140 on the right and 141 on the left. About halfway down the hallway, Holman stopped. That was just as well. I was running out of breath. It wasn't exercise, but anxiety, the kind of awful jolt to the nerves that I hadn't felt in more than a decade.

He pointed at the door at the far end. Standing beside it were Chief Eduardo Martinez and one of his part-time officers, George Bohrer. "That door leads to the west parking lot. It's one of those deals that's locked after nine P.M. under normal circumstances. There's some evidence that the door was used by the assailant."

"Martin," I started to say, but the sheriff held up a hand. He lowered his voice. "I wouldn't have called you over here if I didn't think it was important."

We stopped in front of the door to 167, two rooms from the end of the hall. Holman held up a hand again, like a cavalry trooper halting his patrol. The door was open, and, looking inside, I could see two chairs crashed together against one wall, the mattress askew, and glass from the shattered TV's picture tube scattered across the pale blue carpet.

"Who did prints?" Estelle asked quietly.

"Torrez," Holman replied. "And myself. But we've got a lot more to do." He indicated the outline of the body, white chalk on blue carpet. "There's no one else staying in this wing, which is peculiar. But one of the other patrons who had come down for some ice heard a ruckus. He says one or two gunshots, not very loud. Maybe three shots at the most—he's not sure. And then he heard what might have been a loud groan. He's not sure about that, either."

"Where's this *he?*" I asked.

"Waiting up in the manager's office," Holman said. "The body was lying in a fetal position on its right side, facing the bed." He stepped closer to the outline. "Maybe he was trying to reach the telephone here on the nightstand. I'm not sure." Holman sighed. "At any rate, he didn't make it."

"Who actually came into the room first?" I asked.

"The night manager."

"The victim was dead?"

"No. The manager—"

"Is this DeWayne you're talking about?"

"DeWayne Sands, right. He says he entered the room, and that the victim was gasping and appeared unconscious. At any rate, he didn't respond to questions. The night manager says he saw blood on the victim's shirt and went directly to call police. Bob Torrez says it was a small-caliber weapon, like a twenty-two. Bob Torrez was the first to arrive, and the man was still alive at that time. EMTs transported him, and they said he was alive when they reached the hospital. Still unconscious, but alive."

"No blood on the carpet," I said. "That's interesting. So who the hell is Roberto Madrid, and what was it that you wanted us to see that's connected to..." My voice trailed off, refusing to frame the words.

"Look over here." Holman walked around the outline of the man's body and circled the bed. "We've got a blood splash here," he said, pointing down by the second nightstand, "that continues up onto the wall. There's more blood back here by the sink. And then right here, on the entrance to the bathroom."

I nodded. "Other wounds on the victim?"

Holman shook his head. "He was shot twice, once under the left armpit, once in the back. Like I said, small-caliber weapon. He didn't bleed much."

"Then what accounts for all this?" I said.

"Someone else was here, and got hurt," Holman said. "Badly. Step over here really carefully." He motioned me toward the bathroom. Estelle hung back, her eyes locked on the chalk outline on the floor.

The doorknob and doorjamb were smeared with blood, heavy smears that indicated serious bleeding. A splatter of blood dotted across the counter and the bathroom sink, and there was a partial handprint on the polished vinyl, smeared into the blood as if the person had staggered and caught himself.

"Right here," Holman said, and knelt down. The blood on the floor was more than spots. Whoever had been bleeding had fallen, or slumped here. One of the blood sprays had been smeared by a footprint, so clear and well defined that it sent chills up and down my spine. I could see the imprint of the toes, the narrow curve past the high arch.

"Estelle, come in here," I called. My response to what I was seeing was automatic. It was only after the words were out of my mouth that I regretted them. In a moment, I could feel her presence behind me. I straightened up and stepped out of the way.

She didn't say anything, but I could hear a little sigh of breath. The footprint was tiny, no more than five or six inches long.

Estelle stood for almost a full minute, gazing down at it. I could see that her breath was coming in rapid, shallow spurts. Then she turned back toward the doorway, her eyes fastened on the tile floor. She was deathly pale, and with one hand, she reached out to me like a blind person, fumbling her way. The other hand went to the door-jamb.

"Come on outside, sweetheart," I whispered.

She shook her head. "No. Look. There's only one print."

I hesitated, still holding her hand, not sure what to say.

Martin Holman cleared his throat. "The child was picked up," he said. "If he had walked out of the bathroom, there would be other prints—at least one other footprint."

He knelt down and pointed. "Here's a right foot here. It's almost four feet to the door. That would put a left foot about here," and he reached out and touched the tile. "And the right foot again, just before the threshold. Or even on the carpet." He looked up at me. "But there's just the one print."

"He was picked up and carried out," I said.

"Right," Holman nodded.

"Then whose blood is it?" I asked, and felt Estelle's grip tighten.

"And which child?" she whispered.

Chapter 33

"Any other blood anywhere else?" I asked.

Holman beckoned, and we followed him out of the room. "First of all, there's a small smear right here, on the doorjamb," he said. He pulled out his ballpoint pen and pointed with it. The smear was about five feet up on the jamb, as if someone had leaned there for support.

"And then he turned and went left, out the side door," Holman said.

"Less risk being seen," I said. "If he went back up the hall, he'd risk that intersection where other patrons come down to visit the ice machines."

Chief Eduardo Martinez eased away from the wall as we approached. Eduardo was round and comfortable, given to good humor and easy smiles. He had an endless repertoire of jokes for any occasion. He wasn't smiling. With him was George Bohrer. If straight, square shoulders counted, Bohrer was a winner. Unfortunately, good posture is about all Bohrer had going for him.

"Chief," I said. That was about all I could manage, even though I liked Eduardo. He never presumed to be more than he was—the grand marshal for the Posadas Fourth of July parade. Rumor had it that eons before, he had actually spent a year with the Texas Department of Public Safety.

"Say, it's good to have you back home," Eduardo said, and extended a hand. His grip was warm and friendly. "This is sure a hell of a deal."

"Yes, it is."

"No one's been in or out since you left, Sheriff," Bohrer said. He had a thick Texas drawl and nodded with every syllable, as if each sound needed hatching by the physical motion of his head. I could guess what instructions Holman had left for him.

"The killer went out this way," Holman said. "If you look here, you can see a faint smudge on the door. I'm sure it's blood, but the lab will tell us for sure. And then," he said, toeing the door open with the tip of one polished boot, "it appears that he fell."

"Don't touch the door, George," Estelle said as she saw Bohrer reaching out to hold it open for us. He jerked his hand back as if struck.

Chief Martinez bent down and slid a pebble into the crack between door and jamb.

The man had made it down the carpeted hall successfully, then collapsed on the concrete just outside the door. Blood was puddled thick and dark, as if the man had rested there, catching his breath, taking time to wish that this day wasn't going to be his last. A hand-print had smeared blood on the cement, as if the man had slipped while trying to push himself up.

"There's no sign of a child's tracks out here," Holman said. "None at all. We don't know what happened."

"Did someone process this boot print?" Estelle asked. She knelt and, using the small black flashlight from her purse, bounced light off the print. Just a small curve of featureless sole had broken the margin of the bloodstain.

"We missed that," Holman said. He knelt beside her. "Looks like just a smooth leather sole. Not enough to be sure."

"It could be one of the officers," I said. "There've been people milling around here for an hour."

"Not milling, Bill," Holman said, sounding a little testy. "Anyway, this is as far out from the building as the blood went. Either there was a car waiting or one drove up just then. Or maybe he was able to hold himself together and limp off somehow."

I turned and looked back at the hallway. "This amount of blood means someone is hurt pretty badly. He's not going to go far. You've got everyone who's not sitting a roadblock or checking door-to-door working this?"

Holman managed a trace of a smile. "We don't have anyone else, Bill. We've got some help coming, but it's going to take a couple of hours."

I grimaced. "Who's working the blood typing for us?"

"Skip Bishop. He took about eight doubles from inside the room, and a couple from out here. One set went to the ME's office in Cruces. Dale Kenyon ran it over for us. Skip took the other set to the hospital lab here to get something quicker. Unofficial, but quicker. He'll stay with it until he's got an answer."

I nodded, thankful that Skip worked faster than his older brother, Sgt. Howard Bishop. Howard had finally agreed to attend one of the FBI seminars in Quantico. I knew the sheriff had pressured him into it, figuring that late November was a good, slow time of the year and that we'd be able to spare him for three weeks.

"So tell me about Roberto Madrid," I said, turning back toward the doorway.

"We know nothing about him except what a car-rental paper tells us. He was thirty-four years old. He's a Mexican national, driving a car he rented in Douglas, Arizona. He had a receipt in his suitcase that shows he paid cash for the car rental but used a Banco Central de México credit card as collateral and as secondary identification."

"He came across legally, then."

"Absolutely." Holman shrugged. "There's isn't a clue in the room why he was here. Not a clue what his business was. His wallet has been taken, as well."

"You're sure he had one?"

"No," Holman said uncomfortably. "I guess I was assuming that he had one."

"And we have a child's footprint," I said. We walked back to the room, and Estelle and I meticulously searched the small suitcase that lay on the stand near the busted television. From what I could see, there were a couple of changes of clothes, toiletry items, and one paperback book.

I leaned closer and looked at the cover, a hazy blue design with what might have been the figure of a child standing under a tree. The title, *Cuentos del Soñador*, was in black script.

"What's *soñador* mean?" I asked.

"Dreamer," Estelle said softly. "*Stories of the Dreamer.*" She pushed open the book with the eraser of her pencil and scanned a page at random. "It looks like a collection of short stories for children. Bedtime stories."

She looked up at Holman. "Was someone going to process this for prints? The shiny cover might show us something."

"That's next on the list," Holman said. "As soon as Bob Torrez or Eddie Mitchell gets back here."

She nodded absently. "He hadn't been here long," she said. "He hadn't even unpacked his toothbrush." She pushed at the vinyl toiletry case with her pencil and shook her head. "What time did Sands say Madrid checked in?"

"Shortly after noon."

"How shortly after?" I asked.

Holman pulled out his small notebook and flipped pages. "Twelve thirty-seven is the time punched by the clock on his registration."

I leaned against the door, nestling the edge of it against my spine. "He checks in at twelve thirty-seven, and then just sits here until someone comes and shoots him sometime after six."

"Maybe he was reading," Holman said, gesturing at the book.

"For six hours? Maybe. Maybe it's a good book."

Estelle stood up and closed her eyes, tilting her head back.

"Are you all right?" Holman asked.

"No," she said. She shook her head and slid the pencil back into her purse. "If that footprint is my son's," she said, and paused to take a deep breath, "then that means whoever took him did so in order to bring him down here. The timing fits, if nothing else."

"And it could as easily be a coincidence," I said. "Unrelated. The footprint could be from any other child, or even a woman with very small feet."

"And what if that is my son's footprint," Estelle said. "It could be his. It had a high arch like his."

"If it's his, then there are several possibilities. Maybe Madrid took the boy, and someone else came after him. Maybe there was some sort of arrangement and something went wrong."

"Let's look for something more obvious," Holman said. "Madrid could have brought a child with him from Mexico. Isn't that possible? Let's say the occupants of the room were Madrid and his own son. They come here for whatever reason. Maybe just on a vacation."

"In Posadas?" I said.

"Well, they might have been bound for somewhere else—you can't tell. And then someone breaks in and takes his child." He shrugged. "The MO fits. Someone broke into the Guzman home and took a child. They come here and do the same thing. That's the most obvious answer. Madrid resisted, and pop."

"The child was not Madrid's," Estelle said softly.

"What makes you think not? There's even that book of children's stories, like you said."

She gestured toward the small suitcase. "For one thing, there is no child's clothing in that suitcase." She looked at Holman, her left eyebrow drifting upward. She turned slowly and surveyed the rest of the room. "Or anywhere else in this room. No one travels with a child for any distance and only takes the clothes that the child is wearing. And for another thing, if the child had on only socks, or his pajamas, when he was picked up and taken, where are his shoes now? Where are his clothes? Do you travel with a kid in socks and no shoes?"

"The intruder took them with him."

Estelle grimaced at Holman's train of thought, and I said, "Sheriff, if you were hurt badly enough to be leaking puddles of blood, either shot or stabbed, would you bother to stop and pick up a pair of shoes?"

Holman glanced at me. "I guess not."

"No, you wouldn't. I think it's pretty obvious Roberto Madrid was in this room by himself, waiting. Just him and this small suitcase."

"That means his assailant—"

"Or assailants," Estelle corrected.

"One, two, three, however many. His assailants brought the child with them. If Madrid didn't have the child to begin with, the only thing that makes sense is that someone brought the child with them."

"And left with the child, as well."

"For what?" Holman asked.

"Roberto Madrid knew. And he died at the hospital, without talking," I said.

"Sir?" Estelle said, and I turned. She was looking at me, one hand over her mouth. Her face was pale, and at first I thought the cloying smell of blood mixed with room deodorizer was making her sick. "I need to go home."

I ushered her out of the room. To Holman, I said, "You'll let me know the instant Bishop has some information on the blood types?"

"Of course." He smiled sympathetically at Estelle. "And in another hour or so, there'll be so many FBI agents crawling all over the county that no one will be able to hide a thing. Just hang in there. We'll find your son."

Estelle nodded, but it wasn't the nod of someone seeking either sympathy or help. She set off down the hall, and I hurried to catch up. She remained silent until we reached the car, slid inside, and started the engine.

Then, just as I was reaching for the gearshift lever, she reached a hand over and rested it lightly on my right wrist.

"Sir, we have to consider that the same person—or persons— who took Cody Cole took Francis, too."

I slumped against the door, resting my arm along the window. Estelle was sitting with her eyes closed, and I could imagine the anguish she was going through. The cool, analytical detective side of her wanted answers—straightforward, correct, prosecutable answers. The mother in her simply yearned for a simple, quick solution that would see little Francis safely back home.

And I knew that the real agony of it was that we didn't have time for the mother's side just then.

"I don't see how it could be any other way," I said, and Estelle looked up sharply, surprised. "Until tonight, I was convinced that Cody Cole's disappearance was just a tragic set of circumstances where two hundred searchers had been overlooking one small thing—the smallest little thing. I would have been willing to bet that come next spring, some hiker would have found his bones."

I looked out through the side window into the darkness. "And found them in a spot that would prompt about a hundred search- ers to say, 'Why hell, I walked right over that ground at least a hundred times.'" I watched Estelle's reflection in the glass and saw a hand drift up to rub her left eye. "We've both seen cases where someone was lost close to their base camp, or to the search parties." I shrugged. "But it's too much of a coincidence to be- lieve that the two cases aren't related in some fashion. At the very least, it could be an opportunist, copycat sort of thing. The Cole search has been in the papers. Maybe someone decided to try their hand. Until today, I was even willing to believe that there was a logical explanation for the Cole youngster's jacket turning up where it did. Not anymore."

Estelle looked away, out the window toward the lights of Posadas.

"We're not finding anyone sitting here," I said, and pulled 310 into gear.

"If Madrid was involved," Estelle said, still looking away, "then the boys were headed to Mexico. That's the only thing that makes sense to me."

"And something went wrong." I drove out of the motel's parking lot, trying to think of an easy solution. I knew that Estelle wasn't naïve—she knew as well as I did that children abducted from parents who weren't wealthy were taken not for ransom, but for other reasons. And every one of those reasons was enough to jerk a parent awake in the middle of the night in a cold sweat.

"Cody went missing almost four days ago—sometime Saturday evening. Roberto Madrid checked into the motel today, Wednesday, shortly after noon. If there's a connection, what is it?"

The shake of Estelle's head was just the tiniest of motions.

"I want to talk to Tiffany Cole again," she said.

"Right now?"

"Right now."

We drove north on Grande, and just about at the point where dispatcher Ernie Wheeler could have looked out the front door of the Public Safety Building and seen our headlights, the radio crackled.

"Three ten, PCS. Ten-twenty."

"PCS, three ten is at the intersection of Bustos and Grande."

"Ten-four, three ten. Ten-nineteen."

Martin Holman was fond of summoning people into the office, but he was busy at the motel, making sure Bohrer and the chief didn't ruin evidence.

In less than a block, I turned into the parking lot.

"I'll wait here for you," Estelle said. "I need some time to think."

"You might give your husband a call and tell him we're on the way," I said, and then I trudged up the back steps into the building.

"Ah, line two," Ernie said, gesturing toward the phone.

"Holman?" I said as I started to walk into my office.

"No, Bernalillo," Ernie said.

Chapter 34

I snatched the telephone off the hook. "This is Gastner."

There was an amused chuckle at the other end. "Now that was fast. You must have been right outside the door when Dispatch called you."

"Just about," I said. "What can I do for you?"

"This is Richard Steinberg with Bernalillo County. You've got yourself a mess. I just got the bulletin about the Guzman child, and everyone's got a sharp eye open. I won't take much of your time, but let me shoot this by you. You may remember your sheriff asked us to locate one Paul Cole?"

"Yes."

"Well, the bad news is that we haven't been much help," Steinberg said. "But that may change. We've talked to several people, and the general consensus is that he went elk hunting up in Wyoming."

"The other bad news is that he didn't," I said. "Not unless he went up without a license. Wyoming has no record of him."

"Well now, that's the interesting part," Steinberg said, and his mild west Texas drawl made it sound as if we had all day to chew the fat. "A piece of information from down in Posadas County dovetails in with this Cole business. You have a Deputy Edwin Mitchell working for you?"

"Yes. Eddie Mitchell."

"He asked us to verify a license-plate number for him, and an address. We were able to do that."

"A plate and address for whom?"

"Apparently you have an RV parked down there that belongs to Bruce Elders, a Corrales resident. The tag is Bruce Elders zero zero one."

"That's correct." I wondered how many other officers had wandered around the big RV, each one of them thinking they'd been the first to check.

"I talked to Mr. Elders earlier this evening. I gotta tell ya, under normal circumstances Posadas doesn't get mentioned once a year around here. I'm not much for coincidence."

"What did Elders tell you?"

"Bruce Elders owns a couple of liquor stores here in town. Pretty straight-up kind of guy, as far as I know. Big chamber of commerce booster, big athletic booster, all that kind of good shit. He's also Paul Cole's brother-in-law." The phone went silent as I caught my breath. Detective Steinberg enjoyed the moment and let the silence ride.

"No shit," I said finally.

"No shit. Mr. Elders says that he loaned his brother-in-law his RV for a special elk hunt up in Wyoming. He expected him back this past Sunday, but he says that Cole told him not to worry if he was late. Cole said he planned to stay in the field until he got his elk. Or until the season ended."

"He loaned his brother-in-law an expensive RV to take hunting?"

"They're close," Steinberg said, and chuckled again.

"Must be goddamn Siamese twins," I said. "And he claims that he didn't go with him?"

"Elders says he's not much of a hunter."

"And Cole's wife didn't go with him, either, it seems."

"Apparently not."

"How long have they been married?"

"I couldn't tell you. And so…you folks have that RV parked down there, eh? That sure as hell isn't Wyoming. I wonder if Elders knows that his unit is wandering all over southern New Mexico."

"I don't know. Do us a favor and don't mention anything to him just yet. But that ocean liner isn't wandering, either. It's up on jacks, parked in the yard of a guy named Andrew Browers. I don't know how long it's been there, either."

"Who's this Browers person?"

"He's Tiffany Cole's boyfriend."

"Mother of the missing kid," Steinberg said, making me jealous as hell of his memory for names. I could imagine him hearing Tiffany Cole's name on the television news, then filing it away in some discreet corner of his brain for later reference. "And Paul Cole's ex," Steinberg added. "That sure makes life interesting, trying to unsnarl all that. Deputy Mitchell filled me in. No word on the youngster yet, either, I assume? Either one of them?"

"No."

"How big a village is Posadas?"

"Two thousand on a good day. Give or take."

"Well, if the RV is there, and the Cole kid is missing, then you don't have to be a rocket scientist to figure out that one of those two thousand souls is Paul Cole. Or *was* Paul Cole. And I'll bet this month's paycheck that you don't have two child abductions in a small town in the same week that aren't related, either. Shit, send the whole mess up north to us. We haven't had a really interesting day for months. We're getting tired of drive-bys."

"Believe me, I wish I could."

"Keep me posted, Sheriff. I'll keep nosing around at this end. Let me give you my home phone, just in case."

He did so, and I hung up. I sat with my head in my hands for a few seconds, thinking. I was sure the answer was staring me in the face, but the day was rapidly stretching beyond my endurance.

I turned away from my desk, thrust my hands in my pockets, and ambled out into the hallway, pausing to inspect the coffee machine. I didn't really see it, since my mind was a kaleidoscope of possibilities and ideas.

Ernie Wheeler looked up. "Any news?"

I shook my head. "No news. On Estelle's boy, you mean?" He nodded. "No, no news."

More to give myself time to think than anything else, I scanned the activity log sheet and stopped with a jerk. I reread the entry.

"Tom Pasquale booked Florencio Apodaca?"

Wheeler leaned over, read the entry, and nodded. "He's in the front cell, if you want to talk with him. Tom said that when the call came about Estelle's son being abducted, they were right in the middle of taking the old man's statement. He's not saying

much, I can tell you that. He refuses to talk about his wife."
Wheeler looked rueful. "Sergeant Torrez said that if they could
squeeze in an arraignment with Judge Hobart by this time tomorrow, they'd be lucky."

"They charged him?"

"Murder one."

"I'll be damned."

"They haven't had any time to go beyond the initial processing,
but old man Apodaca just told them he'd be here when they were
ready. He's a cooperative old cuss. Torrez ran out when the call
about the boy came in, and Pasquale had about five minutes until
he had to go get Dr. Guzman."

"What a goddamn mess. Who's working corrections tonight?"

"No one was. We didn't have any population. I called Luis
Romero and he came in and helped me. Tom just sort of dropped
the old man off at a dead run."

"Romero is with Mr. Apodaca now?"

"I believe so. They were talking up a storm."

"Have him stay close to him. Don't leave him unattended for a
minute."

"Suicide watch?"

I shook my head. "I doubt that. But Florencio's an old man.
He's frail. And he's not right in the head. And when he realizes
what he's done, he's going to need company."

Ernie Wheeler nodded. "Luis said he'd stay as long as he was
needed. Oh, one last thing. That guy who was here earlier? Stanley
Willit? He wanted to know the minute something happened. Did
you want me to get in touch with him? I think he's down at the
motel now."

I grinned. "No. Give the old man some peace and quiet. If
Willit should call again, tell him he needs to get in touch with
me." I turned to go. "And you don't know where I am."

"Yes, sir."

"Estelle and I are in three ten. Francis knows that, and so does
the sheriff. If something breaks, give us a call. Otherwise, keep it
quiet."

Ernie Wheeler nodded and glanced up at the clock. The
philosophical expression on his face told me that he knew it was
going to be a long night.

I left the office and returned to the car. Estelle was sitting there, with her head leaning back against the headrest, eyes closed.

"Steinberg says that the RV belongs to Paul Cole's brother-in-law," I said as I got into the car.

"That means Cole's in town."

"There's a possibility that he heard about the search and just drove down here from Wyoming, direct."

"Not likely," Estelle said. "That RV has been there for a number of days. If Cole was helping the search teams, we'd have met him by now." She shook her head, eyes still closed. When she spoke again, her voice was a whisper. "If he's here, he doesn't want to be noticed."

She held up the cellular phone that had been in her lap. "Let's go take their places apart. Both houses and the RV. There's got to be something that will help us establish a connection. Judge Hobart has a warrant waiting for us."

I felt a surge of adrenaline, a buzz about equal to ten cups of coffee, as I started the car and pulled it into gear. "It's a good thing I was driving. If I'd been another couple of minutes longer, you'd have gone on over there without me."

Estelle didn't smile.

We stopped by Judge Lester Hobart's home on MacArthur, and Estelle was inside for only a minute before she reappeared with the folded paper in hand. Minutes later, we were westbound on Bustos and then turned right on Fifth Street.

The streets were November-quiet, the sort of peace that descended at 5:00 P.M., when the sun set, and persisted until dawn the next day. No parties, no loud music, no barking dogs. Folks were practicing hibernation, preparing for our three weeks of winter in January.

Tiffany Cole's sedan was parked in the driveway of 392 North Fifth. Andy Browers's truck and camper weren't. I slowed down as we approached, letting 310 drift along the curb, lights out. Several lights were on in the house, including the light over the front door.

"Browers's truck is up at his house," Estelle said. She pointed up the street. Sure enough, just three houses beyond the intersection the big GMC with the camper was pulled into the driveway. "Let's visit here first."

Her choice of the word *visit* had an ominous ring.

She got out of the car. I grabbed my large black flashlight, the only weapon I had with me, and followed. As she walked past Tiffany's Chevy, she touched the hood lightly. "This has been here awhile," she said.

The porch light was on. We stepped up to the front door and Estelle rang the doorbell. I could hear the chimes inside, a happy little sequence of notes that probably meant something to a listener with half a musical ear. She pushed the button again. The house was tomb-quiet.

"Stay here, and let me circle around back."

Estelle nodded, and I stepped off the porch and made my way around the side of the house. The place was tidy, with nothing to trip over—no toys, no tricycles, no sandbox. It was as if the house had been dropped neatly into a quarter acre of perfect grass and nothing else had ever been done.

Around back, there were no trees, no interior fencing, just evenly clipped grass. I opened the back screen door and tried the knob. I expected it to be locked, and I almost lost my balance when the door swung open easily. "Whoa," I said softly. I stood to one side and pushed the door open with the flashlight, letting the beam jump around the inside of the room.

The back door opened directly into the kitchen, and I realized I was looking at a floor plan nearly identical with the Guzmans'. That shouldn't have surprised me, since much of the western half of Posadas had been built during the heyday of Consolidated Mining, and tract housing was the most efficient way to go—a generic house, plopped on a slab of concrete.

I stepped into the kitchen, found the light switch, and turned it on. On the kitchen table were the remains of what looked like dog food on a blue plastic plate. Half a plastic cup of milk stood beside it, along with a plastic fork.

Nothing else was on the kitchen counter—no knife or spoon or bowl or box of cereal, no toaster or blender or dishes on the drain-board, nothing. The fake wooden butcher-block pattern of the countertop was clean and dry.

I pivoted in place, looking at the kitchen. The floor was as clean as everything else. I walked from kitchen to dining room, pausing only to touch each light switch with the lip of the flashlight. I could just as well have been walking through a house that had never been occupied.

Tiffany Cole was a hell of a housekeeper, I mused, but the house was more than just tidy. The living room was as neat as something out of a catalog, and just as impersonal.

I walked to the front door and unlocked it. "Bizarre place," I said. "No one home, no sign of anyone being home, with the exception of the kitchen."

She stepped inside, and if humans had hackles, hers were up. Her eyes narrowed and her lower jaw thrust forward ever so slightly. She repeated the tour I had taken, but as I watched her silently peruse the house, I noticed that she ignored anything in the upper half of each room. The floor, the furniture, the lower portions of each wall—that's what she examined, until finally she stood in the kitchen.

"That looks gross," I said. "Whatever it is."

Estelle didn't answer, just stood in place, looking down at the plate, fork, and cup. "Did you check under the sink?" she asked after a moment.

"No."

The cabinetry was the inexpensive oak style that didn't have knobs, and Estelle slipped the tip of her pen under the edge and swung the door open. The trash can had a plastic liner, and she slipped the pen under the can's rim and pulled it out. "Best of Texas brand corned beef hash," she said, and pushed the trash can back under the sink. "And that's all that's in the trash bag, too, sir."

She saw where my eyes were looking and nodded agreement. I nudged the refrigerator open. Somehow I wasn't surprised. "This is what you see in those appliance catalog ads for refrigerators," I said. "The unit that's standing with the door open so you can see the shelves inside? All the food perfectly arranged by size, color, type." I nudged the carton of milk. It was nearly empty.

I let the door close. "Estelle, were I to walk through this house any other time, without knowing who lived here, I would be willing to bet a week's pay—hell, make it a year's pay—that no child lived here."

Estelle's lower lip was trembling. "Bedrooms?" She led the way, but we found only more of the same. The master bedroom contained a queen-sized bed, a nightstand and lamp, a chest of drawers, and a clock. That was it.

The carpet was so clean, you could see the streaks from the vacuum cleaner where the pile had been stroked by the brushes. The closet included a neat row of clothing that I assumed belonged to Tiffany and Andy Browers, neatly ironed, neatly hung. And there wasn't much there, maybe half a dozen shirts and an equal number of blouses or dresses.

Estelle reached out and touched a neat, tight pack of empty hangers at the end of the rod.

"Maybe," I said.

The smaller bedroom, where I would have assumed Cody Cole slept, included a single bed, a chest of drawers, a floor lamp, and a pillow with the New Mexico Zia symbol embroidered on the cover.

The closet contained a winter jacket and a single pair of shoes. The chest of drawers was empty.

"They've split," I said. "It's as simple as that. They took most of their clothes and left."

"I don't understand any of this," Estelle said. "If I packed in a hurry and took everything I could think of, my house would still look like two hurricanes lived there, in addition to my husband and myself." She put her hands on her hips and surveyed the small bedroom. "There's no sign of the child."

She stepped to the bed and pulled down the bedspread, a neat no-pattern blue. Underneath the spread was another blue blanket, and then white sheets. She bent down and examined the pillow closely, then bent even closer and inhaled deeply.

"Not for a while," she whispered. "Let's try the other house." She glanced up at me. "And then the RV."

We turned off the lights and made sure both doors were locked, leaving the Cole house a dark, looming shadow.

We could have jogged in less time than it took to climb in the car and drive. I swung into the oncoming lane, easing the county car close to the west curb. No lights were on at 407 North Fifth. I swiveled the spotlight and washed the area in the beam's harsh white glare.

Andy Browers's truck with the camper in the back was parked on the concrete driveway, where the boat and trailer had been.

"Where's the boat?" Estelle whispered.

I stopped the car and switched it off. "Good question. Maybe in the garage."

"Wait," Estelle said. "Pull forward just a bit." I did so and heard her suck in a sharp breath.

"The RV is gone."

"You're kidding."

"No. It's gone."

I leaned forward, hunched over the steering wheel. "Son of a bitch."

"Yes," Estelle said softly. She opened her door.

Halfway across the front lawn, it occurred to me that we might have been smarter to wait for some backup, since I didn't have a gun or my badge, or even the correct pair of glasses. And, like the two veteran officers that we were, with a combined total of half a century of experience, we hadn't even bothered to alert Dispatch.

Estelle reached the front of Browers's truck first and stood in the darkness, listening. I stopped beside her. The place was so quiet that our footfalls on the grass sounded amplified.

She walked around the corner of the garage, turned on her small black flashlight, and bent down to examine the ground where the RV had been parked. "No marks," she whispered.

"What do you mean?"

"No jack marks. Remember before? It was up on jacks—or at least looked like it was. But if the leveling jacks were actually supporting that thing, they'd be driven into the ground enough to make permanent marks."

An uneasy tension began to coalesce in my gut. My own flashlight was about as handy as a small baseball bat. I touched her on the arm. "Let me have your gun." She didn't argue, just swept her hand under her jacket and pulled out the small automatic. It felt awkward in my hand; I was so used to decades of holding the rounded contours of a revolver. "Go back to the car and get another unit down here," I said. "And bring the shotgun."

While Estelle padded back to the car, I slipped along the side of the house to the first window and peered inside. I couldn't see well enough to make any sort of judgment. I heard the door of 310 close, and I returned to the front steps.

"No lights," I said, "and with that thing gone, very likely no one here. If I was a gambler, I'd bet that we're going to find the same thing here as down the street."

Estelle nodded. "The keys are in the truck," she said.

Sure enough, a large wad of keys hung from the ignition of the GMC. It took a full minute to find the one that fit the front door's lock. Finally, it turned with a solid click. I took a deep breath, twisted the key, and applied gentle pressure. With Estelle's small 9-mm in one hand and the flashlight in the other, I nudged the door ajar with my elbow.

The air inside a confined space accumulates its own bouquet, a mixture that, if it could be analyzed in a laboratory, would astonish by its complexity—the personality of all the woodwork, the smells produced by the electrical system, even the chlorine in the treated water. Hundreds of faint aromas would mix with the more massive odors—a dirty T-shirt left hanging over the back of a chair, a carton of past-date milk, carpet mildew, human sweat.

The air from inside Andy Browers's house drifted out through the two-inch crack I'd opened and hit the cool, still night air. I recoiled a step and held out a hand to stop Estelle.

She didn't need the warning. The odors that wafted out were heavy and unmistakable—the smells that human beings create when they die.

Chapter 35

"Sir..." Estelle Reyes-Guzman groaned, and I felt her touch on my right arm, featherlight.

"Stay here," I whispered. Instead of doing as I asked, she started to move forward, as if to squeeze by me to reach the door. "No," I said, and blocked her way. "Now do as I say and stay away from the doorway." Even in a close-quarters whisper, my voice sounded as if it would carry for blocks.

She stopped, holding the shotgun awkwardly in both hands. "Here," I said, taking the shotgun and handing her the pistol. "Put this away." When she had done so, I said, "Move back." When I was satisfied that she wasn't going to charge ahead of me, I touched the edge of the door with my flashlight and swung it open. What was required was something no more complicated than putting my boot across the threshold and stepping inside. It was just a house.

I could not move. I didn't know if I was breathing at all, but I could hear Estelle behind me, her exhalations coming in little choppy bursts.

After what must have been a full agonizing minute, I clicked on my flashlight, keeping it off to one side. "If prayer does any good..." I murmured, and stepped inside.

Across and down the street I heard a door slam and I froze in place, listening. Whatever had happened, the neighbors were blissfully ignorant. The houses on either side of Browers's were vacant, with FOR SALE signs in both yards. He could have had a screaming brawl in his living room and no one would have been bothered as long as he kept the front door closed.

And that's apparently what had happened. The floor of the foyer was vinyl tile, and a blood streak extended from the doorway toward the hall, which turned at right angles and led back to the bedrooms.

I moved a step forward, to a panel of four switches, and turned on the second one. The foyer light came on directly over my head.

Estelle stood in the doorway, looking down at the blood. "It looks like someone dragged a bloody mop across the floor," she said.

"Stay here," I repeated, and advanced to the hallway. There was blood on the floor, smeared in wide swathes. In one spot just beyond the access door to the gas furnace, a bloody hand had reached out and hit the wall, streaking a stain upward, as if when the hand made contact, it had been knocked upward.

The bedroom door was closed, and I tried to flatten my girth against the wall as I pinched the knob carefully between two fingers at three and nine o'clock positions and turned it. If the house had been built like a hundred others just like it, the light switch would be at chest level on the right as the door swung open in the opposite direction.

I could see the empty bed, shadowed by the light that flooded down the hallway from the foyer. I turned on my flashlight and saw the blood.

Estelle had followed me and she heard my curse. I heard her quick footsteps then as she advanced down the hallway.

With the tip of my flashlight, I tipped the bedroom light switch up and the place became as cheerful as any bedroom can be that's a bloody nightmare.

"Let me check the rest of the rooms," I said, and backed out. The remaining two bedrooms were empty and stainless, and I allowed a sigh of relief to escape. The master bedroom's bath was empty as well, but the three-quarter bath opposite the first bedroom still had water puddled in the sink and a blood-soaked towel flung in the bathtub.

I returned to the first bedroom. Estelle stood by the bed, frowning.

The pool of blood had saturated the mattress, covering an area nearly two feet across. Two other towels, both saturated, were flung on the other side of the bed.

"Someone was hurt, and dragged in here," Estelle said. "His bloody hand hit the wall in the hallway." She reached out with her pen and hooked a corner of the nearest towel, lifting it from the bed. "Someone tried to save him."

"Or her," I said. "And then what happened?"

She shook her head. "We need blood comparisons. If this is a match with the blood down in the motel room, then we've got our connection." She bit her lip.

"What?"

"We still don't know for sure if any of this is related to Francis, sir. We have a child's sock print that can't be matched. And that's all." She sagged against the wall. "We're running around in circles, and we don't know where he is."

I put my arms around her shoulders and pulled her close. She was shaking. "We'll find him, sweetheart. Just hang in there."

She said something so quietly, I couldn't catch it, and I directed her toward the hall. "You called for some help?" I asked.

"Yes, sir," she replied, adding, "And we need to go through the camper outside," as if she was forcing some direction and purpose on herself.

I could hear a siren in the distance, and no sooner had I uttered a curse about them running loud than the siren died. Still, in the quiet night, I could hear the big engine working overtime. The patrol car turned onto Fifth and the driver finally pulled his foot out of it, letting the car coast, almost silent, to the curb in front of 310.

I brushed past Estelle and made my way to the door, reaching the step just as Eddie Mitchell worked his way across the yard, keeping in the shadows. He held his service automatic, and I held up a hand.

"It's all right, Eddie." Even after he heard my voice, he didn't drop the stealth pose, just stayed close to the side of the pickup truck, weapon at the ready.

I stepped down. "Here's what we need you to do," I said. "'There's evidence in here that someone was badly injured, brought here for treatment, and then taken somewhere else. We don't have a clue where. The big RV is gone, so we need an all-points put out for that. It shouldn't be hard to find. We need someone here, and we need someone to collect some blood samples and run them to the lab."

"That's all there is?" Mitchell asked. "Blood?"

"No other signs." I hesitated as Estelle walked toward the back of the camper. "No sign of the boy yet."

Deputy Mitchell looked at me thoughtfully. "You're figuring that Mrs. Cole and Browers have the children?"

"That's what we're assuming right now. Somehow, there's a tie-in to the homicide down at the motel. A blood type will bring us closer. But for right now, if we find Tiffany Cole, Andy Browers, or Paul Cole, we'll have some answers."

The door of the camper on the back of Andy Browers's truck was closed but not latched. As soon as we swung it open, we could see the rich brown of dried blood—on the door, the floor, spread between the two small bunks on each side.

Estelle handed the shotgun to Mitchell and stepped up on the first aluminum step. She swung her flashlight around the interior. "A child's been here," she said. "There're some clothes and a partial bag of chips. Even a couple games and toys."

"Anything that belongs to Francisco?"

"No."

"Small child? Like Cody?"

"Yes," she said, and held up a tiny blue-and-yellow-striped T-shirt. Even in the uneven light, I could see the stain on the lower hem. "And we don't know who's hurt," she added. "We need blood tests on this." She held the small shirt in her hand.

I knew there was nothing I could say that would make much difference, but I leaned inside the camper and lowered my voice to the faintest of whispers. "Estelle, you never jumped to conclusions before. Don't start now. Let's go."

"You've got your radio with you?" I said to Eddie.

"Yes, sir."

"We'll be right back."

Every officer we had was on call was occupied in some fashion. Now we had another avalanche of evidence that deserved careful sifting.

There was no one to do the sifting.

By the time I reached 310, Estelle was on the radio.

"PCS, this is three-ten. Have three-oh-eight and three-oh-seven meet this unit at Four-oh-seven North Fifth Street. Silent approach."

"Do you know what Torrez and Abeyta are doing right now?" I asked.

"No, sir. I don't. But I know what they need to be doing. If we find that RV, we find the answers."

"And you can't hide something that big," I said. Even as the words came out of my mouth, I knew they were untrue. With enough head start to carry them out of the initial roadblock area, the RV would blend in with the rest of the snowbird traffic that flowed from one end of the Southwest to the other.

"Why," Estelle said, a statement rather than a question. "If we can find something that tells us why, then we'll know which way to turn."

"Three oh eight, three ten," I said, and then waited, microphone in hand.

"Three oh eight." Torrez sounded as if he'd just come off dinner break on a routine night.

"ETA?"

"I'm there."

As he said that, his county car glided around the intersection of Bustos and Fifth. His headlights were off.

"Three ten, three oh nine is two minutes out." By the time Torrez's car had sidled to a stop nose-to-nose with ours, Tony Abeyta's unmarked Caprice entered Fifth from eastbound Bustos.

"Lights," Torrez said, and instantly Abeyta's headlights winked out. The five of us, exactly half of the Posadas County Sheriff's Department, assembled on the sidewalk in front of Andy Browers's house.

"We need to establish when the RV was last here," I said. "As nearly as we can. That gives us some kind of time frame. If we know what kind of head start they had, we know the search-area radius."

"That vehicle could have gone through any of the roadblocks," Mitchell said quietly. "They're looking for someone in company with a three-year-old Mexican child. And they weren't on the lookout for Baker Echo zero zero one, since it was sitting right here when we put out the bulletin."

"It's possible they drove right through," Estelle said.

"All right, all right," I snapped. "Let's assume that there's a connection with Madrid's death. That's too much of a coincidence not to fly. He was killed sometime shortly after six. If Cole and Browers were involved, and drove back here, maybe one of them hurt, then they could have pulled out anytime between six-thirty and ten minutes ago. That's two hours."

"And two hours at just sixty miles an hour is a hundred and twenty miles already," Mitchell said calmly. "That puts them in Mexico, or Texas, or Arizona. And if they're smart, they've dumped that monster for something else."

"Browers is from Texas," Estelle said quietly.

"But Roberto Madrid is from Mexico, by way of Arizona," Mitchell countered.

"Christ," I said. "All right. Let's do it this way. Eddie, I want you to handle the blood work. Make sure things stay organized. As soon as you can, I want blood-type matches so we can start piecing this mess together. Take a sample from inside, from the puddle on the bed. Take that child's T-shirt, the one that Estelle just bagged. We need a preliminary match with the blood from the motel bathroom. Do it anyway you can, but get back to us ASAP."

"Yes, sir." He spun on his heel and jogged back to his patrol car for his field kit.

"Tony, I want you to go get Jim Bergin and get an airplane. That'll give us some speed and distance advantage. You know what we're looking for, so you fly with him. Take a phone with you so you can stay off the radio."

"We need to track Madrid," Torrez said. "He's the key to this. The sheriff's been on the phone with Captain Naranjo of the *federales*. What he was able to establish so far is that Madrid parked his own car on the Mexican side of the border, came across, and then rented another vehicle."

"Nothing wrong with that," I said. "Under normal circumstances, his insurance may not have covered him in this country. A dozen reasons. A Mexican license plate draws more attention than an Arizona plate does. Maybe he wanted a car that blended in more. What was he driving?"

"Holman didn't say."

"Well, push him that way, Robert. He speaks Spanish about as well as I do. We've got to know what Madrid's connections are. See if you can get Captain Naranjo in high gear."

"That's a trick," Torrez said.

"Perform it," I snapped. I watched him fold his enormous frame into 308.

"You need to talk with your husband," I said to Estelle.

"Yes, I do."

I glanced at my watch. It'd been several lifetimes since we'd dashed out of the Guzman house.

Chapter 36

The night wore on, and on, and on. There had been a few times in my life when the sun simply refused to make any progress around the other side. This was one of them.

Tiny bits and pieces of information dragged in. We were using my office, spacious and removed from the traffic flow in and out of the Public Safety Building.

When Niel Costace of the FBI arrived shortly after ten from Las Cruces, Sheriff Martin Holman and I were alone in my office, trying to establish telephone contact with Capt. Tomas Naranjo of the Mexican *federales*. We hadn't had much success, since Naranjo wasn't in his office in Juárez and wasn't at home—and his wife didn't know where he was. If he had a cellular phone, he was ignoring it.

Costace stood in the doorway of my office, his posture suggesting that he was carrying a sack of cement in each hand.

"What the hell mess have you got going here this time?" he said by way of greeting, and Holman strode across the room to pump his hand like the good politician he was.

"And no word on either the vehicle or the boys yet," Costace said when Holman finished his recap of the case.

"Not a thing."

He turned one of my straight chairs around and sat on it, cowboy-style, resting his chin on his hands.

"We've met this Roberto Madrid a time or two," Costace said. "He's a wheeler-dealer, kind of a free agent. Works most of the time out of Monterrey, as far as we've been able to tell. I can tell you one thing. If he's involved with the missing boys, don't bother sitting around waiting for a telephone call."

"I was afraid that was the case," I said.

Holman looked uneasy. "Why not? What's Madrid's game?"

"No game, Sheriff," Costace said. "Madrid doesn't do drugs, as far as we can determine. Nothing to connect him, anyway. His name came up a couple of years ago in connection with that nasty deal in Matamoros. Remember some of those missing teenagers? Kind of a cult thing? He was connected with that, but we could never nail it down—and neither could the *federales*. The only thing we know for sure is that not all of those kids went down there of their own free will."

"Abducted, you mean?"

Costace nodded. "That's what we think. The next time his name came down the pike was in connection with a deal over in Tampico. That one involved a sixty-five-foot sloop that was stolen out of Hatteras, North Carolina." He rocked the chair forward. "Now, you think it's hard to hide a thirty-foot travel bus? How about a boat twice that big? He pulled it off, and the new owners had been using it for nearly six months before Mexican officials got around to making the connections." He shrugged. "Hatteras to Mexican waters is a hell of a long run."

"Madrid just sailed it down there?"

"He didn't. He had some hired hands. No, old Roberto just does the deals. From the description the boat owners gave, we know it was Madrid. He said he was an insurance agent and he got himself on board the boat for an inspection. That's how he knew the layout."

"I don't care about boats," Holman said. "Why would he be interested in two three-year-olds?"

"Well, I said he was a wheeler-dealer. If there's a market, then he's in there pitchin'."

"You mean sell them? Sell the kids?"

Costace shrugged in that cold-blooded way that suggested that he'd seen it all. "How'd it happen, exactly?"

Holman told him about Cody Cole's disappearance.

"And that happened several days before the Guzman boy was taken?"

I nodded. "Well, see," Costace said, "the Cole youngster's abduction fits. There's no way of tellin' just yet how the Coles made contact with Madrid in the first place, but if they set up a deal, Madrid's style would fit just what happened. They hold the kid—maybe using that big old RV for just that purpose."

"That would mean that the boy's natural father was in on it, too."

"Would seem so. Madrid hits town, and if he thinks the coast is clear, all he has to do is hand over the pesos to the parents and then hit the road."

"Why wait four days to do it?" I asked. "Cody went missing on Saturday night. Why would they run the risk of keeping him around for four days? That doesn't make a bit of sense."

"Madrid might have been planning to hit town last Saturday. Who knows?" Costace said. "Anything could have delayed him— traffic accident, other troubles." He rested his chin on his hands and stared at the floor. "He's late, and whoever is holding the boy is forced to mark time. One day, two days..."

"What about the second boy?"

"That's a problem," Costace said. "We've been getting rumblings now and then that there's a market for children—sometimes a family of *ricos* gets it in their heads that they'd like a little blond-haired, blue-eyes status symbol. They're willing to pay good money for an instant adoption, and that would attract the Roberto Madrids of the world. You want it, he finds it. But the Guzman boy puzzles me." Costace smiled without much humor. "Lord knows, Mexico has its share of cute little black-haired, black-eyed urchins who speak Spanish. I don't see much need to go north of the border to fetch another one, especially a high-visibility target like this little Francis. That sounds like panic to me."

"Panic?"

Costace shrugged. "If the deal was goin' down without any hitch, Madrid would have taken the Cole boy and hit the road. He would have been in and out of here so slick, no one would have been the wiser. Little Cody would have been a Mexican citizen by bedtime Saturday night." He shrugged again. "Nobody would have been the wiser. After a few days, the search is called off; everybody's sad, but eventually everyone forgets. Ma and Pa Cole pocket a trunkful of cash. But it didn't happen that way. From what you say, there was a hell of an argument."

"Someone changed her mind," I said as a lightbulb flashed in my head.

"Who?" Holman frowned at me.

"We went through Tiffany Cole's house tonight," I said. "That woman has a screw loose somewhere. That child's been living with them for all three years of his life, and except for a half-eaten dish of hash and a plastic child's cup of milk, there wasn't any way to tell he'd ever been in that house."

I got up and walked to the window. "She makes a deal to part with the youngster. We don't know how she did; we don't know the circumstances. We know that her ex-husband, Paul Cole, came to Posadas under false pretenses, so only an idiot would ignore his involvement. It couldn't happen under Andy Browers's nose without him knowing, so he's in on it, too."

"A real crop of woodchucks you got here," Costace said.

"They make a deal with Madrid. The time comes to deliver the boy, and someone backs out. Mama, maybe."

"Touching," Costace said.

"Maybe they took some money in advance to secure the deal. They know they have Madrid at the motel, waiting. They figure, Hey, what the hell. Give him some other kid."

Costace rubbed his face. "Do you have some reason to believe they'd know about the Guzman child? Why would they choose him?"

"Sure," I said. "His mother's high profile in this town, as is his father. And his picture was just in the local paper, in a big play they gave the search efforts." I rummaged on my desk and found a copy of the *Register*. "Here it is."

Costace frowned and examined the newspaper at some length. "Handsome boy," he said finally. "But I can just see the look on Madrid's face when they come trooping into his motel room with Francis Guzman, Jr., in tow."

"And so the argument," Holman said. "In all your dealings with Madrid, is he usually armed?"

Costace held up his hands. "Don't get me wrong. I haven't dealt with the man myself. And he's a slick one. He's no strong-arm, if what I hear is right. Sure, he might carry a knife, but the fastest way to get yourself nailed at the border is to be carrying a concealed weapon. No, guys like Madrid come and go slick as an oil spill, because they know what attracts attention."

"Why would he fight, then?"

"Well," Costace said, "if they already had a down payment and didn't want to return it, then he might get just a little testy. Depends on who he was facing, and what they were trying to pull on him. It's all just speculation."

"That's all we've got," I said. "There was blood all over the motel room, and considerable blood in the truck and Browers's house."

"He got in a couple good licks, then," Costace said. "They shot him twice?"

"That's right," Holman said. "The coroner told me tonight that the preliminary shows two twenty-two-caliber wounds. One in the side, one in the back. He lived for about twenty minutes."

"End of his argument," Costace said. "And now your good folks have discovered how easy it is to go from foolproof plan to royal fuckup." He stood up and pushed the chair back against the desk. "Did you find any money in the motel room, Sheriff?"

Holman shook his head. "Nothing. Not even Madrid's wallet. There were a couple of car-rental papers. That's all."

"Then your folks are running around with a bundle of money that doesn't belong to them, and they haven't delivered the goods, either. Someone down south isn't going to be too happy, but there isn't a hell of a lot they can do, either." He glanced at his watch, as if we'd used up his allotment of time. "If what we've been thinking is true, then you can figure it out as well as I can. If I were them, I'd get rid of three things." He held up three fingers, then bent the index. "First is the bleeder. He's hurt bad, maybe dead. There's a lot of empty desert out there, so that's no problem." He bent down the second finger. "The second is the Guzman child. Without that little kid, they're just a nice family. And finally, they've got to dump that RV. They bring top dollar in Mexico, so if they can slip across the border, they've got a chance." He shoved his hands in his pockets. "You been in touch with Naranjo, I imagine?"

"Trying," I said.

He nodded. "There's some good news in all this," he said.

"I'd like to hear it," I replied.

"Well, if Madrid had the boys, I'd bet even money that you'd never see them again. He knows how to slip in and out of Mexico clean as the wind. He's got contacts, and he knows who to pay. But Madrid's dead. You're dealing with a bunch of wild-eyed amateurs. Who knows what they're thinking, or what their logic is? You wait long enough and they'll drive themselves right into a dead end. They can't come back. They can't cross at Regal. The Border Patrol's looking for 'em every foot of the border, and they don't have Madrid's savvy or contacts."

"Maybe that's good news, and maybe it isn't," I said, and eyed Costace. "At least one of those two little boys is excess baggage at this point. And as you say, it's a big desert out there."

Chapter 37

Most of that night, Jim Bergin's Piper Archer moaned in high, lazy circles over Posadas County, spotting headlights. State police took care of the interstate—the interchange at Posadas was blocked, and any vehicle coming on or going off was searched.

We concentrated on two possibilities. First was the notion that they might have ditched the mammoth RV for a more sensible vehicle. If that was the case, then officers manning roadblocks needed to check every vehicle—and they did, with mind-numbing regularity.

The second option was that they might keep the RV, knowing its intrinsic worth on the black market if they ever successfully reached Mexico—or, for that matter, a dozen different chop shops scattered across the Southwest that might specialize in such monsters.

"See, the problem is," Martin Holman said, "the average person just doesn't *look* very closely." We were trying to do just that, me driving and Martin looking *closely*. "Remember that Ditch Witch that the telephone company had stolen right off a job site last year? Machine, trailer, the whole works. Never found it." He turned to find the large handheld spotlight. "You see some guys working out in the field with a backhoe, or Ditch Witch, or jackhammer, whatever, you don't stop and walk out and ask for proof of ownership."

"How true," I murmured.

"We assume that the people using the equipment *own* the equipment. It's that simple. Besides, we can assume they had a choice."

"A choice of what?"

"They could have taken Browers's truck in the first place and left the RV behind. That they didn't do that indicates to me that they want that RV. It's worth a lot of money in the right places. His old pickup truck isn't."

I idled 310 up to the fence of the Consolidated Mining boneyard. High up on the mesa side overlooking the village, the abandoned mine and equipment yard rivaled the landfill for Posadas County's shot of ugly. The gate was heavy steel and chain link, with barbed wire on top. The lock was a length of inch chain with a massive lock inside a plate-steel lock cover. Everything was in place.

Nevertheless, Holman buzzed down his window and swung the beam of the portable spotlight across the vast acreage of mining detritus. Nothing that could have been a disguised RV stood out.

"Turn down the dump road so we can check that tin building," he said. "My bet is that they just drove out of the county and went on their way. They had darn near two hours head start, with no blocks, nothing. By the time we knew something was up, they could have been halfway to the crossing at Douglas-Nogales."

He switched off the light and glanced at the dashboard clock. "And from the time the boy first went missing to when we knew the RV was involved was almost *three* hours, and that is enough time to get across."

"We're just going to have to trust that the *federales* got word to Naranjo and he has his side locked up," I said. "There are far fewer roads down there than up here."

"Unless you count the dirt two-tracks. Stop."

I did so, and Holman scanned the tin storage building. One end was open, and we could see the jumble of fifty-five-gallon drums.

We turned around and headed back to County Road 43 and the winding macadam that led up to the abandoned quarry. I had no expectations of seeing a thirty-foot-long buslike RV parked under the piñons. Hell, there were few piñons tall enough for it to slip under in the first place. But our only hope was to leave no spot in the county unaccounted for, and to that end, every available car and person was working through the night. With the airplane overhead in constant communication, if someone moved with headlights on, we'd know it.

And with that came the nagging realization that Andy Browers, with his experience working for the Electric Co-op, knew every small nook and cranny in the county.

Shortly before midnight, Deputy Tom Pasquale had put together the blood-evidence profile, and it fit Agent Costace's theory. None of the blood in the motel room, except for a small amount immediately associated with the body, belonged to Roberto Madrid.

The blood around the rest of the room, in the bathroom, on the curtain, outside in the parking lot—all the blood evidence at the motel—matched the blood found in the back of Andy Browers's truck and in the bedroom of his home.

Costace and Pasquale—and young Pasquale was in seventh heaven just associating with the taciturn FBI agent—shagged an Electric Co-op official out of a comfortable evening at home and rifled through records. Andy Browers's blood type was listed there as O-negative. The blood evidence in the motel room, his truck, and his bedroom was AB-positive.

Francis Guzman, Jr.'s blood type was A-negative, and that afforded a temporary shot of relief.

Detective Richard Steinberg routed a Bernalillo school official out of his comfortable evening at home and they rifled through school records. Coach Cole's blood type, on file with the school nurse after a recent school-sponsored blood drive, was AB-positive.

Two of the missing party had no blood type on file. We had no record of Tiffany Cole's type, nor of little Cody's. But AB-positive was common enough. Millions of people shared that blood type. A DNA comparison would establish that the blood specimen either did or did not belong to Paul Cole, the only one of the three whose type was on file. But a DNA check wasn't going to happen in the middle of the night, or even by the next day.

I had decided that, based on the evidence of the fight in the motel room, it was Paul Cole's blood. That made sense to me. A distant second choice was Tiffany's. It made no sense that the injury would have been suffered by Cody, either from the placement of the blood splatters or from the amount.

The gravel turnout that led to the shore of the quarry pond was empty. There was no place to hide an RV there, no matter how the driver tried to nestle the thing under the trees.

As I turned around, I saw moisture on the windshield. "No," I said. "We don't need this now." The clouds were glowering, and if the vagaries of New Mexico's weather held true to form, we could expect anything—rain, snow, wind, and mud, the works.

The cellular phone between us chirped, and Holman snatched it up.

"Holman." For the next few seconds, he just listened, and then he shrugged. "Whatever he thinks is best. He's the boss. Check back with me when you're on the ground."

He switched off and sighed. "Bergin says the weather is worse in the southwestern corner of the county, and it's moving this way."

"He's landing?"

"Right. They've seen absolutely nothing in the past half hour except lights on the interstate, and once in a while a local vehicle."

I parked 310 facing downhill. We could see the lights of Posadas below us, and beyond that, a dark inky void that stretched to the San Cristobal Mountains and, beyond that, Mexico.

For a long minute, I drummed my fingers on the steering wheel. "We've got enough people out that every major road is covered in or out. There's no two-track or cattle path that goes anywhere without surfacing eventually on one of the main roads. The border's closed. I don't know what else we can do."

"I think they're long gone," Holman said.

"We don't know that," I said. "No matter who's calling the shots, whether it's Browers or Cole, he doesn't know how much of a head start he had. We've stayed off the radios as much as possible. They can't know for sure what we're doing. That's our only advantage right now."

Holman sniffed. "I'm not sure we know, either. There's got to be something other than sitting and waiting."

"We keep looking," I said, and pulled the car into gear.

Chapter 38

At two minutes after six on Thursday morning, I was dozing in my old leather office chair, my boots up on the desk, hands folded on my belly, and my head slumped on my chest. I'm sure that with two days' growth of beard, I looked like some old hobo off the road.

A few minutes earlier, I had elected not to go home, despite Camille's entreaties. For sure, I knew that her "Dad, you're not doing anyone any good staying here" was probably true. But I felt closer to where something *might* happen, and that was important to me.

Dr. Francis Guzman appeared in the doorway of my office, moving noiselessly. I don't know how long he'd been standing there, but I jarred awake and looked up.

"How are you doing?" he asked, his voice husky.

"You making morning rounds?" I said, trying for some humor on a humorless morning. I glanced at my watch.

"I'm on the way," he said. "Estelle went back over to the hospital for a little while to be with her mother. Then she said she's coming here."

I nodded. "You haven't gotten much rest, either," I said.

He sauntered over to my desk, hands trust in his pockets. "Nothing?"

"No word, Francis. We made a little bit of progress a couple of hours ago." I tried another smile. "There's nothing like the middle of the night to put the screws on people. A Bernalillo detective who's been working with us talked to Paul Cole's new wife. She's co-operating." I leaned back and hooked my hands behind my head. My arms felt like lead.

"She and Paul Cole are so far in debt that she's petrified. They had an argument last week when he broke the news to her about his so-called hunting trip to Wyoming. She says they can't afford gas to drive to the grocery store, let alone something like that. They've paid their mortgage payment with a credit card the past several months. She really believed that Wyoming was where he was going."

While I was talking, Francis Guzman pulled a blood-pressure cuff out of the pocket of his lab coat and advanced on my left arm.

He prompted me when I stopped talking. "And then?"

"She works at an animal clinic, and of course he's a teacher and head coach, so their combined incomes are pretty solid. But she admitted to detectives that they've been living on their credit cards, just paying the interest. And now she's afraid Cole's going to get himself in hot water with the school and lose his job." I pushed up my left sleeve and held it while Francis positioned the cuff. "The most interesting thing she told detectives is that for as long as she's known Paul Cole, his ex wife has been pestering him to take custody of little Cody."

He looked sharply at me. "No kidding?" He patted the Velcro and pumped the bulb, slipping the earpieces of the stethoscope into his ears. I waited until he had finished.

"You need some rest," he said. "Meds?"

"Meds are home, where they belong," I said.

He grinned and shook his head. "A couple of them are important," he said. "We need to keep your pressure somewhere below the boiling point. Are you still taking the heparin?"

"I have no idea what's what," I said. "I took a couple of aspirin earlier. I know what they are."

Francis Guzman listened to my heart and other places where blood still gurgled, then raised one eyebrow at me.

"You ought to be home," he repeated. "Was the aspirin for pain, or discomfort?"

"I've been catnapping here. And the coffeepot was empty, so I had a couple of aspirin instead." Francis shook his head, but I waved off another complaint. "There are more important things to do just now than worry about my shitload of medications, Francis."

He wrapped up the cuff and slid it back in his pocket. "I'll give Camille a call and tell her which ones to express deliver to you, *padrino*." He stared down at my telephone for a moment, as if expecting it to ring. "So Tiffany Cole wanted her ex-husband to take custody of their child. That's interesting."

"According to wife number two, or three, or whatever she is, Tiffany Cole has her own share of troubles. She blames them all on the child. And after looking at her house earlier, I can well agree. There's not a lot of love evident there."

"Do you believe what the FBI agent said earlier? About this being part of a deal to—what, sell children?"

I saw no point in beating around the bush with the young physician. "I think it's simpler than that. If it was some kind of ring, or cult, there'd be more children involved. We'd have heard of more cases. I think someone was willing to pay for a child as a quick means of adoption. South of the border, it would never be traced, or if it did arouse official interest, a little money under the table would take care of it. I think Tiffany Cole, screw loose or not, changed her mind at the last minute. There was a slipup somehow, and she ended up with too much time to think about what she was doing."

"And tried to substitute my son."

"Yep."

"What if that's not what happened?"

I got up and faced Francis Guzman. I reached up and put a hand on each one of the good doctor's shoulders. "Francis, we're all guessing. You know that. Until something breaks, all we can do is dig, dig, dig. Every time we open a little channel of information, we make some progress. We don't know for sure what happened, but we're starting to get a little glimmer of the 'why.' And that's a plus on our side."

"The weather's getting worse."

"Yes, I know it is." We stood and looked at each other helplessly.

"I'll be at the hospital if you…" Whatever Francis was going to say trailed off as Ernie Wheeler, dark circles under his eyes, thrust open the door.

"Sir, telephone for you on two. It's Herb Torrance."

"It's who?"

"Herb Torrance? Out on Fourteen."

"Tell him I'll call him back," I said. I knew the old rancher well, having bailed his wild-haired son out of more than one jam.

Wheeler persisted. "Sir, he says he's got Francis."

I spun around and grabbed the phone. The damn thing slipped out of my grasp and crashed to the desk.

"Herb, you there?" I bellowed when I managed to fumble the receiver to my ear.

"Sheriff, I need me some help out here." My heart nearly sailed out of my chest. "My son found this little boy."

"Is he all right?"

"No, he's busted up pretty bad. He was tryin' to catch him, see, and he slipped and fell."

"Who fell? Your son or the boy?" Francis's face went pale. "Herb, I don't understand what you're saying."

"I'm sayin' my son found that little boy we was all lookin' for up on the mesa."

"Cody Cole, you mean."

"I guess so, 'cept I thought the Cole youngster was a…white kid, you know. I thought I read he was blond. My son says this one looks like maybe some wetbacks lost track of him."

"Oh shit," I muttered. "Is the boy all right?"

"I guess he's fine. My son ain't. I took him over to the house. We're going to have to take him to town."

"Where's the boy?"

"He's out there on the side of the ledge, up behind our west stock tank. That's where my son seen him. He was trying to get him down, and the boy wouldn't pay him no attention. I told the boy just to leave him be. I didn't want someone blamin' us if he got hurt."

"We'll be right there."

"Just come to the front gate. I'll take you back there."

I hung up. "What?" Francis said, his eyes wide.

"It sounds like they found your son," I said, and then grinned. "They can't catch him."

Chapter 39

As we turned westbound on Bustos to head out of town, we could see the leaden gray sky stretching flat and featureless. Dr. Guzman sat in back, behind the security screen. Estelle was silent, eyes fixed outside.

The thermometer on the bank hovered at forty-one degrees, and I had visions of little Francis Guzman standing out in the middle of the prairie in his bunny jammies, shivering, while old Herb Torrance and his sons tried to rope him.

Herb Torrance's ranch wasn't exactly in the hub of all Posadas County activity. We drove west out of the village on 17, the old state highway that roughly paralleled the interstate. Twenty-one miles later and, I'm sure, an eternity for Estelle and Francis, we reached the intersection of County Road 14, the ribbon of gravel that ran north-south down the west side of the county, connecting the east-west state roads like a strand of angel-hair pasta laced across the four tines of a fork.

The route brought Andrew Browers to mind. If anyone knew these roads, it was he. Paul Cole wouldn't know one county lane from another.

The H-Bar-T ranch included more than ten thousand acres, mostly leased from the feds, land that tourists looked at and then remarked about in their various strange accents. "Gee, Elvinia, there ain't nothing out here but cactus." There was more, of course, since cattle couldn't live on cactus. A little stunted bunch of grass here and there explained why Herb needed to lease ten thousand acres for two hundred head of rangy steers.

And somewhere out here, according to Herb, was a little three-year-old boy. I'm sure Estelle and Francis were asking themselves the same string of questions that ran through my mind. Why wasn't the child inside Bea Torrance's snug kitchen, drinking hot cocoa with the other five Torrance children? If cowpunchers could maneuver and catch rangy steers charging through prairie scrub, why couldn't they catch a three-year-old?

Five miles of smooth gravel later, I turned into the H-Bar-T driveway, under the wrought-iron arch that featured a bull chasing a cowboy through yucca.

Herb Torrance stepped out of his front door, crossed the porch, and headed down the steps to meet us even as we pulled under the arch.

He waved us to park beside an enormous crew-cab dualie and 310 was instantly surrounded by four yapping dogs, those variegated blue-and-black things that chase sheep. None of them bit when we got out of the car, and Herb lit a cigarette so he'd have something in his hand when he talked to us.

For the first time since I'd known him, Herb Torrance didn't invite us inside for coffee. I wouldn't have been able to hold the damn cup, anyway—a combination of joy that my godson might be all right and anger that a bunch of adults hadn't been able to corral a three-year-old.

"We'll take my truck," he said. "Wife's taken Patrick into town to have his leg looked at. Rory's got the Jeep. You might make it in car of yours, but you're apt to get 'er stuck." He grinned at me as I grunted up into the cab. "Make 'er? I heard you been under the weather some, Bill."

"A little. You say Patrick found the child?"

"Over yonder past the big stock tank, across the road there." He waved a hand generally toward the south. "The boy's up in some rocks, and the footing gets kinda nasty when it's wet like this."

"He wouldn't come down?" Francis asked.

Herb shook his head and took a deep drag on the cigarette. He glanced back at Francis. "Ain't you one of the docs over at the hospital?"

"Yes."

"This is Dr. Guzman," I said. "You know Estelle." Torrance nodded and butted out the cigarette. "It's their son who was abducted last night. You may have seen the bulletin on television."

Torrance jerked upright and swiveled to look straight at me. The steering wheel twisted to follow his head and we swerved dangerously close to his front gate support. He jerked the wheel back. "Abducted? That right?" We charged out onto the county road and turned left. "Well hell. No, we didn't catch that. How'd that happen, anyways?"

"It's a long story," I said, and let it go at that.

Herb didn't press the matter. "No wonder the child won't come near nobody. He's got to be scared plumb to death, out all night. I left Rory there to keep an eye on him while I called you. I figured another little while wouldn't hurt him none. Better than taking a fall." He turned to Estelle. "I told the boy not to chase after him. Runs like a little rabbit, Patrick was sayin'. He don't want to have anything to do with strangers, that's for sure. I thought that maybe he didn't speak any English."

"He speaks English just fine," I said, not bothering to add that little Francis was also choosy about whom he spoke to.

We drove two miles on the county road and I began to get nervous that Herb's "over yonder" was somewhere in Mexico. The road began to climb gradually as it made its way up the back side of San Patricio Mesa, a broad, flat buttress of land crisscrossed by narrow, deep canyons whose southern boundary was the valley carrying State Road 56 to Regal.

The road wound around several large rock outcroppings that looked as if they shed parts during the infrequent cloudbursts, then, where the country opened up for a bit, we passed by a windmill that was missing all but three of its blades. A small barn, its adobe and stone back wall collapsed inward, stood beside a rusted stock tank. Thirty years before, it might have been an outfit to make a rancher proud.

Fifty yards farther, Herb turned the truck left across a cattle guard and onto a narrow, muddy two-track that slithered through cactus and greasewood for a hundred yards toward an enormous galvanized water tank. The windmill there turned lazily, its Aermotor—Chicago rudder keeping track of the fitful breeze. Twenty or thirty cows stood close by, watching our approach with interest.

"There we are," Herb said.

"Where?"

He pointed off to the right with the butt of an unlit cigarette toward a small black vehicle. "There's Rory's Jeep. And if you look just past that grove of brush, up in them rocks?" I did and saw nothing except brush and rocks.

A figure appeared out of a grove of stunted junipers and lifted a hand in greeting.

"That's Rory," Herb said. The truck slowed to a stop and Estelle and Francis were out and away before I could even find the door handle.

The water tank and windmill nestled in a small amphitheater, the limestone rocks forming a jumbled wall on the east and north. The rocks weren't particularly high, but they afforded ample protection for ground squirrels, pack rats, rattlesnakes, and three-year-old Francis Guzman.

I first caught sight of a small patch of blue, and as I drew closer, I could see that the child was sitting on his haunches, leaning against a boulder that was about the size of a small sedan. "How the hell did he get up there?" I muttered.

When he saw his mother and father, he stood up, and that brought me to a halt. The drop-off in front of him was six or eight feet. "*Mama*," he shouted. He turned and scrambled out of sight for just a moment, then appeared around the side of the rock on top of which he'd been sitting. His father ran to meet him, using his hands to steady himself as he made his way up through the jumble.

Herb walked up beside me and lit another cigarette. "I just figured that it was safer to let you folks handle this, 'cause, of course, I thought..." he said, letting the wetback explanation trail off. "After Patrick took that header, Rory helped him back to the truck. He was hurtin', so they just up and left the child. Didn't figure he'd go anywhere. Patrick busted his leg just above the ankle." The rancher sucked air through his teeth. "He said he saw the boy down by the tank when he was driving in, and the kid just took off. Rory said they called to him, but he sure as hell wasn't going to trust nobody he didn't know. That's why we got to thinkin' that he'd probably been dumped by some wetback family, you know." He glanced at me. "And after Patrick fell, why I just thought, Hell, if he'll just sit there..."

"Thanks, Herb," I said. I watched the two figures merge, and then Dr. Guzman turned around, his son in his arms, and carefully picked his way back down through the rocks. Estelle went up to meet them, and for a while the three of them formed a single huddle.

"I'd sure like to know what sort of person would just leave a kid out in the middle of nowhere, though," the rancher said. He sauntered back toward the truck, muttering to himself. I turned and went with him. The cattle were starting to move toward the truck, their interest piqued. They stopped a dozen yards away, chewing thoughtfully.

"Did you see any traffic last night or early this morning?" I asked.

"No. Sure didn't pay any attention," he said. "What's the deal, anyway?"

I told him briefly what had happened, and what kind of vehicle we were looking for, but he shook his head. "Whole United States Army could have driven by and I wouldn't have noticed," he said. "The kids had a couple of TV videos from town, and that was enough noise for anybody."

"What time did everyone turn in?"

Herb shrugged. "Probably close to midnight."

"And you didn't hear anything after that?"

"No, not that I paid attention to. It's a county road, after all. Fair amount of traffic, especially with the bar down at the main road there."

I turned and grinned. Estelle and Francis were walking back on either side of their son, each holding one of his hands. He was refusing to walk, but he bounced off the ground every second step or so. I could hear his little high-pitched voice jabbering away in Spanish. My blood pressure drifted down a couple notches when I saw that he wasn't wearing pajamas.

"¡*Padrino!*" the child bellowed when he was a dozen yards away. If I had been Estelle or Francis, I'm not sure I'd have been able to let him go. But they did, and he charged forward. I bent down to scoop him up. His jeans and cotton jacket were grimy and damp, and his hair smelled like one of the little sheepdogs over at Herb's house.

"These aren't mine," he said, getting right to the important stuff first. One arm was around my neck, and he reached down with the other to touch the toe of one of his fancy blue-and-white sneakers.

His face was dirty and tear-streaked. "Whose are they, kid?" I asked, taking his tiny hand in mind.

"They're Cody's," he said soberly.

I looked at Estelle. I'd never seen tears in her eyes before. "Were you with Cody?" I asked. The child twisted in my arms and looked over my shoulder toward Herb Torrance and the big pickup. I could feel his grip around my neck tighten. "That's okay," I said. "He's a friend." The grip didn't loosen.

"He's in the bus," the child said.

"Who else was in the bus, *hijo*?" Estelle said. He dug a knee into my belly as he twisted and reached out with both arms to his mother. I handed him to her and he flung both arms around her neck.

He didn't answer immediately, and Estelle brushed the hair out of his eyes. "Were Cody's mommy and daddy in the bus?"

The child nodded. "A man chased me up there," Francis said. "But he fell and hurt his leg." I smiled at the satisfaction in the child's voice. "Then they went away." He pointed at Rory Torrance's black Jeep. "That truck right there."

"You're safe now," I said. "This is Mr. Torrance and his son Rory. They're friends of ours. This is their ranch." Francis nodded and I saw his eyes shift to Rory, skeptical. "Why didn't you stay on the bus?"

"'Cause," he said, as if that was all the answer necessary.

"Did Cody's mommy and daddy make you get off the bus?" I asked, then repeated, "Cody's mommy and daddy?" He nodded. "Where did they stop to make you get off?"

He turned and pointed over Estelle's shoulder. "Right there," he said. "But I runned away."

The "right there" was indicated by a tiny index finger pointing generally off to the west.

"Why did you run away, *hijo*?" Estelle asked softly. Dr. Guzman was holding the door of the truck for us, no doubt hoping the cops in the group would stop their goddamn interrogation and let him take the kid somewhere warm and dry.

Little Francis abandoned English, and most of what he said was whimpered in rapid-fire Spanish into the hollow of Estelle's neck. She cooed something back to him, holding the back of his head tightly as she carried him to the truck.

She sat in the back, with the child in her lap, her arms wrapped around him. Her husband slid in beside her.

"You all want to go back to the house?" Herb Torrance said.

"Please," I said. I twisted in the seat and saw that Estelle was looking hard at me. "What?" I asked.

"He said that Cody's mommy and daddy told him that if he didn't behave, they'd put him in the hole, too."

"Oh my God," I whispered. The little boy's head came up as we hit the county road, and his enormous dark eyes, still filled with tears, watched as we passed the abandoned adobe barn. "In the hole. That's what he called it in Spanish? A hole?"

Estelle put her hand on the top of the child's head. "He doesn't know the word *grave* yet."

"That's where they put that man," little Francis Guzman said, his spine ramrod-stiff. He almost poked a finger in his father's eye in his eagerness to point out the window. He twisted his head and looked at me. "Cody has two daddies. And that's where they put him."

"Herb, stop the truck," I said.

"Bill, please," Dr. Guzman said.

"Just stop, Herb. Let me out, and then take these folks back to the house. Estelle, use the radio to call Torrez and Mitchell out here. Or whomever you can reach. I'll be waiting for 'em."

The truck crunched to a stop. "You sure about this?" Herb said. I looked behind us. The black Jeep idled, waiting.

"Yep. I'll keep Rory with me for company." Just before I slammed the door, I turned to Estelle. "While you're talking to him," I said, indicating little Francis, "we need to know what direction that bus went when they took off. And if he heard them say anything about where they were going."

I stepped away from the truck and beckoned to Rory Torrance.

Chapter 40

"Do you have a shovel with you?" I asked the blond-haired youngster behind the wheel of the Jeep. He looked like a forty-year-younger version of his father, Herb—thin, blue-eyed, big-knuckled, angular features.

"Yes, sir," Rory Torrance said. He watched, maybe expecting a pratfall as I slipped into the Jeep. I'd put in close to a million miles in the damn things during my twenty years in the Marine Corps, back before Humvees took over the world, and despite the modern chrome, fiberglass top, and the CD player wedged up under the dash, the Jeeps hadn't changed much.

"I'd like you to park right in the middle of the road over there," I said, indicating a spot in front of the crumbling building. "There's not going to be much traffic." He backed up not more than a hundred feet.

"Here?"

"Just fine," I said.

"What are we looking for? Were those the kid's parents who went home with Dad?"

"Yes," I said. I got out of the Jeep. A blind man could have seen the deep impressions made by the RV's dual back wheels. Who ever had been driving knew New Mexico's treacherous secondary roads. He hadn't pulled off far, not far enough to risk the slick mud of the shoulders.

Despite the spitting rain of the past few hours, the marks were clear. Someone had dragged a heavy burden over toward the old building. One of the daddies, as little Francisco had said.

"Bring your shovel," I said, "And walk right behind me."

I waited for Rory to dig the tool out of the back, and I noticed that he was wearing boots and short spurs. "You looking forward to Thanksgiving holiday?" I said.

He grinned. "Sure." He glanced at his watch.

"Do you drive in or take the bus to school?"

He looked askance at me. "Don't take no bus," he said. I wondered if he clanked into first-period class with his spurs on.

I walked carefully, staying parallel with the footprints and drag marks. They led us just where I thought they might, over behind the old building, out of sight of the road. It wasn't a spot frequented by bird-watchers, or neckers, or campers. Cattle ambled around the building, rubbing on the crumbling walls and leaving their trademark piles of manure.

"No one's lived here for a while," I said as I moved to the far southwest corner of the structure, the farthest point away from the county road.

"No, sir," Rory offered, and that covered that.

"Do you know who used to live here?" I asked, leaning one hand against the rough stone and adobe, looking down at the fresh grave in front of me. Some of the wall had been kicked loose and pulled down to cover a fair portion of the freshly dug soil. I guessed it was a hurried attempt to keep the coyotes away from the grave for a day or two.

"No, sir."

"Long time ago, huh?"

"Yes, sir." I held out my hand for the shovel, and Rory Torrance gave it to me without hesitation. He was looking down at the dirt. "Somebody steal something?" he asked.

"Yeah, Rory, as a matter of fact, somebody did," I said.

"Why would they bury it way out here?"

I bent down and scuffed at the dirt with the shovel, not bothering to answer. I moved a couple of rocks, and, almost immediately, denim showed. I handed the shovel to Rory and squatted, pushing more of the rocks away. It wasn't difficult. Old Florencio Apodaca knew how to dig a proper grave, if not where. But this one had been finished up in a hurry.

With a gentle tug, the arm came out of the dirt.

"Oh, gross," Rory Torrance said, and backed up a step, suddenly sounding more like a teenager and a whole lot less like a tough leather-slappin' cowboy.

"It's not an 'it' that got buried, it's a who," I said, and stood up.

Rory's eyes were huge as he pointed at the arm. "Was that little kid with these people? He saw all that was goin' on?" I nodded. "Sheeeit," the boy said. "I woulda run, too."

I put my hands in my pockets and gazed around me. The light was stronger, hinting at a thin cloud cover, but the sky made no promises one way or another. Off to the south, ragged clouds hung over the San Cristobal Mountains. To the far west and north, the sky was clear.

"You going to dig it up?" Rory asked.

"No, we need to wait for the detectives. We'll need photographs, identification, all that stuff." I glanced at my watch. "They'll be here in a few minutes."

It was less than a few. Rory and I started back toward the comfortable seats of the Jeep and hadn't covered twenty feet when we heard an engine in a hurry. Seconds later, one of the Posadas County Sheriff's Department's four-wheel drives roared around the corner in a fair imitation of some fairgrounds dirt-track hot dog.

"That would be Deputy Pasquale," I said. Pasquale slid to a stop in front of the Jeep. With him in the Bronco was Niel Costace, and I noticed that the FBI agent took his time getting out of the shoulder harness.

"Have you got your camera bag with you?" I called to Pasquale, and he stopped in his tracks and retreated to the Bronco. "And the heavy shovel," I added. By the time Pasquale had the black bag out of the back, Costace had climbed down. He shut the door of the Bronco with exaggerated care.

"Sergeant Torrez is about ten miles out," the agent said. "But I'm sure we would have gotten here first even if we'd started in Denver." He shot a glance at Pasquale, but the young man either didn't hear the remark or chose to ignore it.

"Over here," I said. As we moved past the Jeep, I added, "And this is Rory Torrance. He's one of the rancher's sons who found Francis this morning."

Costace reached out a hand and grasped Rory's. "Niel Costace. Good work."

"Sir," Rory said to me, "do you want me to go now?"

"I think you probably can, son. We'll be in touch with you for some of the details later in the day." He nodded and looked at the shovel that Deputy Pasquale held. "Unless you want to stay. I'm sure you can be of help when we have to lift him out."

"No thanks, sir," he said quickly, and hustled back to the Jeep.

I led Costace and Pasquale around the building. "I'm guessing that it's Paul Cole," I said. "Just from what I can see of the arm. Browers has darker hair, and he isn't as big."

"You want me to clear away some of these rocks first?" Pasquale said.

"No," I replied. "First, I want you to take a set of photos that shows the grave site just the way it is. Start back here, and make sure you include some of the landmarks in the first couple frames. Then move in closer, including a corner of the building. And then closer still, until you have just the grave in the frame." I held my hands up in front of me and drew a funnel in the air. "Start general, then move to the specific. Just the way they taught you at the Academy."

"Now that we've made it here alive, remember that film's cheap," Costace muttered.

When Pasquale was finished, we cleared away the rocks until the actual perimeter of the grave was obvious. "Photo time," I prompted, then watched Pasquale finish a roll and reload.

It didn't take long to expose the corpse. The man was buried under only inches of dirt, his legs bent back at the knees so that his feet were touching his rump. Despite the dirt, the heavy blood staining high on the right side of his flannel shirt was obvious.

He was blond, probably once ruddy of complexion, and tending to paunch. Well over six feet, he would have weighed 240 at least, perhaps a good deal more.

"Three ten, three oh eight."

Pasquale reached down and pulled his portable radio out of its holster and handed it to me.

"Go ahead, three oh eight."

"ETA about six minutes."

"Ten-four. Robert, did Estelle say anything to you about notifying the coroner?"

"Ten-four. He'll be a few minutes."

I handed the radio back to Pasquale. He holstered it, then pulled out a small notebook and began jotting information about the photos he'd taken.

"What's unclear, Niel," I said, "is whether the child was able to run away on his own or whether they let him go. He told us that he 'runned away.' That could mean a lot of things."

"A three-year-old isn't much of a witness," Costace said.

"Well, this one might be. He's as sharp as they come. He told his mother in Spanish that Tiffany Cole and Browers told him that if he didn't behave, they'd put him in the hole, too."

"Nice folks. He wasn't clear who was who? Or does he know who Andy Browers is?"

"No. He made the comment that Cody Cole 'has two daddies,' and he added, 'And that's where they put him.'" I gestured at the grave. "That's a pretty fair assessment of Cody's situation, if you think about it. To Cody, both Browers and Paul Cole fill the daddy role. I'm assuming that this is Paul Cole. That leaves Andy Browers and Tiffany Cole, with her son."

"So they let the Guzman boy go," Costace mused. "Out here in the middle of nowhere. I wonder where they got that idea."

"He said that he ran away."

"Yeah, well," Costace said skeptically, "it's hard to imagine not being able to catch a three-year-old." He shrugged. "Of course, in the middle of the night, who's to know what happened, exactly. They probably figured he'd either die of exposure out here somewhere or be found come morning. Either way suits their purpose and gives them a good head start." He paused and looked down at the remains of Paul Cole. "Head start to where?—that's the next question." He looked up at me. "Do you think that the youngster will be able to tell us what went on in that motel room?"

"Maybe. I'm not counting on it."

He grunted with disgust, surveying the prairie and hills around us. "Where the hell do they think they're going to go? They think they're going to drive that behemoth through roadblocks without anyone noticing?"

"They have to know better than that," I said. "But we're close to the border. If they can get across and put just a few hours between us and them, the Mexican police aren't going to give them much thought. A token search. That's about it. Especially if they pay the right price."

"Don't be too sure."

"Look at it this way. They got rid of this deadweight, and they got rid of one of the two youngsters—in this case, the one who would cause them the most trouble. They might have figured that a three-year-old wouldn't make much sense of what went on out here. Now they're running, just the three of them."

"If they don't get rid of the RV, they're going to be caught. It's that simple," Costace said.

"Then that's next," I said. "If Paul Cole was using the borrowed RV as a sort of personal motel and base of operations, odds are good that he was planning to return it when the deal was done. He'd get his share of whatever Madrid was supposed to pay for the kid, and he'd be home free."

"But then there's the fracas at the motel," Costace said. "One plan goes out the window. Our lovin' parents know they're in over their heads anyway now, so they take the RV and split." Costace shook his head in disgust. "Hell, maybe they got some fool notion that they'd be able to return to the States after a spell, claimin' that they were abducted. Who the hell knows what people like this really think?"

"If they've got half a brain between them," I said, "they've been listening to the radio. Browers may even have a scanner. The border crossings slammed shut and roadblocks went up before they could slip away. That makes it tough. Now they know they made a mistake, and they're going to be ditching it."

"You got any ideas where?"

I shook my head. "I couldn't guess, but I've got an idea for a place to start."

Chapter 41

By the time I left Paul Cole's final resting place, a fair convocation of folks had arrived, including Dr. Alan Perrone, the assistant county coroner. Deputy Pasquale didn't like it much, but I commandeered his Bronco, leaving him to catch a ride with one of the other deputies.

Estelle had taken her husband and son back into Posadas in my car, and I needed to know what other information she had been able to pry gently out of little Francis. I didn't want to infringe on her time or her privacy with her family, especially with her mother in intensive care. But there was still a whole mountain of information we badly needed.

I drove into Posadas at twenty minutes after eight that morning, feeling an odd combination of immense relief and apprehension. Paul Cole had been an unknown quantity—I had never met him, knew nothing about him. His notion of fooling both wife and school with the fake hunting trip spoke of a kind of brainless, lame bravado—make things too complicated, and then try and bull through. It hadn't worked with Roberto Madrid, either.

But Paul Cole wasn't calling the shots anymore. Andy Browers was. And I knew a little bit about Browers.

I pulled into the Public Safety Building's parking lot and walked quickly inside. To my surprise, Gayle Sedillos was working Dispatch. To my even greater surprise, she rose quickly to her feet, reached me in three quick steps, and enveloped me in a hard bear hug.

"What's that for?" I said, returning the squeeze.

Her smile was brilliant. She was a lovely girl, and I wished that the old department bachelor, Robert Torrez, would look her way once in awhile.

"I just decided that today was a good day to hug everyone I see," she said.

"Fair enough." I grinned. "Has Stanley Willit been in yet this morning? He needs one."

"No." She made a face. "Estelle wants you to call her, though."

"She home?" I asked. Gayle nodded. "How long ago did she call?"

"About ten minutes. And you've got important company waiting for you." She pointed toward my office door.

I went into my office and found my daughter sitting at my desk, playing solitaire on the computer. She was resting her head in her left hand, moving the mouse with her right in dreamy circles.

"Hey there," I said.

"Hey there, yourself," Camille replied. She offered a bright smile, and then her expression turned to one of sympathy. "Is the little boy really all right?"

"As far as I know. I was going to call right now. Estelle left a message that she wanted to talk to me."

"And then am I going to be able to get you to go home?"

"Eventually, I suppose. What's up?"

She shrugged and turned away from the screen. "I just don't want you to keel over in your tracks." She pointed at a small plastic box. "And I brought some of the medications you've been ignoring."

"You and Francis," I said, and reached across the desk to punch the autodialer button for Estelle's number. After six rings, I was about to hang up, but then the good doctor answered, chatty as usual.

"Guzman."

"Francis, how's the kid?" I said without preamble.

"He's fine." There was a slight pause. "Physically, anyway. He only dropped a degree or two in body temperature, so he's just tired. Thank God they put him in some clothes. He wasn't abused in any way, other than a small bruise on his left elbow. But he may have gotten that up in the rocks." He chuckled softly. "Our little mountain climber. He was asleep two minutes after we left the ranch."

"I'm sure the boy's going to have a nightmare or two for a while, but he'll heal. I wish I could have spared him this."

"It's not your fault, Bill."

"I know it's not. I'd just like to have a magic wand sometimes, is all."

"Wouldn't we all. And we've still got one out there, haven't we?"

The photo of Cody Cole flashed through my mind and I grimaced. "Yes, we do."

"Estelle wants to talk with you. Take care of yourself. And by the way, when things settle down a little, I really do need to review your meds with you."

He didn't give me time to object.

"Sir?" Estelle said, so quickly that she must have lifted the other extension, "I caught some of the radio traffic. You found the body?"

"Yes. I think it's Paul Cole."

"That fits, then. Francisco woke up for a few minutes when we got home, and he said a couple of things that might be useful. First of all, it sounds like he was in the motel. He got the idea that Cody's 'daddy' wanted him to go with 'that man,' who I assume was Roberto Madrid, and 'that man' didn't want him. It sounds like they started to fight, and Francis ran into the bathroom. That's all he'll say."

"That pretty much follows what we were thinking," I said.

"Right. What we don't know is if Francis was a last-minute substitute for Cody."

"Or an addition, maybe," I said.

"If he was just an addition to the deal, there would be no reason for the fight. There would be if the Coles were trying some kind of switch. Trying to pull a fast one."

"Maybe so. Would he say anything else?"

"I asked him if Paul Cole was the man who abducted him. Actually, what I asked was, 'Did Cody's daddy come here to get you?' or words to that effect. He frowned that really serious frown of his and said, 'Cody's got two daddies.' And then he nodded. Maybe a photo would help."

"Don't do that, Estelle. Not unless we really have to. We know that either Paul Cole or Andy Browers came and took him. Erma says it was a big man, and that fits Cole, not Browers. Let's not give the kid's nightmares any more ammunition."

"What are you going to do, sir?"

"I'm going to find the sheriff and go over to Posadas Electric Co-op and have a chat with Browers's supervisor. Anyone who would choose the back side of County Road Fourteen to drop someone off is used to thinking about little nooks and crannies in the county. And that makes sense if we're dealing with Andy Browers. He knows every electric pole, every transformer, every little scratch in the sand that calls itself a road. Costace and I agreed—the first thing Browers is going to do now is get rid of that RV. It's a liability now, and he has to know that."

"He could just abandon it anywhere, sir."

"True enough, but then he has to get away clean. So he can't just drive it into downtown Posadas. We've got his old pickup truck, so he can't get that. And I've got a couple of ideas."

"Will you pick me up on the way?"

"No, sweetheart, I won't."

"Sir, please. Francis is here. He got someone to cover for him. Erma's here. Even the lady next door came over at seven-thirty. I can break away for a few minutes. It's all right."

"When the kid wakes up, you need to be there, Estelle. Don't be ridiculous."

There was a long silence. "Do you know what I keep seeing, sir?"

"What?"

"I keep having this image of Cody Cole as just a little bump in the snow down in the San Cristobal Mountains. Remember when we were all up on the mesa and I was holding Francis? Remember that?"

"Yes."

"And I asked him if he'd run down to the fence and back?"

"Right. He wouldn't go."

"Right. I don't think any of us can imagine what it's like being three years old and spending the night out, all alone."

"I've thought about that more than once, sweetheart. And that's my point."

"One of the things Francis said when I was tucking him into bed was that last night he could hear all the 'doggies' around him. Three years old, sitting by a rock, and listening to coyotes."

"Estelle…"

"He's safe now, sir. Cody Cole isn't. I don't think there'd be much *paz en mi alma* if something happened to him that I could help prevent. Please stop by and pick me up. Francis says I should go, so you know I'm right."

"You win." I sighed.

She heard it and actually chuckled. "Promise?"

"Yep."

"See you in a few minutes, *padrino*."

When I hung up, Camille asked, "Is everything all right with the boy?"

"He's home and asleep. He'll be fine." I took a deep breath. "One down, one to go."

Camille frowned. "With one big difference, Dad." She reached around and turned off the computer. "Cody Cole won't have much to come home to, if he makes it at all. What will happen to him?"

I rubbed my face, trying to think clearly. "I don't know, Camille. Let's find him first. Then…" I groped for the right words. "Then …I don't know what happens."

Chapter 42

The receptionist at the Posadas County Electric Co-op smiled uncertainly at the four of us. Sheriff Holman put on his most diplomatic manner, but the tapping of his class ring on the plastic counter hinted at his impatience.

"Good morning. I'm Sheriff Holman. We need to talk with Matt Tierney," Holman said. The receptionist closed the folder of papers she was wading through and looked up at the clock.

"I don't think he'll be free until after nine. They're having their morning staff meeting, and that's usually the time they finish up." She smiled at Holman, and he smiled back. I saw his eyes drop to her name tag ever so briefly.

"Loni, do me a favor and buzz him, will you? Their meeting can wait. I can't."

Before she could answer, the door at the far side of the office opened and Matt Tierney stuck his head out. He held on to the doorknob as four other men filed out, discreetly disappearing into other offices. "Sheriff," he said in a deep, powerful voice, "come on in."

Holman, Estelle, Camille, and I trooped through the middle of Loni's turf, and she gave each one of us a pleasant smile and nod.

"I saw you drive up," Tierney said. "I was going to call you this morning if you didn't call me." He shut the door and gestured toward the still-warm chairs. Like a good service-club member, he stuck out his hand to Camille and said, "I don't believe I know you."

"Camille Stratton. I'm Undersheriff Gastner's daughter."

"Oh. That's great. Visiting or working?"

"Visiting. A nice relaxing visit," Camille said.

"I bet. Sit down, sit down." He moved to the chair at the head of the conference table. "I've been hearing all sorts of stories, and I gotta tell you, none of it sounds good. What the hell is Browers up to, anyway? We spent a hell of a lot of time, man-hours, equipment—you name it—on that search, and now I'm hearing all kinds of crazy things. When the deputy came over last night asking to look at the personnel files, I didn't know if I should let him or not without a court order. What the hell's going on?"

Holman glanced at me, and I said, "It appears that Andrew Browers was involved in the abduction of Detective Reyes-Guzman's son last night. It also appears now that Cody Cole's disappearance last week was a scam."

"A scam?" Tierney's heavy eyebrows shot up behind his glasses.

"That's right. What we need from you now is information."

"I'll be happy to help in any way I can—you know that."

"First of all, it would be helpful to see a map of the entire Posadas Electric Co-op area. We'll go from there."

Tierney stood up and indicated the far wall. "Right here's the system," he said. The map was six feet wide and nearly as tall, a mass of lines, dots, squares, and other symbols.

I moved close and pushed up my glasses. Every house in the village was indicated by a small black square. Out in the county, the squares were few and far between.

I circled my finger around an area just south of Herb Torrance's square. "This is where the Guzman child was abandoned last night," I said. "He was found by some of the Torrance family who were out tending livestock. Browers is—or was—driving an RV—not his. It's one of those huge self-contained things. But we know that he drove down this road. We've got deputies working this entire area," and I circled the remainder of County Road 14, down to where it intersected State Highway 56. "The tracks where he pulled off the road here"—and I tapped the spot by Torrance's ranch—"were clear enough. We're hoping that investigators will find more on down the road. The county road is gravel, but if he strays just a few inches onto the shoulder anywhere, that thing is going to leave prints."

Tierney wiped his eyes. Despite the cool room, he was already sweating. "You have no idea which way he's going to go once he hits Fifty-six?"

"No, we don't. I was hoping you could shed some light on why Browers might choose that route. Why County Road Fourteen?" I ran my finger from the village of Posadas southwest along State Highway 56 thirty-four miles to the tiny hamlet of Regal on the other side of San Cristobal Pass. "The border crossing at Regal is blocked. He's not crossing there. And it's been blocked since last evening."

"What about to the east? Like over at Columbus? Or El Paso, even?" Tierney asked.

"The roadblocks are going to make that almost impossible, unless he changes vehicles and is very, very clever. The Border Patrol assures us that their aircraft will keep the border covered, but we all know that's impossible. There aren't enough men and planes to do that. We've had an airplane up off and on, and they haven't spotted the RV. What I think is that Browers has a spot or two where he's holed up. That's why we came to you."

I stepped back and pulled a chair close to the map. Seated, I was looking right at the intersection of Country Road 14, where it wound down from the mesa, and the state highway.

"The staggered dash-dot blue lines are the transmission lines along the highway?"

Tierney bent down beside me. "That's right. Basically, you can see our entire grid there. These are transformers," he said, pointing with the tip of his pen at a red triangle.

"What do the little flags mean?" Estelle asked.

"That's where crews are currently working. We do that so that anyone who comes in here can glance at the map and see where our resources are. We keep it updated with every job ticket we send out. The initials on the flag represent the actual crewman who's working."

"Each man has his own flag, then," I said.

"That's right."

"Where was Browers working last?"

Tierney took a deep breath. "We had his flag up at the search site from the day that the boy was reported missing. Then he took some annual leave, so the flag came off the map. On the personnel board out in the office, he's shown as on leave."

"Tell me about this," I said. To the east of Regal, up in the rugged San Cristobal Mountains, was a collection of five personnel flags and another small number flag. I bent close. "Number one oh nine," I said. If I extended Browers's route south from the intersection of County Road 14 and State Highway 56, the arrow would point roughly at site 109.

"That's a major repair site," Tierney said. "We have a block of transformers there. You can see that's a junction of several lines. The main transmission line from our Posadas substation follows the Guijarro wash there. That's a pretty good cut through the mountains, and it saves us having to make an end run all the way around the west side of the San Cristobals. Then, right where those flags are, one line goes to Regal itself, another heads east over toward Maria, and one shoots west, sort of following the county line, over into Arizona."

"This solid line..." I said, pointing south from State Highway 56.

"That's a service road. We've either got a service road or clear land easement along every one of our lines."

"But it's not a road," Holman mused.

"Well, not what the highway department calls a road," Tierney said. "But it's clear enough that a four-wheel-drive vehicle can usually get through. Sometimes we have to use a Cat."

"And a big RV?"

Tierney laughed. "No way. Certainly not down there. Those rocks would tear the tires to pieces. It wouldn't have the clearance or the traction."

I sat back. "What if after he hit the state highway, Browers just crossed the road and took the electric easement straight south, following the transmission lines."

"He'd probably be able to bump along for about three miles. As soon as the lines started up through the pass there, it'd be much too rough."

"And then he'd be about what, five miles from this work site where they're messing with the transformers?"

"Closer to seven."

"And there would be vehicles there, wouldn't there?" I looked at Tierney. "And if he got one of your utility trucks, there wouldn't be much to stop him from following this line east toward Maria. It parallels the border, and he'd have no trouble finding a spot to cut the fence."

Tierney wiped the sweat off his forehead again.

"And those are nice trucks, too, as I recall," I added. I looked back at the map. "Would Browers know about this work crew?"

"Sure," Tierney said. "As I recall, he would have been assigned there. And he's worked there before. We had to juggle things around when we had the search for his stepson. A lot of our men were in on that."

"He would have been assigned there?"

Tierney nodded. "He's one of our transformer techs."

I ran a finger south, along County Road 14, frowning. My finger dropped across the state highway and trailed down into the mountains. "Bingo," I whispered.

"Which way do your work crews go to that site?" Holman asked. "It almost looks shorter to go to Regal and then cut over to the east and into the hills."

"That's the way they will go," Tierney said. "Especially with the weather the way it's been." He pointed at a spot just north of the San Cristobal ridge. "There's a lot of clay right in through here. We usually don't go that way unless we're using a Cat."

"Does Andy Browers know that?" I asked.

"I'm sure he does. He's been with us for seven years, so he's seen most of the county in that time. And like I said, he's worked down there before."

"If they're on foot, it won't make any difference," Estelle said. "If Browers abandons his vehicle and decides to walk to the top and then over, he'll run right into the work crew when they drive up the other side from Regal."

"Let's look at the time," I said. "They took Francis at six-oh-three. The ruckus down at the motel was sometime around six-thirty. Cole is stabbed or shot, or whatever happened to him, and they return to North Fifth Street. They take him inside and try their best to patch him up. It doesn't work. Or maybe they think they've succeeded. They load him into the big RV and head out.

They may have thought at first that with out-of-town plates, it would be ignored. That would still be only about seven o'clock—and we were still ignorant of what was going on. By the time Erma managed to alert us, it's going on eight. By that time, Browers could already have been out beyond the Torrance ranch. Even if he hadn't heard about the roadblocks, this area would make sense to him as a place to ditch the body."

"Francis has no concept of what time anything happened, sir," Estelle said. "It was dark—that's all he'll say."

"We had the airplane in the air by nine o'clock, nine-thirty at the latest, as soon as we discovered that the RV was gone. So he had time. Lots of time. He drove out here, buried the body. He had time to drive all the way down here," and I tapped the intersection of County 14 and State Highway 56. "By then, he must have known that the borders would be closed and that the highways would be jammed with cops looking for Francis.

"I don't know of any place along County Road Fourteen where he could hide that thing, although as long as his lights were off, the airplane wouldn't see him."

"What if he crossed the state highway and continued on ahead?" Tierney said. "He's got just a mile of pretty hard-packed prairie, and where the power lines cut across the wash, there's even been some dozer work done. It's conceivable that he could have worked his way to about Wilson's Tank, with just a little luck."

I peered at the map. The San Cristobal range was one of just a handful in the continental United States that ran generally west-east for part of its length. The range looked like an upside-down crescent, with its western end just northwest of Regal, and then curving east and south, down into Mexico. The north slope of the range drained into the same valley that was the roadbed for State Highway 56.

Parked at the intersection of County Road 14 and State 56, Browers would have been looking at the back side of the San Cristobals, with Mexico just on the other side, tantalizingly close. To him, the mountain wasn't a barrier; it was an opportunity.

"Wilson's Tank is right here," Tierney said. "We used that area for a while as a staging spot for equipment and supplies when we ran the new line across."

"What's there?" Holman asked.

"The Guijarro cut is pretty narrow there, lots of trees down in. There's an old corral, some stock chutes, and the water-collection platform and tanks. That's about it."

"Suppose he was able to make his way there," I said. "That's about two and a half miles?"

"About that."

"He could have been there by nine o'clock. If he had to walk the rest of the way, how far is it?"

Tierney wiped his forehead again, looking pained. "First of all, it's one hell of a walk. I mean, that's rugged country, even staying right under the power lines. It's the sort of track that'll jounce your teeth out, using compound low in a four-by-four." He put his hands on his knees and got his bifocals into position. "I'd have to guess seven or eight miles. Uphill. Tough walking." He stood up and looked at me.

"Bill, he's got a woman and a three-year-old boy with him," Holman said. "He wouldn't try something like that with them. For one thing, he'd have to carry the boy most of the way."

"Maybe," I said. "He might have them with him. He's dumped his other complications along the way. He might continue the habit. But you're right. He's certainly not going to do it in the dark."

"I don't know," Tierney said. "Walking from pole to pole, it's hard to get lost. Our crews work at night all the time."

"But it's sure hard as hell knowing where to put your feet," I said. I frowned, knowing damn well that Andrew Browers was still young enough to know exactly where his feet where.

I looked at the map again. "All right. Here's the deal. He knows the work crews will be right here"—and I stabbed the map just south of the ridge—"when?"

"They pull out of here about eight-thirty, normally. They were a little late today. Say closer to nine. It takes 'em an hour and a half to make the drive. One hour to Regal and beyond, the last half hour up the power line to the relay and transformer station."

"So, ten-thirty." I looked at my watch. "It's nine-fifteen right now. If Browers spent the night at Wilson's Tank and then, come dawn, made the hike up hill, he'd make that seven miles by ten easily. He'll be there waiting."

Tierney frowned again. "How many men are on that crew?" I asked, and counted flags.

"Four, right now," Tierney said. "But what makes you so sure that he's going to go that way?"

"We're not, except for one major thing. There's nowhere else for him to move without being seen. And it makes sense that he'd stick with familiar turf. And he knows exactly where to find himself a tough, dependable vehicle—and it's just the kind he could easily sell across the border."

"One of our trucks? But they've got our logos all over 'em."

"A little paint takes care of that, or a heat gun," I said.

"What do you want me to do?"

"First, I want you to get on the radio, and order your work crew to stop in Regal." I pushed myself to my feet. "We don't know what kind of radio Browers has, but make it sound innocent, in case he's listening. Some kind of repair that just got called in that they need to do before going up in the hills. You know your system. Make something up. Just don't say anything to tip Browers off. Tell your men that another work crew is going to meet them at the church in Regal just as soon as they can get there."

Tierney looked sideways at me. "Then what?"

"Then I'd like permission to borrow a couple of your trucks for a little while."

Chapter 43

At ten minutes after ten that morning, three white Posadas Rural Electric Co-op trucks ground their way up a steep, narrow two-track that angled eastward, working its way up the south slope of the San Cristobal range.

The second and third vehicle in line were standard one-ton four-wheel-drive utility trucks, their beds including enough gear and utility boxes to make a plumber drool with envy. Leading the pack was a high-slung Chevy Kodiak, a big blunt-snouted diesel-powered monster that carried the cherry picker and about four tons of other expensive equipment, including a generator big enough to power half of Posadas.

Behind in Regal, six bemused Electric Co-op workers sat on the steps of the Iglesia de Nuestra Madre Catholic church, watching us rumble off into the distance, leaving behind as collateral a handful of high-mileage patrol vehicles, my daughter Camille, and Deputy Skip Bishop.

I rode in the lead truck and tried to make myself comfortable while at the same time fighting not to crush Estelle every time the Kodiak waddled and jolted over another set of rocks. Half the time, I needed the palm of my hand up on the roof liner to keep my skull from making dents.

Bob Torrez idled through a particularly dense stand of junipers, their limbs raking the side of the truck. The trail curved north into a narrow canyon, switchbacked out again, and then actually ran downhill for a while before angling up into a dense thicket of scrub oak.

"This road is supposed to fork somewhere up there," I said.

"Supposed to," Bob grunted. He looked right at home with the yellow hard hat. I looked in the rearview mirror and watched the two trucks behind us—Eddie Mitchell and Tom Pasquale in one, and Martin Holman and Tony Abeyta bringing up the rear.

I had a nagging apprehension that we were putting all our eggs in one basket, but we now knew that Andrew Browers had driven south, just as we had suspected. There had been no way to conceal the tire tracks of the heavy RV when he had turned off of the state highway and headed south.

With one of the department Broncos, Deputy Tom Mears and Dale Kenyon had set off to follow the tracks. As they worked their way south and we formed a pincer coming north, Andrew Browers would be caught in the middle.

I chose to put the largest truck first because I wanted to be able to see, and its windshield being six or seven feet off the ground made that easy.

We drove out of the canyon, and for a moment, directly ahead and below, Mexico stretched out to the horizon. The clouds were beginning to break, the last strands of moisture burning off. To the east, I could see an airplane making lazy circles as it worked its way along the border.

We turned left, following the terrain, the oak brush as high as the doors of the truck. Another hump in the side of the slope brought us to an old slag pile, where years ago someone had hoped to strike it rich. "Tierney said that once we went by the stone foundation, the fork was about six-tenths of a mile," I said.

The miner had managed to dig a great scar in the earth, but then he had ran up against granite so hard and empty, he'd gotten discouraged. He hadn't gone deep enough to bother with shaft supports. Just beyond the slag pile was a small heap of rubble that still showed some organization.

"That's the foundation, I assume."

Torrez nodded and pointed. "I've been hunting down this way. Got a eight-pointer about four miles south of here. This trail would have to cut downhill a bunch. I wasn't anywhere near this far upslope."

"Tierney promised a fork," I said.

And sure enough, as the odometer rolled six-tenths, the trail did split. The right fork angled into another grove of oaks, and the left switchbacked up so steeply that we all held our breath as the big truck reared and bucked, its all-wheel-drive system clawing for purchase on the loose rocks. The other two vehicles held back until we'd cleared the top. The two-track crested a rise almost immediately and then skirted a grass and cactus meadow.

We rolled for a hundred yards on packed soil, almost highway-smooth.

"This is better," I said.

"Until up there," Bob said. I could see jagged rocks ahead, and then the power lines as they appeared in the saddle-back. "About another mile and a half."

I glanced in the rearview mirror and saw the second truck pull over the hill and accelerate across the smooth grass.

"Pasquale wants the lead," I said. "As always." He pulled up within ten feet of our back bumper.

Torrez took the opportunity to rest his arms on the steering wheel, leaning forward and gazing up the side of the mountain toward the cut. "I wonder where he is," he said. "What do you suppose he'll do?"

Estelle's mouth was set in a grim line. "That depends on how smart he is, or thinks he is," I said. "He won't know it's not the electric company until we're on top of him."

Bob slowed the truck to a walk, and I glanced at him. He was looking in the rearview mirror. "The sheriff may be having trouble with that last switchback," he said.

Sure enough, Holman's vehicle hadn't crested the rise to the meadow. Torres stopped the truck and I said into the handheld radio, "Hold up for a minute, Tom." We sat for thirty seconds, the big diesel idling.

That thirty seconds was Pasquale's limit of patience. I could imagine the taciturn Eddie Mitchell enjoying the ride.

"We'll go check," Pasquale said. The kid could drive backward as well as forward, and he reversed across the meadow. I had visions of him losing it at the last moment, the fifty-thousand-dollar electric company truck sailing ass-end-first right off the edge, crashing to junk on the rocks.

He jarred to a halt, skewed sideways, and I saw both doors fling open. From a hundred yards away, it looked as if one of the deputies was pointing, but then I saw several puffs of smoke, followed eventually by the rapid *pop-pop-pop* of pistol fire.

"What the hell," I said, and almost instantly the radio cracked to life.

"He's got the truck!" Mitchell shouted.

Torrez jammed the Kodiak into reverse and we jolted backward off the trail, sod and rocks flying. He spun the wheel and floored the accelerator, and we shot forward, cutting back onto the ruts. I saw Mitchell's stocky figure race over the edge while Pasquale dashed to the truck.

Even with the diesel of our truck bellowing for all it was worth, Pasquale had the smaller unit turned around by the time we arrived. He headed downslope without a moment's hesitation, and I could see the tires of his truck crashing over rocks big enough to high-center a passenger car.

We crested the hill in time to see Holman and Abeyta standing by the side of the road, gesticulating. Their truck, without them in it, had already backed far enough down the two-track that it had reached the fork, and it was now heading south on the other trail.

"Go get the son of a bitch!" I heard Holman shout over the radio. Tom Pasquale needed no more incentive. We had a grand-stand view as the two Electric Co-op trucks careened pell-mell down the narrow two-track that would along the foothills of the San Cristobals. The Border Patrol aircraft that had been orbiting farther to the east had swung overhead, a fast Cessna Sky Master that was going to be of little use other than providing eyes in the sky.

Torrez eased down the hill, keeping the pace at a crawl as the heavy truck shifted this way and that on the rocks. Holman sprinted up the hill to meet us, his face purple with rage.

"He's alone!" Holman shouted as he jumped up on the driver's side running board of the Kodiak. "He doesn't have the child or the woman with him!"

"Oh Christ," I said, "what's he done with 'em?"

"He must have left them behind, with the camper," Estelle said.

"Or under any number of humps in the sand along the way," I said. "He knew exactly what the hell he wanted."

Tom Pasquale had slowed just enough for Eddie Mitchell to jump back aboard, and Mitchell certainly deserved a medal for bravery. No more than a hundred yards separated the trucks, and Pasquale was gaining.

"I don't think he hit him," Holman said. "There was just an instant when Browers was out in the open, and Pasquale got off three shots."

"He was waiting for you?"

"I don't know," Holman said ruefully. "One minute we're fine, and the next instant he's standing right where I am now, on the running board of the truck, sticking a pistol in my ear. He wanted us out, and I didn't argue with him."

"Wise," I said. "Bob, if we go any farther, we won't be able to see them when they get below that swath of oaks." He stopped the truck and the four of us climbed down.

"He's got Tony's gun now, too," Holman added. With a pair of binoculars, Bob Torrez watched the race.

"It looks like Pasquale is chained to his back bumper," he said, and below us and to the east we saw the two trucks dive into a copse of elm scrub where a mountainside spring had created a tiny patch of green. "He's got a quarter of a mile, and he's at the fence."

And, at that particular point, that's all that separated the United States from Mexico, a well-made steel-post six-strand barbed-wire fence. Torrez raised the glasses and swept the view. "No *federales*, either."

The Cessna swooped low, entering a hard bank, keeping the two roaring trucks in clear view.

"There will be," I said.

The two-track swerved out onto a flat, dry section of prairie, and Andrew Browers saw his chance. He skidded right, off the road, roaring through the low brush, hitting hummocks so hard that half the time his truck was airborne.

And less than a hundred feet behind him were Pasquale and Mitchell. I knew that trying for a spectacular tire shot was impossible. All Mitchell could do was hang on with both hands and feet and hope that Pasquale didn't miscalculate and put them on their roof.

"He's going to go for it," Torrez said.

I held up the radio and thumbed the transmit button. "If he goes through that fence, you just go right after him," I said.

"They can't go into Mexico," Holman said.

"Sure they can." I glanced at him and held out the radio. "Do you want to tell Pasquale to stop?"

"Hell no," Holman said.

Browers crashed the fence dead center, taking one of the steel posts right on the massive power winch on the front bumper of the truck. We saw a burst of sand and flying metal, and the two trucks had themselves a doorway into Mexico.

"Veracruz by nightfall," I muttered, but I had spoken too soon. Tom Pasquale had other plans. Even as one vehicle swerved violently to the left to avoid a deep arroyo, the second merged with it. We saw a cloud of dirt fly heavenward, and the two vehicles jarred to a halt.

For a moment, it was impossible to tell what was happening, but then Torrez said, "They've got 'em," and a wide grin split his features. He shifted the glasses a fraction. "And here come the troops."

I looked in the direction he was pointing and saw two vehicles approaching on the Mexican side of the fence. "This should be interesting," I said.

Chapter 44

"PCS, three oh three is ten-fifteen."

I laughed with delight. "God, he must have paid Mitchell to get to say that," I said. "He's got Browers in custody."

It took us a half hour to cover the same ground that the two fleeing utility trucks had covered in five or six minutes. Martin Holman and Tony Abeyta balanced on the running boards, clinging to the door and mirror frames. By the time we reached the break in the fence, Capt. Tomas Naranjo's tan Toyota Land Cruiser was parked beside the two white trucks, with a tan Suburban just arriving.

"You want to go in?" Torrez asked, hesitating.

"Hell yes," I said. "I'm not going to walk."

Tomas Naranjo leaned against the fender of his Toyota and grinned as we approached.

"I remember seeing that break in the fence last week," he said as we approached. "You know, those range cattle sometimes can be a real nuisance." He shook hands with Holman and then me, and his grip was firm and friendly. "Señora," he said to Estelle, and touched the brim of his cap.

"We appreciate your cooperation, Captain," I said, and turned my attention to the others. "Are you guys all right?" Pasquale clearly was. I could count every one of his teeth, his grin was so wide. Mitchell looked as if he was glad to be standing on solid ground. Andy Browers sat on the running board of the truck he'd taken, his hands cuffed behind his back and his ankles locked together with a heavy nylon zip tie.

He didn't look up, just stared instead at the Mexican sand under his feet.

"Where are Tiffany and Cody Cole?" Estelle snapped.

"I have no idea."

I bent down and grabbed his shoulder. "You're cute, you son of a bitch. Now where did you leave 'em last night?"

He looked up at me, his face impassive.

"Perhaps you could leave him with us," Naranjo said mildly. "We have several experienced interrogators on our staff."

"They were at the camper," Browers said, and spat into the sand. "They couldn't keep up, so I told 'em to go back." He looked up at me again. He licked his lips. "They were just in the way."

"Who's idea was this whole thing?" I asked.

"Cole. Paul Cole." Browers looked off into space. "He had this whole big deal cooked up."

"I'm sure," I said. "And conveniently, he's dead." I saw a muscle twitch in Browers's cheek. "Yes. We found the body, thanks to the little boy who you figured would never show up again—alive, anyway."

Browers looked up suddenly. "He run off," he said. "If he'd done what I told him, everything would have turned out all right." He turned to Naranjo. "I got twenty thousand dollars in there."

Naranjo tipped his head and regarded Browers with interest. "Twenty thousand? American dollars?"

"That's right."

Naranjo flashed teeth. "That's enough to fix one of these trucks," he said. "I don't know about the other." He reached out and patted a torn and battered fender.

I straightened up and turned to Estelle. "Let's get this creep back to town."

※

It took the rest of the morning to clean up the mess. Despite the shattered fence and 640 yards of clear southbound tire tracks, Capt. Tomas Naranjo, still amused, remained adamant that no one had trespassed on Mexican soil.

Torrez, Estelle, and I elected to ride back to the church in the Kodiak. Considering the circumstances, returning one of the three vehicles wasn't too bad. The others piled into the *federales'* Toyota and the accompanying Suburban, to be chauffeured back to the formal border crossing at Regal.

Eddie Mitchell volunteered to stay behind and wait for the Posadas County wreckers to arrive and pull Matt Tierney's trucks back. I think he looked forward to the stationary peace and quiet.

We rumbled into Regal about ten minutes after the others, and Camille waved a greeting and broke away from the crowd.

"Just another normal Posadas morning," she said as I stepped down out of the truck. "And they've got Tiffany Cole and the boy. They're both all right."

Estelle let out a deep sigh.

"Where were they?" I asked.

"Sitting on the step of the RV, at the spring, where you thought they might be." She turned and gestured toward one of the patrol cars. "They were trying to raise you on the radio."

"I had it turned off," I said.

"So I gathered. Apparently, Tiffany decided just to sit and wait it out until someone came and got her."

"But the child's all right?"

Camille grimaced. "As good as he's going to be, I guess. Physically, anyway." She reached out and touched my arm. "I talked to Gayle on the cell phone. Tiffany Cole told one of the deputies that they would have made it across the border if they hadn't been slowed down by having to drag the kid along."

"Wonderful people," I said.

Holman approached. "You heard?"

I nodded. "Did someone call the wreckers?"

"On the way," Holman said. "Good work, folks. We'll wrap this up and then head on back to Posadas to face the music."

I smiled at his worried expression. "I'm sure Posadas Electric has insurance. Or we do."

"I don't mean about the wrecked trucks," Holman said. "I just talked with the office. Stanley Willit's been sitting in my office for the past two hours."

"Well, that's a nice way to spend the rest of your day," I said.

"He's going to want some answers. Do you want to talk with him?" Holman asked.

I looked at him sideways. "I leave it entirely in your capable hands, Sheriff. You don't need me to figure out who hit whom with a shovel. Your investigators will have that sorted out by nightfall."

Camille heard that and understood my intentions perfectly. She hooked her arm through mine. "Do you think I can get you to come home now, Dad?"

"Yes, you can," I said.

To receive a free catalog of other Poisoned Pen Press titles, please contact us in one of the following ways:

Phone: 1-800-421-3976
Facsimile: 1-480-949-1707
Email: info@poisonedpenpress.com
Website: www.poisonedpenpress.com

Poisoned Pen Press
6962 E. First Ave. Ste 103
Scottsdale, AZ 85251